Michelle Smart's love aff... when she was a baby and v... in her cot. A voracious rea... ... ... found her love of romance established when she stumbled across her first Mills & Boon book at the age of twelve. She's been reading them— and writing them—ever since. Michelle lives in Northamptonshire, England, with her husband and two young Smarties.

Lorraine Hall is a part-time hermit and full-time writer. She was born with an old soul and her head in the clouds—which, it turns out, is the perfect combination for spending her days creating thunderous alpha heroes and the fierce, determined heroines who win their hearts. She lives in a potentially haunted house with her soulmate and a rumbustious band of hermits in training. When she's not writing romance, she's reading it.

BOUND TO AN ENEMY

MICHELLE SMART

LORRAINE HALL

MILLS & BOON

First published in Great Britain 2025
by Mills & Boon, an imprint of HarperCollins*Publishers* Ltd,
1 London Bridge Street, London, SE1 9GF

www.harpercollins.co.uk

HarperCollins*Publishers*, Macken House, 39/40 Mayor Street Upper,
Dublin 1, D01 C9W8, Ireland

This book contains FSC™ certified paper
and other controlled sources to ensure responsible forest management.

For more information visit www.harpercollins.co.uk/green.

Printed and Bound in the UK using 100% Renewable Electricity
at CPI Group (UK) Ltd, Croydon, CR0 4YY

SPANIARD'S
SHOCK HEIRS

MICHELLE SMART

MILLS & BOON

CHAPTER ONE

DIAZ MARTINEZ STRODE through the lobby of his Mayfair hotel and descended the wide stairs to the restaurant. He noted with unsmiling satisfaction that every table was occupied, the hum of chatter only slightly higher than the specially chosen melodious background music. A number of diners were taking pictures of their food. Their expressions suggested their social media postings would be favourable. As it should be.

In the kitchen, ordered chaos ensued. The head chef, whose famous name was on the restaurant door, 'Tom Carlow at the Martinez,' noticed Diaz's appearance but was too busy to do anything but nod an acknowledgement. As it should be.

When Diaz had bought the worn-down hotel two years ago, he'd known it would take time and money to bring it up to the standard of his other hotels. The previous owners had driven it to the wall. By the time they'd been forced to sell, their client base, fed up with overinflated prices for substandard service and crumbling decor, had deserted them, the hotel reduced to ridicule.

No one was ridiculing it now. A full-scale refurbishment followed by stringent hiring and an unrelenting attention to detail meant the grand reopening, filled with specially curated guests, had been hailed a spectacular success. Hiring the Michelin-starred Tom Carlow as head chef had been just one of many components that had seen the latest chain in Diaz's empire pay back tenfold the investment he'd put into it.

Back in the lobby, he climbed the cantilevered stairs two at a time to the first floor and swept past the doormen and into the hotel's real money pit. The casino.

Almost nine o'clock on a Saturday evening and already the atmosphere was thrumming. Where the music in the restaurant was kept low-key to enable his diners to relax, the volume in the casino was upped, the tempo fast. In another hour, all the gambling tables would be full and would remain full until the early hours. People would have to wait their turn to play on the slots. As it should be.

Satisfied that standards hadn't slipped in his absence, he headed for the door at the far end, using his fingerprint to open it.

Imagining the large Scotch he'd have when he retired to his suite for the night, he walked the narrow corridor to the far end, then used his fingerprint and inputted the access code to enter his security hub.

The Hub, as it was known, was the unseen heart of his casino, containing almost as many monitors as patrons. Not an inch of the first floor went unobserved. Everyone, from the guests to the croupiers to the tellers, knew they were being watched. None of them knew just how closely.

'Has it started?' Diaz asked, taking his usual seat.

'Eight minutes,' Jorge answered, not averting his eyes from the screens in front of him.

Once a month, Diaz hosted a private poker event that was the most sought-after ticket in the gambling world. He rotated the venue. Last month he'd held it in Madrid, next month it would be in Paris. To gain entry, you had to apply. For your application to be successful, you had to produce proof of a minimum ten million euros or equivalent in a deposit account. To play, you needed to bring that ten million euros—or equivalent—in cash. Sixteen players. Winner takes all. One hundred and sixty million euros. Ten per cent handed to the casino—Diaz—in fees.

Diaz always made sure to be there, not to gamble— to his mind, only fools gambled—but to oversee. When that kind of money was at stake, anything could happen.

He studied the monitors surveying the private room the event was being held in. Chyna, hostess that evening, was welcoming the selected fools into the room. 'Usual faces?'

'Mostly. A couple of new ones.'

Diaz nodded his approval. Fresh blood was always welcome.

To apply, you needed to know about the event and only a very select number of people were in the know. Those who attended did not like to risk their places by widening the competition pool. It was Jorge's job to vet the applicants and rubber-stamp their place.

'Coffee?'

Jorge didn't look up from the screens. *'Por favor.'*

There were three coffee machines strategically located in The Hub. The work in here being too important to distract the staff with trivialities, Diaz always sorted his own coffee.

A couple of minutes later and he placed Jorge's coffee in front of him, peering over his shoulder to see what was happening in the private room. The players had taken their seats. Two tables. Eight players per table. Top four players of each table went into the final…

A jolt of electricity zinged through his veins. He blinked to clear his vision and moved his stare to a different monitor, which was fixed, face on, on players seven and eight from table two.

He swore.

Jorge gave him a quick side-eye. 'What's wrong?'

'Player fifteen.'

'Ms Gregory? What about her?'

His throat had gone dry. 'What the hell is she doing here?'

'She passed all the checks. Do you know the lady?'

The lady in question, as if sensing their attention on her, lifted her gaze to the monitor they were watching her through.

Diaz's heart thumped.

Clenching his jaw, he gave a grim laugh. 'That's no lady. That's my wife.'

He'd seen her. She could feel his stare on her. She'd always been able to feel it, a fuzzy electrical sensation like nothing else on this earth.

Rose had been fourteen when she'd first experienced it. She'd been hiding at the bottom of the garden under the cherry tree, headphones on, listening to music, trying to drown out the noises…screams…in her head and calm the terror that had gripped her so tightly. As young as she'd been, she'd known she couldn't fall apart. Her mother needed her. Mrs Martinez needed her.

She'd felt Diaz's presence before she'd seen him, like an internal antenna had come to life and started softly buzzing, and hurriedly pulled her headphones off.

He'd stopped a good distance from the tree. Even then,

a decade past, he'd not wanted to get close to her. She'd repelled him from the start.

His hands had been jammed in his shorts pockets, she remembered, a black T-shirt of a punk rock album cover covering his gangly torso. 'I'm sorry to hear about your mother,' he'd said stiffly.

She'd wanted to throw her phone at him. 'Did your grandmother tell you to say that?'

'I would have said it anyway.'

'Well, you've said it now so don't let me keep you.'

He'd turned away and then turned back. Hesitated before quietly asking, 'How are you holding up?'

Her response had been to stare at him defiantly and ram the headphones back on. She would not give Diaz Martinez the satisfaction of seeing her cry. Any hint of vulnerability and he'd use it as a weapon against her.

It was with the same defiance eleven years on that she gazed into the monitor now. The same knowledge that she had to remain strong for what was to follow, whatever the turbulence beneath her skin.

The first cards had been dealt. She looked at hers and looked at the table cards. She had possibly the worst poker hand it was possible to have. She pushed all her playing chips into the pile. 'All in.'

There were audible gasps from her fellow players.

Only the American player, number eleven, matched her. He had a full house.

Ten million euros poorer than she'd been ten minutes earlier, Rose smiled gracefully and got to her feet at the same moment the door opened. She'd played her cards with perfect timing.

Head held high, she strolled past the remaining players, all gawping incredulously at her, towards her husband.

The gangly nineteen-year-old who'd been shamed into giving her words of sympathy over a decade ago had filled out over the years. Diaz Martinez had transformed into a six-foot-two slab of pure rangy muscle, the dark brown hair that eleven years ago had been worn long like the surf dudes who hit Devon's beaches in droves cut short at the back and sides, the longer top squiffed up and to the side.

The green eyes that had never bothered to disguise their loathing skimmed hers before he stepped aside to let her through the door.

Without exchanging a word or a glance, they crossed the casino floor. It didn't surprise her that he led her to the back offices rather than take her up to his suite.

The office he selected had 'Accounts' on its door. It smelt stale, as if its occupants never bothered to open the windows. She was quite sure he'd chosen this one deliberately.

Inside, he propped his backside on the nearest desk, folded his arms across his chest and gazed at the ceiling. In perfect, barely accented English, he said, 'I have seen some stunts in my time but throwing ten million euros away in one hand just to get my attention is a new one on me.'

The agony at his indifference came within a breath of poleaxing her.

'I had to get your attention somehow, didn't I?' she said tremulously. 'I mean, you've blocked my number.' She'd woken to an empty bed and a note that read:

My lawyers will be in touch about the divorce.

And they had been.

Of Diaz, she'd seen and heard nothing.

That note had lodged like a taunt in the forefront of

her mind. She'd read it so many times the sharply executed letters had etched themselves into her retinas and into her broken heart.

'I'll do everything else through the lawyers but this you need to hear from me and not a suit. Not that I particularly think you *deserve* to hear it from me, but then, I'm not the vengeful narcissist of this so-called marriage. Keeping track of your itinerary is impossible, but I knew you'd be here tonight so took my chance. Luckily I kept my maiden name otherwise the security checks would have picked up that I had the same surname as you, which would have quite ruined the surprise.'

The firm, sensuous lips twisted. It was a twist she'd seen too many times to count. 'Spit it out.'

'Notice anything different about me?'

'I do not have time for games, Rose.'

'Neither do I, so why don't you look at me and see for yourself why I pulled that stunt?' It shouldn't hurt so much that he refused to look at her. She should have expected it—she *had* expected it.

Diaz hated her. Shared grief had pulled them together that night, nothing more. While she'd fallen asleep locked in his arms and with a sense that the world's axis had righted itself, he was already deep in regret. He'd extricated himself from her arms and her bed with such darkness in his heart that he'd been compelled to leave a note about their divorce. The final cruelty had been where he'd left the note—on the pillow where his head should have been.

The night that had meant everything to her had meant nothing to him, and she would never, *never* make the mistake of allowing emotions to play any part in their relationship again.

Teeth gritted, heart furiously pumping, Diaz let his stare fall to the face he'd last seen in the flesh four months ago while she'd been sleeping.

She looked the same as she'd done then. Same large blue eyes ringed and enhanced with dramatically applied eyeliner and mascara. Same too-long nose. Same wide mouth and high cheekbones. Same long, dirty blonde hair. The same captivating beauty that had mesmerised and repelled in equal measure.

He shrugged roughly. 'What am I looking at?'

She lifted up her index finger, then pointed it downward.

His still dry throat had closed even before his gaze followed her finger's direction.

Same slender neck. Same slender shoulders. Same high breasts. All covered in a silk dress he didn't recognise, black and long-sleeved, more like an oversized shirt than a dress, and which shouldn't cling to her slender waist and flat belly...

His heart made a sudden cold, hard thump.

She pressed a hand to the belly that was no longer flat.

He shook his head in disbelief and lifted his gaze back to hers.

She nodded.

Another disbelieving shake of his head.

Another nod. The slender shoulders rose. She expelled a long breath. 'Sorry for ruining your life again, but I'm pregnant.'

A distant emergency services siren pierced through the siren roaring in Diaz's ears.

He grabbed tightly to the side of the desk that was the

only thing stopping him from slumping to the floor. His limbs had turned to water. 'How?'

Her answering laughter contained no humour. 'How do you think?'

'But… We…'

'No, we didn't.'

An image flashed. Rose pinned beneath him. High cheekbones slashed with colour. Blue eyes liquid with the same desire that had liquidised his loins…

The siren ringing in his ears increased tenfold.

He hung his head and tried to breathe. Tried to think coherently. That night. He never allowed himself to think about it, had locked it away.

He'd woken with the soft weight of Rose pressed against his skin and a suffocating weight pressing down on his chest. All the emotions that had taken him over when making love to her…so many emotions had broken free…had compressed under the sense of doom throbbing in the back of his head and he'd known before opening his eyes that he'd made the biggest mistake of his life.

Forgetting that mistake had been the hardest task he'd ever set himself.

He met her stare. 'How can you be sure it's mine?'

The face that grew more captivating with each passing year spasmed. For the first time he caught a barely perceptible glimmer of hurt. 'How can you even ask that?'

There was a strong chance he was going to be sick.

Rose, pregnant?

'Oh, and just for extra fun, we're having twins.'

A wave of nausea flooded his system. He blew out a long puff of air and clasped his cheeks. 'Twins?'

'You never do anything by halves, do you?' she said in another attempt at a joke, which was Rose all over. In all the years he'd known her, he'd only caught her with her defences down three times. The last time had been four months ago when both their defences had been down.

And now she was carrying his child. Children.

Unless this was her idea of a sick joke; vengeance for the way he'd left her?

But no. That wasn't Rose's style. Not even Rose would stoop so low as to fake a pregnancy. That bump straining against her dress...

Diaz was going to be a father. Not a father to just one child, but to twins. And Rose, the woman he was counting the days until their divorce could be filed, was their mother.

'I need a drink,' he muttered, rubbing the back of his head.

This was too much.

He'd thought he was finally freed from Rose's toxic spell, that he could live the rest of his life and never have to hear her name or share her air again.

She gave a short laugh. 'Have one for me. Believe me, there've been a few times these last four months when all I've wanted is to bury myself in a bottle of gin but I've got these little lives inside me to think of.'

He stared at her, dumbfounded. 'How can you be so calm?' Calm when he felt like a rug had been yanked out from under his feet. Scratch that. Felt like his whole *world* had been yanked out from under him.

Dios, Rose was pregnant with his babies.

'I can't say I was calm when I did the test,' she admitted with a rueful shrug. 'And when two heartbeats were detected on the scan...' She gave another laugh and shook her head. 'Two babies to bring safely into the world? Only a *tiny* bit terrifying. But it is what it is, and all I can do is my best.'

'You didn't think to...?' He couldn't bring himself to say it.

She recoiled in horror and covered her belly with both hands. 'Abort them? Absolutely not. They didn't ask to be conceived, so don't even think of suggesting it.'

'I didn't...' His voice had become hoarse. 'I wouldn't.'

'Good.' She gave a tight smile and readjusted the strap of her handbag. 'I should go.'

'Go?' What the hell was she talking about? *Go?*

'You need to digest the bombshell I've just thrown at you. Get in touch when you're over the shock of it all and we can talk properly then. And don't worry—the pregnancy doesn't change anything as far as you and I are concerned.'

Rose, desperate to get away without Diaz realising just how desperate her need for escape was, left him staring at her with the expression of someone who really had suffered a grenade explosion at close quarters.

The moment the door shut behind her, she slumped against it and clasped her thighs to stop herself sinking to the floor. She was shaking, inside and out.

That had been easier than she'd imagined, and yet a hundred times harder.

Easier because Diaz had been too shocked to erupt with the anger and accusations she'd prepared herself for. Harder because all the mental preparations she'd made to be with him in the flesh again had gone to nothing.

But that was the story of her life. Diaz had always been capable of eliciting emotions in her with nothing but the mention of his name, and it destroyed her that the pain she'd tried so hard to bury had risen back up again, fragmentary memories of their night together floating like whispers to the surface. She didn't dare risk exposing herself to those fragments, not now, and she blinked hard to push them away.

She had to get out of here. She couldn't stay slumped against the door, not when he was on the other side it. She'd thrown a grenade into his life but Diaz was not the kind of man to stay shellshocked for long. She'd much rather be safe in Devon and in control of her surroundings for when the shock wore off and he demanded they talk. She needed every ounce of advantage she could get.

Pulling herself together, she went back into the casino and headed for the exit. As she descended the stairs she couldn't stop herself thinking of the first time she met him. She'd been eleven, a lonely girl on the cusp of adolescence, excited that Mrs Martinez's grandchildren were going to spend the whole of the summer holidays in Devon with them. Well, not with *them*. With Mrs Martinez. After all, Rose's mother was Mrs Martinez's live-in housekeeper. Rose was just the housekeeper's daughter. But Mrs Martinez had never seen her like that. Certainly never treated her like that. She'd made Rose feel welcome in her home. Wanted. Only two months living there and, to Rose, it had felt like she'd finally found a grandmother.

Surely a woman as wonderful as Mrs Martinez would have wonderful grandchildren? She'd been half right.

Twelve-year-old Rosaria had been thrilled to make a friend of Rose, had marvelled at the similarity of their names and declared they would be best friends for ever.

Sixteen-year-old Diaz had been a different proposition. He'd made no effort to hide his resentment of Rose's presence. Only days after his arrival, she'd overheard him complaining about the 'feral' child of the hired help leading his sister astray.

'Why does your brother hate me?' Rose had asked his sister after he'd flatly refused to let her walk with them to the local town for ice cream.

Rosaria had shrugged. 'Don't take it personally. He hates everyone.'

'He doesn't hate you.'

'That's because I'm his sister.'

She'd been confused. 'But I thought brothers and sisters were supposed to find each other annoying?' At least, that was the impression she'd always got from her old friendship group, where she'd been the only only-child. The others always used to say how lucky she was. They wouldn't have thought her lucky after the move, when she'd failed to make a single friend in her new school and didn't even have an annoying little sister to fall back on for company.

'Diaz thinks it's his job to look out for me,' Rosaria had explained.

It had taken a few more years for Rose to understand why Diaz thought that way, a few more years of long school holidays spent with her favourite person—Rosaria—and the sulky presence of her least favourite—Diaz—for her to consider that if they spent their terms at their English boarding school and most of their holidays with their English grandmother, then how much time did they actually spend in their native Spain with their parents? The answer to that was not a lot.

Not her problem, Rose thought defiantly when she reached the ground floor of the hotel. She was long done with trying to understand what made Diaz Martinez tick or understand why, despite his sister's long-ago assertion that he hated everyone, it was just Rose he abhorred. Just Rose his hackles lifted for. Just Rose he watched with distrust and suspicion.

She wished she could scratch away the memory of the night when he'd looked at her with a tenderness that had made her heart fill like a balloon.

Thanking the porter for opening the door for her, she stepped out into the early autumn air. She should have brought a jacket with her. It had been a long time since she'd been outside this late in an evening.

A black cab was approaching. The porter hailed it and opened the back door for her. He was closing it when it swung back open and Diaz slid in beside her.

CHAPTER TWO

THE DOOR CLOSED, enclosing them in the cab. A little of the tension contained in Diaz released. Enough to snatch a breath. And inhale a trace of Rose's beautiful, toxic scent.

'You think it acceptable to cut and run after dumping that on me?' he demanded tersely.

The woman who'd dumped the bombshell rested her head back and gazed at the cab's ceiling. 'You are hardly in a position to complain about me cutting and running after what you did.'

There was a pounding in his head. 'So this is pay-back?'

'No.' She turned her gaze to him. 'Just pointing out your hypocrisy. I left so you could digest what I'd told you in your own time and without my hateful presence there to distract you.'

'How can I digest that? You tell me you're pregnant with twins and then you disappear?'

'I didn't disappear, Diaz. I left. Even if you've deleted my number, you know how to get hold of it and get hold of me. You certainly know where I live.'

The implication being that he'd done the opposite and made it damn near impossible for her to get hold of him.

That it was an implication that happened to be the truth did nothing to still the tempest raging in him.

The cab driver rapped loudly on the plastic-glass thing separating them from him. 'Where to?' By the impatience in his voice, it was a question he'd already asked.

Rose closed her eyes a moment then gave the name of a hotel in Westminster. The cab set off.

Diaz twisted in his seat to face her. They'd both positioned themselves at the furthest point to the other. He made an effort to speak in a cordial tone. 'You're staying in London?'

'Only for tonight. I'm going home in the morning.' There was weariness in her voice.

'I'll drive you home.'

'I've got a train booked.' She didn't look at him.

'If I drive, we can talk. We have a lot to discuss.' The lives of the two babies currently nestled in her belly. His babies. Their babies. Created during the one night of his whole life he'd never wanted to have to think of again.

He'd crept out of her bed and walked out of their Devon home with a stomach full of lead knowing he must never see her again.

How could he have not considered the possibility that their carelessness—*his* carelessness—could have had such huge, life-changing ramifications?

'And many months to discuss it,' she said.

'Months? Rose, you're pregnant *now*.' In the blink of an eye, the future he'd created for himself far from the toxicity of all the feelings she evoked in him had been ripped away. Far from excising her from his life for good, he was going to be tied to her for ever.

He'd despised her from the start. It had been irrational then, he understood that now, but his grandmother's Devon house had been the one place that had felt like home to him. The one place he and Rosaria could simply be. Their parents' home—and he used that word loosely—in Madrid had felt more like a high-end, stylish museum than a place to live and relax. Like many high-end museums, visits were by appointment only, even for the fabulously chic owners' children.

Diaz's fabulously chic parents had sent the usual driver in the Bentley to collect their two children from their respective hideously expensive boarding schools, and the two Martinez children had been driven to their grandmother's full of plans for how they would spend their summer. Diaz had seen it as his responsibility to keep Rosaria entertained. Keep her safe. Her uncomplicated adoration of him had made him feel like a prince in comparison to how their parents' indifference had made him feel.

And then they'd arrived and discovered a new housekeeper had replaced the retired Joan. A new live-in housekeeper with a skinny daughter in tow who was a similar age to Rosaria. That had been it. His little shadow had left him without a thought and attached herself to Rose, and, *Dios*, had he resented Rose for it. Resented that this stranger had treated the place he'd considered his home as her home. Resented, too, his grandmother's obvious adoration of this wild child who'd had no volume control, a seeming allergy to footwear, never walked when she could skip or run, and whose presence had infected the entirety of the one place he'd felt he belonged.

Diaz liked to think he'd have got over his irrational resentment if she hadn't become such a bad influence on Rosaria, an influence that had grown as the girls strode through adolescence. If not for Rose, his sister would still be a part of his life, not living in a hippy cult in Nevada, poisoning her mind and body with all manner of drugs and refusing to take his calls.

It was almost beyond credulity that the wild child who'd led his sister astray would be the one to lead a clean adult life. He almost wished he had evidence that she'd never really changed her rebellious ways and so could go for sole custody, but having lived with her for months while they shared the care of his dying grand-mother, and having watched her like a hawk throughout, he had to accept that, in this regard, Rose had changed.

Besides, if he was to try and take the children from her, his grandmother, may she be resting in peace, would see that he was sent to hell for it. He knew damn well she was already looking down on him with sorrow that he'd never intended to keep his marital promise.

His grandmother had always been blind to Rose's faults. Always forgiven and excused every transgression.

'Indeed I am,' Rose agreed. '*I'm* pregnant, not you, so don't think you can start throwing your weight around.'

'I don't *throw my weight around.*'

She speared him with a stare.

'Don't give me that look,' he said angrily. 'I don't know what you want from me but—'

'Nothing but a bottle of gin, but that'll have to wait until I finish breastfeeding.'

'Enough of the jokes,' he snarled.

'It's either make jokes or let myself lose my rag like you're on the verge of doing.'

He hated that she was right.

Breathing deeply, he rolled his neck. 'Let me make one thing clear,' he said tightly. 'You might be the one carrying them but they are my children too, and I *will* be a father to them.'

Her blue eyes flashed. 'I know. That's why I told you.'

'Then as we are in agreement in that regard, I *will* drive you home tomorrow because I'm moving back in.'

'No and no, and before you explode, let *me* make one thing clear.' There wasn't the slightest shred of amusement on her face. 'When our year of marriage is up, we're still divorcing.'

'I'm counting the days until I can file the divorce papers, but you are not keeping me from my children,' he bit back. 'Try it and I will fight you, and don't think I won't, and I will win.' Even if she did have the funds to fight him right back. Funds she'd inherited from his grandmother.

'For heaven's sake, Diaz, will you stop assuming the worst of me?' she cried in exasperation. 'When the babies are born you can be as involved as you want to be, but I'm carrying twins and that means extra risks and I'm not willing to risk their health or mine with the stress that living with you would bring.'

His barely controlled temper rose back up his throat. 'You are calling me a health risk?'

'Quite frankly, yes. My blood pressure has already risen and I'm barely halfway through the pregnancy.'

'You can't stop me moving back in. The house isn't in your sole name yet.' Unbeknownst to either of them, his grandmother had long ago transferred the house deeds into their joint names, long before she'd made her one request that neither of them had been able to refuse—that they marry.

'You're right, I can't, so I'm going to appeal to whatever shred of decency you have left inside you and ask—

beg—you, for the sake of our babies, to let me get on with the pregnancy alone.'

'You have a responsibility to bring the babies safely into the world but I have a responsibility, as their father, to help you do that.'

'And how is it going to help me when you and I can't even be civil to each other?' she demanded. 'You can come to all the scans and appointments and other medical pregnancy stuff, but please, nothing more than that. Just sharing the same air as you raises my blood pressure and that isn't good for them or for me.'

The cab came to a stop. In the distance, Westminster Abbey. He barely registered it.

Neither of them moved.

'Please, Diaz,' she beseeched. 'I've put our babies first by telling you about the pregnancy when I could have kept you in the dark, and now I need you to put them first too. Please. For their sake.'

And this was the danger of Rose, he thought dimly as he gazed into the large blue eyes brimming with an emotion that made his heart pump far harder than it should. The flashes of vulnerability. They affected him in a way nothing else did, caused a painful ache in his chest he'd never learned how to erase.

Dios, how could one woman inflict so many contrary emotions in one man?

He'd been rash in his declaration that he move back into the Devon house with her. And that was another danger of Rose. The burning toxicity that flowed through his veins when he was with her. It always stopped him thinking rationally and brought out the impulsive side to his nature.

Rose was his personal poison, and there was no antidote.

'Let me be sure I understand things,' he said, speaking
quietly as he gathered his thoughts and made another attempt to quell his inner turbulence. 'You are saying that
I can accompany you to all pregnancy-related appointments but that is the extent of my involvement with the
pregnancy? But when the babies are born you will not
try to stop me being a father to them?'

'All I'm saying is let me bring them safely into the
world without any pressure or stress and then yes, of
course, you can be as hands-on a father as you wish to be.'

'There is no *of course*, not with you.'

She closed her eyes and expelled a slow breath. 'You
have just proven my point. You assume the worst in everything I say or do. You always have.'

Now he was the one to expel a slow breath. 'Not always,' he rebutted softly.

Their eyes locked back together, shared memories
flowing between them of those months when they'd
pulled together and worked in harmony for his grandmother's sake, and he remembered how his grandmother's blind faith in Rose had been paid back tenfold in the
tender love and care Rose had given her, and he felt it
again, that ache, that yearn to cross the invisible divide
they'd both erected between them…

They'd crossed that divide four months ago. Smashed
it into pieces. The price they both had to pay for it was
more than either of them could ever have imagined.

He cleared his throat. 'And the birth? Am I allowed to
share that with you?'

Her chin wobbled. Blinking hard, she swallowed and
nodded. 'They're your babies too. You should be there to

greet them into the world. All I ask is that you put aside your loathing of me for it.' The semblance of a smile broke free. 'I've heard that labour can be a bit painful so I'd much rather not have you glowering at me while I'm going through it.'

Rose sat on a rock in the small, private cove reached through the bottom of the garden, and watched the waves crash onto the shore. Despite living by the coast for so many years, she'd never had much interest in the sea. Since discovering she was pregnant though, she'd found herself taking long beach walks, the fresh sea air clearing the demons in her head as she marvelled at the changing nature of it all, how one day there was barely a ripple as far as the eye could see, the next a swirling tempest.

It had been weeks since she'd found the energy for her daily walk. Now it took all her reserves just to reach the cove. That morning had taken more of her reserves than normal.

Diaz was coming over.

It would be the first time he'd been to the house since that night.

She'd not felt that she could refuse. Not when he was coming with a specially commissioned twin cot for the babies.

Only four weeks to go and then their babies would be sleeping in it. The complicated nature of Rose's blood pressure and other warning signs meant she'd been advised to have a caesarean at thirty-eight weeks. She hadn't argued. All she wanted was for her babies to make it into the world whole and healthy. Diaz hadn't argued either. On this one thing, their thoughts were perfectly aligned.

She hadn't seen enough of him to know if their

thoughts aligned on other aspects of parenthood. He'd accompanied her to all her medical appointments but that had been it. He'd taken her request to go through the pregnancy without his blood-pressure-raising presence seriously, and for that she was grateful. She was grateful, too, for the regular thoughtful messages he sent, checking in that she was okay. His primary concern was the health of their babies but she knew in his own sick, twisted way, that there was an underlying concern for her health too. She just wished her heart didn't skip to see his name flash on the screen. Wished she didn't have such a strong awareness whenever she sat in the cove that a twenty-minute walk along the beach would take her to the house he'd bought a few months ago so he could be close at hand if she needed him.

She wished a lot of things, none of which could ever come true.

Her phone pinged a message.

Be with you in ten.

Her heart thumped, and she closed her eyes with a long sigh.

There was a pain beneath her ribs, and she rubbed it as she walked—waddled—up the gentle path to the garden. Her head was hurting too. She'd long resembled a beached whale but today she felt especially bloated.

Passing the small housekeeper's cottage she'd lived in with her mother, she blinked back the tears that had been swelling more frequently than they'd done in years. Grief, Rose had learned, was like the sea. Some days you barely felt a ripple. Others, it was like a tempest of it had unleashed. There had been more tempest days than calm in recent months. She'd never needed her mother more.

Wiping a falling tear, she sniffed the emotions back and continued to the house where her every memory of the man who haunted its walls had been born.

And there he was, his tall rangy figure coming round the side of the old manor house, dark brown hair blowing in the cold breeze, wearing dark jeans and a tan leather jacket. Despite being only a quarter English, he'd never felt the cold like she had.

Her breath caught in her throat and for a beat she wished she had her camera around her neck.

There had been a day, years ago, when she'd been sixteen and thrilled with her first professional camera, a Christmas present from Mrs Martinez, and she'd taken pictures of anything and everything. Diaz had been alone in the old-fashioned drawing room reading something on his tablet. The Christmas decorations had been taken down but he'd filled the room so well with his still presence that Rose had barely noticed their absence. She'd taken the photo of him without thinking.

He'd looked up at her, she remembered. Remembered too the long pause before his lips had twisted and he'd asked what she thought she was doing, taking sneaky pictures of him.

Mortified, not just at being caught but at the compulsion to take his picture in the first place, she'd given him a sulky smile and said it was only the one picture and that it was for her dartboard.

Now, nine years later, she saw him clock her again. Noted the hesitation in his gait before he crossed the lawn to her.

He rammed his hands in his jeans pockets. 'You have been for a walk?'

Feeling suddenly and unaccountably awkward, she looked down at his expensive black boots and answered quietly, 'Just to the cove.'

She felt his stare pierce her but he made no comment. She could only imagine what the restraint of keeping a civil tongue in his head around her was costing him, and wondered how long after the babies were born he could keep this civility up. Probably until he judged she was fully recovered from the birth. Her head was hurting too much for her to think how she would play it when that happened and normal loathing resumed.

Walking in step, they reached the boot room in silence. Rose swallowed as she pulled her house keys out and unlocked the door.

Instead of following her into the cramped space, Diaz took a step back. 'I'll get the cot.'

She nodded. 'I'll unlock the front door.' Silly, really, as he still had his own keys. She should ask for them back, especially now that he'd signed his share of the house over to her.

Mrs Martinez's dream of them making this house a proper marital home had lasted less time than their marriage. Another four months and their marriage would be dissolved, and the dreams that had come vividly to life for one passionate and beautiful night would dissolve with them.

Those dreams had already dissolved, and Rose blinked the remnants away knowing they'd only resurfaced because this was the first time Diaz had entered the house since that fateful night.

'Do you still want it in your room?' he asked once he'd brought the huge box inside.

'Please.' She couldn't meet his stare. 'Next to the bed.' The bed they'd conceived their babies in. 'Either side will be fine.'

Carrying the box to the stairs, he stopped before taking the first step and looked directly at her. 'Are you feeling okay?'

She shrugged. 'Just feeling very pregnant today. Why?'

His green eyes narrowed in speculation before he gave a short smile. 'You must look more pregnant than last time. Rest your feet. I won't be long getting this together.'

Rose turned away so she wouldn't have to watch him climb the stairs.

For all that he'd pre-set his mind into 'get done and get out' out mode, Diaz still found he needed to brace himself before crossing the threshold into Rose's bedroom.

How he'd resented his grandmother for giving this room to her. It had been the room his parents used when they visited. His grandmother's dry, 'But they've only visited once in the last four years and there are three other rooms they can use if they ever grace my door again,' had cut no ice with him. The interloper had inveigled herself even more tightly into their lives. That his grandmother had allowed the move into the bedroom to be a permanent thing once Rose finished senior school, even after she'd caused his sister's near-death and been the catalyst for Rosaria cutting him from her life, had angered him like nothing else ever had… Apart from when Rose denied culpability.

He breathed deeply, refusing to let memories of that

sickening row surface. Especially the way it had ended. Especially that.

Except he was now in her room for only the second time since she'd taken occupancy of it and having to fight the memories from that one other time from surfacing too.

He should have got one of his team to bring the cot over and put it together, not let his caveman instinct of doing it himself override his rationality.

He wanted to put together his babies' bed but didn't want to see the bed they'd been created in and deal with all the memories that came with it, and so he blurred it from his sight...but couldn't blur the neat, white dresser with the baby change mat on it, or the pretty box filled with tiny nappies. Couldn't blur the calming, feminine aesthetic of a room that had once been more functional than lived in.

Despite his intention to 'get done and get out' his gaze was drawn to the photo tiles artfully placed on the walls. Rose and her mother, Amelia. Rose's mother alone on the beach with her eyes closed and her face tilted to the sun. Rose and his grandmother. Rose's father and his wife and children in what Diaz presumed was the garden of their Australian home. Rose and Rosaria...

He tore his gaze from the pictures and got to work.

In the kitchen, Rose had turned the radio on so she didn't have to hear Diaz move around her bedroom and be consumed with the memories of the one and only time he'd stepped foot inside it since his grandmother had insisted it be Rose's all those years ago.

He'd been furious when he'd found out, she remembered painfully. Not that he'd said anything. He hadn't needed to. Diaz's fury had been etched on his face. He'd accepted Rose moving out of the housekeeper's cottage and into the manor house after her mother's death so she could complete her final school year, but hadn't expected the move to become permanent. He'd thought she would complete her exams and then go to her father in Australia, a man she'd never lived with and hadn't seen in the flesh since she was a baby; she was perfectly certain Diaz would have paid a one-way ticket to be rid of her for good.

Mrs Martinez had had other ideas.

'This is your home, and I want you to stay. You've got your university place, and Plymouth's only a short drive so you can still do your degree and still have all the fun that comes with student life, but you're too young to be out in the world on your own,' she'd said, even though Rose had recently turned eighteen. 'And I'm too old to be in this rambling place on my own.' She'd smiled. 'Besides, I'd miss all your noise.'

'That's a really lovely offer,' Rose had said, covering the elderly woman's hand, 'but what would Diaz say? You know how he feels about me.'

Mrs Martinez's face had hardened. Clearly, she was remembering the terrible evening and terrible row that had taken place only weeks earlier. 'I love my grandson but when it comes to you, he has a blind spot. I can do whatever I want in my own home, and what I want is your young, lively presence to live vicariously through.'

'He'll think I'm trying to take Rosaria's place in your affections,' Rose had warned.

'Then he's a fool because you earned your own place in it a long time ago. I don't want to live on my own, Rose. Diaz is too busy conquering and travelling the world to visit as often as I'd like, and Rosaria...' She'd sighed sadly. 'Rosaria has chosen her path.'

Indeed she had, Rose now thought wearily. And it was a path Diaz still blamed Rose for Rosaria taking.

She squeezed her eyes shut, not wanting to think about that awful confrontation. Seven years had passed. It shouldn't still have the power to hurt.

Movement in her belly was just the distraction she needed...except the accompanying stabbing sharpness wasn't the usual discomfort she'd become used to since the babies had grown so big inside her. Close to tears with the pain, she rubbed at the spot with one hand, and stared intently at the other hand. Was she imagining it had swollen even more?

'All done... What's the matter?'

Rose looked from her swollen hand to Diaz, who'd appeared at the kitchen door. Tried to smother the panic suddenly gnawing at her. 'I think we need to phone the midwife.'

CHAPTER THREE

DIAZ COULD NOT stop pacing the corridor.

How long had she been in the operating theatre? It felt like hours.

He could not stop his mind racing to what was happening in there.

This was not the way the birth was supposed to go. He wasn't supposed to be shut out.

Rose wasn't supposed to be unconscious.

She was supposed to have a spinal anaesthetic and Diaz was supposed to be sitting beside her not glowering at her. That had been the plan.

The midwife had told them to go straight to the hospital. Diaz had never driven with such distracted concentration before, the urge to put his foot down fighting with the need to make the drive as smooth as it could be for her. Only thirty minutes could have passed from the phone call to their arrival but they'd entered the maternity wing with Rose complaining the lights were hurting her eyes.

Pre-eclampsia. Deadly if left too late.

'We need to get these babies out now,' the obstetrician had said, and it had been the barely detectable urgency in his voice that had alerted Diaz to just how serious the situation was.

Rose had recognised the seriousness too.

From the hospital bed they'd wheeled her to the theatre room on, those captivating blue eyes had locked onto his. Fear had rung from them. 'Don't let our babies die,' she'd whispered. 'Please, Diaz.'

At the door, he'd clasped her hand and kissed her fingers. 'Nothing is going to happen to our babies and nothing is going to happen to you, okay?'

And then she'd been wheeled inside and he'd been barred from following, and since then he'd heard nothing, had no clue as to what the hell was going on in there, had only been able to torture himself with terrible thoughts that turned his blood to ice and stopped his heart from beating.

'Mr Martinez?'

He spun around and found the obstetrician at the door.

'Rose?' he asked hoarsely.

'She's in recovery.'

'She's okay?'

'She's out of danger. It will be…'

But the obstetrician's next words evaporated through the ringing in Diaz's ears as a wave of relief so powerful he doubled over under its force punched through him. *'Gracias a Dios,'* he muttered reverently to himself. *'Gracias a Dios.'*

It took a long moment to compose himself.

'And the babies?' he asked, straightening.

'You daughters will be just fine too…'

'They are girls?' His heart caught. Neither of them had wanted to know the sex but Rose had confessed when they'd been in the waiting room for one of her medical appointments that she had a feeling she was carrying girls.

Just a passing comment but it had stuck with him, and from that point he'd always imagined their babies as girls.

The obstetrician smiled. 'Two girls. They're tiny, naturally, given how premature they are, but they're fighters like their mother. They've been taken to the neonatal unit. One of my team will take you to them shortly.'

'Can I see my wife?'

'Soon. Let her come round from the anaesthetic first.'

It took effort for Rose to open her eyes.

She heard her name and slowly turned her head. Diaz was sitting on a chair beside her.

She had to swallow to croak, 'Hi.'

'Hi yourself.'

Exhaustion made her sigh. 'Have you seen them?' When she'd first come round from the anaesthetic, the nurse had been quick to assure her the babies had made it safely into the world.

He smiled. Even through the blurriness of her vision, she could see the awe in his eyes. 'They're beautiful, Rose. Just perfect.'

Her heart swelled. She longed to see them and hold them. Part of her wish was answered when Diaz brought pictures of them up on his phone for her.

'I've forwarded them to you and I've got one of my team printing them off so you can hold them until you can hold our girls for real.'

Tears filled her eyes. 'Thank you. That's a really thoughtful thing to do.'

'It is the least I can do. I'm afraid they're not up to your standard of photography, but you can rectify that when you're better.'

She blinked back the tears and tried to smile, but the

anaesthetic and pain relief were still working their magic in her. 'Will you kiss them for me?' Her eyes were getting heavy again. 'And tell them I love them and will be with them as soon as I can?'

'I promise.'

'Thank you.' It was becoming a struggle to speak. 'And, Diaz?'

'Yes?'

'Can we call them Amelia and Josephine?'

His shoulders rose and the strangest smile curved his cheeks. 'I guessed you'd...' He gave a low laugh and admitted, 'Those are the names I've been calling them in my head.'

Her eyes closed and she fell back into sleep with a contentment in her heart and a soft smile on her lips.

Amelia and Josephine were her mother's and Diaz's grandmother's respective names.

She didn't register the lingering brush of warm lips on her forehead.

Five months later

Diaz let himself in through the front door. 'Rose?'

No answer.

After checking all the rooms downstairs, he headed up to her bedroom. She was sprawled face down on the bed, fast asleep, one hand dangling in the cot, which had been pushed against the bed so she could comfort the twins through the night when needed. But this wasn't night time. It was three in the afternoon.

Amelia was asleep too, but Josephine—Josie as they both called her—was awake and kicking her legs. He scooped her up. Immediately she went for his nose. If ever he was confused over which twin was which, all he had to do was bring them to his face. If she tried to suck his nose then it was Josie.

His almost noiseless movement woke Rose, and she lifted her head. When she saw Diaz, she blinked in confusion.

'Go back to sleep,' he mouthed.

Another confused owl-like blink and then she put her head back on the pillow.

Carrying Josie downstairs, he took her into the kitchen and, holding her securely with one arm, made himself a cup of instant coffee. He disliked instant but there were no fresh coffee beans. Other than half a loaf of bread, some teabags, an empty box of cereal and some dried pasta, the cupboards were bare.

He sighed.

Rose thought she was a superwoman who could do it all. The only person she permitted to share the childcare load was Diaz, who she let come and go as he pleased. He limited his travels as much as he could but he had an international business to run. When he wasn't around, she was alone with the girls. He always knew when she'd had no sleep at all because he'd walk through the door and she'd mumble the time for the girls' next feed before zonking out. When she was awake around him, it was as if he faded into the background for her, a presence that blended into the walls.

The current status quo couldn't continue. It wasn't good for any of them, least of all Rose.

The current status quo also meant that when he was around to share the load, he returned to his home in the next town once the twins were in bed, even though neither twin slept through the night. He'd stayed full time the month after they'd all been discharged from hospital, sleeping in his old room, but then one morning Rose had declared herself recovered from her caesarean and that it would now be better if he slept under his own roof. Knowing how fragile she was, he hadn't argued. Back then, with newborn twins who refused to sync their feeding or sleeping schedule, he'd only been concerned with getting through each day too, and had agreed to leave on the proviso they employed a nanny to help her. Preferably two. One for each child.

Every nanny interviewed had been rejected. Rose had found fault with each and every one of them. She'd flatly refused a live-in housekeeper to take the domestic burden off her shoulders too, even though she was living in a three-thousand-square-metre, seven-bedroomed house. It had taken weeks of cajoling before she compromised and allowed him to hire a daily cleaner.

He checked the fridge. Empty except for some butter and four made-up bottles of baby milk. It had broken Rose's heart that all her efforts to breastfeed had proved fruitless.

Josie clocked the bottles and made grabby hands, which Amelia, with the scarily strange telepathy that bound the twins, took as her cue to wake up and start screaming the house down.

Things had to change, he thought grimly, putting a bottle in each of the bottle warmers, and when Rose appeared with Amelia in her arms, he passed her a warmed bottle with a smile as grim as his thoughts.

Yes, things had to change. He'd bent to Rose's wishes for five months, knowing it would take time for her to recover from the birth and adjust to the seismic shock of the reality of newborn twins.

Luckily, he'd been working on a plan to enact change, and the time to enact it was now. He just needed to tread carefully.

'You're back early,' she said tiredly.

'Just as well,' he said, trying not to sound too pointed. 'What are you planning to feed yourself?'

She pulled a face and raised a shoulder before sinking onto the kitchen sofa and feeding Amelia her bottle. 'Toast probably. I forgot to order a food delivery.'

He settled Josie in his arms at the kitchen table. 'Shall I get take-out?'

'If you like.'

He hated this lethargy. Hated to see her hair lank, unbrushed and bedraggled, her clothes crumpled, her usually bright complexion pasty. Especially hated the dullness in her eyes. She was too thin too. In the last two months, all the baby weight had suddenly fallen off, and he knew it was because she too often forgot to eat. He didn't know how to approach any of this without sounding like a critical monster. Rose was neglecting herself because all her energy was devoted to their daughters. Whatever state she'd let herself fall into, when it came to their daughters, she really was a superwoman. Their daughters were happy, healthy and thriving under her loving care.

'Chinese or Thai?'

Another listless rise of the shoulder. 'How was Paris?'

'Athens,' he corrected, then wished he hadn't when he saw her dismay.

'Oh. Sorry.'

'Don't be. Listen, I have been thinking and I would like to take the girls to Spain. It is time that they got to know the other half of their heritage.'

Even greater dismay rang clear. 'Not yet, Diaz. It's too soon.'

He made sure to keep his tone even. 'Not in the least. The sooner they are introduced to flying, the sooner they will get used to it.'

'But they're only five months old,' she pleaded. 'They won't understand any of it. Please, wait a few more months.'

'Their brains are like sponges.' Even if they would try and eat an actual sponge if given half a chance. 'And the sunshine would do us all good.' This early English summer had, so far, been a wash-out.

'I know it would but...' Her eyes filled with tears. 'I'm not ready to be parted from them yet.'

Her upset set off an ache in his chest, which he smothered by kissing the top of Josie's sweet little head. 'I'm not taking them without you,' he assured her steadily through the thumping of his heart. 'You'll be coming with us.'

There was a moment of blankness before comprehension dawned. 'Oh. I misunderstood.'

'Rose, I wouldn't take the girls anywhere without you.' Even if he wanted to, which he didn't, it wouldn't be fair to Rose or the girls. Rose was their world.

Her tear-filled eyes widened until, chin wobbling, she dropped her stare from his and wedged Amelia's now empty bottle between her thigh and the arm of her chair. After brushing a lock of dirty blonde hair out of her eyes, she moved Amelia onto her lap and began gently patting her back.

He pretended not to notice the effort it took for her to keep the tears at bay. Being a superwoman mother to twin babies came at a price, and the cost for Rose was major sleep deprivation. Safe in her own home, she was too tired to see how exhausted she was.

Her voice not quite steady, she quietly said, 'If you want us to go to Spain, the girls will need passports.'

'They already have them,' he confessed. He'd antici-pated this argument and so had fixed it before it arose. 'I arranged it.'

Her gaze flew back to him, eyebrows drawn together in confusion. 'When?'

'Two weeks ago. I signed for them the other morning before I left for Athens. They're in the safe in the study.'

'You never mentioned it.'

'I wanted it to be a surprise.'

She didn't look convinced. 'I didn't know fathers could apply for baby passports.'

'I have the same legal parental responsibility as you.'

'Oh, yes…' She suddenly jerked her chin and blinked. 'Has our divorce come through?'

It was not the first time she'd asked this. 'Not yet.'

'I thought it would be done by now…' Her voice trailed off as anxiety flittered over her face. 'You did file the papers, didn't you?'

Their one-year anniversary had passed six weeks ago.

'Yes,' he lied smoothly. The birth of the twins had changed everything as far as Diaz was concerned…not that he'd voiced this to Rose, not with her mental and emotional state being what it was. One step at a time. Getting her to Spain was merely the first step.

Her nod was absent, her thoughts clearly busy.

'So, that's settled, then,' he said decisively before her thoughts could get *too* busy. As much as he wanted the old Rose back, he knew it would be better if she returned while they were in Spain rather than under this roof where the ghosts of their shared past lived.

'What's settled?'

'Spain. I'll make the arrangements. We can leave tomorrow.'

Rose clutched at her hair. 'But we *can't* go yet,' she wailed. 'I haven't got a suitcase for my own stuff.'

She could scarcely believe how quickly Diaz had made this trip to Spain happen. She'd woken in the early hours to Amelia making snuffling sounds in her sleep, certain she'd dreamed the entire conversation. Most of her life had felt like a waking dream since she'd brought the girls home from hospital. She'd never known such exhaustion existed.

Her precious girls were worth every hour of sleep lost.

It wasn't until Diaz had turned up while she was giving them their morning feed and asked if she'd started packing that she'd realised their discussion about Spain had been no dream. Things had moved at a rapid dreamlike pace ever since, which was a bit of a shock to a system grown accustomed to taking one long day at a time.

Uncertain what was best to pack for the girls, she'd played it safe by stuffing her cases with the entirety of their wardrobes, which Diaz's driver had already put in the back of the car, and now she had nothing to stuff the bundle of her own clothing currently heaped on the bed into other than an old beach bag.

Strong hands clasped her shoulders. The physical contact made her start. Diaz was around so much that she never really noticed him as anything but the one person who loved her daughters as much as she did. She didn't have the functioning brain cells to see him as anything but their father, so to feel such solid contact from him when the most they'd shared in five months was brushed arms as they passed the babies between them was another shock to her system.

Stern green eyes locked onto hers. 'All you need is your passport and I have packed it with mine and the girls'. We will buy whatever you need when we get there, but we have to go now or we will miss our slot.'

'We can get another slot,' she protested.

'No,' he said firmly, hands still grasping her shoulders. 'It is the summer. Flight slots are scarce, even private ones. We need to leave. Now.'

Before she could argue again, he let go of her shoulders and expertly lifted both girls out of the cot. Holding them securely in each arm, he headed out of the room without a backward glance.

Trying not to cry—she had no idea where the tears came from—she snatched an armful of clothes from the bundle, shoved them into the beach bag and hurried after them, just as Diaz knew she would. It didn't improve her mood to catch a glimpse of her reflection in the mirror as she left her room. With her black jeans and light black sweater, she looked like she could be cast as a member of the Addams Family. They wouldn't even need to bother with gothic make-up. She looked a wreck.

She didn't want to leave the safety of her Devon home. That was the problem. As tired as she was—and she was very much aware her exhaustion made her more emotional than she would normally be—travelling to Diaz's territory made her feel all antsy, like there was an undertone of motives, a reason for his determination to get them all to Spain being kept from her. Although what that something could be, her exhausted mind couldn't begin to envisage.

* * *

Rose's first trip on an aeroplane had been for a visit to Diaz and Rosaria's parents in Spain when she'd been seventeen. Rosaria had begged for Rose to be allowed to go with them. Mrs Martinez hadn't needed persuading.

Diaz had graduated from university the year before. To celebrate, his uber-rich parents, the celebrated faces and brains behind the Tinez luxury beauty brand, had given him a large pot of cash with which to make his own way in the world. As a result, his visits to Devon had substantially decreased, the long weeks of his presence throughout the year reduced to the weekends he could fit them into his busy schedule. Strangely, Rose had found herself missing him, although when he did turn up she quickly resorted back to loathing him in the face of his unrelenting hostility towards her.

The return flight eight years earlier had been the height of luxury. First class! It had blown her mind. No doubt if Diaz had booked it, she'd have been stuck at the back in cattle class.

This journey, travelling on Diaz's private jet, which made the luxury of first class seem like the cattle class he'd have chucked her in all those years ago, she was too exhausted to appreciate the sumptuousness of it all. Both girls screamed their heads off during take-off but then quickly quieted, and with Amelia asleep in her secured carrycot and Josie contentedly trying to eat Diaz's nose, there was nothing to stop Rose from obeying her body's yearn for sleep…and nothing to stop the most potent memory of her last visit to Spain from weaving into her dreams…

'Sure you don't want a puff?' Rosaria asked, waving the spliff over Rose's face.

'I'm sure.'

Rose had tried dope once, over the Easter holidays, from the small stash Rosaria had brought home with her from boarding school. She'd hated the way it made her feel all woozy. Rosaria, though, liked the way it made her feel, and having unlimited funds from her generous but neglectful parents meant she could afford to buy it whenever she chose. And afford to buy other narcotics too, Rose suspected, despite Rosaria's denials. She knew lots of people smoked dope but it made her increasingly uncomfortable to see her best friend smoke it. Worried her too. Rosaria had changed in the last year. The one time Rose had tried to voice her concerns, Rosaria had brushed them away with an airy, 'I'm eighteen. I make my own choices now. Don't worry,' she'd added in a placatory tone, 'I know what my limits are.'

And maybe she did, Rose thought as she closed her eyes and enjoyed the feel of the sun on her bikini-clad body. The girls had the Martinez villa to themselves and were sunbathing around the pool.

She was probably worrying about nothing. They'd been in Spain for four days and had spent every waking hour together. This was the first time Rosaria had done anything she shouldn't since they'd arrived, so maybe she should cut her some slack and...

There was the strangest prickling of her skin, and then Rosaria swore under her breath. 'My brother. Quick, take it.'

Rose shot upright and found the spliff stuck between her fingers before her brain caught up to realise what she was doing.

Striding past the pool, Diaz. Diaz wearing nothing but a pair of black swim shorts and black shades, his atten-

*tion firmly on the screen of his phone...until he realised
he wasn't alone and came to an abrupt halt.*

*Rose had frozen. The beats of her heart had gone hay-
wire. When Diaz's stare locked onto hers, a fuzzy, electrical sensation danced over her skin and all of a sudden
she was filled with a sticky awareness she couldn't begin
to understand. What she did understand in that frozen
moment, though, was that Diaz, her best friend's hateful
older brother, was no longer a boy. At some point, when
she hadn't been watching, Diaz had turned into a man.
A beautiful, broad-chested, sculpted man and, oh, she
could hardly breathe to look at him.*

*She'd barely noticed he'd started walking again. Not
until he stood before them and his nose twitched and
his gaze dropped to the spliff held in her frozen fingers.*

*'How dare you bring that filth into my parents' home?'
he accused tightly.*

*In an instant, the spell he'd cast her under was broken.
'I...' Feeling Rosaria's pleading eyes on her, Rose's denial
caught on her tongue. 'I'm sorry,' she finished lamely.*

*'Sorry you got caught,' he snarled before glaring at
his sister. 'Did you share this with her?'*

*'No, of course not,' Rosaria denied. 'You know I
wouldn't touch that stuff. Rose brought it.'*

*The rest of Diaz's diatribe was lost through the
whooshing in her ears at Rosaria's betrayal.*

*'Did you hear what I just said, Rose?' he demanded,
compelling her to look back at his furious face through
sheer force of will. 'I will be telling my grandmother
about this and will let her decide whether your mother
should be informed. Considering the gravity of your
mother's condition, I am disgusted you would do anything to make the time she has left harder. Thank God*

you're going home tomorrow—when you get back, you stay away from my sister, do you hear me? I always knew you were bad news. This friendship ends now.'

He stormed away, his poison still ringing in Rose's ears.

'Rose?' Rosaria whispered.

'Don't say anything,' she managed to drag out, hugging her knees tightly and fighting back tears of humiliation and hurt and betrayal. 'Just...don't.'

'Rose...'

'No.'

A hand lightly touched her shoulder.

'Rose. Wake up.'

She snapped her eyes open. Diaz was hovering over her. Diaz of now, not the Diaz of then. He had one of their daughters in his arms. Amelia. She couldn't read the expression on his face. If it was anyone else, she'd guess it might be concern.

'You were crying in your sleep,' he said slowly.

She touched her wet cheek. 'Just a dream,' she whispered.

'Must have been a bad one.'

She nodded and looked away, grateful when a member of the cabin crew stepped in and announced they would soon be landing.

CHAPTER FOUR

For some reason, Rose had imagined Diaz's Spanish home would be an ultra-modern villa in the heart of a bustling city like his parents' home. Instead, they were driven to a whitewashed layered Moorish-style villa framed by high palm trees, and cut into the rocks of a cove where the sea lapped up to the travertine marble steps that in turn led to sprawling lawns and the vast outdoor living areas.

'What do you think?' he asked when they were standing in the part-shaded outdoor dining area with its own bar, an industrial-sized barbecue and huge inbuilt pizza oven, gazing out over the sun slowly setting on the horizon of the calm sea. The babies were by their feet, sleeping in their carrycots.

Still unable to look properly at him after all the memories dredged up by the horrible dream that had been no dream but a replay of a time it hurt her heart to remember, she could only answer truthfully. 'It's beautiful.'

'Inspiration to start taking photos again?'

The studio she'd created for her photography had been closed since Mrs Martinez's stroke. Rose hadn't picked up her camera since the night the twins were conceived. She'd taken hundreds of pictures of the girls on her phone but her camera remained stored away.

'One day,' she answered, before changing the subject. 'Coincidence that you're living in a private cove?'

'Devon always felt more like home than Madrid. I always knew I wanted something with a similar feel to it.'

'Even though I tainted the feel of it with my malign presence?'

'Don't say that.'

'I didn't. You did.' The fog of the last five months had acted like a blanket on their history. The only time she'd vaguely shaken it off had been when she'd put a stop to Diaz sleeping over at the house, a scratching awareness that she must not allow herself to become accustomed to or reliant on his constant presence. He was the father of her children and proving himself an amazing father but she'd be a fool to think the *entente cordiale* they'd unspokenly entered could last. At some point, Diaz's inherent loathing of her would resurface, even if he did temper it for their daughters' sake.

That's what her dream had been about. A needed reminder and warning.

'Then I apologise.'

So shocked was Rose at this unexpected apology that she whipped her gaze to him.

His stare continued to take in the horizon before he gave a brief nod. 'Let me introduce you to the staff.'

As unnerved by the apology as the dream, she tautly quipped, 'Do they know I'm the daughter of your grandmother's housekeeper? Or shall I tell them I belong downstairs too, so to speak?'

'Rose, stop it,' he said quietly. 'You know I never thought that.'

'Do I?' Lifting Amelia's carrycot, she gave a quick smile. 'Not that it matters any more. The only thing that does matter is our girls, so make the introductions and then you can show me to our room. I want to get their stuff unpacked before they wake for their bottle.' If she'd known travelling was a sure-fire bet to make them fall asleep, she'd have taken them out for evening drives before bed.

She headed inside the way she'd come, into the magnificent living area, chiding herself for letting emotions surface when she needed to keep them locked away, especially from him.

But her resolve lasted only until they reached the bedrooms.

'Where's the cot?' she asked as she scanned her appointed room, uncaring of its feminine beauty when all she could see was what wasn't there. Diaz had assured her he'd had the same cot commissioned for the Devon house installed here.

'In the adjoining room.'

'Can you get it brought in here please?'

She heard him take a deep breath. 'No.'

'But there's plenty of room in here for it.'

Diaz folded his arms across his chest and braced himself for what must come. 'It is time for them to move into a room of their own. You need to sleep.'

She rounded on him, her captivating beauty dark with anger. 'That is not a decision for you to make. Bring the cot in here, right now.'

'No. I'm sorry, Rose, but we need to start as we mean to go on. They will only be in the room next to you and—'

'I'm not going from room to room when they wake when all I have to do is lean over when they're right next to me.'

'I don't expect you to. Their nannies will go to them.'

Her furious shock was so powerful he felt it like a slap to his skin.

'Their *nannies*?' she yelled. 'You've gone behind my back and employed *nannies*?'

On cue, the girls woke up. In unison, their faces screwed up and they began crying.

'See what you've done?' she said, her voice only a few decibels lower. 'You've upset them.'

No, you have with your shouting, he wisely decided not to say. He'd prepared himself for upset.

When they'd taken a girl each and were pacing the room, gently bouncing them to soothe them, he said, 'I didn't want to go behind your back but I didn't see an alternative.'

'What, other than the alternative of letting me be a mother to my own children!'

'Nothing and no one can take that from you, Rose, but you're exhausted. You've been raising twins without any family to ease the pressure when I'm away—'

'That's because I don't *have* any family, unless you want to count my father, who lives on the other side of the ruddy world!'

'I know that, and I also know how badly you missed being able to hold them those first few days and how badly you feel about being unable to feed them yourself.'

Her face crumpled.

He moved closer to her. He'd had a feeling it was those issues that had been driving her to exhaustion. 'None of that was your fault, Rose. You have nothing to make up for. You have done your best and you are a fantastic mother for it. All that matters is the love and care you've given to them, and you've given it in abundance and as a result we have two healthy, happy little girls.'

As if to prove his point, both girls had stopped crying. Josie's mouth was aiming for Rose's nose and Amelia was trying to insert a finger into Diaz's ear.

'It's time you gave yourself a break,' he continued. 'Surviving on such little sleep isn't good for anyone— much more of it and you'll be a walking zombie.' If he'd had doubts about employing nannies behind her back, Rose crying in her sleep on the plane had fortified his resolve. Even in the days when he'd despised the air she breathed, he would not have been able to endure that whimpering sound. 'Just give the nannies a chance. You don't have to use them every night if you don't want, and if after, say, two weeks, you're still not happy with the arrangement then we'll rethink it.'

He could see her finally taking his point in. It was there in the dejection of her shoulders and the wobbling of her chin.

'What if the girls don't like them?'

Knowing he'd won, he relaxed. 'Let's introduce them and see how they take to them.'

Growing up, Rose had never thought of herself as poor. Her mother had been a whizz at making a little money go a long way and Rose had never gone without. They'd lived in a rented house in a Somerset town where everyone had to stretch their money and the local primary school's used uniform sale had a queue before it opened. Rose and her mother had often been the first in it.

Moving to Devon and into the little cottage that came with her mother's new job had been like entering a whole new world. The riches in Mrs Martinez's manor house had been mind-blowing, a wealth Rose had never imagined. The sumptuousness of Diaz's parents' Madrid home, though less surprising by that point, had nonetheless been impressive.

None of what she'd experienced had prepared her for Diaz's home. She'd known he'd created his own vast fortune in the nine years since his university graduation but, restlessly exploring in the early hours while the house slept, the baby monitor clutched in her hand, she realised his wealth was something else. In the underground garage, a fleet of supercars she couldn't name but instinctively knew cost the price of a decent house each. That was on top of the cars he drove and was driven in when in England. Where his grandmother had been content to employ a housekeeper and his parents a handful of domestic employees, Diaz had a fleet of staff that rivalled his fleet of cars in numbers.

The villa itself was deceptive. Anyone looking at it from the outside would assume someone incredibly rich owned it, but it was only when you were inside and able to focus on all the detailing and the abundance of seamlessly blended ancient and modern artwork, and the labyrinth of airy, white-walled rooms the external dimensions only hinted at, that you realised this was the home of someone with unimaginable wealth.

Rose supposed her inheritance from Mrs Martinez meant she would be considered unimaginably rich by most people's standards. Even after throwing away half her inheritance to access the poker game and force Diaz's attention, she had enough left in the bank to see her comfortably through for the rest of her life. But nothing like this. Not even close. In comparison, she was like her mother making a little go a long way.

It was unnerving for reasons she couldn't comprehend. As were the little touches she'd noticed to make the place more toddler friendly. Their daughters were a long way from being toddlers. Months and months. So why the safety locks on the kitchen cupboard doors and the clear plastic corner protectors on all the tables?

And why a freshly painted playroom filled with more unopened boxes of toys than would be found in a toddler toy store and the clearly new fencing around the kidney-shaped swimming pool area?

Overactive imagination, she told herself when she reached the top of the staircase that led to the sleeping quarters. Overactive imagination and sleep deprivation...

The door opposite her appointed room opened.

Her heart had already jumped into her throat before Diaz emerged, tousle-haired, wearing only a pair of navy swim shorts. He had a towel slung over his shoulder.

He paused. Took her in with a long stare. Quietly, he said, '*Buenos dias*, Rose. You're up early.'

Painfully aware that she was wearing night clothes—having failed to chuck night wear in with her beach bag of clothing, a pair of silk shorts pyjamas and mid-thigh-length silk robe had been delivered and laundered for her before she'd gone to bed—and even more painfully aware of Diaz's even greater lack of clothing, she self-consciously tightened the sash of her robe. 'I could say the same about you.'

'I like to swim before the world wakes up and de-mands my time.' His gaze narrowed as he studied her face. 'Did you sleep?'

'A little.' She didn't know where to put her own gaze. The sexual awareness she had for Diaz, born that awful day in Madrid when she'd been seventeen, had all but disappeared since the birth. Being this close to him virtually naked, his tanned, rangy muscular body with its smattering of dark hair across the perfectly defined chest and abdomen only feet from where she stood…

Her awareness must have been blanketed in the same fog as their shared history because she could feel it awakening, and as prickles danced on her skin and her veins thickened, an even stronger charge pulsed, an image forming, of gently encircling his flat, brown nipples with her tongue, and suddenly the memory of his taste was right there in her mouth, as vivid as it had been the night they'd made their babies.

Her heart racing into a burr, she hurriedly fixed her stare on the terracotta flooring beneath her feet and wished for its coolness to seep into her heating bloodstream and freeze the memories into oblivion.

'And the girls?' he asked in the same low voice.

God only knew how she was able to speak. 'They've been asleep since eleven.' It was the first time they'd slept through the night.

'Spanish air must suit them.'

'That, or they're exhausted from the travelling.'

From the periphery of her vision, she saw him raise a non-committal shoulder. 'Time will tell. So why didn't you sleep? Keeping one ear open in case they woke up?'

She nodded. She'd agreed to testing out the nannies but cold feet had seen her put her cold foot down about them attending the girls through the night until they'd got used to them. Luckily for Diaz's perfect nose, he hadn't argued. 'I should check on them.'

'It's only six o'clock. Let them sleep a little longer.' Casually, he added, 'Join me for a swim?'

Taken aback at the offer, Rose's gaze shot up before she could stop it and locked onto his. Locked fast.

A pulse of electricity shifted the air around them... and pulsed in his eyes.

Powerless to break the hold of their stares, a wave of scalding heat rose inside her from the tips of her toes to the roots of her hair.

The pulse in his eyes darkened into a hooded, unmistakably sensuous gleam.

Slowly, he straightened.

Shivers let loose inside her. The scalding heat intensified, the act of breathing suddenly impossible.

His chest and shoulders rose, strong neck extending.

Rose tried to speak but her heart was thrashing so hard the beats were slamming into her throat.

Time stood suspended until, finally, he took a long inhalation and gave a short decisive nod. The smallest smile curled his lips. 'You know where to find me if you wish to join me.'

And then the air shifted again as his mostly naked body moved past her and disappeared down the stairs.

It was a long while before Rose was capable of moving her own body.

Diaz swam his usual lengths of the pool. He'd always enjoyed swimming but since becoming master of his own destiny, he'd taken to doing fifty laps daily wherever he happened to be in the world. For years he'd kept the routine, right until he'd moved back to his grandmother's home after her stroke. It was Rose's presence that had stopped his daily swims. And it was Rose fully in his mind now as he thrashed through the water. Rose, a year after he'd caught her smoking drugs by his parents' swimming pool.

The charge of awareness he'd felt that hot day in Madrid had kept him away from Devon for much of the following year. That, and his singular failure to eradicate the image of Rose in a white bikini.

Dios, he'd watched her blossom from a skinny waif into a captivating beauty without even noticing, and he'd been sickened with himself for the way he'd finally noticed. Sickened with the way it had made him feel.

Six visits he'd made home that following year. The first had been for Amelia Gregory's funeral. He would never, for as long as he lived, forget the white-faced desolation of her only child. Rose's grief had been so complete that not even Diaz had complained when his grandmother insisted she move into the main house. Not at that point, anyway.

The fourth visit to Devon had been for Rosaria's nineteenth birthday months later. She'd just completed her first year at university and Rose, recently turned eighteen, had completed her final senior school exam. His intention to take his sister out to celebrate her birthday had been thwarted when she'd announced she would be going to Rose's school prom as Rose's plus one, then going to an after-party, overbearing big brothers most definitely not invited.

He'd known something bad would happen that night. Some sixth sense weighing down in his guts had stopped him sharing a bottle of wine with his grandmother that warm summer evening. And so, when his phone had rung with his sister's name, he'd taken a deep breath before answering. 'Rosaria?'

'Diaz, it's Rose,' a panicking voice had said.

'What's happened?' he'd snapped.

'Rosaria's overdosed. The ambulance is on its way...'

'Where are you?'

He'd arrived at the address to find his baby sister being wheeled into the back of an ambulance and a group of crying partygoers huddled by his car.

'Who provided the drugs?' he'd demanded as he'd slammed his door shut. 'Tell me now or I will hold each of you culpable.'

'Rose brought them,' one of them had said tearfully.

In the back of the ambulance, his unconscious sister. Sobbing beside her, Rose.

'Get out,' he'd snarled.

'Diaz, I...'

'I said *get out*,' he'd roared.

White faced and shaking, she'd obeyed.

She had still been white faced and shaking when he'd returned many hours later to his grandmother's, after it had been established his sister was expected to make a full recovery. To that day, he had no idea how Rose made it from the party address to his grandmother's house. At the time he hadn't cared to ask. At the time he'd been too intent on releasing his fury, shouting so loudly and viciously that his grandmother had intervened.

'Diaz, it wasn't Rose's fault.'

'Not her fault?' he'd shouted. 'She provided the damned drugs!'

'I *didn't*,' she'd protested.

'See, not only is she a drug dealer but she's a liar too!' he'd yelled at his grandmother before rounding back on Rose. 'It's already been confirmed that it was you, and I'll make damned sure the police know it too...'

'You will do no such thing,' his grandmother had cut

in. 'Whoever provided the drugs—and if Rose says it wasn't her then I believe her—no one forced Rosaria to take them. Your sister has developed a drug habit, Diaz.'

'Bull.'

'You've not been here.' It was Rose who'd said that. Rose, who had been very much responsible for his avoidance of Devon and subsequent failure to notice his sister's unhappy relationship with narcotics.

'Rose, go to bed,' his grandmother had said. 'I'll deal with this.'

And so Rose had disappeared upstairs to the bedroom he'd thought of as belonging to his parents, and his grandmother had sat him down and given him the truth about his sister's drug habit, a habit both she and Rose had been increasingly concerned about and Rosaria increasingly devious about. His grandmother had told his parents but their attitude had been that all young people experimented and that she wasn't doing anything they themselves hadn't done, and that she'd grow out of it in her own time. The typical laxness he'd expected from his feckless parents.

His grandmother had been the one who'd decided not to tell Diaz. She'd feared he would overreact and that Rosaria's rebellious nature would see her rail against him and push her deeper into a habit that could easily flip into an addiction. Even as angry as Diaz had been, he'd known his grandmother had acted for what she'd—mistakenly, in his opinion—thought was the best.

Not long after his grandmother had gone to bed, Rose had crept back down, and cringed when she'd found him alone in the unlit kitchen, the only illumination that early morning coming from the full moon.

'That's right, run away,' he'd sneered when she'd turned to flee.

She'd turned back to face him. She'd been wearing a short nightdress, her braless high breasts jutting against it, her dirty blonde hair loose and messy... Bed hair. She'd cleaned her face but remnants of make-up had ringed her eyes. She'd been as dishevelled and sexy a sight as he'd ever seen; a sight that had only made him hate her more.

'You're poison, do you know that?'

This time she hadn't cringed. She'd folded her arms, pushing her high breasts even higher, and looked him square in the eye. 'No, it just suits you to believe that.'

'You fed my sister drugs.'

'No. Rosaria brought them.'

Rage burning back up in him, he'd kicked his stool away and prowled over to her. 'You might have my grand-mother fooled, but you don't fool me. My sister was an innocent until you came into our lives.'

She'd stepped back against the counter and lifted her chin defiantly. 'Then you must be the fool if you really believe that.'

He'd clasped her shoulders and brought his face down to hers. He'd been so close the mintiness of her breath and remnants of the sultry perfume she'd drenched herself in before she'd led his sister away to near death had swirled headily into his senses. 'You are like Circe,' he'd whispered, sliding his hands up her throat and spreading his fingers over her silky-smooth cheeks in a clasp. He'd felt the beat of her pulse beneath his little finger. 'Beautiful on the outside but filled with malignancy.' He'd brushed his mouth against her wide lips...such succulent lips... Heard the quickening of her breath. 'I pity the man who falls under your spell and tastes your poisoned fruit.'

Headily aware of how close he was to taking a taste of the fruit for himself, he'd let her go and walked away.

And now, seven years later, his body still vibrating from the charge of awareness that had pulsed between them outside their bedrooms, Diaz hauled himself out of the pool and castigated himself for how nearly he'd succumbed to the irresistible temptation that was Rose again.

For the first time in so very long he'd watched the flame of awareness reawaken in her. Felt the flame that lived inside him rouse in response.

Only the instinct that came from knowing her so well had enabled him to temper that flame.

It was too soon.

When he made his move, he needed it to be with the real Rose, not the Rose with eyes bruised from exhaustion and a fog in her brain, but the Rose who didn't shy away from confrontation and always, *always* matched fire with fire.

The Rose whose near-death still brought him out in a cold sweat just to remember.

Diaz had spent half his entire adult life fighting the toxic spell she'd cloaked him with but, as he'd learned that fateful night, one taste of her poisoned fruit created a singular hunger that neither time nor distance could erase. God alone knew how hard he'd tried to erase it.

Some fights could not be won.

For good or ill, Rose was as much a part of him as their babies were. And he was as much a part of her.

She must have imagined it, Rose told herself fretfully as she paced her bedroom and wished her babies to wake for the distraction they would provide. She'd had a little more sleep than she'd become accustomed to but nowhere near enough. She would need to sleep for a week to catch up on all the sleep she'd missed these last five months. Sleep for a month!

Sleep deprivation was proven to cause hallucinations, so that's what the look she'd seen in Diaz's eyes must have been. A hallucination evoked because her awareness of him had uncoiled from its dormancy and for the first time since the birth of their daughters, she'd been entirely alone with him. That was the only explanation.

She'd known since that awful night Rosaria almost died that he desired her and that he despised his desire almost as much as he despised her. The chemistry between them had simmered like poison for seven long years until it had finally taken possession of them both.

It made her want to weep to remember how beautiful it had been. His tenderness. The care he'd taken of her once he'd realised…

She squeezed her eyes shut to block the memories. Remembering was unbearable. It only brought home her desolation when she'd found his note where his head should have been.

In all those years his desire had always been wrapped up in resentment, the pulse of attraction in his eyes always accompanied by a twist of his lips.

There had been no twisted lips when his hooded stare had met hers that night.

And there had been no twisted lips when their eyes had collided that morning and that electrical pulse had ensnared them.

CHAPTER FIVE

'ARE YOU NOT enjoying your meal?' Diaz asked politely that evening.

Rose, realising she was just aimlessly pushing food around her bone china plate, quickly popped a lemon potato into her mouth. She didn't want him to guess how excruciating this meal had been for her.

She'd been skittish the whole day, her heart jumping into her throat every time footsteps approached. None of those footsteps had been Diaz's so she'd been on tenterhooks for nothing, right until a maid entered the girls' nursery with the request that Rose join him for dinner.

She couldn't believe she was back to being on tenterhooks around him. Couldn't believe how swiftly awareness had cloaked her again, and now she was eating what she knew to be a delicious meal but could hardly taste because she was too busy trying to tune out Diaz's deliciously masculine scent and the fact of his strong thigh being only inches from hers.

Trying. And failing miserably. Failing, too, to stop herself side-eying his long, tanned fingers and the crisp white shirt covering his muscular torso.

She should have moved her place setting. The mahogany table was huge. If she'd moved her stuff to the far end, he'd have been only a blur in her vision. They could have shouted their polite, stilted conversation.

'You need to relax,' he chided. 'The girls are fine.'

Easy for him to say. She'd never had a meal without them being in the room with her before. Not a proper meal. Snatched slices of toast or bowls of cereal wolfed down in the rare moments both girls were asleep at the same time didn't count.

She'd never shared a meal alone with Diaz before either, and it was tying her in knots to know her inability to relax had little to do with the girls' being upstairs, fast asleep under the supervision of the on-shift nannies.

Her inability to relax was entirely down to Diaz, who'd been coolly polishing off his courses and drinking his wine as if they'd dined alone together a hundred times.

His impeccable politeness wasn't helping either. If anything, it was increasing her tension. The more amiable Diaz was towards her, the louder the alarm in her head rang about his motivations for bringing her here.

The best analogy she could come up with to explain how she was feeling was as someone being played by a kid-glove-wearing puppet master...

And *that's* what felt so wrong, she realised with a start. In all the years she'd known him, Diaz had never hidden his feelings towards her, and she'd taken the full spectrum of them. Hate. Desire. Fury. Passion...

Whatever he was feeling and whatever was going on in his head, the man who never masked his emotions was hiding behind a smooth façade that rang so false she could scream.

She could scream, too, at how desperately aware she was of him wrapping his fingers around his wine glass, and she stabbed her fork into a roasted baby tomato and said the first thing that came into her head. 'Why four nannies?'

He answered as if he'd been waiting all evening for that very question. 'Two each working in shift patterns.'

'I get that but I don't get why it's necessary.'

'It gives you options if you want them. At some point when you are less exhausted, you will want to reclaim part of your life for yourself, even if it is just a trip to the shopping boulevard.'

'If I want to go shopping, I'll take them with me.'

'This gives you the option to leave them behind if you wish. And as we are discussing shopping, I was thinking we should go out tomorrow and buy you some clothes.'

And have to travel in a car with him? It was bad enough sharing a meal in this magnificent dining room with staff discreetly bustling around them, and trying to stop her needy stare from falling onto him for longer than a second, never mind being stuck in a confined space with him. 'No, thank you. I'll find some stuff online. Give me your address and I'll get it delivered.'

'Forward your choices to me and I'll arrange it all— and I'm paying,' he added firmly.

A wave of tiredness washed through her and she shrugged, covering a yawn. If he wanted to pay, then fine. It was his fault she didn't have enough clothes with her. 'How long are we staying here for?'

'We've only just arrived and already you are looking to go back?'

'I just want to know how many T-shirts and stuff I should have delivered.'

'My parents are planning a visit at the weekend so I would suggest adding a cocktail dress to your list—as

I'm sure you remember, they are great enthusiasts for dining formally.'

Her gaze finally landed on his. 'Your parents are coming?'

Green eyes holding hers, he raised his glass of white wine and gave an ironic smile. 'They are keen to meet their grandchildren.'

'Still?'

A glimmer of amusement passed between them, both remembering how his parents' eagerness to meet the twins had been booked to coincide with London Fashion Week, only for them to bypass travelling to Devon due to an 'invitation they couldn't refuse', a Hollywood hell-raising movie legend's eightieth birthday party. Their busy schedule meant it had been 'impossible' for them to fly over and meet their grandchildren since. They had, however, got their lawyers to set up incredibly generous trust funds for the girls.

At least the glamorous Martinezes were true to form, Rose thought with a pang, remembering how sad she used to feel for Rosaria that she spent such little time with her parents. Sad for Diaz too, when she'd had enough weeks away from his loathing for her own loathing to have become diluted, and as their gazes held, a stray fragment of memory floated into her senses before she could snatch hold of it and squash it into oblivion, a memory so vivid she could feel the caress of his lips against her mouth as if he were kissing her now.

The beats of her heart accelerated and, suddenly terrified he could see the memory reflecting in her eyes, she dropped her stare back to her half-full plate and shoved her knife and fork together on it.

'Excuse me but I'm shattered,' she mumbled, pushing her chair back. 'Please give my apologies to the chef.'

He gave an easy shrug but the heat of his stare intensified. 'No apology needed. Your appetite will return when you are no longer sleep deprived. If you find yourself hungry at any time, put a call to the kitchen. They will make whatever you like.'

Clutching the baby monitor, she had to stop her feet from running out of the dining room door.

She felt his eyes follow her every step.

After a good sleep, Rose woke feeling much better in herself. With all quiet in the adjoining nursery, she brushed her teeth and hair, and dressed quickly in a pair of denim shorts and a white vest top covered with a pretty loose-fitting cream crocheted top. Then, with equal speed, she used her phone to select enough clothes to last her a couple of weeks. Surely they wouldn't be staying any longer than that?

It was amazing, she mused as she forwarded her choices to Diaz, how sleeping well could change a mood and perspective. The evening before she'd been a bag of nerves and over what? Diaz? She'd spent years living with all the tumultuous emotions he brought out in her without turning herself into a wreck.

All the same, she refused to add any underwear to her clothing selection. Just to imagine him browsing through it all and envisaging her wearing them was enough to make her stomach churn and her skin tingle. She'd rather go knicker-less.

All her mental bravado nearly came apart at the seams when she pushed the adjoining door open and found Diaz already there.

In the process of lifting Amelia out of the cot, he was dressed in a tailored pinstripe suit that subtly accentuated the length and muscularity of his body, and, from the scent emanating from him, freshly showered and shaved.

When his gorgeous stare turned to her, the thumps of her heart became a thrum as her pulses soared.

'*Buenos dias,*' he said, his eyes narrowing slightly as he took her in. 'You are looking well.'

Relieved one of the nannies was already in there too, Rose took Josie from her and, refusing to let herself return to the bag of nerves she'd been the night before, managed a tight smile at the man who'd made her a bag of nerves. 'Thanks... You're going out?'

'I have back-to-back meetings in Madrid over the next couple of days.'

She'd never known it was possible for relief and disappointment to rush through a person at the same time.

Disappointment? Why on earth would she feel that? she thought fretfully. She should be dancing a conga.

Thankful he was too busy tapping Amelia's nose to spot either emotion on her face, she pithily said, 'Just as well I didn't take you up on your shopping offer.'

His shoulder lifted nonchalantly. 'I would have rescheduled if that had been the case.'

'No rescheduling needed. I've emailed you the clothes I want.'

'*Bueno.* I will ensure they are delivered by tomorrow.'

'Thanks. I ordered enough to keep me going for a couple of weeks. I don't imagine we'll be staying here any longer than that, will we?'

'Did you remember to select a cocktail dress?'

'I did...'

'Great.' He expertly looked at his watch without loosening his hold on their daughter, who was starting to wriggle. 'I need to go.'

In a flash, he'd kissed Amelia's forehead and passed her to the nanny, then crossed the divide Rose had deliberately created between them to engulf her all over again in his delicious scent as he bent his head to kiss Josie's cheek.

Only then did his gaze rest fully on Rose.

The instant their eyes locked, the air shifted.

For one breathless moment she thought he was going to kiss her too.

On Rose's fourth morning in Diaz's villa, she stretched her waking body and realised she felt fully refreshed for the first time since about six months into the pregnancy. Yawning to shake off the last vestiges of sleep, she padded to the adjoining door and checked on her babies. Both opened their eyes when she leaned over the cot and gave the identical gappy smiles that never failed to melt her heart.

After changing and feeding them, Rose called the on-shift nannies in and asked them to watch the girls while she took a shower. She was determined the four nannies Diaz had employed would be the most underused nannies in existence but, standing under the powerful spray of water, had to admit that having all the time in the world to shower was bliss.

Teeth brushed, and wrapped in a huge, fluffy white towel, she checked again on the girls and smiled to find them on their backs on a giant stimulation mat, swiping at the toys dangling in an arch over them, the nannies on the floor beside them.

'I'm just going to get dressed,' she murmured, revers-

ing back into her own room. The dressing table drawers she'd shoved the few items of clothing she'd brought
with her were empty, and she remembered Diaz's butler
mentioning the day before, just before she'd set off for
a late afternoon stroll along the beach with the girls in
their plush double pushchair, that her clothes delivery
was due at any moment and would be unpacked in her
dressing room for her. Still delighting in making up for
all her missed sleep, she'd gone straight to bed without
bothering to check.

The one time she'd had a quick nose in her dressing
room she'd idly thought that if she'd brought the entirety
of her wardrobe with her it would only have filled a tenth
of the available space. The last thing she expected to find
when she opened the first fitted cupboard was a vast array
of dresses hanging in it.

A few minutes later and her heart was racing as hard
as her brain.

The entirety of her dressing room was filled with
clothes. Expensive clothes. Clothes for all occasions and
all seasons. Including underwear. Dear heavens, it was
sexy underwear. Enough to set up her own lingerie shop.
Make-up too. And perfumes. Shoes. Boots. Sandals. Everything.

Unable to find the few items she'd brought with her or
identify the items she'd chosen for herself, she pulled on
the first pair of lace knickers that came to hand and, not
bothering with the matching bra, donned a pale yellow
summer dress with spaghetti straps, still thinking hard.

Why would Diaz go out of his way to buy all this
stuff for her? It made as little sense as toddler-proofing
the place.

And why hadn't he mentioned it?

There was only one way to find out.

But that meant seeking him out, something she really, really didn't want to do.

She'd seen little of him in recent days and been thankful for it. Two full days working in Madrid meant she'd only been subjected to sharing her evening meals with him, meals conducted with scrupulously polite conversation and intense, watchful green eyes observing her every movement.

It all felt so different from how things had been in Devon since the girls were born, and she knew it wasn't just because *she* felt different, as if she'd come back to life.

The blanket that had covered her awareness of Diaz for all those months had lifted in its entirety and she had the awful feeling Diaz knew it and was simply biding his time, and that all the time he'd been spending in Madrid had been an excuse for space away from her until he was ready to make his move.

But make his move for what?

Something was going to happen. At a time of his choosing, the mask Diaz had been wearing since her arrival in Spain was going to be ripped off. She could feel it in her bones. She just wished she knew what that something was so she could arm and protect herself.

She almost hoped the removal of his mask would reveal his old loathing and that he'd start throwing barbed comments at her. At least then she'd know where she stood and could throw her own barbs back at him, a good old screaming row to release some of the tension currently tying her in knots.

Even though she didn't know what *it* was, it was time

to have it out with him, before he left for the two-day trip to Sweden he'd casually mentioned over dinner.

Telling the nannies she wouldn't be long and planting a kiss on both her daughters' cheeks, Rose pulled her big girl knickers up and set off to find him.

After much searching, Rose eventually found Diaz in a shaded seating area by the swimming pool working on his laptop, a pot of coffee and a jug of water on the table close to hand. Clothed in a pair of dark tan cargo shorts and black polo shirt, his face unshaven and his dark brown hair messily styled, he was so undeniably, mouth-wateringly sexy that just to look at him was to make the beats of her heart accelerate and her veins heat and her determined steps falter.

She caught the scrutinising narrowing of his eyes before he said in the pleasant tone she so distrusted, 'You are looking for me?'

She managed a short nod and stepped closer.

Not even nine a.m. and already the sun was warm, the shade in the form of a heavily flowering, heavenly scented pagoda a welcome relief, a relief countered by having to be that bit nearer to him.

He indicated the seat across from him. 'Drink?'

Ignoring the gesture and question, she folded her arms across breasts that were inexplicably tingling, and wished she'd put a bra on. 'How long are you planning for us to stay here?'

He continued to scrutinise her. 'Why do you ask?'

'Because I want to know and every time I've asked, you've fobbed me off.'

'Is there a reason you're so keen to return to England?'

'Yes. I want a meeting with my lawyers to discuss the

delay to our divorce,' she stated pointedly. 'And I notice you still haven't answered my question.'

His stare became shrewd. Her heart thumped under the weight of it.

She raised her chin and stood as tall as she could. 'Diaz, what's going on? Why have you filled my dressing room with enough clothes to last me a lifetime?'

He tilted his head. 'Are they not to your liking?'

'That isn't the point.'

'Good, because I sent your selection to Spain's top stylist and asked her to supply you with a wardrobe using that selection as a base guide to follow your own style.'

'But why? I have my own clothes in my own home.'

Instead of answering, he continued scrutinising her. 'How did you sleep last night?'

'What's that got to do with anything?'

'A lot.'

'I don't see how.'

'Just answer the question.'

She had no idea why she felt so reluctant to admit, 'I slept well, if you must know.'

There was a flickering in his eyes. 'You slept well. The girls slept well—they were fast asleep when I checked on them before my morning swim. We are all sleeping well. Already you are looking much better in yourself and, I think, feeling better in yourself too.' He raised an eyebrow, clearly expecting her to comment on his assessment.

'Yes,' she agreed with a calm she was not anywhere close to experiencing inside. The fluttering in her belly was telling her loud and clear that whatever Diaz had been biding his time over was about to be revealed. 'I'm starting to feel a lot more like my old self.'

He nodded slowly, now studying her with an intensity that made the pulse between her legs throb.

How was it possible she could still want him so much that just to be trapped in his stare was enough to fill her with a heat that roused only for him? she thought with something close to despair. So potent was his effect on her that she half wished to still be cloaked in exhaustion and all her senses muted to everything but her babies.

Bringing her here was Diaz's way of lifting that exhaustion, she knew that with the same certainty she knew her birth date, and it took all her courage to maintain the lock of their eyes. 'Can you stop being evasive for a moment and give me a straight answer for when we're going home?'

He gave a long exhale and as he breathed out, his large frame loosened a fraction and the mask he'd been wearing since their arrival in Spain finally slipped off.

Green eyes swirling with a meaning she couldn't decipher but which made her stomach plunge and her hands grip her arms tight enough to bruise, he quietly said, 'There is no need for you to meet with your lawyer. There has been no delay. I lied about the divorce papers being filed.'

Head suddenly swimming, her mouth dropped open. Then closed. Then opened again. 'You did wh…? But… *why*? Why would you do that?'

His green eyes didn't so much as flicker. 'Because I no longer wish to divorce.'

CHAPTER SIX

DIAZ WATCHED ROSE absorb his words.

As hard as it had been to keep his distance from her and by extension their daughters these last few days, he'd known it was necessary to wait for the Rose he'd known all these years to emerge from the fugue of exhaustion that had cloaked her all these months.

As much as he'd wanted to wait a few days more to get his business affairs in order before having this conversation, one look at Rose had told him the time was now.

She really did look remarkably better, from the colour on her cheeks to the straightness of her back when she walked, but it was the return of the spark in her eyes that convinced him she was ready to deal with what he had to throw at her.

'You have got to be kidding me?' she finally blustered. 'Stop giving me the run-around and file the papers already.'

He shook his head. 'I appreciate this has come as something of a shock to you and that you will need time to digest it, but I want our marriage to continue and—'

'We don't *have* a marriage,' she snapped.

'Then it's time we did. Our girls deserve to be raised by both their parents.'

'They already have that.'

'But not always under the same roof. Not as a real family.'

She visibly blanched but didn't back down. 'When you're around, you spend all the time with them that you want. I have never denied you access or even tried to deny you access. For heaven's sake, Diaz, I didn't even ask you to return your keys once the house was put into my sole name. You come and go as you please.'

'Yes,' he agreed evenly, 'but only until night falls and then I'm expected to sleep elsewhere.'

'So for the sake of you getting a few extra hours with them, you think we should pretend to play happy families, even though those extra few hours are spent with the girls fast asleep?'

He held her stare so she could not misunderstand his meaning. 'Who said anything about those night-time hours being spent with the girls?'

For the second time in as many minutes, her mouth dropped open. Dark colour slashed her cheeks and, shaking her head as like was in a daze, she took a step back. 'Absolutely not.'

He could have written her script.

Having set his plan in action, the last few days a form of torture, sensing her attraction unfurl back to consciousness but not allowing himself in all good conscience to do a damn thing about it.

The only way through it had been to bury himself in work and wait for the Rose he'd experienced the whole gauntlet of emotions for over the years to unfurl the whole of herself back to life. And now she was here, barefoot and more beautiful than should be human.

With a blink like the shutter of the camera she always

used to have slung around her neck, Diaz finally allowed himself the luxury of taking the whole of her in with the appreciative eyes that had known better than to devour her while she was postpartum and exhausted.

It felt like he was finally allowing himself to breathe again.

All those months of pretending not to notice the sexiness of the legs currently on display before him in that chic but pretty dress, pretending not to catch glimpses of those high breasts in the times when she'd not noticed the V of her robe gaping open. He'd deliberately put his own desire to sleep but now he could let it wake again and, *Dios*, the rush that came from it…

He recaptured the blue eyes that had turned to liquid as she'd come undone in his arms and which in turn had turned *him* to liquid. 'We don't have to fight it any more, Rose. Our night together—'

'*Don't,*' she interrupted, her voice suddenly tremulous. 'Don't ever bring that night up. I never want to speak of it or think of it again.'

His hands curled, a heaviness settling in his chest.

Diaz had always known walking out on her the way he'd done after everything they'd shared had been cruel. Unforgivable. But it had been completely necessary, and if not for their daughters he'd have spent the rest of his life forbidding himself to ever think about their night together. At some point he might even have found the energy to take a lover to aid this forgetting.

The birth of their daughters had changed everything for him. He could not endure the thought of his daughters being raised under the same roof as another man, not even on a part-time basis. And he could not endure the thought of Rose with anyone else.

He'd spent what felt like his whole life fighting his feelings for her but it had taken her near-death for him to understand and accept that Rose was a part of him and there was not a damn thing he could do about it.

'We don't have to speak of it, but you cannot pretend it didn't happen or that it wasn't out of this world.' He'd always known that if the chemistry between him and Rose was ever given an outlet, it would be good. He'd never dreamed just *how* good it would be or how deeply it would mark him. 'We can have that again, Rose, for the rest of our lives, and we can be a family.'

She took another unsteady step back. 'No. It would never work. Families are built on love, not hate, and you hate me. You've always hated me. And I hate you,' she added as an afterthought.

Did he hate her still? He had, for a long, long time, but for years his hate had always been mixed with other equally virulent feelings, a sickening combination that had stopped him sleeping whenever they shared a roof and kept him alert to her every sound, like he possessed invisible antennae attuned only to Rose's frequency.

He worked hard to keep his voice even. 'What would you say if I told you I loved you? Would that change your feelings on the matter?'

She flinched as if he'd slapped her.

The tension in the silence that followed was loud enough to hear the air enveloping them crackle.

Slowly, she lifted her stare back to him. Her voice barely rose above a whisper. 'If you were to say that then I would say you're a warped, cruel bastard and that I'm taking the girls and going home. In fact, I'm going to do that right now. I don't know what sick game you think you're playing but I want no part in it and I will not allow our daughters to be used as pawns in it.'

Filled with more clashing emotions than any woman could bear, Rose turned her back on him and aimed her trembling body back to the villa.

She'd known there was more to this trip than a simple break, but *this*?

The worst of it was that she knew Diaz was being serious. He really thought, after everything he'd done and all the poisoned water that had passed under the bridge between them, that she would consider turning their sham of a marriage into something real.

But to play with her emotions by mentioning love of all things? How *could* he? To request a real marriage in one breath and then stab her in the heart the next?

She'd barely left the seating area when he called out. 'Rose, I don't want to have to play it like this but you cannot take the girls back to England without my consent.'

She froze in her tracks.

'We have shared legal responsibility, remember? You cannot take them out of the country without my permission.'

Feeling like ice had been injected into her veins, she turned to face him.

He'd risen from his seat, arms folded over his broad chest, all his upper muscles flexing.

'They're British citizens,' she dragged out. 'You can't stop me taking them home.'

'They are half Spanish. They have dual passports and those passports are in my possession.' He gave a visible deep breath. 'If you try to take the girls without my permission, I shall notify the authorities and have them barred from leaving the country.'

* * *

Rose felt the blood drain out of her, from the roots of her hair all the way down to her toes as everything fell into place.

'Oh, my God,' she whispered hoarsely. 'You had this all planned.'

His handsome features taut, he inclined his head in agreement.

'You've trapped me.'

'No. You are free to leave—I cannot prevent that if that is your wish.'

'But not the girls?'

'Not the girls,' he echoed. 'I would never take them from you, Rose, but I had a sense you would refuse to hear me out so took preventative measures to ensure—'

The roar in Rose's ears was too loud to hear anything more. She didn't even feel her feet move. One moment she was on the path, the next right in front of him with her arm raised, shouting obscenities. She didn't even know what her arm was raised for until Diaz snatched hold of her wrist and, in one deft move, spun her around so she was trapped between the hulking great slab of muscle that was Diaz and the table.

'Calm down,' he ordered tersely, his breath hot in her hair.

Hating the thrills careering through her to be held against him like this as much as she hated him, she kicked him with her bare foot. 'Let me go.'

'When you are calm.'

She twisted her face so she didn't have to breathe in his hateful, heavenly scent or have his strong, tanned neck so close to her mouth. The way she felt right then, she didn't trust that she wouldn't bite deep into the skin and draw blood. 'How can I be calm when you've effec-tively kidnapped me?'

Without giving her the space to escape, he loosened his hold and moved an inch back to gaze down at her. 'This isn't a kidnap and it isn't for ever unless you want it to be. All I'm asking for is time.'

'Time for *what*?'

'For you to consider making our marriage a real one like my grandmother always wanted.'

But that only twisted her heart into a sharp ball, and she slammed her hand into his chest and shouted…was a whisper away from sobbing… 'We could have had that. You're the one who walked away from it without a word of goodbye.'

The intensity of his stare didn't diminish. 'I know I did, but now I'm walking back to it and I want you to walk back to it too.'

She kicked his leg again. *'Never.'*

She barely registered the stinging in her bare foot from where it had connected to his shin bone for in the breath of a moment she was lifted onto the table with her thighs pushed apart and Diaz filling the space.

'Stop trying to hurt me,' he ordered.

'You're the one trying to hurt *me*,' she half snarled and half cried, skimming his calf with her heel at the next lash of her foot. Hurting her with words that would once have made her heart soar not weep, and hurting her with the closeness of the body that had made such tender love to her, and she pounded a fist into the rock-hard arm that had cradled her while she sobbed.

A large hand clamped onto the top of her thigh and his handsome face closed in on hers. 'Rose, you need to calm down,' he warned.

Panicked at how close their faces were, she reared away from him, but, with the hold he had on her, succeeded only in pushing her pelvis forwards. In the beat of a moment his groin was against hers.

Her breath caught in her throat as the world came to a juddering stop.

Every inch of her tensed.

And every inch of Diaz tensed too.

Jaw clenched, nostrils wide, he breathed in heavily, and then she felt it, the hard jut of his arousal.

The throb in her pelvis came from so deep inside that another breath of air caught and her body, stiffened in resistance, began to melt at the same speed as the steel in his stare.

His pupils dilating and pulsing, the firm mouth that had kissed her into senselessness inched closer.

Her aching lips pleaded to be crushed to his again.

Stifling another sob that came from nowhere, Rose turned her face before their mouths could come together.

It was the hunger on his face. She couldn't bear to see it. Couldn't bear the reminder of the last time he'd looked at her like that and the ache of his absence she'd lived with ever since.

'Don't even think about it,' she whimpered, her voice nowhere near as strong as she wanted it to be.

'Believe me, I have spent years trying not to,' he said hoarsely as the hand on her thigh skimmed down an inch to the hem of her dress. 'Years fighting it. We both have.' Strong, warm fingers slipped beneath the skirt of her dress, and she jolted at the sensation of flesh upon flesh. 'You have weaved through my dreams for years, Rose Martinez.'

'Gregory...' She had to swallow hard to continue, had

to fight to think coherently. Diaz's fingers were tiptoeing up her inner thigh, gentle caresses trailing fire over her vulnerable skin and deepening the burning pulses alive inside her.

She needed to push his hand away and tell him to stop, but she was melting too fast, too furiously, his touch dispelling the last of the tension that was her only resistance to him.

'My surname is Gregory...' Her words became a gasp as his fingers tiptoed higher still.

Gently, he stroked her pubis and huskily murmured, 'It should be Martinez, and our marriage should be real.'

Barely aware of what she was doing, she raised her thighs and grabbed at his chest, making a fist of his polo shirt. 'How...' She gasped as he adjusted his hand and slipped his fingers beneath the lace. '...can it be when...' His fingers skimmed over her hidden nub. 'When we...' Oh, heavens. Oh, God. 'We...'

But she couldn't finish her plaintive argument, not with the wondrous things Diaz was doing to her. His fingers were caressing her with increasing pressure, coaxing her, stimulating the need for him living beneath her skin that had been building for days into a burn of blazing life.

His mouth pressed into her hair, soft words whispered in Spanish she didn't understand but which sent thrills racing through her that were as bone melting as the clever manipulation of his fingers. When he moved his fingers from the source of her pleasure and slid first one then another into her sticky heat, she cried out, half from the loss of the pleasure where she most needed it and half from the new waves of pleasure he was filling her with until he pressed his palm on her nub, giving her the stimulation she craved, and Rose was lost.

All sense gone, she threw her arms around his neck and rocked into him, her mouth pressed tight into his shoulder, conscious of nothing but the maelstrom of sensation being evoked by the incessant movement of his pleasuring hand and the heat of his breath against her hair.

'Oh, God… *Diaz*…'

'That's it, *mi corazón*,' he encouraged softly, burying his mouth even tighter into her skull as he intensified his movements. 'Let it go. Let it all go.'

'Oh, *God*…' With a loud cry, her entire being splintered and she was engulfed in waves of pleasure so powerful she was helpless to do anything but ride them until she was nothing but limp skin and bone clinging to him.

Sanity returned slowly.

Rose could feel the strong thud of Diaz's heart echoing through her breasts and cheek. Hear the raggedness of his breathing. Feel the manic thuds of her own heart.

Oh, God, what had she just *done*?

She wanted to cry. Really, really wanted to cry.

Mortification over what had just taken place creeping steadily through her, she tried to disentangle herself from him but he tightened his hold… since when had he wrapped both arms around her…? and kissed the top of her head.

'It's okay,' he said quietly, as if he knew how close to tears she was. 'Everything will be okay.'

'How can it be?' she choked into his shoulder.

How could it *ever* be okay?

Loosening his hold, he slid his hands up her arms and gently cradled her cheeks, forcing her to meet his stare.

'Give us a chance, Rose. That's all I'm asking for—a chance, for our daughters' sake, because they deserve the full family neither of us ever had. Give us until the end of the summer. If we can't make the marriage work and you still want to walk away then I will not stop you taking the girls back to England.'

There was sincerity in his stare but she knew to her cost that Diaz was as capable of lying with his eyes as with his mouth. Actions spoke louder than words and his actions had come close to breaking her.

Blinking back tears, she shook her head. 'How can it possibly work when we've spent half our lives hating each other?'

His jaw clenched then loosened with a low laugh. 'We've also spent half our lives fighting this thing between us. We've both fought it but always it refused to die, and you cannot pretend it isn't still there.'

Fresh mortification burned through her veins.

How could she deny this when she had literally just lost complete control of herself with nothing but his touch?

'Is it not time to stop fighting and see if we can create something good out of it?' he asked, intensity returning to his gaze. 'I don't know if we can make it work but I know we owe it to our daughters to try. If we can't make it work by the end of the summer and you want to take the girls back to Devon then I will not stop you, and as a sign of good faith I will give you their passports now.'

She could have laughed. There hadn't been an ounce of good faith between them in fourteen years. 'You can still stop me leaving the country with the girls, even with their passports.'

'That works both ways.'

'I'm not a billionaire with all the power.'

'Stay married to me and you will be.'

Despite all the churning emotions wrecking her, a

short burst of laughter did break free, an amusement briefly matched in Diaz's stare, and for one tiny breath of a moment, lightness cut through.

But only for the breath of a moment.

He brushed his thumb across her cheek. 'You agree to try?'

Her stomach plummeted.

Oh, but her thoughts were a muddle of confusion, her heart feeling as if it were being yanked on a yo-yo.

How could she possibly say no when she'd been so successfully backed into a corner?

More importantly, how could she look her daughters in the eye when they reached an age to question why their mummy and daddy didn't live together? How could she tell them she'd been the one who'd refused to even try to create a proper family unit?

But how could she live even for a few short months as Diaz's wife? she wondered with something close to desperation. To share his bed and his life knowing that if not for their daughters, she would never have seen him again, that their wedding certificate would already have been replaced with divorce papers and that he'd be getting on with his life forgetting she existed?

He must never suspect that she would never have been able to do the same, and it was with this thought and their daughters' faces lodged in her mind that Rose fortified her spine with steel.

Heart beating fast, she summoned her courage to meet Diaz's dark, questioning stare. 'Okay. I agree we owe it to our girls to try and make a go of our marriage, and I know exactly what you mean by it, but...' She swallowed. 'Don't expect miracles. I promise to try but I can't promise more than that.'

His stare continued to bore into hers.

'What I'm trying to say is don't push me.'

The tension of his features finally loosened. The sides of his eyes crinkled as he gave a short laugh. 'As if I have ever been able to push you into doing anything you don't want to do.'

She thought of all the years of his fury at her unbreakable friendships with his sister and grandmother, and shook her head with a small smile. 'My refusal to comply with all your demands over the years must have driven you crazy.'

His lips made a wry twist. 'You can have no idea.'

'Oh, I think I can.' She'd taken bitter satisfaction from never letting him drive her out of the lives of the women she'd loved.

He expelled a long breath then captured a lock of her hair and gently pulled down its length. 'When I return from Sweden I'll be taking a few weeks off. Let's use that time for making peace.'

Peace? How could there ever be peace between two people who'd spent half their lives at war?

Reading her thoughts, he gently caught her chin. 'Our past doesn't have to determine our future, Rose. Not unless we let it.'

Trapped all over again in the stare that had haunted her waking and sleeping dreams for so long she couldn't remember a time when he hadn't been a part of them, she whispered, 'Can you really let it all go?'

'I only know I owe it to all of us to try.'

How her poor, foolish heart *longed* to believe him.

The loud ring of his phone broke the spell cast over them in one trill.

With a rueful smile, he brushed his thumb against her

chin before stepping back to pull his phone out of his pocket. Reading the message, he captured her stare one more time. 'It is time to change for my trip.'

That strange alchemy of relief and disappointment collided all over again.

CHAPTER SEVEN

A NOISE SHOCKED Rose awake. In an instant she'd thrown her duvet off and was padding quietly to the adjoining door. Her racing pulses already knew before she reached it that it hadn't been the girls who'd woken her. It had been Diaz closing his bedroom door.

He was back from Sweden.

Heart in throat, she tiptoed back to bed and buried herself under the duvet.

This was the last time she would sleep under this duvet.

From tomorrow night she would be sharing Diaz's bed.

It destroyed her to know the hot, knotted sickness low in her belly was the sickness of anticipation. Excitement.

It destroyed her even more to know that, even in sleep, her subconscious had been waiting for him.

Early the next morning, Rose sat on the sill of her bedroom window hugging her knees as she waited for the rest of the world to wake up. Her room overlooked the sprawling, romantic garden and she watched the flowers respond to the rising sun. She knew how they felt.

She'd spent half the night awake, on tenterhooks that Diaz would come to her. She still didn't know if she was relieved or disappointed that her door remained closed.

There would be no closed door between them tonight.

She hugged herself tighter and tried to breathe through the ripples of her thumping heart.

A real marriage. That's what he wanted. What she'd agreed to, even if only for a few months. What her tingling body yearned for.

If she could separate her body from her heart she would have few qualms about the agreement, would happily go to his bed and use him with the same shamelessness that he'd used her until the summer ended and she took the girls back to England and divorced him.

When it came to Diaz though, Rose's heart and body were inextricably linked, and she had no idea how she was going to sever that link when she was sharing his bed every night.

Movement in the grounds caught her eye.

Her breath caught in her throat.

Striding over the path towards the swimming area, a towel slung around his neck, Diaz, wearing nothing but grey swim shorts.

As if sensing her stare, he stopped and looked up.

She ducked out of sight.

A few moments later her racing heart skipped wildly to see his name flash on the screen of her phone. A simple message.

Join me?

The *longing* that ripped through her…

It was a longing reawoken on her arrival to Spain and now back with a vengeance.

His absence had brought no respite. He was always there in the back of her mind by day and weaving through her dreams at night, just as she'd long weaved through his dreams.

He'd been the one to reject those dreams. He only wanted to live them now to provide their daughters and himself with the real family he'd never had.

Rose turned her phone off without replying.

Breakfast was mercifully Diaz free, and Rose snatched the opportunity for more Diaz-free time by taking the girls for a walk on the beach before the sun burned away the thinning clouds gathered above them.

For the first time she wished she were back home in Devon, just so she could walk along the unpredictable sea. The picture-perfect blue Mediterranean was too perfect for her mood. She needed a tempest to match her emotions and help quell it before she came face to face with him again.

Since she'd arrived in Spain, a wide ramp had been installed next to the marble steps that led up to Diaz's gardens, and she pushed the double buggy back up it thinking there was nothing he hadn't thought of…

She almost stopped in her tracks.

Had that really been the first time she'd wished herself back home?

She never got the chance to answer herself for a tall figure appeared in the distance and scrambled her thoughts before he'd taken his first stride towards her.

Diaz hadn't known it was possible that two days' absence could enhance beauty so greatly, not until he stood before Rose, dazzling under the rising sun in a short pale blue summer dress, dirty blonde hair wild and loose.

He'd thought about her every minute of his time away.

Recalled over and over how she'd lost control in his arms, turning from passionate fury to passionate desire in a breath.

As their daughters had fallen asleep, he simply stood there and soaked her in, filling his senses with the woman who would, finally, after all these years of fighting and all these months of waiting, be sharing his bed.

Whether she would be sharing it on a permanent basis was something he could not predict. From the defiance ringing out of the brilliant blue eyes soaking him in with the same degree of intensity, she was far from reaching the point of acceptance he'd reached all those months ago.

She'd given him her word to try and make their marriage work but she wasn't going to pretend it was what she wanted. Rose never put on a front. In that respect, she hadn't changed since she was eleven. She was doing it for their daughters, not for herself and definitely not for him.

But at one point she *had* wanted a real marriage with him, something she'd unwittingly admitted between furious kicks to his shins.

His actions that early morning had hurt her greatly, a knowledge that sat increasingly heavy in him, but if he could put the past behind him and separate Rose, the mother of his children, from the Rose who'd led his sister on the path to destruction, then in time she would learn to make a similar separation too. It was the only way to make it work. Draw a line in the sand and step into the territory marked *future*.

A future where neither of them had to hide away from the passions and desires that had bound and repelled them for so long.

'I take it from the happiness on your face that you are thrilled at my return,' he commented, breaking the silence and its accompanying tension, and was rewarded with a twitch of Rose's wide, perfect lips.

'Ecstatic.'

'I thought as much. I was nearly convinced by the way you rushed to join me for a swim earlier but now it has been confirmed.'

'I would have joined you but I had a prior engagement with a book.'

Chest lightening at her irreverence, he laughed. 'Is it one of those big photography tomes you always used to have your nose stuck in?'

'It's a thriller, about a woman on a quest for vengeance.'

He raised an eyebrow. 'Reading it for tips?'

Her laugh was a short melodic burst that stopped almost as soon as it started.

It was a sound he hadn't heard since his grandmother died. Not like that. Unforced.

'Assuming you don't already have a prior engagement with your book, I thought we could take the girls to a nature reserve for the day,' he casually suggested, watching her reaction closely.

'Today?'

'The weather is supposed to remain relatively cool and it is never too early to introduce them to the joys of nature.'

He could see the internal war she was fighting, see her scrambling for a reasonable excuse to refuse and coming up with nothing.

No longer looking at him, she gave a short nod of her head. 'Sure. When do you want to leave?'

'As soon as we have everything we need packed for the girls.'

* * *

The nature reserve, a thirty-minute drive away, turned out to be a twenty-square-mile wildlife park with free roaming, endangered species living the best lives they could outside their natural environments.

Diaz drove, and in the reserve itself they took a child each onto their laps and pointed out the exotic creatures, some basking in the sun, others hiding in the shade, as they crawled along with the air conditioning keeping them nice and cool.

For the first time in a long time, Rose wished she had her camera to hand. For years, she'd kept it almost permanently around her neck, always ready to take a shot if something caught her eye. Although the park, created out of a former open-pit iron mine, was filled with beautiful and diverse natural colours that contrasted brilliantly with the cobalt sky and had a real air of tranquillity that it would be a pleasure to immortalise in one snapshot of time, it pained her to admit it was Diaz her camera hands itched to immortalise. Diaz, exactly as he was in that moment: sexy, relaxed and engaged with their daughters, filling their heads with knowledge they were way too young to remember. They were too young to appreciate any of it and there was zero chance of them ever remembering any of it, and yet they seemed to be taking everything in, so surely they had to be getting something out of it, whatever that something might be.

She wondered if her own father had ever engaged with her like Diaz did with their daughters. She'd never thought about it before. He'd moved back to his native Australia before her first birthday and while they'd kept in touch over the years, the original intention of him making regular visits back to England to see her had never materialised. Flights from one side of the world to the other were expensive. That was the reason she'd always been given. The reason she'd always accepted. The reason she had no memories of her father in the flesh.

It was painful to admit that if her father had loved her like Diaz loved their daughters, he would have found the money.

Diaz would always be a true father to their girls. He was hands-on with them because he wanted to be. Because he loved them.

He would never do as her father had done. Or as his parents had done to him, leaving him to be dragged up by nannies until he was old enough to be shoved off to an English boarding school. She remembered Rosaria telling her Mrs Martinez had initially moved back to Devon from Madrid so someone was close by if Diaz needed them.

Whether the widowed Mrs Martinez had known she would become his and later Rosaria's de facto parent was something Rose had never thought to ask. Having known and loved her, she strongly suspected that not only had Mrs Martinez known it would happen but that she'd wanted it to happen, for the children's sake, so they could have stability and continuity in their lives.

For all Mrs Martinez's love and attention, it was his parents' love and attention he'd needed.

Diaz loved their daughters so much that he was prepared to tie himself to his nemesis for life for their sakes, so they could have the full family he'd always craved. And it was for this reason that when they returned to the villa, all Rose's stuff would have been moved into his bedroom.

Was she being selfish for being so emotionally resistant to his wishes for them to have a proper marriage and be a family? Rose wondered miserably as she made sure to keep her happy face on and pointed to a warthog rooting about, closer to their car than any of the other animals had been.

Once they'd finished driving around the wildlife reserve, they parked up and took a walk around the reservoir to the picnic area. While Diaz pushed the girls in their double stroller, shades on, his height, athleticism and rugged good looks turning heads from all who passed them, Rose found her camera hands tingling again.

It felt strange to be out and about. Since the girls had been born, she'd only left her home for medical appointments and walks along the beach with them. Diaz had come along on a couple of the walks but those had been in the days of newborn baby brain fog and all she'd seen him as was a capable extra pair of hands.

It was frightening how quickly everything had turned around; old feelings and desires resurfacing, old hurts freshly wounding.

And it was terrifying that her awareness of Diaz's every movement and gesture was more acute than it had ever been.

Even more terrifying that the excitement of what the night would bring buzzed in her pulses at a rapidly increasing tempo.

The rest of the day had to rank as the longest hours of Rose's life. She went through the motions of behaving like a functional human being but beneath the skin she was a bag of heightened emotions living on her nerves.

Soon, very soon, she would be climbing the stairs and

opening the door to her new bedroom. She would be sharing a mattress and bedsheets with Diaz.

How—*how*—was she supposed to separate her heart from her body and protect herself? she despaired for what had to be the hundredth time.

'Do I need to have a talk with my chef?' he asked lightly, interrupting her despairing thoughts. 'This is the third meal we've shared that you've hardly touched.'

That evening they were dining under the stars. Diaz, sitting excruciatingly close to her, had been holding a steady stream of conversation about his plans to open a hotel in Iceland and steadily clearing his plate whilst Rose pushed the fresh seafood paella around hers.

Beneath the amiable conversation ran a strong undercurrent that pulled and tugged at the nerves in her stomach making it impossible to eat, no matter how divine the food tasted.

So strong were the nerves that she was close to wishing they'd skipped the pretence of dinner and gone straight to bed once the girls had fallen asleep. Got it over with.

It was the thought of *it* feeding the undercurrent. Tugging her nerves into a frenzy.

Not that *it* had to happen. Nothing did. If she chose, she could get into the bed and turn her back to him. If she trusted him with anything, it was that. He wouldn't force her.

'No, it's lovely,' she refuted. 'I'm just not very hungry.'

Warm fingers touched her hand.

She didn't want to look at him but his touch compelled her.

The green eyes that captured hers were stark but steady, his hand warm as he enveloped her clenched fist. 'Relax, Rose. It's just me.'

Her short burst of laughter contained no mirth. 'And that's exactly why I can't relax. We've never had the kind of relationship where we relax around each other.'

'Point taken.' He gazed at her a long moment before raising his wine glass with a wry smile. 'To being able to relax in each other's company.'

She didn't think she was imagining his accent had become more pronounced as the meal had gone on. Usually, it was barely detectable.

The undercurrent was pulling and tugging at them both.

Slipping her hand away from his, she lifted her glass of untouched wine. 'To getting through the summer without wanting to kill each other.'

His eyes glittered, amusement and something less definable. He took a drink. 'We have made it this far. I will take that as a win.'

'Always best to take your victories where you can.'

'Undoubtedly… Are you going to eat any more?'

She glanced at her mostly full plate and shook her head.

'Would you like dessert? Coffee?'

Another wordless refusal.

After a beat, he gave a sharp, decisive nod and pushed his chair back. 'In that case, I shall go up to bed.'

Her stomach crashed to her feet, her heart, which had been incapable of beating a normal rhythm the whole day, flipping over on itself.

On his feet, he extended an open hand to her and, his voice even, said, 'Are you going to come up too?'

His meaning was clear. The meaning ringing in his eyes was clear.

The thrashing of her heart and the longing in her veins were even clearer.

Rose picked up her glass of wine and drank the contents in two giant swallows. And then she pushed her own chair back.

CHAPTER EIGHT

DIAZ'S BEDROOM WAS BREATHTAKING. As with the rest of the villa, the walls were painted brilliant white, the marble flooring a softer white with subtle blues and terracotta threading in natural random patterns throughout. The main colour came from the dusky blue drapes of the ceiling-high double aspect windows and long velvet sofa and ottoman of the same hue, but it was the enormous bed and its cream and gold-threaded bedspread that was the real focal point, and Rose's belly quivered just to look at it.

There was something inherently sensual in the simplicity of this breathtaking room, a femininity, too, that she hadn't expected from a man as soaked in testosterone as Diaz. Nowhere near as feminine as the guest room she'd been using but a dreamy blend of masculine and feminine combining to create a room both sexes could come together and find either pleasure or sanctuary...

Pressing tight to her stomach in a futile effort to contain the butterflies loose in it, she was relieved to escape into the privacy of her own bathroom.

It, too, was divine, a gorgeous feminine blend of traditional Spanish tiling and ultra-modern luxury combining to create a sanctuary as complete as Diaz's bedroom. She gazed at the sunken bath, unable to nullify the image of sharing it with him, and of them...

Closing her eyes, she inhaled large gulps of air and reached for the hair clip she used when she didn't want to get her hair wet when showering. It had been placed on the left-hand side of the sink unit with her hairbrush. Taking a closer look around, she saw her toiletries had all been placed in exactly the right positions for their purposes, her shampoo, conditioner and shower gel lined up on the long ledge running alongside the waterfall shower. Everything placed as if they'd always been there. As if they belonged.

Shaking the strange thought off, she stripped her clothes, pinned her hair and stepped under the shower, blocking the memories of the last time she'd showered before bed from surfacing.

But she couldn't block herself from the painful acceptance of why she was showering now.

She was cleaning herself for him. She was soaping flesh abuzz with an anticipation that burned strong enough to melt bone.

She couldn't pretend to herself that she was going along with this solely for the sake of her daughters. She was going along with it for her own sake too. Because she couldn't not.

Any attempt to resist would end in failure. Diaz only had to touch her for her skin to melt.

Her body had bound itself to him when she was seventeen and it had belonged to him ever since.

Somehow, though, she had to find a way through this night…the whole summer…possibly her whole life… without giving him everything again. Without losing the whole of herself to him. A way to give him everything and take everything while keeping the most essential part of herself safe.

Teeth and hair brushed, face moisturised, she looked

at her fevered reflection. The pretty cream negligee she'd selected was virtually transparent, her dusky pink nipples a shimmer of colour through it. She shivered to know that soon, very soon, he would be stripping it from her, and soon, very soon, he would be taking those nipples into his mouth...

She swayed as a tight, heavy sensation formed in her breasts, and unthinkingly cupped one, imagining it was his hand holding it. The flush of colour on her cheeks deepened.

An impulse that came from nowhere had her tugging the negligee off, and she stepped out of it and stepped to the door before she could change her mind.

It was only her heart she needed to shield from him.

He was already in bed. His hair had that freshly washed and towel-dried messiness she'd seen so many times over the years, his jaw that freshly shaved smoothness she'd seen all those times too...but never in a bedroom. Never when he was propped against a headboard, sheets draped to his waist, the soft lighting creating shadows over the beautifully honed torso with its perfect smattering of fine dark hair. Never when he was clearly naked.

There was a stillness about him, the illusion of flesh wrapped in marble. The only sign of life was in his eyes. Even with the distance between them she could feel the heat contained in them, as if he'd stretched an invisible arm and stroked the flesh above her pounding heart.

The heavy tingles in her pubis thickened. Deepened. All the tentacles spreading from it thickened and deepened too.

The sheets on her side of the bed had already been turned over so she could slip in beside him unhindered.

Unhindered by anything except her own fear.

She must, must, must keep a lock on her emotions, she dimly beseeched herself.

Almost sick with longing, she unrooted her feet from the cool flooring and walked towards him.

The statue on the bed made no movement but the heat of his stare burned through to her core.

She slipped between the silk sheets with closed lungs and faced him.

Eyes locked.

The unbreathable air of the silence engulfing them was so highly charged it threatened to choke her.

The strong throat moved and then the statue came to life as if in slow motion, a hand reaching through the charged atoms enveloping them to spear through her hair.

Slowly, slowly, he trailed fingers down her neck and onto her shoulder, sending shivers of delight fizzing through her entire being, and she moaned softly when those same fingers skimmed at the same unhurried pace over her unbearably heavy breasts.

Consumed with the need to touch him as he was touching her, Rose pressed a shaking palm to the base of his throat, saw the pulse flare in his pupils and felt the subtle shudder of reaction. With the same rigidly contained pace his fingers were caressing her, she tiptoed her fingers up his smooth neck to scrape through hair that was the only softness to be found on the whole of his beautiful body.

Unable to tear her stare from his face, she drank in every last detail with an openness she had only permitted herself that one night.

Diaz was beautiful. The entirety of him. As masculinely beautiful as it was possible to be.

His breaths heavy, the stare locked on hers molten, the sensuous mouth that had been her gateway to heaven inched forwards. Lips buzzing with the same franticness as the beats of her heart, Rose closed her eyes.

The brush of his lips against hers sent a shock of electricity through her…and an equal bolt of terror, strong enough to make her turn her face so their cheeks came together instead of their mouths.

This was how she must protect herself, she realised dimly over the pounding in her head and heart.

She'd lost control, heart, body and soul to Diaz before. Her body was beyond her control but her heart and soul needed her to do everything possible to protect them from the fresh agony only he was capable of inflicting on her, and of everything she'd spent so long trying to forget, his kisses had haunted her the most. The tenderness and passion contained in them had opened the gateway to her heart when all along they'd been speaking his lies the loudest.

There was a long moment of stillness before he moved his head back and locked his searching gaze to hers, an infinitesimal hold but one that stretched to the moon until she placed a finger to the lips she *ached* to kiss and gave a small shake of her head.

Another infinitesimal stretch of silence and then his eyes pulsed and his nostrils flared in silent acceptance of her wordless condition…followed by another pulse, a resolve that brought the statue fully to life.

In one fluid movement he'd wrapped an arm around her waist and laid her down as if she weighed nothing, pinning her beneath him with a barely restrained force that knocked the little air she had from her lungs.

She stared up at the taut face hovering over her, gazed into the hooded green eyes blazing with a sensuality she felt all the way to her bones, and pleaded with herself to hold on.

'You have no idea how long I've been waiting for his,' he whispered gutturally. And then he bowed his head to her neck.

The ravaging of her delicate skin sent a shock of sensation rippling right down to her toes. Lips and tongue devouring her neck and shoulders as if they were laced with edible sweetness, he slid a hand down her side and between her legs, skimming the heat of her desire with a stifled groan before scraping the tips of his fingers up and over her belly and ribs to cup a breast, and when he rubbed his thumb over a taut peak, she cried out at the pleasure, crying louder when his hungry mouth closed over it.

Greedily, he sucked first one breast then the other, tongue encircling, teeth grazing, tantalising the oh-so-sensitive flesh until the pleasure became so acute it became a form of pain and she was cradling his head and writhing beneath him, moaning helplessly, her moans becoming cries of protest when he abandoned this sensory assault.

But there was no abandonment. Not an inch of her enflamed flesh went untouched. He kissed and stroked every inch of skin, sought every hollow, explored every hidden part before lifting her thighs to kiss her most intimate, feminine part, stroking her inside and out with his tongue and fingers until all sense was abandoned and she was nothing but a coiled flame of hot, sticky need desperate for release.

She'd forgotten, she thought, in the deepest recess of what remained of her consciousness. Forgotten…deliberately…just how painfully, gloriously intense the pleasure had been.

Cruelly, as if sensing she was on the brink, he shifted

his attentions away from where the flame burned brightest. Fingers biting into her skin, he caressed his way back up her body, taking a breast almost whole into his mouth with a barely controlled savageness that made her want to weep at the darts of painful pleasure it induced.

Clasping his skull, she scraped her fingers through his hair, and when he brought his face back to hers and his demanding arousal pressed urgently into the top of her thigh, she was a breath away from fusing her lips to his.

It took all her strength to turn and deny herself this, her desperation for his possession of her mouth as acute as her need for his full possession of her. Swallowing hard, she lifted her head and pressed her cheek to his, nuzzling into him, soaking in the musky scent of his skin, fingers dragging over the plane of his chest and abdomen to take hold of him.

He mumbled something unintelligible as she moved her hand up and down the hard velvet length, his groans of pleasure feeding her arousal until the pain became unbearable. Raising her thighs to encircle his hips, she guided him to the place they both desperately needed him to be.

In the beat of a heart, he'd filled her with such completeness it shocked the breath from her lungs.

There was a long moment of stillness before he lifted his head to gaze into her eyes, and suddenly she could *see* it, all the passion and emotions that had been there their one other night together.

Just as suddenly, fear she could barely comprehend gripped her heart, and she pressed her mouth into his neck and closed her eyes, tightening her hold around him as she blocked out everything but the incredible feelings that had taken possession of her, and encouraged him with her body to make love to her.

He withdrew slowly then drove back fully, again and again, over and over. Slow, driven thrusts that she fell into and savoured, the powerfully heady sensations washing away all her fears.

This was what she'd craved. What she needed.

Diaz inside her. A part of her.

Slowly but surely, the tempo increased and her craving grew with it. Rose followed her body's demands slavishly, holding him tightly and wrapping her legs around his waist, inviting his ever deeper penetration until a groan came from his throat and he lost control, thrusting into her without restraint, driving a rhythm that swept her away on a relentless tide of bliss that had her giving as much as she was taking, aware of nothing but the assent to rapture building with each hard, demanding stroke until she tipped over the edge and shattered into a thousand pieces.

As she clung to his sweat-licked body, clung to the convulsions of ecstasy, he drove into her one final, drawn out time with an agonised cry of her name.

The descent back to earth took so long Rose had the time to wish to never land back there. To just stay like this, with delicious thrills racing through her veins and the delicious weight of Diaz on top of her, his ragged breath hot against her skin and their hearts beating in perfect heavy unison.

Don't think like that, the voice of sanity urged. *Never think like that.*

It didn't matter what the voice of sanity said though. When Diaz went to move his weight off her, her primal reaction was to clamp her limbs around him to keep him exactly where he was.

He gave a hoarse laugh and kissed her shoulder. 'I'm going to squash you if I don't move,' he said, easily escaping her hold and rolling off onto his side of the bed. When he hooked an arm around her to pull her close to him, her limbs and brain were still too liquid to resist.

For a stretch of time that seemed to pass without beginning or end, she lay replete, tucked in the safety of Diaz's arms, breathing in the scent of his skin and luxuriating in the feel of his chest against her cheek and the slow strokes of his hand through her hair.

She sighed sleepily when he traced a finger over her cheekbone before shifting his body so they were face to face, still holding each other.

Trailing her fingers over his back, she marvelled at the smoothness and strength, and the way the muscles bunched and flexed at her touch, marvelled that the sensations she experienced at his touch were shared so perfectly and completely.

He pressed the tip of his nose to hers and huskily asked, 'Am I allowed to kiss you now?'

All the happy, relaxed sensations and thoughts that had filled her disintegrated, and memories of their last post-coital conversation replayed itself with its unerring ability to slice her heart open into a fresh wound.

Stomach churning with fear at how easily she'd slipped into contentment with him, she said as evenly as she could manage, 'What makes you think that?'

The hand gently kneading her lower back stilled. The eyes that had been gazing at her with a sex-satisfied gleam dimmed like a light being switched off.

Disentangling herself from his hold, she sat up and tugged at the sheets to cover herself with shaking hands.

'Rose...'

'What?' Mustering all her strength and channelling all the pain the fresh wound had given her, she met his stare. 'Did you think that one bout of great sex would suddenly make me decide that everything's all hunky-dory?'

Incredulity flashed in his stare. 'That meant more than sex.'

Her heart thumping, she eyeballed him. 'Did it, really?'

His lips tightened.

'Don't bother answering,' she said before he could speak, tearing her stare away. 'I'm not in the mood for a dose of déjà vu.'

He took a long breath and kneaded his temples. When he spoke, it was with patience underlaid with an edge. 'Rose, I know I...'

'Don't bother,' she interrupted again. 'I don't want to hear it. You got your way—I'm in your bed like a good little wife. I was even a willing partner in sex with you, and I'll happily be a willing partner again because it really was wonderful—congratulations, you're a great lover—but you don't get to bully and blackmail your way into taking all of me. Not after what you did.'

Charged silence surrounded them; a different charge to the one that had been holding them in its spell.

This charge tasted of poison.

The charge broke when Diaz swung himself off the bed and strode across the bedroom floor, disappearing into the dressing room.

Her heart now in her throat, Rose puffed out a short breath of stale air and blinked vigorously to clear the tears prickling her eyes, guilt already stabbing at her for her outburst.

She'd deliberately provoked him but she'd had no choice. The fear had been too great.

She needed to protect herself. When it came to Diaz she was more vulnerable than she could ever let him know, and she couldn't let herself forget that he had essentially blackmailed her into staying here with him...

But he'd given her the girls' passports, she reminded herself wretchedly. He'd stuck to his word in that respect. If there was blackmail, she'd gone along with it. She'd agreed to try. Whether he'd have let her go home with the girls if she'd said no was an unanswerable question because she'd said yes.

Blackmail aside, it didn't change anything else.

That didn't stop her heart lurching when Diaz reappeared wearing a pair of undone jeans and holding a black T-shirt.

His eyes met hers across the divide. There was nothing knowing or sensual in the glitter firing from them. For the first time in so very long she saw his mouth twist in loathing. 'I'm going out. Don't wait up for me—I would hate for you to think it necessary to add sleep deprivation to my list of crimes against you.'

She watched him tread to the door, trying her hardest to keep her composure.

She'd known it was only a matter of time before Diaz's true feelings for her resurfaced but there was no satisfaction in proving herself right. Only wretchedness... and a flare of anger that burst out when he turned the door handle.

'Are you really going to run away and leave me alone in a bed *again*?'

Rose's furiously delivered words sliced through Diaz like barbs.

The pulse in his jaw throbbing, he turned slowly,

breathing heavily to smother the turgid emotions boiling like a cauldron in his guts. 'You push me away and accuse me of blackmail and bullying, and expect me to *stay*?'

At her tight-lipped response, he dragged his fingers through the hair her own delicate fingers had threaded through only minutes ago.

'I accept that I blackmailed you into staying here for the summer, but only because I know how impulsive and stubborn you can be,' he said tersely into the silence. 'Without that threat, you would never have given me a fair hearing, but I never bullied you into agreement. You agreed to try and make our marriage work.'

'I *am* trying,' she burst out. 'I'm here, aren't I?'

'You are here in body but not in spirit. Not when you hold yourself back and then push me away at the first opportunity.'

'What do you *expect*?' she cried. 'I gave you every-thing before and look where it got me. Can you really blame me for wanting to keep something back now?'

Her heart bumping painfully, Rose closed her still-stinging eyes and willed herself not to cry.

The silence that enveloped them, so complete she could have heard a feather falling, was finally broken by a deep sigh.

Footsteps neared. The bed moved as he sat beside her.

Quietly, he said, 'Of all my regrets, how I left you that morning is my greatest.'

Taking a tremulous breath, she met his stare.

The frustrated anger had vanished. 'I know building a sustainable relationship between us is going to take time but it will never work if you hold yourself back.'

'But I need time, Diaz,' she whispered. 'We both knew we wouldn't find harmony overnight. You can't expect me to just forget everything that's happened between us or stop being on my guard for the next time you turn against me.'

'That will never happen.'

'It just did. You promised not to push me.' She sniffed back a threatening tear and clutched at the sheet. 'I know I overreacted. You're not a bully and I never should have said that, and for that I'm sorry.' She raised her shoulders helplessly. 'It's just that everything's all so overwhelming. The past still feels so present...' She shook her head, frightened to finish, frightened he would see just how deeply she still felt the wounds of the past.

A large hand palmed her cheek. 'I overreacted too, *mi corazón*, and for that I too apologise. I did promise not to push you. I know I need to be patient.' He gave a low, rueful chuckle. 'This might come as a surprise but I sometimes struggle to find patience.'

A floating atom of amusement danced into her veins and she covered the hand on her cheek without thinking. 'I might have got that impression on occasion.'

The atmosphere between them lightened perceptibly.

With a loosening of his shoulders, Diaz turned his hand to thread his fingers through hers, and pulled it down to rest against his chest.

Gazing into the blue eyes no longer threatening him with fire and brimstone, he took a long breath before admitting, 'I think it is possible I sometimes struggle to deal with rejection too.'

There was a flare of compassion he didn't deserve.

'Anyone with your parents could be forgiven for that,' she said with a softness he also didn't deserve.

Somehow surprised and yet not surprised that she'd

associated rejection with his parents, he tightened his hold on her hand.

It shouldn't be possible that such a small gesture as the taking of a hand could lift a weight off a heart or possible that, after all the years of bad feeling between them, they should know and understand each other better than anyone else ever could.

He'd behaved like a spoilt, entitled ass, he realised heavily. He'd known it would take time to break Rose's barriers down, but in his arrogance he'd compressed the definition of time into nothing. At the first hurdle, he'd assumed the worst, just as he always had with her.

'Did I tell you they're now coming next weekend?' he told her.

'Not this weekend?'

'They had a better offer.'

Another flare of undeserved compassion. 'I'm sorry.'

'So am I. I try to accept them as they are, as my grand-mother always told me I should, but they are such self-ish bastards and I don't understand how they can be that way.'

'At least they want to see the girls,' she said with a light shrug. 'My father will never meet them.'

'He's said that?'

'He doesn't need to. Neither of us have suggested it and we never will. We're strangers to each other. When Mum was alive she'd make me video call him every two weeks but since she died we don't even video call twice a year.'

He knew this. Of course he did. And yet he'd never really thought about it before or considered what it must have been like for Rose to have been so comprehensively rejected by her father. At least Diaz had never doubted that his parents loved him in their own selfish way.

The clasp of her fingers tightened. Her voice dropped even lower whilst growing in fierceness. 'He's the reason why I will never stop you having a relationship with our daughters. Whatever happens between you and me, Diaz, I don't want them growing up without a father. They need you, and the reason you will never understand your parents' selfishness is because you don't have that gene in you—you proved it a hundred times over with your sister and grandmother, and you've proved it a hundred times over with the girls. You put their needs first and you always will.'

Moved beyond belief at this assessment from the woman who not even an hour ago had accused him of bullying and blackmail, it was a long time before Diaz felt capable of clearing his throat to speak. 'And what about you, *mi corazón*? Do you think there will ever come a day when you need me too?'

Her fingers tensed in his before she slowly pulled them away. Instead of pulling away altogether as he braced himself for, she shuffled closer to put her head on his chest and wrap her arms around him.

'I don't know,' she said starkly. 'There are times when…'

Her voice caught.

He pressed his mouth into the top of her head and held her close. 'When what?'

She shook her head. 'I won't make any promises other than to try. Just… Just try to be patient with me in return.'

CHAPTER NINE

AFTER A DAY spent as a family at one of Valencia's foremost art galleries, Diaz as adamant about it never being too early to introduce the girls to culture as he'd been about nature, Rose kissed her babies goodnight.

Since living in Spain, she'd got into the habit of changing for dinner each evening. Nothing formal like how Diaz's parents, who—surprise!—had cancelled their visit again, liked to dine. More slightly dressy-casual. Clothes she'd prefer not to have splattered in baby milk or sick. Clothes, it pained her to admit, she could imagine Diaz peeling off her.

In the dressing room they shared, she rifled through her abundance of drawers, shelves and rails and tried to dampen the panic nibbling at her chest at how important their evenings alone together were becoming to her. How she would put the girls to bed with a quivering of anticipation low in her belly, not just of the pleasure that would soon be hers but what came before it, the shared meal and idle conversation. His company.

And yet for all the surface harmony currently existing between them, an undercurrent of tension remained, much faded but still there, the sense that one wrong word could bring everything crashing down.

The biggest eggshell for Rose was his sister.

The biggest eggshell for Diaz, she was certain, was her continued refusal to kiss him on the mouth.

In many ways, the marriage they were slowly creating together was the fairy tale of her dreams coming to life, but, as she knew to her cost, believing in fairy tale endings with Diaz ended in destruction.

He must never know how desperately her senses yearned to be filled with his dark taste.

Everything he was doing here, all his thoughtful gestures, everything, was to satisfy his craving for them to be a family. Nothing more.

Without the girls, she wouldn't be here, she thought bleakly. Diaz would have filed the divorce papers. She would have spent the rest of her life without seeing him again.

None of this was about her. It was all about Diaz wanting the real family he'd never had, and she must never let herself forget that, and when he joined her in the dressing room and gave her the smile that never failed to make her heart bloom, she had to ground her bare toes to the floor to stop them skipping to him.

Diaz didn't know which of them reached for the other first. He had no clear memory of climbing on top of Rose but knew he must have done because he awoke to the most incredible sensation of being inside her and her soft mews of pleasure soaking into his ears.

Opening his eyes to early morning dusk, he found her half-open eyes already on him, sleepy sensuality blazing from them.

The hand clasping the back of his neck skimmed up, fingers diving through his hair.

He could kiss her now, he thought dimly as he continued the deep, slow rhythm they'd found together. She would accept it. The sweet tongue that had once danced with such passion against his would…

She raised her thighs, deepening the penetration to levels beyond pleasure. It was all he could do to hold on.

Kiss me, he silently willed.

Eyes still fused together, she tightened the clasp on his head and lifted her face, but the ultimate fusion he craved remained as out of reach as ever when she pressed her cheek to his. Clinging to him tightly, her breaths now shallow pants, she ground her groin to his, her body demanding more and more until convulsions thrashed through her and his name echoed as a whisper on her tongue as she dragged him over the edge and into oblivion.

The sun rising high above them was growing in strength. Even though they were slathered in factor fifty, sun hats on and covered from neck to ankles in all-over swimsuits, Rose sighed to know it would soon be time to take the girls out of the pool. The shade keeping it cool and adding protection to their delicate skin was lessening, Diaz chasing it as he pushed them through the water in their baby floats. She didn't know which sight made her heart sing the most—Diaz's tanned perfect body glistening with water, his handsome face alive with joy, or the gummy beams of delight on their daughters' faces. Their love of the water was wholly down to their father.

The first time they'd taken them into the pool, both girls had screamed in protest. Where Rose had been ready to put an immediate stop to it—nothing could freeze a mother's heart more than her babies' screams of terror—

Diaz had been entirely unfazed. Each morning, before the sun got too hot, he'd carried them on his lap into the shallow end and gently dipped their tiny toes in the water with crooning encouragement that there was nothing to fear. And look at them now, only twelve days from that first disastrous attempt!

From Rose's vantage point on the side of the pool, she raised her new camera, a gift from Diaz, and took a snap of the three of them laughing as he spun the pair of them in circles.

Maybe she could do something along these lines when she was ready to start working again, she thought idly as she captured more images of her babies with their father. Forget the arty stuff she'd always aspired to and just capture moments in time of pure family joy.

The love alight on Diaz's face was as pure as their daughters' thoughts and burned brighter than the sun.

It was a love that made her chest clench into a fist to witness.

She had no idea how she was going to make her choice at the end of the summer.

Take the girls home and break Diaz's heart? Or stay and run the real risk of breaking her own?

Rose finally settled on what she hoped was a suitable dress for a society party, put it to one side, sat at her dressing table, and got to work on her face.

Five weeks since she'd arrived in Spain, she'd gained enough confidence with the girls' nannies to know they'd be in safe, loving hands if she left them for an evening, and now she was preparing herself to go out into the big wide world and socialise properly for the first time in close to two years.

Having postponed their visit yet again, Diaz's parents had finally swept into the villa that afternoon, two hours late, in a cloud of perfume and aftershave. They'd proceeded to fuss and pet and coo over their granddaughters for a whole fifteen minutes. That fussing, petting and cooing hadn't extended to actually holding them. Camila's excuse had been that her nails were too long to safely hold them, an assessment Rose had been entirely in agreement with—Camila Martinez's fabulously decorated fingernails could easily be classified as lethal weapons. Julio's excuse was that he was afraid of dropping them. However, they did both deign to place goodbye kisses to their granddaughters' foreheads. Rose had needed to use baby wipes to gently remove the bright red lipstick stuck on their foreheads from it, something she'd done whilst still giggling over how Josie had almost ripped Camila's dangling, blingy earring out.

It was while they'd been finishing their extremely late lunch and readying themselves to leave that they'd mentioned the party they were attending that night. A famed Spanish film director was throwing a birthday party for himself.

'I know him,' Rose had said before hurriedly clarifying, 'not personally. His work.'

'You should come. Everyone will be there,' Camila had said, before turning to Diaz. 'You were invited, yes?'

'I've already sent my apologies,' he'd replied coldly. 'Rose isn't ready to leave the girls yet.'

'Nonsense! You want to go, don't you, Rose? Pedro hosts the *best* parties.'

Rose had tried to remember the last time she'd gone to a party. Gone anywhere that wasn't a shop or restaurant or a place for them to enjoy as a family.

Her thoughts must have expressed themselves on her face for Diaz's gaze had locked onto hers without expression. 'You want to go?'

A sliver of excitement had unfurled in her belly. She'd nodded.

And that had been that. All settled.

And now here she was, the girls already tucked up in bed, getting ready for her first proper night out since Mrs Martinez's stroke.

The dressing room door opened and Diaz came in, a towel around his waist, smelling of citrus shower gel and shaving foam. One glance was enough to make her heart bloom and her pulses surge. One glance was enough to see he still wore the tension he'd been carrying the whole day.

'We don't have to go if you don't want to,' she said. It was the first chance they'd had to talk about it. By the time his parents had gone, it had been time to bathe and feed the girls. One thing they never did, by unspoken agreement, was talk about anything slightly contentious in front of them.

He pulled a dapper suit off the railing. 'I never said I didn't want to go.'

'You turned the invitation down.' Without even mentioning it to her.

'I didn't want to put you under any pressure. I know how you feel about leaving the girls.'

'They'll be asleep. They won't even know we're gone.' The royal *we*.

When, Rose wondered, had it all slipped into something that was starting to feel real? Natural. Her and Diaz. Her, Diaz and their two babies. A family.

Swallowing the swell of emotion that had risen from

nowhere, she added, 'You've put your social life on hold since we arrived here. If you'd rather not go out with me then just say. I'm a big girl…'

He'd crossed the room to stand behind her before she could finish speaking. Hands on her shoulders, he stared at her through the mirror. 'Don't think like that, *mi corazón*. Never think like that. Yes, my social life has been on hold, but that was the choice I made so I could devote my time to you and our daughters.' Resting his chin on the top of her head, he slid his arms around her waist. 'Believe me, no one is happier than me that you feel settled enough here to leave the girls in the nannies' hands for an evening.'

'Then why…?' Understanding flashed. 'Because your parents will be there?'

He was angry with them.

Diaz's ultra-glamorous parents were the most un-ashamedly selfish people in existence. Uncompromising about living their lives on their own terms, they refused to feel guilt or contrition about putting their own needs and wants first.

Rose could no more comprehend their selfishness when it came to their children—and now grandchildren—than Diaz could. Seeing them in action for the first time since Mrs Martinez's funeral, at which they'd stayed for the service and an hour of the wake before jetting off to Los Angeles, only served to increase her appreciation for Diaz's determination to be a proper father to their girls. He had some of his parents' traits, that was for sure, from his uncompromising, single-minded nature to his love of the finer things in life, but he wasn't selfish when it came to those he loved. When Diaz loved, it was with a fierce loyalty and a deep-rooted protective instinct. The latter, she suspected, had come to life when Rosaria had been born, and the wound in Rose's heart that had never healed throbbed to know the love he held so deeply and fiercely would never be for her.

He desired her. He respected her as mother to his daughters. She suspected he was even growing to like her. But love?

Their shared history was every bit as much of a barrier for him as it was for her. It loomed between them in everything never said.

Diaz dropped a kiss into Rose's silky, fragrant hair before unwrapping his arms and stepping away to dress.

If he wanted...and he did want, as much as he'd ever wanted anything...he would lift her out of that chair, carry her into the bedroom and lay her down on the bed. Rose understood his feelings towards his parents better than anyone else. They could spend the evening making love and forget all about his anger towards his abhorrently selfish mother and father.

He shoved his arms into a black shirt and tried to quell the rage still flowing through his veins by watching Rose ring her eyes with dark eyeliner.

He'd spoken to his parents numerous times since his grandmother's funeral but today was the first time he'd seen them in person. He hadn't realised how angry he was with them for this, especially at their failure to meet their granddaughters, not until they'd breezed into his home acting as if no time at all had passed since they'd last been under the same roof. They'd shown the exact amount of interest in their granddaughters as he'd known they would. Reality had matched his expectations perfectly.

For them to so casually mention the party and then encourage Diaz to take Rose along to it and spend hours of an evening socialising at the same party they'd be attending when they'd shown such little interest in their beautiful granddaughters had provoked such anger in him that if he hadn't seen the expression on Rose's face he might well have exploded. They'd afforded their granddaughters, babies of their own blood, less than two hours of their time since their birth. A third of the time they would spend at one party.

But he *had* seen Rose's expression in the unguarded moment when the party had been suggested and the spark of longing that had flashed in her eyes, and had quelled his temper and agreed to go.

He could not deny her anything.

Continuing to dress, he watched her expertly coat her lashes in thick mascara then reach for a round pot before her stare caught his reflection again.

Instead of opening the lid to the pot, she held his stare and softly said, 'Diaz, I don't blame you for being angry with them. They neglected their responsibilities to your grandmother so they could waltz around the world without any cares, and now history's repeating itself with our daughters.'

'They're selfish narcissists,' he stated flatly.

'I know, but all this suppressed anger...' She lifted a slender shoulder into a rueful shrug. 'It isn't healthy. They're not going to change. Wouldn't it be easier and healthier to just learn to accept them for who they are?'

His hand stilled at the knot he was forming in his tie. It took all his control not to snarl at her. 'You think I should forget all their neglect and move on?'

'You'll never be able to forget it, but moving on? It's possible. But you'll only be able to do that if you can put the past behind you. The fact you haven't cut them from your life suggests you do want a relationship with them, and, in their own selfish way, they do love you and want to be involved in your life too. Only you can decide if that counts for something.' Her lips curved into a sad smile. 'You can hold onto your resentment over their terrible, selfish parenting and let it eat you up or you can try and enjoy the time you get to spend with them because I can tell you this much—I would bite your hand off for five minutes with my mother. I would give a kidney just to hear her voice.'

Diaz's brief flare of anger at her unwelcome observations evaporated. His chest tightened into a point so painful it was difficult to breathe as he remembered Rose's complete devastation at her mother's funeral. She'd been hollow with grief. Barely able to support her own weight.

He remembered, too, the ache to wrap his arms around her and hold her tight to him that had gripped him that day. He'd watched her every move, afraid her fragility would see her dissolve into vapour if she left his sight, the compulsion to promise her everything would be okay and that he would take care of her alive on the tip of his tongue.

Maybe if his sister and grandmother hadn't taken such great care of her, he might have done all those things, but between them, they'd supported her the whole day, never leaving her alone for a second.

Was that the day it had all changed for him? He couldn't say for certain. It had all come about in increments. The only thing he could say for certain was that the overwhelming tenderness he'd felt for Rose on the day of her mother's funeral hadn't lasted because he hadn't let it. He hadn't wanted to let it.

'And what about you?' he asked quietly, working on

knotting his tie again without dropping his stare from the woman who shared his bed every night, who gave herself to him every night, who curled herself into him for sleep every night, but who still turned her mouth away from his. 'Do you think the day will come when you can put the past behind you and move on too?'

Her eyes closed, something—pain?—spasming over her face before her throat moved and she rested her gaze back on him. 'I don't know,' she whispered.

Now he closed his eyes, taking a moment to find air.

What would he do if she couldn't?

It didn't bear thinking about. He just had to be patient and give her the time she'd asked for and trust that she would find trust. In him.

There were days when everything felt so perfect he would forget he was waiting for her to decide if she would stay with him for ever, but then his lips would ache for a kiss that never came and he was forced to confront the reality of his situation and swallow back all the turgid emotions that came with the reality check.

He'd promised patience and, as much as it killed him, he needed to enact it for as long as needed.

Nodding to show he understood, he stood before a mirror to straighten his tie and decided to discard it. They were going to a party not a business meeting.

While he finished dressing, Rose, her make-up done, took off her robe and then, wearing only white lace knickers, her high breasts bare, slipped her arms into what first appeared to be another silk robe.

Dios, she was so graceful in her movements. So beautiful.

It was only when she'd fastened and tied it at the waist that he realised it was a long-sleeved knee-length dress.

White with large peach roses and vibrant green stems and leaves embroidered on it, it gaped from shoulders to midriff but was so cleverly tied her seemingly exposed breasts were tantalisingly concealed and the exposure of her thigh managed to be both daring and modest.

Feet in high silver ankle boots with open toes, she sprayed perfume onto her exposed cleavage, fluffed her wavy dirty blonde hair around her shoulders, then opened a drawer and selected a small silver bag.

She faced him. 'Ready?'

For the second time since entering the dressing room, Diaz found his chest tightening into a painful point.

After the birth of their daughters, Rose had stopped caring about her appearance. There had been subtle changes since their arrival in Spain, her outfits selected with care rather than the first outfit that came to hand being thrown on, but her make-up the rare times she bothered with it was kept minimal.

She'd always loved make-up. Dark, dramatic black liner and dark grey shadow to ring her eyes while keeping her lipstick subtle had been the Rose Gregory 'look'. It had always made her beauty more striking, forcing you to look, forcing you to see the large blue eyes that always brimmed with whatever emotion she was feeling. That's how it had always been for him, in any case, and he'd added it to his long list of things to despise her for.

He'd hated her intoxicating beauty and truculent sexiness. The way it made his blood heat and his pulses thicken. The fantasies it provoked. After his sister's overdose, the times he slept under the same roof as Rose were spent alone in his bed consumed with awareness of how close her room was to his, despising himself for being so beguiled by someone so poisonous.

Looking at Rose now was to see her come fully back to life in all her vivacious glory and beauty.

Looking at Rose now was to accept that there had never been truculence to her sexiness. That had been what he wanted to see, and it came to him with a punch in the guts that the poison had existed only in his mind too.

'Diaz?'

The dramatically ringed blue eyes were gazing at him. There was a tiny crease of concern in her forehead.

His heart was pounding so hard into his throat that it was an effort to speak.

He'd fed the poison. He'd fed it with a cruel ruthlessness to stop himself facing a truth he hadn't been equipped to handle.

He pulled a smile together and reached for her hand.

Fingers with shapely nails painted the same black as her toenails threaded into his.

She stepped to him.

For a breathless moment he thought she was going to kiss him.

Instead, she pressed the palms of their entwined hands together. 'What do you say that we just forget all the bad stuff and let loose for the night?'

He traced his thumb gently over her wide mouth. He remembered so vividly how soft her lips had felt against his.

How could he have believed someone who kissed with the whole of her heart, and who loved and cared with the whole of her heart, could have even an ounce of poison in their veins?

She placed a hand on his chest, right above *his* thumping heart.

A blue-eyed gleam speared him. She smiled with the

whole of her wide mouth. 'What do you say, Señor Martinez? Shall we go and have some fun?'

It came to him in a bolt that Rose didn't just want to go out for the evening, she wanted to go out for the evening with *him*. After everything he'd done, it was *his* company she wanted.

Spirits lifting absurdly high, he returned the smile and only just held himself off from cupping her face to kiss her. '*Sí, mi corazón.* Let's go and party.'

CHAPTER TEN

THE HELICOPTER LANDED on the roof of the private club the party was being hosted in. When Rose stepped out of it, she felt like the heroine of an action movie. All she needed was a gun in her knickers and she'd be ready to take down the villain of the piece.

She didn't imagine action movie heroines had to make the short walk from helicopter to entrance holding their dress down to stop it lifting from the force of the spinning rotors though.

A short ride down, the elevator opened into a huge gold lobby and then they were climbing winding stairs and walking a wide corridor lined with doors and the kind of arty, atmospheric black and white photos she'd once loved to take herself. Up another set of stairs and then, finally, they entered a sprawling, darkly lit but glittering room with copious mirrors that immediately brought to mind the Hollywood glamorous gangster ideal.

One quick skim revealed an abundance of faces she recognised from the big screen and small, and from the glossy fashion magazines she used to buy to study how photographers created mood and atmosphere in their shoots.

Suddenly feeling every inch the mother of twin babies

amongst such glamour, she slipped her hand into Diaz's and pressed herself closer to him.

'Relax,' he murmured, perfectly understanding her nerves without her having to say a word. 'These people don't bite. Champagne?'

'Do they serve it by the bottle?'

Laughing, he swiped two flutes from the tray of a smiling host.

Feeling a bit more grounded with her hand clasped in his, Rose let Diaz lead the way, noticing his nods of greeting at some of the familiar faces and his gestures to others that he would be back to talk to them soon. Once they'd passed the main throng, she realised he was leading her to a large crowd by the bar, and thought how handy it must be to be as tall as Diaz and able to see over everyone's heads.

A bald, diminutive man wearing horn-rimmed glasses holding court spotted them and immediately stopped whatever he was saying to beam widely. 'Diaz!'

'Pedro!' he replied with an identical beam before embracing him in a bear hug.

So this was the birthday boy and director whose films she so admired. He was exactly as Rose had imagined.

After a short exchange in Spanish, Diaz switched to English. 'Pedro, meet Rose.'

Pulling her into a tight embrace, Pedro said in heavily accented but perfect English, 'Thank you for agreeing to come and forcing Diaz here—I have been dying to meet you.'

That took her aback. 'You have?'

'Who wouldn't want to meet the woman who turned Diaz Martinez into a recluse?' He beamed again. 'But I understand it. My sister was the same when she had her first baby. Two for you. No wonder you are so slim. They must keep you very busy.'

'They do,' she agreed. 'It's the first time I've left them.'

'Don't think about them,' he urged. 'Otherwise you will spend the night checking your phone and be boring like my sister.'

'Rose could never be boring,' Diaz interjected with a faint wink at her.

Rose's brain was reeling so much she had no idea how she was able to hold the long conversation that followed between her, Diaz and Pedro, the other guests dipping in and out, the topics ebbing and flowing between movies and scripts and salacious gossip.

She'd never really thought about if or how Diaz had explained their situation to his friends and acquaintances. And now she knew. He'd dropped off the social calendar with the simple truth that he had twin babies and their mother wasn't ready to leave them.

He'd turned down this party with a man who was clearly a great friend for her sake. He really hadn't wanted to put her under any additional pressure.

'How do you know Pedro?' she asked after Diaz had extricated them with the excuse that they were monopolising Pedro's time and found them an empty booth to sit in.

'I was the main investor in one of his films six years ago. None of the studios wanted to touch it because it wasn't in English. I heard about it from a friend of a friend and approached him. We hit it off and now I provide most of the finance for all his films.'

She thought quickly. *'La Viuda Blanca?'* It had swept the movie industry awards for best foreign language film.

He raised an eyebrow. 'You know it?'

'I love Pedro's films. They're all so dark and twisty and have such great cinematography.'

'I thought you meant his English-speaking ones. I never knew you'd watched his Spanish-speaking ones too.'

Glad the lighting meant he'd be unlikely to see the blush she knew was burning her cheeks, she said, 'And *I* never knew you were involved in any of them.'

'I'm not, I'm just the finance behind them. It's good to diversify. If you watch the Spanish ones, does that mean you now speak my language?'

'I use subtitles.' She drained her champagne so she didn't find herself admitting that she'd initially started watching Pedro's films in the wake of her night with Diaz, a form of self-torture, immersing herself in the language he'd whispered to her when he'd made love to her.

That had been in the days when she'd held onto the faint hope that his English whispers had come from his heart and that he would come back to her.

By the time she'd taken the pregnancy test, she'd long come to the crushing acceptance that his words, Spanish and English alike, spoken in the heat of passion and in the stunned aftermath, had all been a lie, and for the first time in so very long, she was unable to block her heart from beating the pain as if the wound were as fresh as it had been all those nights spent curled on the sofa watching films in a language she didn't understand.

She could have kissed Diaz's parents for choosing that moment to appear at their booth.

'There you are!' Camila said, sliding in beside her son without invitation. 'Pedro said you'd arrived. Why are you hiding away?'

'So you wouldn't find us,' Diaz replied drolly.

Camila slapped his thigh with a, 'We need to work on your sense of humour,' and beckoned a passing hostess for more champagne.

Fresh flutes before them, Diaz put his to his mouth.

'Wait,' his mother commanded. 'We must make a toast.'

'To what?' he asked. 'The joys of grandchildren?'

She fixed him with a beady stare. 'To family.'

Even Rose winced.

The beat of the music being played by the famous DJ changed. Bodies began gravitating to the dance floor.

'How is business going?' Julio asked his son.

Rose squeezed Diaz's hand and braced herself for another cutting remark. It never came. Diaz returned the squeeze and answered his father cordially, and soon he was deep in conversation with both his parents, business talk that went completely over Rose's head. She was grateful for the time it gave her to compose her emotions.

More memories were pushing like a tidal wall at her brain, and the only way to push them back was to concentrate and focus her mind on people watching.

'You must wish you had your camera with you?' Camila observed, breaking Rose's mental attempt to put a name to the Hollywood actor gyrating on the dance floor with three scantily clad women.

'Could you imagine if I started taking pictures now?' she said with a wry smile.

'You would be escorted out and your camera destroyed,' Camila hooted. 'When will you start taking commissions again?'

'I haven't really thought about it.'

'But you must miss it, surely?'

'Having twins doesn't leave much time for missing things.' She didn't add that she hadn't taken any commissions since Mrs Martinez's stroke. Caring for her substitute grandmother had been a full-time occupation and one she had never begrudged, not after everything that wonderful woman had done for her.

Diaz had cared for her too. Between the two of them, they'd nursed her through her final months while Mrs Martinez's son and daughter-in-law had continued their jet-setting life.

She'd always accepted the selfish nature of Diaz's parents. They weren't going to change, something she'd pointed out to Diaz just hours ago, but sitting in this booth, absorbing the heat of Diaz's body, their fingers entwined, a little swirl of anger unfurled at the damage their selfishness had caused.

Camila waved a dismissive hand. 'You have staff for the twins. It is a crime to let your talent go to waste.'

'I'm sure I'll get back into it again one day but, for now, my priority is the girls.'

'But children are so boring and messy, and a career is so fulfilling. With your talents, you could be travelling the world and making a real name for yourself.'

The little swirl of anger grew but she tempered it into a pointed rebuke. 'I'm not like you, Camila—I could never leave it for other people to raise my children for me.'

Both her in-laws looked at her in bemused confusion. She had no idea what Diaz's expression was as her attention was entirely on his parents, but the hand clasping hers had tightened.

Giving a put-upon sigh, Camila finished her champagne. 'Oh, well, I can see your mind is made up so I will not argue about it, but I think you're making a mistake.

Now, tell us about your wedding. Diaz refuses to tell us anything. Am I right in thinking it was just the two of you and Josephine?'

'Nearly—we had the registrar and two witnesses there too.' Rose looked at Julio and, again pointedly, said, 'Your mother wanted to be a witness but she wasn't well enough to sign the certificate. She wasn't well enough because she was dying.' Something Julio and Camila had both known perfectly well.

They'd known perfectly well, too, that Rose had been Mrs Martinez's only visitor when she'd been admitted into hospital with the stroke that had been the beginning of the end for the wonderful woman, and she thought back to all the calls she'd made to Julio to enable his mother's discharge into her care. Thought back, too, to Julio and Camila's failure to let Diaz know about the stroke and its seriousness for over a week even though they'd promised to let him know immediately.

The moment Diaz had, finally, been informed, he'd dropped everything to be there for the woman who'd been more of a mother than a grandmother to him, and as all these thoughts and memories reeled through Rose's head, the building anger morphed into pure rage, and she wondered what the hell she'd been thinking spouting about *acceptance* and *moving on* to the one who'd most suffered at Julio and Camila's neglect.

Julio made the sign of the cross and, without an ounce of contrition for neglecting his mother with the same zeal that he'd neglected his children, said, 'She got to see you two married though.'

'Which is more than we did,' Camila added, now the one speaking pointedly, her attention on the son she'd rarely shared a roof with to kiss goodnight or been there for during a single one of his—or her daughter's—child-hood nightmares. 'We didn't know anything about it until you told us we were going to be grandparents.'

Rose's rage-induced impulse to chuck her champagne over the abhorrently narcissistic pair was only thwarted by the fact she had no champagne left to throw.

Diaz was the one to respond, smoothly saying, 'The last thing we wanted was for our wedding to be turned into a circus, but if you'd made the effort to visit while she was so gravely ill, one of us would have told you about it.'

Naturally, neither of his parents absorbed his reproach any more than they'd absorbed Rose's.

Rose was right, he realised. They were never going to change. Which made the anger he could feel vibrating from her all the more mystifying.

She'd been the one to stop him exploding in temper at the funeral. His parents had breezed in late to the service and taken their seats next to him. It was the first time they'd set foot in England since his grandmother's stroke. About to let rip at them, he'd been caught off-guard by the lightest of taps on his thigh.

He'd whipped his head to Rose, sitting to his right. She'd pulled her hand away, shaken her head, and quietly said, 'Not today.'

Those two words had been enough to bring him to his senses.

A hostess appeared with more champagne. Diaz thanked her with a smile and took a drink, his thoughts drifting even further back, to the evening he'd agreed to marry Rose.

They'd been in the drawing room. It had been three weeks since the hospital had released his grandmother into Rose's care. Diaz had reworked his diary to keep his international travel to a minimum so he could be there as much as possible. Rose had made them all a simple omelette, something his grandmother could chew without difficulty. Diaz had fed her.

They'd formed an unspoken, temporary truce.

It had been once the plates were cleared and they'd settled in what was by then their usual seats either side of her bed to watch a film that his grandmother had quietly said, 'I want you two to marry.'

He could still feel the shocked silence that had reverberated around the room.

His grandmother had slowly spread her hands out for them to take one each.

In perfect unison, they'd risen from their seats and carefully sat on the edge of the bed clasping a hand each and facing her. Facing each other too. All three able to see each other clearly.

His grandmother had looked directly at Diaz with a plea in her eyes. 'Don't let Rose be alone when I'm gone.'

His stare had darted to Rose. Her face had drained of colour, eyes wide with the same disbelief he'd known resonated in his.

'Will you marry her?' his grandmother had rasped, clutching his hand with all her limited strength. 'For my peace of mind?'

His heart had beaten so hard he could have sworn he'd felt it thumping to escape his ribs. 'Do you know what you're asking of me?'

To marry Rose? To make the most toxic woman alive, the woman he held responsible for his sister's near-death and estrangement, his wife?

His grandmother had nodded and smiled. 'Grant a

dying woman her last wish and marry Rose. Stop this war. The love is there if you will only give it a chance.'

'You're not dying,' he'd denied, lying to them both, too stunned at what was being asked of him to correct her on the love she'd spoken of.

They'd married four weeks and a day later in that same room, the tiny wedding party crowded around his grand-mother's bed so she could bear witness.

Two weeks after that simple wedding where the bride wore black and the groom wore the first suit that came to hand, his grandmother had died with Diaz and Rose holding the same hands they'd held when she'd made her final request to them, and he'd still been blind to the truth of her words.

The love is there if you will only give it a chance.

He hadn't given it a chance. He'd run from it. And he'd left her on her own.

The truth had only come when Rose had been close to death and even then, knowing he loved her, knowing he needed her, still he'd resisted the fullness of it, still running, running, running from the full truth of his feelings, still letting himself believe her responsible...

His mother's voice cut through his pounding thoughts. 'Have you heard from Rosaria lately?'

For a moment he was certain his darkening thoughts had conjured his sister's name from his mother's mouth.

She repeated the question.

He stared at her as if she were a stranger. She knew he hadn't spoken to his sister in almost eight years.

And then Rose quietly answered, 'A few weeks ago,' and he felt his whole world lurch.

Rose was very much aware of Diaz's stiffening beside her. Aware of his thumb, which had been gently stroking the top of her hand, freezing before he slowly pulled his hand from hers. Aware of his stare turning to her.

Bracing herself, she faced him.

His expression was incredulous, his voice hoarse. 'You are in touch with my sister?'

It was the first time Rosaria had even been alluded to since they'd arrived in Spain. Longer.

But she'd been with them the entire time, one of the eggshells to be avoided, the largest elephant never addressed for fear of the poison that would be unleashed through it.

Quivering inside, Rose nodded and confessed, 'We've always been in touch.'

She held her breath and waited for the explosion. It would be tempered—they were at a party surrounded by his friends and acquaintances—but it would come. It would be in his cutting words and the tone of his voice.

But the green eyes, narrowed as he searched her face, betrayed no hint of anger. Only the pulse ticcing on his jawline betrayed any emotion. 'How is she? Is she well?'

She expelled the breath with another nod. 'She's doing great.'

A crease appeared in his forehead. 'Really?'

'She keeps bees.'

The crease in his forehead deepened. 'Bees?'

'She's a complete hippy but where she lives…it's not a cult or anything. She still smokes pot but doesn't touch the hard stuff any more.'

He breathed in through his nose. 'You have seen her?'

She hesitated before admitting, 'I stayed with her three years ago.'

'You never said.'

Rose had debated for months whether to tell him that

she'd visited Rosaria. She knew Diaz kept tabs on his sister but also knew he would want to hear first-hand how she was doing. The problem was, he wouldn't want to hear it from the person he blamed for her drug addiction and the estrangement. To tell him she'd visited Rosaria would only reopen wounds that had never fully healed.

Their history was littered with wounds.

Had he become so good at masking his feelings that she couldn't read his anger and loathing any more?

Or had time and their babies finally…?

Don't think like that, she told herself with a panicking voice as she downed half her champagne in one swallow. *You fell into this trap before and inflicted the deepest wound of all.*

The wound was a thread away from being ripped wide open again.

As blissfully unaware of the undercurrent running between his son and daughter-in-law as he'd been of Rose's surge of anger towards him, Julio laughed and said to his son, 'And you always said Rose was the wild one of the pair.'

Rose tried to enjoy the rest of the party but it was hard when she felt herself on tenterhooks for Diaz's rage and questions when they were finally alone.

She didn't know how she'd endure the scathing insults. Not now.

Before their night together, a part of her had revelled in standing up to his loathing and matching it with her own.

Too much had passed between them since to find that revelry again.

Thankfully, any talk over the rest of the evening was Switzerland in its neutrality. Shortly after the Rosaria conversation, his parents disappeared to mingle with other guests, their seats taken by a steady stream of famous faces wanting a few minutes with Diaz, most barely hiding their interest at the woman who'd supposedly tamed him.

If only they knew the truth, she thought miserably. She hadn't tamed him. His love for their daughters had; a love that had seen him settle for and make every effort to build a relationship with his nemesis for the sole reason that she was their mother.

Her tenterhooks sharpened on the drive back home.

She wished they were flying back in the helicopter.

They sat positioned as far from the other as humanly possible, just as they'd done when Diaz had jumped into her taxi after she'd told him she was pregnant.

She sensed his brain whirling through the long silence. Was he condemning her in his thoughts? Remembering all the things he despised her for? Hating her all over again for his sister packing a bag a week after her overdose and, instead of going to the rehab facility Diaz had arranged for her to stay at to straighten out, losing her head and accusing him of being a control freak and saying that she wanted to live the life she wanted and not the life he wanted.

The life Rosaria had wanted included all night partying and as many drugs as she could consume.

'You want to control everything,' Rosaria had raged at him. 'Well, you don't get to control me any more. This is my life and my choices and if you don't like it you can go to hell. I'm not going to that stupid facility—the only person there's anything wrong with is *you*.'

Even then, Rose had felt a stab of pain for him. Even

when he'd blamed her for the life and choices his sister had made.

What had Mrs Martinez been thinking when she'd asked them to marry? Had she really thought fourteen years of bile and acrimony could be consigned to history?

It made her want to weep to remember how her heart had swelled in those months when it had been just the two of them and his grandmother. The months Rose had managed to fool herself that their long history of bile and acrimony could be finally put to bed.

They'd pulled together and worked as a unit to ensure Mrs Martinez's final months were filled with love and care.

Rose was so lost in her thoughts that she blinked in surprise when they turned into his long driveway.

The driver opened their doors.

The silence that had consumed the drive home broke when they walked into the villa to the sound of one of their daughters' cries.

They raced up the stairs.

Hearing them, Giselle, one of the on-duty nannies, appeared from the nursery. She had a wailing Amelia in her arms.

'What's wrong?' Rose asked, taking her daughter and cradling her to her chest, her heart rate trebling at Amelia's obvious distress.

'Teething,' Giselle said with kindly authority. 'I've just given her some baby paracetamol and put some of the teething powder on her gums. She should settle soon.'

'Go back to bed,' Rose told her gratefully. 'I'll look after her.'

Carrying Amelia into her old bedroom, Rose sank onto the rocking chair. Her daughter was already quieting.

After hanging by the door watching them, Diaz came into the room and crouched down to stroke Amelia's hair.

'I'll stay with her until she goes back to sleep,' Rose whispered.

He glanced up from their daughter's flushed face and gave a short nod. 'You'll wake me if you need me to take over?'

'I will,' she promised, blinking back tears.

They'd had that same innate understanding when they'd cared for his grandmother. There had never been a need to discuss any of it. Their minds had been in complete alignment.

He kissed Amelia's forehead then straightened. 'I'll have a glass of water brought to you,' he told Rose.

'Thank you.'

It was when he reached the door that he turned back to her and quietly said, 'We will talk in the morning, yes?'

Her stomach lurched but she met his stare and lifted her chin. 'Yes.'

It was only when he'd closed the door that a tear rolled down her cheek.

Rose couldn't settle. Amelia had gone back to sleep shortly after Diaz left the room but, not wanting to be far from her, Rose had decided to sleep in her old bed even though it was the same distance as the room she shared with Diaz. When she'd crept into their bedroom for nightwear, he'd been awake, staring at the ceiling.

His gaze had captured hers through the light seeping into the room from the landing.

'I'm going to sleep in my old room in case she wakes,' Rose had whispered.

His features had tightened but he'd nodded. Thinking,

she knew, about the elephants of their past they could no longer ignore.

She'd dozed on and off but her brain refused to switch off enough for proper sleep to take her, and now the birds were singing their early morning chorus.

Climbing out of bed, she slipped her robe on and padded across to the adjoining room.

Her babies were cuddled together, fast asleep.

She messaged the nannies, telling them to call her when one of the twins woke up, then crept out of the silent villa and escaped into the headily scented garden.

For the longest time she stood barefoot on the edge of the sprawling, manicured lawn, soaking in the faint rays of the rising sun, trying to expel all the thoughts crowding her mind.

It felt like every thought and memory she'd ever had had converged and were fighting for supremacy in her head. But there was one memory fighting the hardest, and it was this memory she'd fought the hardest to resist. She'd resisted letting this particular memory form for fourteen months.

She didn't have the strength to fight it any more.

She'd reached the gate of the fence surrounding the swimming pool area without any awareness of crossing the lawn to it.

Opening it, she stepped to the poolside and dipped a toe into the water. That one little action caused a ripple.

So many ripples, she thought bleakly as she sank onto the poolside and submerged her legs into the cool water.

Some ripples would always be felt, and she closed her eyes and abandoned the fight, and finally allowed herself to relive the night her daughters were conceived.

CHAPTER ELEVEN

Fourteen months ago

THE LAST OF the catering vans disappeared. The house that only hours ago had been filled with Mrs Martinez's family, friends and neighbours sharing food and drink and memories now contained only Rose… And Diaz. Every last trace of the wake had been wiped away by the efficient staff.

Rose sank onto a stool at the kitchen island and hung her head. She felt as drained and bereft as she'd ever felt.

Diaz's footsteps neared and his shadow appeared in the kitchen doorway before his full figure emerged. He'd showered, changing from his black suit into black jeans and a black V-necked T-shirt. Unshaven, damp hair mussed from a towel being run over it, he looked as drained as she felt.

He held up two crystal glasses in one large hand and a bottle of what looked like Scotch in the other, and raised an eyebrow in question.

Longing filled the ache in her heart. A longing to touch his face. To press herself close to him and find comfort and strength in his strength.

In the two weeks since Mrs Martinez had died, they'd

continued sharing the house as they'd done in the months leading up to her death, but the only times they'd come together had been when making all the funeral arrangements and touching briefly on the divorce they would file when the first year of their marriage was up. There had been no debate about it. There had been no debate, either, when they'd divided the house into two territories: his and hers. Only the kitchen had been Switzerland and even then, by more unspoken agreement, they'd only used it when the other wasn't.

They'd been like two ships deliberately giving the other a wide berth, and yet she'd been acutely aware of Diaz's course, always knowing where he was in the house, feeling his absence like an ache during the long hours he left to conduct business that needed the personal touch, lying in her bed at night consumed with his physical closeness and tormented by his distance.

Today though, they had come together one last time for his grandmother, and stayed by each other's side until the last guest left. The need to clasp his hand had, at times, been overwhelming.

And now he was offering her one last drink.

Come tomorrow, it was unlikely their paths would ever cross again.

She nodded and attempted a smile. Her mouth refused to cooperate.

He took the stool beside her. Filled both glasses with a hefty measure of the amber liquid, pushed one in front of Rose and raised the other. 'To my grandmother.'

She lifted her glass. 'To Mrs Martinez.'

He smiled faintly. Rose's insistence on addressing Mrs Martinez formally had been a long running in joke between her and the woman who'd loved and cared for her so greatly, a joke Diaz had come to be part of during the last weeks of his grandmother's life.

It didn't feel real that she'd been gone two weeks already.

Glasses clinked together; they drank.

'Thank you for stopping me earlier,' he said after a long passage of silence.

Her bruised heart filled again. She didn't blame him for having wanted to erupt at his parents. They should have been the ones holding Mrs Martinez's hands when she took her last breath. The ones to organise every aspect of the funeral. Not their son and the dead housekeeper's daughter. 'You're welcome.'

He swirled what was left of the liquid in his glass and grunted a laugh. 'You would think age would bring perspective but I don't know how I will ever find perspective over those two.'

'Now's not the time to try and find it,' she pointed out softly, wishing desperately that she could just *touch* him.

Rose didn't just ache for comfort from Diaz's strength but ached to give him comfort of her own. It was an ache that had grown stronger and stronger these last few weeks.

Diaz was her husband and she'd only voluntarily touched him once her whole life, that simple tap to his thigh in the church earlier when she'd instinctively known he was on the verge of erupting at his narcissistic parents.

Every single involuntary brush of their hands and arms as they'd cared for his grandmother in her last months had seared through her skin and into her heart.

And soon it would all be over and she would be all alone in the world without the one person left in it that she loved, and she didn't know how she could begin to endure it.

He refilled his glass and topped Rose's up.

Closing her eyes, she inhaled the potent liquid before drinking it in one large swallow and climbing off the stool.

To prolong this moment would be to add to her torment.

'I'm going up,' she said, then, as casually as she could muster, added, 'What time will you be leaving?'

He hesitated before replying. 'Early. I've a meeting in Milan.'

'If I don't see you before you go, safe travels.'

'Thank you.' A long pause. 'Sleep well.'

'And you.'

She didn't look back.

Her heart ripping and rippling, Rose went up to her bedroom needing to scrub the day from her skin and cleanse her emotions, and took a long shower under the highest temperature she could bear.

Don't think about him, she told herself despairingly as she scrubbed her face and fought with equal desperation to hold back the tears.

It was a battle she won only until she climbed into her bed and a wave of desolation grabbed her with such strength she could have more easily stopped the sun from rising.

With a moan of despair, the tears poured out in a torrent.

She wept for her mother who she missed desperately. Wept for Mrs Martinez whose loss suddenly felt so very real. And she wept for Diaz and the love that had taken such a strong hold in her heart and the future that could never be hers.

She barely heard the click of her door as it opened or the footsteps padding across the room but her body reacted, huddling even tighter into itself like a small child hiding from the monster in the room, but, in Rose's case, the monster was the despair she had never wanted Diaz to see, and she buried her face even tighter into her soaked pillow.

The duvet moved and the mattress dipped. A muscular arm wrapped around her waist and then, as if he really were manipulating the small child hiding from the monster, Diaz gently turned her round and enveloped her in his strength.

Her sobs grew stronger.

Clinging to him, Rose bawled into his chest, purging herself of everything she'd been carrying inside her for so long that she couldn't remember a time when her heart hadn't hurt. And all the while, Diaz's mouth tight in her hair murmuring broken words in Spanish, his legs entwined in hers and the palms of his hands stroking her back.

She would never know when the strokes stopped being given for solace and took on a different meaning. Or when she became fully aware that she was exploring the planes and muscles of his back with her hands…his naked back.

She lifted her face out of his chest without thinking and tilted her head back.

Diaz's gaze locked onto hers, a gaze filled with the same pain that had convulsed her. And with the same longing…

For a time that hung suspended, they simply drank each other in, their faces so close Rose could see every individual dark, stubbly hair covering his strong jaw and feel the heat of his breath with the same strength that she could feel the heat of his body.

With a soft groan of her name, he brought his sensuous lips to hers.

The shock of sensation burst the dam inside her. Inside them both.

His silken tongue swept into her mouth and in an instant Rose tumbled into a dark fusion stunning in its intensity, pinned beneath the hard length of Diaz's body and being kissed with a passion that sucked the air from her lungs.

The heat that exploded through her burned hot enough to incinerate every ounce of the pain and misery that had gripped her, and she wrapped her arms tightly around his neck and dragged her fingers through his hair as the dark fusion of their mouths took control of her body and drew out all the love and desire she'd so desperately hidden inside herself onto the surface of her melting skin.

In her deepest, most secret dreams, she'd dreamed of Diaz's kisses, fantasised about the day he would look beyond his loathing of her and see what she saw and feel what she felt, and now it felt like she'd fallen into that most secret dream and her senses were free-falling under the assault of his taste and scent, feeding the need that had been waiting all these years to be woken.

Diaz broke the fusion of their mouths only long enough to lift her up and remove her cami top, the skim of his fingers trailing fire over her skin. There was barely time to breathe before she was pinned back beneath him and the urgent, almost primitive demands of his mouth and tongue.

The world beyond the two of them had ceased to exist.

All Rose was aware of was Diaz, kissing her with the hunger of a starving man. Together, they worked impatiently to rid themselves of her cotton pyjama shorts and his undershorts, and then they were naked, lips entwined, her hands clasping the back of his neck, his hands lifting her bottom and his heavy arousal pushing at...

A moment of sanity broke free.

Panic shot through her and made her tense at the exact same moment Diaz murmured her name into her mouth and drove inside her, and when she cried out, it wasn't with pleasure but with pain.

Shocked to her core, she froze. The last thing—the very last thing—she'd expected was that it would hurt.

Diaz had become very still.

Breathing heavily, he lifted his head. His concerned face hovered over hers. A question creased his forehead. 'What's wrong, *mi corazón*?'

She couldn't speak. Could do nothing to stop the tears from leaking.

Understanding rang out as his eyes widened in horror. 'You've never done this before?'

'I'm sorry,' she whispered, turning her burning cheek onto the pillow and closing her eyes so she didn't have to look at him. She couldn't begin to guess how he was going to react.

Silence enveloped them.

He shifted his position, lifting himself out of her.

She closed her eyes even tighter, waiting for him to lift the whole of himself off her and leave the room.

'Rose, please look at me,' he commanded gently.

She didn't want to obey.

Her body gave her no choice.

Opening her eyes, she turned her face back to him.

He gazed down at her. His expression was troubled but there was so much concern and tenderness in his stare that the fears in her heart evaporated.

This was the Diaz she'd fallen in love with. The gorgeous, sexy hulk of a man capable of such great empathy and tenderness.

Only in her dreams had that tenderness ever been directed at her.

'I hurt you,' he said, his voice breaking.

She attempted a smile to ease his self-recriminations. 'No.'

He raised a disbelieving eyebrow.

Without thinking, she palmed his cheek. The sharp stubble made the most vivid contrast to the softness of his hair. 'I'm to blame, not you. You didn't know.'

He placed the gentlest of kisses to her mouth before drawing back again. 'Why didn't you tell me?'

'I forgot.'

'You...? How could you forget that?'

She stared into the green eyes that had haunted her dreams long before she'd accepted her love for him and, her heart turning over, sighed. 'Because in my head you've made love to me a thousand times.'

Shock etched his gorgeous face. Shock and then new understanding.

And still he didn't run away. Still he continued to drink her in as if she were the most precious thing in his world.

She ran her fingers over the stubble on his jaw. 'It's always been you,' she confessed in a whisper.

Always had been. Always would be. A love born without rhyme or reason but which had stopped her ever looking at another man.

Hate and love bound on the sides of the same coin.

Her heart had bound itself to Diaz before she'd hit adolescence. Her body had bound itself to him that awful day by his parents' swimming pool. Her soul had bound itself to him during the long weeks spent together nursing his grandmother.

He lowered his weight onto hers without crushing her and threaded his long fingers through her hair. *'Mi amor...'* he breathed before his sensuous mouth came back down on hers in a featherlight kiss. And then another. And another.

He lifted his head to gaze at her again. *'Eres muy hermosa.'* At her unspoken question, he breathed in deeply and gave a tortured smile. 'You are so beautiful. So very beautiful.' Palming her cheeks, he caressed her lips in another light kiss. 'I wish I had known. I would have been so gentle and given you the pleasure that should have been yours.'

'You did give me pleasure,' she whispered. 'I didn't know I could feel like that.'

'And now I will make you feel much more.' He pressed his mouth to hers again. 'And this time there will be no pain.'

Gently, his lips parted hers. All the urgency that had gripped them in the hedonistic madness gone, he explored the contours of her mouth with an unhurried seduction, coaxing her responses, lighting the sparks of her desire back into life and opening the gateway to heaven.

If their kisses before had been a fever of combusting lust and desire, this was restrained softness but its effect on her was equally as powerful, and she ran her hands over his back, still barely able to believe that this was Diaz in her bed, Diaz she was touching, Diaz's naked body upon her, Diaz's seductive mouth kissing her as if she were infinitely precious to him.

She'd ached for this for so long. Ached for him. Her only hate. Her only love.

And now there was no hate. Only love.

She moaned in protest when he moved his mouth away, a moan that softened into a sigh as his lips caressed featherlight kisses across her jaw, deepening when he flicked his tongue on the sensitive hollow beneath her ears and over the pulse of her throat, shivers flaming through her skin.

Closing her eyes, she surrendered herself to his love-making, soaking in his murmurs of Spanish as he worshipped her with his lips.

The sensation in her breasts when he took them into his mouth and circled the taut peaks with his tongue, achingly bringing each one to life, had her mewing and lifting her chest to him in a wanton plea for more, a plea answered with slow, voluptuous strokes of the tongue and grazing bites.

His lips moved languidly downwards, trailing fire over her ribcage and stomach, his hands stroking and exploring, all the sensations making her writhe at the liquid heat burning inside her.

Only when his mouth reached her silken pubis and she realised where he was headed did she tense, would have automatically pressed her thighs together if Diaz hadn't been lying between them.

Sensing her fears, he lifted his head and gave her a look of such tenderness that her heart cried.

'Trust me, Rose,' he whispered huskily, taking her hand and threading his fingers through hers. 'I will make this good for you, I swear.'

Tears that came from nowhere and which she would never in a thousand years understand except to know they weren't tears of unhappiness stabbed the backs of her eyes. Squeezing his hand, she gave a short nod.

A smile pulled at his mouth. 'Close your eyes, *mi amor*, and let your mind go. Put your trust in me.'

Her crying heart thrumming loudly, her breaths catching, she put her head back on the pillow at the same moment Diaz shifted himself lower until his face was level with her groin.

With infinite gentleness, he slipped a hand beneath her bottom to raise her, and coaxed her into parting her thighs further.

The liquid in her core had thickened into molten. Her pulses were raging fire as anticipation and fear collided, but the fear weakened at the first caress of her most intimate part.

Slowly, worshipfully, Diaz explored her secret flesh, his tongue probing and flickering, opening her to him.

It was when he sought out her most hidden part and patiently urged it to swollen arousal that the last of Rose's inhibitions at this most intimate of acts vanished into the ether and she was taken into a world of unknown pleasure.

He'd lied when he'd said there would be no pain, she thought dimly as exquisite, all-consuming sensation built inside her. This was pain. Rose was lost in it, drowning in a maelstrom of the most intolerable, glorious pain imaginable, each stroke of his tongue sweeping her higher and higher on the crest of a giant wave towards an undiscovered pinnacle...

The wave smashed and in the beat of a heart, Rose was thrown into a vortex of shimmering, spasming pleasure that had her crying out and clasping Diaz's head as she rode the ripples of her climax until her body was nothing but tingling atoms.

She opened her eyes.

Diaz lifted his head.

She opened her arms to him.

He crawled up her until he was covering her with his body.

She wrapped her arms around his neck and gazed into his eyes.

He inhaled deeply, his stare filled to the brim with emotion-laced hunger.

Their chests were so tightly fused she could feel the rapid thumps of his heart.

Her heart soared. All the tingling atoms that made Rose soared with it.

She lifted her head and pressed her mouth to his. 'Make love to me.'

He closed his eyes and took another deep inhalation. 'Rose…'

She raised her thighs. His arousal jutted hard against her pubis.

Eyes still closed, he gritted his teeth. 'Rose…'

'Make love to me.'

His stare opened back to her. There was a starkness to it. 'I don't want to hurt you again.'

She kissed him and whispered, 'You won't.'

Not now. Not when she was floating on a cloud of bliss.

She unhooked an arm and slid it down his smooth back. 'Love me, Diaz.'

His eyes pulsed and he bent his head to kiss her. 'Always.'

Trailing his fingers down her side, he slid his hand

between their groins and took hold of his arousal. Rose could feel it pressing into her opening and raised her hips higher, brand-new anticipation and excitement building inside her.

His stare not leaving hers, Diaz guided his thick length slowly inside her velvet heat, releasing his hand and driving the final few inches in with his hips.

Eyes widening at the new sensations stretching and filling her at this ultimate fusion, she sucked in a long breath.

'Are you okay?' he whispered unsteadily.

She nodded. She couldn't speak. She was trembling. She could feel him throbbing inside her. Could see the restraint he was exerting.

'Any time you want me to stop, you...'

She cut his words away with a kiss.

He groaned into her mouth, and then, slowly, gently, began to move, raising his head, watching her for signs of discomfort.

There was no discomfort. Her body melted into his possession as if it had been specially made for this moment...made for him.

'Dios, mi corazón,' he dragged out raggedly. 'This feels...' His words trailed off, left unsaid in a deep moan.

The tempo of his movements increased but still she sensed his restraint, knew he was holding himself back, and her heart swelled all over again in time with the sensations the smooth ebb and flow of his lovemaking was arousing inside her, and as the fire inside grew, the need for more, the need to feel everything, grew, and she cupped the back of his head and pulled him down for a deeply passionate kiss, and wrapped her legs tighter around him.

'*Te amo,*' he groaned raggedly. '*Dios, te amo,*' and she sensed his control teetering as he thrust even harder into her, a new driving rhythm that swept her to another realm where thoughts ceased to exist and she was aware of nothing but the deep throbbing of sensation building like a tidal wave into a crescendo until the first convulsion had her clinging to him and crying his name as she shattered into ecstasy with the crack of her own name ringing in her ears and Diaz's shuddering body collapsing onto hers.

It was a long time before Rose was capable of even opening her eyes.

Her brain fired slowly back to life. She stretched out a leg. Her entire body was tingling.

Diaz's head lay in the crook of her neck, a hand buried in her hair. She could feel the heavy thud of his heart against her breast.

He lifted his head and gently lifted his weight to gaze down at her with dazed eyes. 'Are you okay?'

She ran her fingers through his hair and smiled, still too stunned to speak.

A smile slowly curved his mouth and then he bent his head for a gentle kiss before attempting to pull himself out of her. She hooked her legs back around his waist to stop him. 'Stay,' she croaked.

He smiled more widely and stroked her hair off her damp forehead. 'Believe me, I'm not going anywhere.'

Her smile widened to match his. 'Good.'

He kissed her again. 'Are you sore?'

'No.' She was many things but sore wasn't one of them. 'That was…' She couldn't find the word to describe just how incredible it had been. 'Is it always like that?'

His smile dimmed into seriousness. 'No. Rose… I've never known anything like that before.'

Her fluttering heart soared anew and she sighed to release it. 'I love you.'

Eyes glittering, lips twitching, he breathed in deeply through his nose before slowly lowering his face back down to hers.

His tongue slid into her mouth and she closed her eyes…

CHAPTER TWELVE

FOOTSTEPS BROKE ROSE out of the deep reverie she'd fallen into.

She closed her eyes tightly and prayed for control.

She didn't have to turn her head to know who was approaching her.

Diaz paused a moment to compose himself.

Rose's body language told him she knew he was there. It was in her stillness.

Sickness lay heavily in his stomach. Exhaustion soaked his brain.

He hadn't slept. Too much history being replayed crowding his head until he'd thrown on a pair of jeans without thought and staggered out of his room to find her.

He knew what he had to do.

Without any acknowledgment of his presence, she lifted her legs out of the pool and twisted her body around. Pressing a hand to the tiled flooring for support, she got gracefully to her feet.

One look at her face was enough to know she'd had as little sleep as he'd had.

'We have coffee coming,' he told her quietly.

She nodded. There was defeat in the gesture. Defeat, too, in the shadows of her eyes.

A member of staff appeared with a tray of coffee and pastries for them. With quiet efficiency, she laid it on the poolside table for them, then disappeared.

They settled themselves at the table in silence. Diaz poured the coffee. He had to control the tremor in his hand. Control, too, the tightening of his throat to speak.

'Rosaria brought the drugs she overdosed on, didn't she.' It was a statement of fact, not a question.

Bloodshot blue eyes locked briefly on his. There was a hint of deserved accusation in them.

Rose had always denied being the one to buy them. He'd always refused to believe it.

He nodded slowly then quietly said, 'After you came into our lives, she started shortening her name to yours. I asked her why once, and she said it was because it was prettier than her name.' He gave a short, bitter laugh. 'I told her she was being ridiculous to want anything of yours but she was enthralled by you. I never understood it. I would watch the two of you and ask myself what she saw in a skinny child a year younger than she was, who had zero decorum and ran wild about the place barefoot.'

He let his stare fall to Rose's bare feet. She'd never lost her preference to be free from footwear.

His chest tightened at how pretty her feet were.

Breathing hard, he added a spoonful of sugar to his coffee. Usually he drank it black but that early morning he needed all the sweetness he could get.

'You thought I was feral,' she stated expressionlessly.

He turned his gaze back to her.

Her features were tight but her eyes…those expressive big blue eyes brimmed with hurt.

His nausea strengthened.

He'd caused that hurt.

The magnitude of everything he'd put her through had finally hit home to him. Everything he'd done to her. Everything he was continuing to do to her.

He would never forgive himself for any of it.

She blinked and looked away from him.

'I did think that,' he admitted, his voice as heavy as his heart. 'I hadn't met anyone like you before. I went to an exclusive private school until I was old enough to be sent off to an exclusive English boarding school. I mixed with children from the same kind of monied, privileged background. It was the same for Rosaria. Meeting you was like meeting a creature from another planet. You were just so...free, and unfiltered. I was as fascinated by you as Rosaria was.'

Her voice rose barely above a whisper. 'You hated me on sight.'

He clasped his coffee cup tightly. 'No, I hated how my sister fell in love with you on sight. And I hated that my grandmother had fallen in love with you. You were an interloper in the only place I'd ever been able to call a real home and stealing the affection of the only two people in the world who truly loved me.'

Her stare caught his and she tightened the sash of her robe.

He cleared his closing throat. 'That joint I caught you holding at my parents'? That was Rosaria's, too, wasn't it?'

Her chin made the faintest wobble.

'She made you take the blame.'

'She didn't make me.'

'She let you take all my anger and pretended to be blameless.'

Rose closed her eyes. She was too numb to feel any

sense of vindication at Diaz's acceptance that he'd been wrong about her. Finally allowing the memories of their night together to surface had wrung her dry.

It was all she could do to speak.

'She knew how you'd react. She knew you would hit the roof and have watched her like a hawk to stop her doing it again. She was angry at the world and drugs were the only way she'd found to blot all her anger out. She didn't want to stop.'

'And I did hit the roof,' he said heavily. 'I made everything worse with my heavy-handedness and drove her away.'

'No,' she disagreed. When it came to Rosaria, Diaz was blameless. 'You forget she has the same parents as you. All her angst goes back to the neglect she suffered at their hands, but because they're so indifferent to everything the only person she was able to rail at was you, because you're the one who loved her most.' At his disbelieving expression, she dredged a faint smile. 'You were the one most likely to forgive her.'

She hated to see the pain in his stare. Hated that it had the power to cut through her numbness when the torment of her memories made her never want to feel again.

'Then why does she still block all my calls and messages and refuse to see me?' he asked. 'Why did she boycott our grandmother's funeral when I made damned sure my mother told her about it?'

'She wanted to come but she was scared.'

Dismay and pain glittered. 'Of me?'

'Of causing a scene. She didn't know how you would react.' Cupping the base of her neck, Rose kneaded her thumb into the tensed muscle. She'd never felt this tight before, as if every muscle in her body had seized up and the rest of her had coiled in on itself.

Only her heart felt like it was working properly but the steady erratic increase of the beats was the warning sign that she was a hairpin away from the coil springing free.

She needed to keep it together and keep a tight hold of herself because to release the coil would be to release the clamouring demons and bring the whole world crashing down.

As evenly as she could manage, she said, 'Diaz, she's not the nineteen-year-old girl you remember. She's found her place in the world and she's happy. She's a spiritual, beekeeping, pot-smoking hippy, living off her trust fund with a long-term boyfriend, but she still fears your disapproval.'

Rose snatched a breath and willed her phone to buzz with a message from one of the nannies so she could end this conversation and hide away from Diaz until she had the demons under control. 'I think, too, that she's deeply ashamed for everything she put you through and that she misses you as much as you miss her, and I think if you were to fly to Nevada waving a white flag, she would embrace you back into her life.'

He sat in silent contemplation for the longest time before turning a bleak stare back to her. 'How can you be so calm and reasonable talking about this after all the years of blame I put on your shoulders?'

She gripped the sash of her robe. 'Whatever you did or said to me, you didn't deserve to be treated like that when all you were doing was trying to save Rosaria from herself.'

'Don't tell me you forgive me for my treatment of you,' he said in scathing self-recrimination.

The beats of her heart had risen to her throat. 'You both suffered at your parents' neglect.'

'You've been neglected your whole life by your father but that hasn't screwed you up and turned you into a monster.'

A pounding had formed in her head. 'I had my mother. She loved me enough for them both.'

'And then she died and instead of being a support to the girl who'd been such a large part of my life for so many years...' Diaz swallowed in an effort to contain the self-loathing consuming him. 'I was never able to see you truthfully. Always there were emotions mixed in it. It started with jealousy. You infected my whole life and I hated you for it. Even my parents on the few visits they bothered to make to Devon fell in love with you. When I started developing baser feelings for you...' His lips twisted. 'I hated myself. I hated that I could do nothing to stop them.

'Do you remember that weekend when your mother was at the hospice and I drove my grandmother to collect you from it?'

As still as he'd ever seen her, Rose gave the jerkiest of nods.

'As soon as I walked into the house, I knew you weren't there. You were always there. For years I'd resented you for that but that one time you were gone, there was an emptiness that I've never been able to explain. I insisted on driving my grandmother to the hospice on the pretext that she didn't like driving, but the truth was that a part of me needed to see you. I think that was when I first started falling in love with you.'

Rose jumped to her feet so quickly she knocked into the table, spilling coffee all over it. 'Don't.'

He gazed at her suddenly ashen face. 'I'm sorry, *mi corazón*, but this needs to be said. I need to clean my conscience and beg your forgiveness because I can't do this any more. I can't put you through this any more.'

She was trembling from head to toe. 'I don't want to hear it.'

'I know you don't, and I don't want to cause you any more—'

'No!' Spinning on her heels, arms folded tightly across her chest, head bowed, she hurried away from him.

Kicking his chair back, he followed her across the lawn, his longer strides easily closing the distance. 'Rose, I know I've behaved terribly to you.'

Her pace didn't slow. She gave no impression of hearing him.

'I know I can never take away the hurt I've caused you—'

She came to an abrupt halt. Her back straightened and stiffened, and then, slowly, she twisted around.

Colour crawled over her disbelieving face. 'Hurt? You call that *hurt*?'

His heart splintered, all words of apology lost under the agonised contortion of her face.

'Hurt? *Hurt?*' she screamed, slamming her hands into his chest. 'You didn't hurt me, you bastard, you *destroyed* me! Do you understand that? *Destroyed* me. I gave you my heart... I gave you my *everything*, and you took it all with words of love and then you crept out of my bed and walked out of my life without a backwards glance.

'You didn't just break my heart, you broke my soul, and now you want to clean your conscience?' Tears streaming down her face, she threw her hands in the air. 'Well go on then, clean it. Purge yourself. Tell me all the lies you've dreamed up to justify treating me like the nothing you've always thought me to be.'

The sickness in his stomach spread through his veins, infecting the whole of him, and it was all Diaz could do not to throw himself at her feet. 'I will spend the rest of my life repenting every wound I inflicted on you, but you have never been nothing to me. You've been a part of me for so long that I couldn't even try to tell you when you first seeped into my soul.'

She was swiping at the falling tears, shaking her head. 'No.'

'When I left you that morning, I didn't just destroy you, Rose, I destroyed myself and any chance I ever had of happiness because you *are* my everything.' He needed her to know that. Needed her to believe it. Needed her to leave his home with the truth because the truth was the very least she deserved.

'I woke that morning feeling like I was suffocating. You were asleep in my arms and everything I was feeling was just too much. I couldn't breathe. I hadn't intended to come to you that night. I'd spent months—*years*— doing everything in my power to stop myself stepping into your room. I'd spent years hating you and the toxic allure you'd spun around me, and to admit to myself that I'd been wrong about you was too much to allow myself, not just because I'm an arrogant bastard but because of what it would have led to.'

Her lips were still trembling but the rest of her had frozen.

'Deep down I always knew that there was no real rationality behind my loathing of you. I turned you into the evil heroine of my mind because I needed to. Once my attraction for you came to life, I was terrified of how deeply my feelings for you ran. But I couldn't keep it up, not once my grandmother had her stroke. The way you cared for her...' He shook his head, more memories flooding him. 'No one could devote themselves to giving such care to someone who wasn't even of their blood if they had anything but love in their heart, but I would never have come to you if I hadn't heard you crying.'

Those cries had touched him like nothing else, compelling his feet to her room and compelling his arms to wrap around her and hold her tightly.

'Nothing could have prepared me for what we shared that night. I cannot tell you how it felt to learn I was your first, and my words of love...they came from my heart, you must believe that, but in the morning I went into denial. I justified walking out on you without saying goodbye and leaving that note by telling myself that we'd got carried away on all the emotions of the funeral. I could not face the depth of my feelings for you or the possibility that your feelings for me could be of the same weight. I had to rebuild you back into the evil heroine to stop myself coming back to you. And then you told me you were pregnant.'

She visibly flinched.

He felt it like a flinch to his own heart.

Pinching the bridge of his nose, Diaz breathed deeply, needing to get control of the emotions boiling inside him.

He wished as hard as he'd ever wished that he could turn back the sands of time.

He had never hated himself as he did then.

It took everything he had not to flinch from confessing the rest. But he needed to say it, and, whatever Rose might say, he knew she needed to hear it.

'I have never had unprotected sex before and I think

the reason neither of us even mentioned contraception that night was because when we were holding each other, the future my grandmother had wanted for us and that we'd been running from was right there for us to take. If I hadn't run away from it, we would be living that future now, but, coward that I am, I did run, and I did everything humanly possible to block you and the night we'd shared from my thoughts.

'I couldn't block you from my dreams though. That has always been impossible, and when the girls were born, that was it. I couldn't run from my feelings any more.' He pinched the bridge of his nose again, this time to hold back the stinging tears the mere memory of that day always provoked. 'I have never experienced such cold fear in the whole of my life.'

Her throat moved and she bleakly croaked, 'I was terrified they wouldn't make it too.'

He held her stare and shook his head. 'No, *mi amor*, my terror was at losing *you*.'

Shock widened her eyes, and she hugged her arms around her chest.

'I thought you were going to die.' He blinked hard and pressed a hand to his chest, and starkly said, 'If I had lost you, I don't know how I would have gone on. It took your near-death for me to come to terms with the fact that a world without you in it is no world at all for me, but even then, even knowing I couldn't live without you in my life, I still could not bring myself to admit the truth and see you for who you really are rather than the warped version I'd always fed myself.

'You are my life, Rose. My sun. My moon. My stars. The future I ran away from is the only future I want but I see now that it's a future I can't have. I know you still love me but I know now that the hurt I've inflicted on you is too deep to heal. I have destroyed any trust you had in me beyond repair. I thought all I would have to do was be patient and you would come to see that my feelings for you are true and unbreakable but I was lying to myself, just as I have always lied to myself about you, and I continued to hurt you just as I have always hurt you.'

Self-loathing filled him like rancid bile. 'What kind of love blackmails to entrap a heart it had so cruelly rejected and abandoned?'

Her wide eyes flickered and closed.

He took what was possibly the biggest breath of his life. 'My plane is on standby for you to take the girls home. I will instruct my lawyers to file the divorce papers immediately and have primary custody made over to you.'

There was a long moment of stunned silence before she gave a dazed shake of her head and choked, 'No, Diaz. No. You can't do that.'

'Yes, I can. I see it now.'

'*No.*'

'Rose, *yes*. It has to be this way. Our history will always be an open wound and there will come a point when it will infect our daughters too. They need stability and they need their mother.'

Her face crumpled. A tear rolled down her cheek. 'But you're their father. They need you.'

'I will always be their father and they will always have me,' he insisted with a firmness he had to force his vocal cords to make, 'but this arrangement is the best one for them and the best for you. You deserve the world, Rose, and you deserve your freedom, and this is the only way I can give it to you.

'I will still be involved in their lives but this means you can start again and live your life as you choose, and one day find someone who can love you how you deserve to be loved without years of toxic history poisoning it. But if…' He had to swallow to say the next words. 'If you find you are pregnant, then I will be there for you in whatever capacity you need me to be.'

All those weeks of making love unprotected. Never mentioned between them. His arrogant hope that it meant Rose wanted nature to send her a signal that they were meant to be together and tie her irrevocably to him.

Still shaking her head, she burst into tears, different tears from her earlier sobs, formed by a different kind of pain, a pain he shared right down to his marrow. Without any forethought, he hauled her to him.

'It has to be this way, *mi amor*,' he said into her silken hair, squeezing his eyes to hold back his own threatening tears. 'My feelings for you have always been extreme and my reactions in fighting it extreme, and I want you to know that I am beyond sorry. I've behaved monstrously to you and now I have to put things right, as much as I can.'

For the longest passage of time they did nothing but hold each other tightly, Rose's tears slowly subsiding into dry heaves.

He kissed the top of her head. 'I love you, Rose. I will always love you.'

'I love you too,' she choked.

Disentangling their arms, they gazed into each other's desolate eyes.

'Please go,' he whispered. 'Don't drag this out.'

Chest and shoulders still heaving, she made a short nod and pressed her fingers to her lips and then pressed her fingers to his mouth. Her voice was barely audible. 'Goodbye, Diaz.'

He trailed his thumb along a high cheekbone for the final time. 'Goodbye, Rose.'

Diaz hauled his leaden legs up the stairs. He'd drunk enough bourbon to tranquillise a horse and could only hope it would have the same effect on him.

He craved oblivion. If not for his daughters, he would crave to never wake up.

The villa was deafening in its silence.

With drunken, blurry eyes, he found the nursery door.

He didn't know if it was better or worse that much of the girls' stuff had been left behind. The items left were for when they came to visit him.

From now on, his daughters would only be visitors in his home. He would no longer share the daily routines with them. No longer share their daily life.

No longer share Rose's life.

He staggered to his bedroom and through to the dressing room.

The dressing table at which he'd watched the Rose he'd fallen in love with all those years ago come back to life just a day ago had been cleared of the beauty products she didn't need but adored using.

He opened its drawers. All empty...except for the pencil that rolled out of its hiding place at the back of the top right drawer when he started closing it.

Rose's eyeliner.

He slumped onto the dressing table chair and picked the eyeliner up.

Just to touch it was enough to rip the fissure that had been steadily growing in his heart wide open. Holding the eyeliner tightly to his chest, he opened his lungs to expel all his agony in a roar before he slumped over the table and bawled like a child.

The girls were settled in their double cot, holding hands and on the cusp of falling asleep.

Rose crept out of the room and crossed the landing to the bathroom.

Even though the cramps that had been gripping her on the flight back to England had told her what was coming, she still found herself shaking to have started her period.

Shaking and then sobbing.

CHAPTER THIRTEEN

ROSE CLOSED THE nursery door until it was slightly ajar and blew out a long breath of air. A week since returning to Devon and she still had trouble breathing properly.

Downstairs, she curled up on the sofa in the living room and switched the TV on with the remote.

Her phone buzzed.

Her heart jumped.

It jumped at all her messages and alerts.

She pulled it out of her cardigan pocket and held her breath as she swiped it, then slumped when it wasn't Diaz's name on the screen. It was Rosaria.

He's on his way. Should land by late afternoon. Wish me luck!

She wrote back an equally jaunty reply.

Good luck!

Reply sent, she grabbed a cushion, held it tight to her belly and closed her eyes. She wished the girls were awake so she could cuddle them.

Knowing Diaz was flying across the Atlantic only

made the distance between them feel wider, and not just because the physical distance between them was widening.

A whole week without him.

She supposed it was natural that she would miss him after being in his near-constant company since the girls were born.

The emptiness of the house didn't feel natural though.

She supposed the emptiness would soon start to feel so natural she wouldn't even notice it.

She didn't think she would ever stop noticing the gaping wound in her heart. Not until it healed, which so far it showed no signs of doing. It was a different kind of wound from the wound Diaz had inflicted when he'd abandoned her but the pain from it hurt with equal intensity. And was getting worse, not better.

At least she had the girls. They were as happy back in Devon as they'd been at home in Spain. Happy to be in their new nursery rather than sharing their mummy's old room.

The twins were always happy as long as they had each other to hold onto.

She couldn't begin to imagine how much Diaz must be missing them.

Another message pinged.

What do I say to him?

Just tell him that you're sorry for everything and that you love him.

At least that was one salvageable relationship, she comforted herself. She was glad she'd made that call to Rosaria and told her to stop being a scaredy cat and let her brother back into her life. Within two days of her call she'd received a message from Diaz thanking her and asking if he could visit the girls soon, after his visit to Rosaria and his short trip to Vienna for the monthly high-stakes private poker game.

She'd come within a whisker of calling him and begging him to come to them now.

It had to be this way. They both knew it.

But, God, she missed him desperately.

The distance she'd hoped would ease the gaping wound of her heart had eased nothing.

Her period had finished and she still felt bereft at the conception that had never been. A conception she hadn't even known she'd been longing for, a deeply rooted yearning from the heart that had never stopped loving Diaz, a yearn for another chain to tie herself to him.

It had to be this way. What chance of a future did they have with their history? How could they just wipe it all out and forget it? How could either of them move on?

But how could she move on without him?

And how could she find the love he said she deserved when her heart belonged in its entirety to him and their daughters?

Her heart suddenly doubled over and she sat up sharply, swiping at her phone to reread her last message to Rosaria.

Just tell him that you're sorry for everything and that you love him.

What was Diaz doing that very minute? Flying thousands of miles to the sister he'd loved and protected his whole life and who'd cut him from her life as repayment.

The same Diaz whose parents had never shown him the love a child needed to thrive. If his love for Rose was a fraction as strong as her love for him, then no wonder it had terrified him. To his parents he'd been an encumbrance. His sister had rejected his love and protection. Knowingly or not, Diaz associated love with rejection. All things considered, it was a flipping miracle that he'd come to accept his love for Rose.

He'd unflinchingly admitted to his sins against her and set her free even when it had destroyed him to do so. He'd been making amends for those sins all along but she'd been too frightened of waking up again to an empty bed to realise. Too scared to trust him. Too scared of trusting what every single one of her senses had been telling her.

Diaz loved her. Truly loved her. As much as she loved him.

And when you loved someone as much as they loved each other...

Rose jumped to her feet and raced up the stairs to her room.

Diaz climbed out of the hire car.

The farmhouse was exactly as he'd imagined, a two-storey sprawling wooden ranch with a wraparound porch encircled by a white picket fence, and surrounded by fruit trees.

The front door opened.

A buxom brunette wearing denim dungarees appeared.

If he'd passed her in the street he wouldn't have recognised her.

Rosaria walked to the porch steps. 'Hello, Diaz. How are you? Good flight?'

He reached the bottom of the same steps. 'The flight was good, thanks. You're looking well.' Looking healthy.

'So are you…although you look like you haven't slept in a month.'

'More like a week.'

He climbed up the steps.

His baby sister gazed up at his face. He gazed down at hers.

A moment later the years of their estrangement melted away under the force of their embrace.

Diaz strolled through the Michelin-starred restaurant of his Viennese hotel. He noted with unsmiling satisfaction that every table was occupied, the hum of chatter only slightly higher than the specially chosen melodious background music. A number of diners were taking pictures of their food. Their expressions suggested their social media postings would be favourable. As it should be.

In the kitchen, ordered chaos ensued. The head chef, whose famous name was on the restaurant door, noticed Diaz's appearance but was too busy to do anything but nod an acknowledgement. As it should be.

In the spacious lobby, he descended the stairs two at a time to the basement, and swept past the doormen and into the hotel's real money pit. The casino.

Almost nine o'clock on a Saturday evening and already the atmosphere was thrumming. Where the music in the restaurant was kept low-key to enable his diners to relax, the volume in the casino was upped, the tempo fast. In another hour, all the gambling tables would be full and would remain full until the early hours. People would have to wait their turn to play on the slots. As it should be.

Everything in his business empire was exactly as it should be.

It was only in Diaz's heart that everything was wrong.

Before heading to his security hub, he checked his phone in the faint hope he'd missed it vibrate a message.

Nothing. No reply to the message he'd sent Rose early that morning in reply to her own message. It had been a sweet message saying she hoped his visit to Rosaria had gone well and asking if he still planned to come to Devon after Vienna.

He could not credit how badly he missed her.

It was all he could do to get out of bed each morning.

He could no longer give his soul to have her back. His soul had gone. All that was left was emptiness.

'Has it started?' he asked, taking his usual seat in The Hub.

'Four minutes,' Jorge replied, not looking up from the screens before him.

Diaz skimmed with disinterested eyes the fool currently being welcomed by Stefan, the evening's host. 'The usual faces?'

He barely registered the hesitation before Jorge answered. 'Yes.'

'Okay. Coffee?' He was off his seat and heading for the nearest coffee machine before Jorge could answer.

Coffee made, he placed Jorge's in front of him and took a sip of his own, wishing it were a large Scotch or bourbon.

Had to maintain the façade that everything was business as usual.

The players had taken their seats. Two tables. Eight players per table...

A jolt of electricity zinged through his veins. He blinked to clear his vision and moved his stare to a different monitor, which was fixed, face on, on players three and four from table one. Player three was a slender woman with long, dirty blonde hair worn loose around her shoulders. She was wearing a sparkling gold strappy-sleeved dress, high breasts showing just a hint of cleavage.

His throat ran dry.

As if sensing his attention, player three lifted her stare to the monitor Diaz was watching her through.

He'd seen her. She could feel his stare on her.

All her pulses were racing.

The first cards had been dealt. Rose looked at hers and looked at the table cards. Her hand wasn't as bad as the hand she'd been dealt the last time she'd played poker but it wasn't a good hand. She didn't care. She wasn't here to win money.

She was here to win her husband.

She pushed all her playing chips into the pile. 'All in.'

There were audible gasps from her fellow players.

Only the Greek player, number seven, matched her. He had a royal flush.

Ten million euros poorer than she'd been ten minutes earlier, Rose smiled gracefully and got to her feet at the same moment the door opened. She'd played her cards with perfect timing.

Head held high, she strolled past the remaining players, all gawping incredulously at her, towards Diaz.

Only when she stood before him did her performance come unstuck and her feet glue themselves to the floor.

His shoulder was propped against the doorway as if he'd fallen into it.

The green eyes that had only looked at her with love for so long she could no longer remember what his loathing had looked like locked onto hers. His handsome features were taut, his chest and shoulders rising and falling in rapid motion.

There was no way of knowing how much time passed before he straightened and stepped aside to let her through the door.

Without exchanging a word or a glance, they crossed the casino floor.

This time, it wasn't to the administrative offices that he led her. This time it was to an elevator.

Still without either speaking or looking at the other, he pressed the button and in silence they rode up to the penthouse.

Inside his private suite, Diaz slumped against the nearest wall and closed his eyes.

He wasn't entirely sure he wasn't dreaming. To dream, though, you had to sleep, and he couldn't sleep. Hadn't slept since the night he'd drunk himself into a stupor.

He felt like he was in that stupor again.

A warm hand touched his cheek.

He held a breath he couldn't exhale.

A warm hand palmed his other cheek.

The soft swell of breasts pushed and rose against his chest as the clasp on his face tightened and then the softest lips in the world brushed fleetingly against his mouth.

Heart thumping intolerably, still unable to breathe, he opened his eyes.

Big blue eyes bored into his.

The softest lips pulled into the softest smile and then she lifted onto her toes and pressed her mouth to his, fingers sliding across his cheeks and ears to bury into his hair as she seduced his lips apart and her sweet tongue slid into his mouth in a slow, deeply passionate kiss that spoke more eloquently than words ever could.

'Love me, Diaz,' she whispered.

He gazed into the eyes brimming with the same love and desire consuming him in its flame, and brought his mouth back to hers. 'Always.'

Diaz carried Rose to the bed they'd failed to reach before their desperate hunger had overpowered them. She was perfectly capable of walking. He just wasn't capable of letting her go. He needed to keep the physical connection, a shadow of fear in his head that she would disappear if he stopped touching her.

She cuddled tightly into him. Her silky hair tickled against his throat.

The enormity of what she'd done was just starting to penetrate. What it meant…

He hardly dared believe what it meant.

'I love you,' she whispered.

He tightened his hold around her and pressed his mouth tightly to the top of her head. 'I love you too. So very much.'

But their love had never been in doubt.

'Where are the girls?'

'At home with the nannies and staff.'

'You've employed staff?'

She wriggled free enough to raise her head and brush his cheek. 'I didn't need to. You've already employed enough of them.' She kissed him gently. 'They're at home in Spain, waiting for their *mami* and *papa*.'

He stared intently into eyes brightening with a lightness he hadn't seen in them for so many years. 'Rose...'

'I'm really sorry, but I've not got any choice,' she interrupted. 'We have to move back in with you, I'm afraid, as I'm now officially skint. That hand of poker was the last of my money and now I can't afford to run the house in Devon and am at the mercy of your generosity to feed myself.'

Incredulity meshed with the spark of realisation.

She sat up and threaded her fingers through his with a beam. 'Yes, Diaz, I have instigated things so you have no choice but to take me back, and as you have to take me back, we might as well stay married, so I've sent instructions to cancel our divorce. If you want to divorce me then you'll have a proper fight on your hands because I'm not going anywhere.' She lifted his hand to her mouth and kissed it. 'I've been in love with you for so long I don't even know when it started, and I'm not going to spend the rest of my life in purgatory just because of our past. You're the one who said the past doesn't need to determine the future, and I've decided our future is going to be together.'

He raised an eyebrow. 'You've decided?'

Her beam widened, the whole of her face as bright as the lightness in her eyes. 'Yes, but you decided it first.'

'I did?'

'Yep. Remember you said that thing about me deserving the world? Well, you're my world, so that means I deserve you, which means you've got to take me back, whether you like it or not.'

He groaned. 'Rose, it was never about me. I never wanted to let you go.'

The lightness dimmed a little but the brimming love didn't. 'I know. Because you're selfless when it comes to those you love. And you said something else too, about my father's neglect not screwing me up, but in a way it did. Not like the number your parents did on you, but I think it's made me more self-protective. I learned when I was little that the best way to stop someone you loved from hurting you was to build barriers. My father and I will never have a proper relationship partly because I've never let my barriers down for him—I wanted him to knock them down and force the relationship, and it took a long time to accept that he never would.'

Gazing into the eyes that still contained the last vestiges of disbelief, Rose pressed his hand to her breast and flattened it right where her heart was beating its love for him. 'I was so terrified of falling in love with you again and being hurt by you again that I couldn't see over the barriers I erected to protect myself. I was too frightened to dare trust you again or see you were no longer hiding from your feelings for me and that everything you were doing was for me.'

The hand not pressed against her heart lifted and stroked her chin. The smallest smile of belief began to form.

She leaned down and kissed him. 'It's always been you for me,' she whispered. 'When you're not with me, all the lights go out. I don't want to be in the darkness any more.'

His green eyes were intense with emotion. 'I swear I will never do anything to hurt you again.'

'I know,' she said simply.

'You are my life, Rose. My heart. My soul. My everything.'

Every atom of her body filling with sensations that fizzed like fireworks were being let off in her, Rose fused her mouth to Diaz's and, wrapped tightly in his strong, protective arms, let the light fill them both.

EPILOGUE

ROSE'S HANDS WERE spread over Diaz's naked chest, one of his hands clasping her hip, the other cupping a ripened breast, eyes locked together as she rode his thick length, moaning at the pleasure saturating her.

Feeling the sensations tighten, she ground down harder, chasing the release that would shatter her into the most glorious pieces.

She would never, ever get enough of their lovemaking, and when her release finally came, Diaz, holding himself back as he always did, let go too, thrusting up and gripping her hips tightly as he climaxed deep inside her with a shout of her name.

Unable to flop and collapse on top of him as she so loved to do, she eased herself onto her side and cuddled into him as well as she could.

Holding her securely to him, Diaz bent his head for a kiss and placed a gentle palm on her swollen belly. *'Te amo,'* he murmured into her mouth.

She smiled sleepily. 'I love you too.'

Their fourth baby woke from its slumber and kicked against his hand.

* * * * *

THE BRIDE
WORE REVENGE

LORRAINE HALL

MILLS & BOON

For my very own work wives.

CHAPTER ONE

"YOU DON'T HAVE to keep taking this job."

Lynna Carew continued to assemble her brownie sundae as a last hurrah before she traveled to Mykonos for a job. Her coworkers—and friends—were all on video chat as she worked.

The four of them made up Your Girl Friday. Freelance assistants who operated with the upmost discretion. They assisted the richest of the rich with different aspects of their lives, Irinka managed personal affairs, Maude handled the rehabilitation and management of the elaborate grounds of ancient estates, and Augusta, better known as Auggie, was a jill-of-all-trades, and oftentimes the driving force behind the business.

And of course, her friends were right in this instance. She didn't have to keep taking this annual job, as Irinka *always* reminded her. But Lynna would take it, as she always did, just the same.

"I feel like we've been over this," Lynna said, adding the homemade chocolate sauce she always kept stocked in the fridge.

"We just don't get it," Auggie groused. "You *hate* him. You complain about this job every time. And we all know he's hiring you just to be an ass."

He was indeed doing it just to be an ass. That's what

Athan Akakios did best, in Lynna's opinion. Well, maybe not best. His *best* skill was being a backstabbing villain. The *ass* just came naturally along with that.

But that was just the thing. He wanted to twist the knife in her back. Why? She didn't have a clue. Her father's untimely death, after the Akakios empire had ruined him, was punishment enough, Lynna figured. But Athan wanted something more from her.

She refused to give it—whatever it was. Refused to let him hold anything over her. Even though he continued to try. "The best revenge is a superior dish served to haunt his dreams for the remaining days of the year I'm cooking for someone else."

"That is *not* how the saying goes," Maude said grimly.

"It's how *my* saying goes," Lynna returned. She surveyed her brownie sundae. *Perfect.* She grabbed it and the tablet where her friends were faces in boxes. She moved into the living room of her cozy flat in London and settled into her overstuffed armchair. "Besides, this isn't the normal month of work for him. I'm leaving tomorrow. I'll prepare for the wedding, cater the wedding, then I'm just on call for the remaining two weeks."

"You're catering the *wedding* of a man who destroyed your family. It's an affront."

Lynna took a bite of her sundae, reveled in the homemade whipped cream. The brownie and ice cream she'd made lovingly from scratch. "I happen to like catering weddings, Irinka. Regardless of the bride and groom."

She supposed this was something of a ritual. Her friends and coworkers protested. She listened to each of their concerns and dismissed them one by one.

Because Lynna Carew did not need anyone's approval. She never had.

Maybe she didn't *relish* the feeling of *waiting* on Athan. But the higher insult would have been if he'd forgotten her and her family entirely. Clearly, the Carew name—or at least the dishes she made—still haunted him in *some* way, or he wouldn't keep hiring her, year after year. He wouldn't have asked her to handle the food for his very private, very exclusive and expensive if small, upcoming wedding.

Maybe he thought he was torturing her by hiring her a few weeks out of every year, but she never let on that she hated him. Never made a bad meal to punish him. She behaved like the consummate professional every year for the past five years.

And then took her paycheck straight to the bank.

If he wanted emotion, he was barking up the wrong tree.

"You're going to poison him this time, aren't you?" Maude asked. With just a little too much hope in her tone.

"Not at all. That hardly helps business. But do you know how many people are going to want *me* to cater weddings like this, make cakes like this after I succeed? It's going to set me, and *us*, up for life. I happen to think there's a kind of poetic justice to the whole thing."

It didn't bring her father back, but nothing did. It didn't pay for her brother's education, but her work at Your Girl Friday was doing that. It didn't change what the Akakios family had done, but nothing would.

So why not profit off them?

Perhaps once upon a time she might have considered Athan a friend—a family one, if not a personal one. She might have thought of him and his father as good men, just like her father.

And then almost six years ago, they'd both betrayed her father so deeply—stealing away from him every last share of the business he'd built from the ground up. Making the public think Aled Carew was a criminal and the mighty Akakios family had righted a wrong.

They had succeeded. Her father had not recovered. Financially or from the shock and pain and stress of being treated this way by people he'd not just trusted, but loved like family.

An aneurysm had taken his life not six months later. It had nearly destroyed her family. Would have if Lynna hadn't determined that no one else got to destroy them.

So no, she didn't mind her yearly job for Athan. She didn't mind catering his wedding. She might hate him. She might hope to one day see his and his father's end.

But for now, she would happily take his money to do what she was good at, to do what she loved and to set her on the path to her own wealth. Eventually.

A wealth no one else, especially an Akakios, could take away.

Athan Akakios had arranged everything almost exactly as he wanted it. He would be marrying Regina Giordano, daughter of his father's current business partner, in two days' time. And once he had taken over the Giordano half of the company, he would oust his father.

Once and for all.

It seemed only fitting that Lynna Carew be involved, all in all.

For five years, he had watched for some crack in her armor. He'd waited for her to refuse the job. To approach him, accuse him, tear him into pieces.

He'd deserved it.

And maybe, what he really wanted, was *some* reaction from her to wipe away the memory of her crying at her father's funeral. Hidden in a little room because she'd remained strong for her mother and brother all through the burial.

She had never given him the satisfaction of outwardly hating him, and part of him couldn't help but respect her for it.

Sometimes, he worried that she was a little too much the personal touchstone from which he'd made every choice since. Because the moment of her father's death had changed him, set him on a new course, and her crying in a corner had started that change.

Except it wasn't *her*, he reminded himself. It was simply what she had represented.

A realization that his father was a viper. There was no amount of *business acumen* Athan would ever employ enough to earn his father's respect, no matter whom he betrayed. And if he couldn't get that respect, he did not want to continue down the path to be *like* his father.

Athan Akakios would be his own man. Maybe his past transgressions would never be forgiven—by Lynna or anyone else—but he had set out to be a *good* man in the time since.

Well, once he got his revenge.

After the wedding, he would pull the rug out from under his father. He would do to his father what Constantine Akakios had once done to Aled Carew.

Maybe Lynna wouldn't pretend she didn't care so much then.

Athan had gotten word she'd arrived this morning, but he hadn't seen her. Usually he liked to seek her out, try to get a rise out of her. She never took the bait, but he tried all the same.

Tonight, his father was arriving at the estate to prepare for Saturday night's wedding. Along with Athan's bride, they would all sit down to a dinner where they pretended to laugh and celebrate over one of Lynna's incomparable meals.

But Athan would know it was all a lie. His father wasn't *happy* for him and would be even less so once the papers were signed. Because once they were, Athan would have the shares to handle the company *his* way.

And it would be without Constantine. In any role. Anywhere. Athan would make AC International legitimate. Respectable. No more shady deals to save a dollar. No more questionable alliances. Athan would make everything as it had once been, before he'd been young and naive enough to betray a good man.

A good family.

Thinking about that good family had him going in search of his hired chef. She was in the kitchen, dressed as she almost always was on these jobs. Head-to-toe black, and a colorful apron. Her thick brown hair was always pulled back in some complicated twist with colorful fastenings Athan wouldn't have the first idea the names of.

"Good evening, Lynna. So good to have you back."

She didn't immediately turn. She didn't stiffen. She, in fact, did not react to his presence or his voice in any way. She finished what she was doing—something fussy looking with herbs over some *tiropitakia*.

She made him wait—he liked to think it was on purpose, but she was a focused soul. Once she was satisfied with her work, she motioned for one of the kitchen staff to add them to a platter of hors d'oeuvres.

Then, very slowly and with the blandest of pleasant smiles, she turned to face him. Though he liked to think her blue eyes reflected a malice she tried to hide. "Hello, Mr. Akakios."

He scowled at her, unable to stop himself. He tried to have as little of reaction to her as she did to him.

He never succeeded. "I have asked you not to call me that. Repeatedly."

Her eyes went wide—she always had a flair for the dramatic, though she did such a good job of pretending otherwise. "My apologies. I must have forgotten. I have *many* clients."

He wanted to point out that they'd known each other since she'd been *born*, and he was hardly just another client. But she would just say something else equally infuriating.

Besides, a staff member came in and hailed him.

"Mr. Akakios is here."

Athan nodded. "What about Miss Giordano?"

"I will have someone track her down."

"Very good. Have my father seated at the dining room table. I will be there momentarily." He looked over at Lynna, wondering if the mention of Constantine might be enough to see a crack in her armor.

No such luck.

"This is your first time feeding my father," he said to her, needling the point. "I hope we won't require medical intervention after eating your food."

She didn't so much as blink. It was as if her *blandness* intensified. The all-black outfit that hid any hint of a figure, boring brown hair pulled up and away aided in her attempt.

But her apron was still the color of the Aegean. Her eyes had just the faintest hint of silvery-gray flecks in all that blue. There was *something* deep inside her expression close enough to hate to suit him.

"I would never risk Your Girl Friday in such a way," she said. Pleasantly. Then she hefted the platter beautifully appointed with a wide variety of offerings, despite the fact only three of them would be dining tonight.

Unsatisfied, and knowing sparring with her would never bring any satisfaction because she refused to fight back, Athan grunted and moved his way from kitchen to dining room. Lynna followed, carrying her fancy and no doubt delicious platter of hors d'oeuvres.

But when they entered the dining room, there was only one person.

Athan regarded his father. The great, feared and ruthless Constantine Akakios. Sometimes Athan wished he knew how to be more like his father. To have absolutely no regard for anyone or anything besides his own success.

But mostly, he understood. His father was as close to evil as one got without full-on murdering people—not that Athan would put it past the man given the right circumstances.

Constantine stood by the exit, still wearing a jacket, like he wasn't planning on staying.

"Did Christos forget to take your coat, Father?"

"I'm afraid not. I can't stay as planned, Athan. Well, that isn't true. I could, but I doubt that's going to be on the table."

An old foreboding feeling, one that spoke of a lack of agency and control over his own life, wriggled to life deep in the pit of his stomach. As a grown man, he'd done everything short of leaving his father's company to solve that feeling. To grasp his own life by his own hands. All so he could change the fate of AC International.

But his father had flipped some kind of script, and Athan knew the only answer in the moment was to brace himself.

"Regina won't be attending your little dinner either. To start."

Athan stood, a head taller than his stylish father these days, and still it was like he was already shrinking.

"What do you know of Regina's plans?"

"I've put her on a private jet back to Athens. You see, it turns out, she's decided to marry me instead." Constantine said it with a kind of offhanded, charming smile, as if this new information was *accidental. Unavoidable.*

Athan stared at his father for far too long, trying to understand how those words in that order made any kind of sense.

Marry…

"I am sorry, son," Constantine said, and that was his great skill. To sound genuinely sorry, when Athan knew he wasn't at all. He'd never been actually sorry a day in his life. He reveled in other people's suffering—especially if he was the one to cause it.

"It's a shame to have to do this. But you didn't really think you'd pull one over on me, did you?" Constantine shook his head, as if saddened when it was clear he was actually enjoying himself. "You were never quite smart enough for subterfuge. Regina will be mine, and so will the Giordano shares. And it will be *you* out of AC International."

Athan's hand curled into a fist, but he knew better than to advance on his father. Constantine reveled in playing the victim, particularly physically. He'd had more men than Athan could count thrown in jail for the weakest of punches.

"You can't kick me out of AC." Athan had spent the past few years making certain his position was protected.

"It'll be interesting to see if that holds true once I control the Giordano shares." His gaze darted to Lynna. And he smiled in a way that had Athan wanting to move between the two.

"If you've forgotten how the shares and control work,

I'm sure you can ask the Carew girl how me controlling the majority of shares turns out for my second-in-command."

Athan was sure he had a million strong comebacks when it came to his father, but in this moment, he'd been rendered utterly speechless. He'd thought he'd won already.

He should have known better.

"*Adío*, Athan. And sorry about the wedding costs. Perhaps you can get partial refunds if you beg enough." Then Constantine exited with his usual dramatic flair.

And Athan was left standing in his dining room, all his plans thwarted, and his father winning.

Yet again.

CHAPTER TWO

LYNNA HATED FEELING *any* sympathy for Athan. After all, why should she? He was just getting a taste of his own medicine. If anyone else had done this to him, she would be popping marinated olives and laughing herself all the way home.

But it was Constantine Akakios who had delivered this blow, and she couldn't celebrate *that*. She wished Constantine would get his comeuppance too. But she'd spent the past five years trying to make peace with the lack of fairness in the world. You couldn't change the whims and arrows of ruthless, careless men. You could only learn how to build your own life, protect the people in it at all costs, and roll with all the consequences of other people's actions.

She let out a slow breath. She'd been prepared to see Constantine, and still there'd been a visceral initial response of wanting to hurl the tray of food at him. Among other things.

The impulse was still there, so she moved forward and carefully set the tray down on the dining room table. She turned to Athan, who looked shell-shocked. That little wriggle of compassion was trying to gain a foothold, but she *refused*.

He deserved to be shell-shocked. No matter the instigator, he *deserved* to be destroyed. His karmic reward.

"A dinner for one, then?" she asked, innocently enough.

Athan straightened, as if her voice was the antidote to a spell. The shock slowly morphed into something sharper on his face. He was plotting, and that should be just alarming enough for Lynna to beat a hasty retreat.

But she found herself pinned to the spot when he aimed his dark gaze at her.

Because the problem was… He *was* handsome. Outrageously so, really. It was the sharp angles, the aristocratic nose, the dark eyes that were no doubt reflective of the depths of hell he'd crawled out of.

No doubt the devil was this attractive as well, when he wanted to be.

Get out! Her brain seemed to shout at her. But her feet were resolutely rooted to the spot, her heartbeat kicking up as Athan's expression went from one of shock, to a slow, sly smile.

"I know exactly what we'll do," he said, his voice dark. *Like the devil himself,* she told herself. Resolutely. And it was *worry* that had her heartbeat picking up, not anything else.

Particularly when it sounded like he was bringing her into the *we*. That was ridiculous. Surely he meant some royal *we* that had nothing to do with her and she needed to *leave*. Now.

But his attention seemed solely on her. A kind of demonic tractor beam she was incapable of escaping.

"It seems you'll have to marry me instead."

The peal of laughter was bright and unexpected. She actually threw back her head and laughed and laughed. Enough that he was more irritated by the dramatics than distracted by the slim column of her throat or the shocking punch of seeing true amusement on her face.

"It isn't a joke," he said. Maybe later he could find the

humor in it, but right now he only had rage. But it wasn't molten, out of control. No, he'd learned how to control it.

Careful, sharp, deadly ice.

His father would not—could not—win.

"Then you've had a break with reality," Lynna said. "And my answer is a hearty *no*."

"I didn't *ask*, Lynna."

Any humor melted off her face. Temper snapped into her eyes. Color mounted in her cheeks. "Oh, were you under the impression I am one of your minions because you paid for my culinary expertise? Bad news for you." She stepped toward him, finger raised in an aggressive point. "No. You cannot order me about. Particularly to *marry* you. Are you insane?"

He supposed it sounded a bit insane. To *her*. But she didn't understand. He needed the shares. If he couldn't get them out from under his father, if he couldn't get them with an in with Giordano, then he would need to rely on the one name that was like a specter in the halls of AC International.

Carew.

"People in the company still respect your father, his name. They know it was my father's shady dealings that hurt his reputation. People at AC respect me for my efforts to fix it."

"Surely not the same people."

But he ignored her barb. The idea was forming, taking shape in the moment. The way the best ones did. Evolving into something even better than the original.

It would be better. He would still destroy his father by pulling together disparate parts, instead of one big share. His father couldn't stop an insidious campaign if Athan had an actual Carew on his side.

And he would have AC International come hell or high water. Giordano shares or no. He hadn't given up at the first few roadblocks his father had put up, why would he give up now?

Here she stood, the answer to his problems. He needed Lynna. The nostalgia of the Carew name was his last chance at undercutting the fear and intimidation his father led with.

Two *years* of working toward marrying Regina up in smoke. It grated, but he wouldn't take another two years. He wouldn't waste the planned wedding on Saturday.

No, Lynna would marry him, and he would begin his coup that way.

Of course she didn't *want* to marry him. He knew her, though. Her family. Her situation. Perhaps he did not have as much positive interaction with her as an adult, but that did not change the fact he knew what was important to her.

Her family. Stability. And even if she wanted revenge against him, surely his father ranked at least a little bit higher.

He could use it. Not *against* her. It wasn't so sordid as that. He could use it to bargain a *deal*. A mutually beneficial deal. Where they both got something out of it.

Because he was not his father.

"You will take Regina's place and marry me on Saturday. Prior to the I dos, we'll draw up an agreement. You give me…" He considered the amount of time it would take. "Three years, and I will afford you a lump sum to pay for any and all of Rhys's education. A position for him in my company once he's done at university, with contractual guarantee he can't be outed for a specific period of time. A house for your mother wherever she'd like." Her brother's education and a job, stability for her mother. She'd want nothing more.

But she remained stubborn. "And what would *I* get out of the deal?"

"Satisfaction."

She laughed again. "Have you had a head injury lately? Helping you would not be satisfying in the least."

"You hate my father."

"I hate you both. I'd hardly help one to hurt the other when I'd rather see you both fail."

He'd wanted her to outright say that for five years, and now the moment was here, and he felt no satisfaction. Because he needed her to avenge this. There was no other way. Not right now. Perhaps he could build another plan in a year or so, but by then his father would find a way to oust him.

He could build his own company. He could do a lot of things, but he wanted his father to suffer as much as he wanted to win.

So he needed to act fast. "Everything you do is for Rhys. And your mother."

Her chin went up. Her shoulders back, but when she spoke it was with that same calm detachment that always made him want to roar, like a lion in a cage.

"Yes. And remarkably, I have handled everything for them. I don't need your help." She turned on a heel. No doubt not just to leave the dining room, but to leave his villa and Mykonos altogether.

But he knew *everything* about her. Had kept ruthless and detailed tabs. Not that he'd ever let on, even going so far as to pretend he'd just *happened* to hear about Your Girl Friday from some friends.

But that wasn't true. Ever since her father's funeral, he'd known her every move. He'd never been able to articulate to himself exactly why, but it didn't matter. Now the information would come in useful.

"The interest on that loan is rather high," he called after her.

She stopped on a dime. Then she whirled around to face

him. That anger and temper he'd wanted from her for *five* years right there in her expression.

She really was beautiful. She kept it understated, perhaps she even hid it the same way she always hid her real reaction to him.

But it was there. With her eyes flashing and color in her cheeks. Her shoulders back and her fists curled like she might physically fight him. A roar of something like triumph rumbled through him.

He could almost forget about his own anger, his own fury, his own revenge.

Almost.

"Think of it, Lynna. The next three years could be easy. You wouldn't have to work yourself to the bone."

"I like my work."

"All right, work away. But you could work how *you* wanted. No missing Christmases, or Rhys's sporting events. You could take the jobs that suited *you* and leave the rest. You could pay that loan off in full. Immediately. You could spend time with your mother. All you have to do is—"

"Marry the devil?" she tossed at him.

"Come now, *paidi mou*. I think we can both agree my father is the devil. I am perhaps a lower-level demon. This could be my redemption right here."

"Redemption my…" At his raised eyebrows, she trailed off. "I would never in a million years marry you or any Akakios." And she turned on a heel as if that was it.

It was not it, could *not* be it. He followed her into the kitchen, recalculating. His staff had already cleaned up much of the dinner preparation mess, but there were unserved dishes sitting there. Lynna went for them, began to pack them away.

Still working. Sometimes, she made no sense to him.

But that was the thing about business. People didn't have to make sense if you knew their weak spots.

"Two years of wedded bliss, then you may divorce me. Another significant payoff there. Schooling for Rhys. A guaranteed job for him, *and* I will mentor him. A house for your mother—hell, make it two."

"This is ridiculous."

"Money is no object, Lynna. I need you. I need your name." Which gave him the idea that might actually win her over. "And once I have ousted my father from AC completely, I will deliver a public apology. To your father and your family. Splashed across every news outlet in the world, clearing his name once and for all."

CHAPTER THREE

LYNNA FROZE. She wouldn't deny that the money was tempting. It solved a lot of problems, but she was a problem solver. She hadn't needed anyone's help before this moment, why would she need it now? With enough hard work and determination, she could give Rhys and her mother everything they deserved.

Or at least close.

Maybe she *wanted* that to be true more than it was. Regardless, there was one thing Athan was offering that no amount of her hard work would ever accomplish.

No matter what she did, she would never be able to clear her father's name from the accusations Constantine and Athan had leveled against him. Crushing his spirit, ruining his reputation, filling a once loving and generous man with bitterness…and putting a black spot on Rhys's future.

A public apology. "You would only do that to make your father look bad."

"Does it matter why I would do it if I would do it?"

She didn't dare look at him. Because the question was simple and her answer was not. Did it matter? To her it did, she wanted *nothing* that helped either man, but she did not think her mother would have such qualms if it cleared her father's name. Her mother would make that deal with the devil. And Rhys would be free of that stark black stain.

Of course, her mother would possibly have her own aneurysm at Lynna marrying an Akakios.

She was not considering this. It was lunacy. *Lunacy.*

A public apology. A guaranteed job and mentorship for Rhys.

How could she deny him that chance?

How could she feed him to the lion's den that had essentially killed their father?

"Sleep on it." Athan said this with that thread of silk and coercion in his tone that had no doubt fooled her father, that had once fooled her into thinking he was a *friend.* Why would she listen to him? She knew what he was.

"We will breakfast together. Feel free to put together a counteroffer."

She looked at him then, focused on being calm, cool, and completely unaffected by him and his outrageous offer. Because, no. This just wasn't a realistic offer or choice or *anything.*

He was just…shell-shocked. By his father stealing his fiancée out from under his nose. A man like Athan didn't do shocked and upended like other people did. He went into scheme mode.

But this scheme was just…not possible.

"My counteroffer is no." And since he didn't have the good sense to nod or accept or look the least bit like he understood, she didn't have the good sense to shut up and leave. "It also involves you taking a long walk on a short pier."

His mouth curved, and something deep inside of her seemed to curve in response. She was quite certain it was a feeling associated with hate since no one else she'd ever encountered had caused that strange tightening sensation so deep within her.

"Think on it, Lynna. If your answer is still no in the

morning, I will respect that. I will pay you for the full three weeks, and you may return home or enjoy a vacation in Mykonos at my expense."

She narrowed her eyes. It was a trick. She knew a trick when she saw one. But didn't that mean she could be immune to the trick part of it? "At your expense?"

"You only have to spend the night and give me your answer or counter in the morning." He shrugged, as if it was oh so simple. "You were going to be staying here for the week anyway. What's one night?"

She knew better. She *did*. And still…all the things he was offering kept shuffling through her mind. She couldn't make a deal with the devil, or even a lower-level demon. No one came out of those unscathed.

But did she need to be unscathed? She was resilient. If it got Rhys and Mom what they needed… Could she withstand a little damage?

Maybe it wasn't ridiculous to sleep on it. To go to her room, where she'd been planning to stay the next week anyway, as he'd pointed out, and write out a pros and cons list. Really sort out the smartest choice, taking all of her mixed-up feelings out of it.

Because while she was an excellent decision-maker, and coolheaded in most things, she knew Athan brought out more emotions in her than she liked. Time and space was *sensible*, and how she made every major life decision.

Carefully. Mathematically. Emotions, feelings—both positive and negative—led to catastrophic decisions. She had watched her parents lose everything because they'd trusted kindness and love. She'd watched her father dig himself deeper into suffering by being so obsessed with bitterness and betrayal that only alcohol had quieted his mind in his last months.

The only reasonable option was to take all that *feeling* out of it. No revenge. No knee-jerk refusal. And certainly no reckless acceptance. She inhaled deeply. "All right. You'll have my answer in the morning."

And it would be no, because of course that was the *only* answer, but she would be certain of her no and would have absolutely no regrets or second thoughts, because by tomorrow morning she would have looked at it from every angle.

And come to the correct conclusion.

Athan didn't bother to retire. He wouldn't sleep. Not tonight. So he went to his study—not the kind of dark, medieval type of study his father preferred, but a bright room full of natural light and colorful art. Comfortable chairs instead of old stuffy ones.

He poured himself a drink and considered his options. He needed a backup plan. He would find a way to make Lynna say yes, but he had to be flexible enough to understand it might not look exactly as he liked.

This, he had determined, was his father's greatest flaw. Sure, being an inflexible, demanding monster could build you an empire, it could get you far enough, but it would also eventually be the source of your downfall.

So, Athan was determined to handle this with all the flexibility it required. He could keep twisting the deal until Lynna took it. As long as it made AC International his, it was worth any price.

When his phone rang, he looked at the screen readout and frowned. He could ignore it. It would make the most sense.

But he'd never been a man to back away from a challenge. He answered it. "Well, good evening, my darling. Have you landed in Athens? Cleaned the knife of my blood? Or did you leave it in my back to twist it?"

"I am sorry, Athan," Regina said quietly. He wouldn't say she sounded *contrite*, but there was a certain solemnness to her tone.

He studied the amber liquid in his glass. Considered hurling it at the wall. But he kept the bitterness out of his voice and settled for dry and underwhelmed. "Well, an apology changes everything."

"His offer was better. Surely you of all people can appreciate that."

"You didn't give me the chance to counteroffer." He thought of Lynna. Would she? Was there any way his offer had gotten through that thick skull of hers?

Regina laughed. "Part of his offer was not allowing you the chance to counter. It was *very* lucrative, and I'm sure I'll be very happy. So would you be if you just accepted your father has a better grasp on things."

Athan took a deep drink from his glass. Had his father spearheaded this phone call? Because not that long ago, Regina had believed in *his* bid to take over. Which, he supposed, meant she didn't care about the business side of things at all. She was just looking for the best deal.

He didn't *blame* her, exactly, but that didn't mean he was happy about it. "He's twice your age, Regina."

"He's a handsome, powerful interesting man. My father loves him. It's hardly a downgrade."

"Your father is terrified of him."

"Well, *I'm* not."

"You should be." And Athan could not think of a simple way this conversation came to a productive conclusion, so he hung up on her.

Because she should be terrified. No woman came away from his father's clutches unscathed. No matter how smart or strong, silly or weak, beautiful or plain.

Constantine Akakios was a user. An expert user, but a user all the same. Anyone who didn't escape was bled dry—one way or another.

Athan pushed to his feet and stalked over to the balcony, its bright white gleaming in the golden light of a fading day. Beyond his extensive villa was the impossibly blue bay, the rocky shoreline and hilly fingers of land that seemed to reach out for the sea.

He looked out over the crashing waves. Darkness encroaching, but light holding out there on the horizon. For a little while longer yet.

Lynna would agree to marry him. And then he had two years to make certain that his father paid.

For everything.

CHAPTER FOUR

LYNNA AWOKE IN the prettily appointed room, gritty eyed and *exhausted*. She had slept for maybe an hour. Most of her night had been spent making lists, thinking through every scenario she had the imagination to come up with.

No matter how she'd tried to sway the outcome, the answer remained the same.

If she took this deal, her brother and mother would have everything they desired. And all she had to do was marry a demon for two years.

No. He expected a counteroffer, and she'd give him one. One year. Six months. A day. More stipulations. She would make sure the deal outrageously favored her and her family so that Athan would *never* go for it.

And if he agrees?

She blew out a breath. She would not go to the lion's den unsure. She had to be certain that this was something she was really going to agree to if she got everything she wanted. *And* certain of her sticking points. What she would not compromise on, even if it meant walking away from all that money and opportunity for Rhys.

She was in the position of power. If she went into that room with that kind of confidence, knowing what she wouldn't compromise on, this would all be fine.

She was in charge.

She got ready for the day, dressing as she would for any personal chef job. She assumed when he said breakfast that she would be in charge of making it, and perhaps she'd even counted on that as something to steady her before she faced Athan down.

But when she arrived in the kitchen, his staff had clearly already taken care of everything. There were platters of food being carried out of the kitchen.

"Mr. Akakios is waiting for you on the terrace, Ms. Carew."

Lynna didn't scowl. It wasn't the fault of anyone in this kitchen that she'd been ousted from the one thing she'd *wanted* to do this morning.

Besides, there was no way Athan would go for her counteroffer and then she could be on her way home. She could plan out her next job.

So, she walked through the kitchen and a hallway toward the terrace. Five years of coming here meant she knew where she was going. She'd served Athan out there on the terrace enough times.

Last time, in fact, a very scantily clad Regina Giordano had been his companion. Lynna had nothing against Regina—except her taste in men, obviously—but she could admit that seeing the perfect bronzed goddess wandering about in a very small bikini had given her some unpleasant thoughts about her own pale, soft body and reminded her why she'd never be caught dead in a bikini.

But Regina wasn't here, and Lynna didn't need to worry about swimwear because she'd be on her way home to rainy London by tonight.

She stepped outside onto the terrace and squinted against the bright morning sun. All that white and blue Mykonos was famous for. Her parents had been born and raised in

Wales, but Lynna had been raised in the warmth and sun of Greece. She had visited Wales enough growing up, and lived in London for the past few years, to know she was glad for it.

In the midst of the terrace was a table. Athan lounged in one of the chairs, sipping coffee. His shirt wasn't quite buttoned all the way, and she wanted to tell him he looked ridiculous, like some sleazy playboy.

But of course he only looked relaxed and gorgeous and every inch the powerful and magnetic billionaire he was.

But *she* was in charge. She lifted her chin. "I assumed I would be making breakfast for the amount you're paying me," she offered as she stepped out into the sun.

He stood and turned to her. "You assumed wrong." He pulled a chair out for her. Gestured for her to take a seat.

She inhaled, quietly but deeply, trying to let the smell of the beautiful flowers mixed with sea calm her.

She knew what she wanted out of this, and if he would not give it, she did not have to take his deal. There was no reason to be nervous.

He poured her coffee. Gave it a dash of cream. She did not trust the fact he knew how she liked her coffee. No doubt it was some insidious Akakios trick.

She would fall for *no tricks*.

"It's a beautiful day, is it not? Then again, it is always beautiful here. I don't know why anyone lives anywhere else."

"We're not all billionaires, I suppose."

He chuckled at that, but she hadn't been making a joke. And she did not want to make *small talk* about beautiful days.

So she laid out her counteroffer. "Six months. A percentage of shares from Akakios not just in Rhys's name, but my mother's and mine as well—announced to the public when you give your apology to my father."

For a moment, he only looked at her. His posture betrayed nothing. He didn't move. But she saw the *flare* of something, there in his eyes. Triumph.

Run, some sensible voice in her head whispered. But she simply sat.

"One year," he replied. "I've done the math, run the numbers, we will need a full year to ensure my father is ousted and stays that way."

Well, if it was *mathematical*.

She didn't *have* to compromise, but she could if it was logical. Factual. No emotion involved. Just getting what she wanted.

"I must be able to tell my family the truth. And my friends. It cannot be a secret why I'm doing this to the people I love. Even if I could get them to believe it, my mother would be devastated, and my friends would be…" She managed a smile—sharp as she could. "Vengeful."

She thought that would be the sticking point. Maybe she hoped it would be.

"I can agree to that, if we work in an addendum that if any one of these people knowing the truth gets to people who use it against me, the deal will be called off with absolutely no compensation for anyone in your family. I'd choose your trustworthy companions wisely."

No. She wasn't going to do this. She *wasn't*.

She leaned forward. "Rhys is a genius. He's capable and *good* and would be an amazing asset to any company once he graduates."

Athan leaned forward as well, so they were practically nose to nose with only the table between them. Lynna's heart thundered in her ears, that prickling heat she refused to name spreading its serpentine way through her bloodstream.

"Then we'll be glad to have him at Akakios," Athan said, his voice low and smug. "Because once my father is ousted, we will need an infusion of *good* to fill the vacuum of all his evil."

"You're evil too," Lynna said. Or maybe not so much *said* as whispered, because it was hard to breathe normally this close to those dark eyes, that egotistical smirk. Hate was the thing worming around in her gut. *Hate, hate, hate.*

"I have been," he agreed. So damn easily. So there was nothing to fight against. She knew he did that on purpose. He did every annoying thing on purpose.

"And if you hire Rhys, mentor him, as you said. Then someday he rips AC International out from under you, what will you do?"

"I suppose that would be its own poetic justice. Wouldn't it?"

Panic was beginning to flutter at her breastbone. Why was he agreeing? Why wasn't he refusing? Why was this happening?

"And…what? We'd get married tomorrow night, and then just…live here while you use my name to convince people in your father's company to go against him?"

"We can live here if you like. There's also my place in Athens. Provence. New York. I have a charming little place amongst the fjords in Norway."

"Norway?"

"I like variety." He grinned. "But I spend most of my time in Athens. There will be a period of time I will need you with me, to wine and dine your father's sympathizers to my plight. But otherwise, we need not be together, and you may do as you please as long as you wear my ring and do not engage in any affairs that might look poorly on our union."

Something about the way he'd said I like variety had this commentary hitting her all wrong. "And you?"

"And me what?"

"Will you be engaging in any affairs that look poorly on our union?" she said, mimicking him a little bit with his own words.

"Businessmen do not quite have the dim view of such things as…"

"The victims in their little games?"

Athan sighed, as if she was very tiresome or boring.

She wanted to stab him. "I will not be the butt of a joke, even for a payment."

"Very well. I will remain devoted to you and you only, *latria mu*." He reached across the table and took her hand— but only for a second before she jerked it away.

"Would you like to invite anyone to the wedding?" he asked innocently.

She hadn't agreed.

But you're going to, aren't you?

She didn't want to, but she didn't know how to say no to something that would potentially set Rhys up for life. It would make Mom's life easier, her own as well. She wouldn't constantly feel the need to take every single job. Maybe, just maybe, she could ease the pressure that sat on her chest every single day whispering to her that she was failing everyone while desperately treading water.

Sinking a little deeper every year. Keeping the over-whelming loan for Rhys's education from her friends so they didn't worry. From Rhys. He was so sure he was grown, so sure he could take care of himself.

But he had no idea. At *nineteen*, he had absolutely no idea.

All she had to do to make sure he never found out was pretend a little bit for one year. Was that really all that different than working her ass off for years? It would still be work. She'd just be working for the devil.

Temporarily.

Temporarily.

A person could withstand anything—evil, pain, et cetera—temporarily.

"I will not be inviting anyone. This will be the most embarrassing and lowering moment of my life. I wish to have no witnesses."

He laughed at that, deep and resonant. As if anything about this was anything to laugh at, to enjoy.

"I will need to see all the papers first," she told him tersely. "Everything spelled out, just as you've said. I want my loan paid off before I say I do, as leverage."

He didn't balk. "I live to serve."

"You live to ruin."

"You're going to have to work on your pillow talk."

It was more than enough. She hadn't eaten anything, but still she pushed back from the table and stood. "I have to go somehow break the news to my mother. I want the papers. By tonight. I won't say 'I do' until they satisfy. Until the loan is paid off."

"Aye, aye, captain."

She didn't trust his easy agreement at *all*, but she didn't know what else to do about it. She'd have Your Girl Friday's lawyer look over the contract, no doubt find whatever underhanded thing he was trying to accomplish, and then she could laugh in his face.

Hopefully after he paid off her loan.

She turned to walk away. To not be in his orbit so she didn't have to think too deeply on what she'd just agreed to.

"Oh, there's one little thing we did not discuss," he called after her, his voice lazy.

"What?"

"Consummating the marriage."

She whirled around to face him. Was he *mad*? But he was smiling at her, in that very…male predator type of way. Like he'd even want to… Well, *she* didn't and never would. So. "Never."

"Don't issue a challenge, Lynna," he said, still so lazy and unbothered. "I *love* a challenge."

For a moment she felt simply caught in the laser focus of his dark gaze. Then she remembered herself and whirled away again. "You'll love being a corpse then," she offered as her parting shot.

And then she hurried back to her room so she could call her mother, call her friends and have everyone talk her out of this insanity.

Athan straightened the tie of his tux in the full-length mirror. Everything had worked out. After longer than he'd liked, and a few more negotiations than he had planned on, Lynna had signed the papers. He had paid off her loan.

Now they were getting married.

He couldn't categorize the strange feelings that seemed to stir up. There was satisfaction, of course. His father hadn't bested him yet. Money was no object, so it wasn't as though helping Lynna and her family had any effect on his bottom line.

But he had the strangest sensation of *nerves* accosting him. No, not nerves, because he refused to accept he was nervous. It was anticipation. For the next step in his plan. It was an uneasiness born of the fact Lynna was not exactly…predictable.

He wouldn't be surprised if she simply did not show up. If she'd taken the money and run. But it seemed cowardly.

Lynna was no coward.

He appreciated that about her. She might hate him and think him the very devil, but he held a certain amount of respect for the way she'd dealt with her life since her father had passed. A certain amount of fascination with how she'd found a way to thrive.

He would even hold her up as a kind of example. He would thrive in this place where he'd been put at a disadvantage.

He was told it was time to begin the ceremony, so he made his way down to his private portion of the beach. A platform had been set up with an elaborate arbor at the end, filled with vines and colorful tropical blooms. The officiant waited there, and they would be married under the arch.

So long as Lynna did not back out.

Athan went over to the officiant and thanked him for coming. Made some small talk while staff moved around setting everything to rights. The sun had begun to set, a beautiful sunset with riotous colors painting the sky. A truly beautiful setting.

Most of the plans were Regina's—the flowers, the colors, the beach setting. He didn't think Lynna would mind since this was her version of hell.

Since she had not invited anyone, and obviously his father and Regina's family were no longer coming, there were no guests. Only the officiant and the staff—his own and those he'd hired to handle the event.

"Ah, there's the bride," the officiant offered, nodding toward the end of the platform.

Lynna walked out by herself, though a staff member in

all black helped her up onto the platform she would have to walk down to meet him at the end with the officiant.

He hadn't seen her in anything other than careful black with colorful chef accents since they were young. Perhaps her eighteenth birthday party that he'd been roped into going to. They'd shared a dance. She'd been pretty and charming. A completely different person.

Now she wore white. An elegant white gown he had tasked one of his assistants with procuring since he knew Lynna would likely try to marry him in black if he let her. It nipped in at the waist, highlighting what she usually hid— an hourglass figure with curves interesting enough to be distracting. She was on the taller side, but still she wore heels. Her hair was in careful waves around her shoulders, though some strands were pinned up with sparkling gems and some fell around her face.

She looked like an angel in a painting. Soft and ethereal. Regal and majestic. He could watch her walk down this aisle forever. Even with that scowl on her face. Or maybe the scowl was part of it.

When she made it to the end of the aisle, she regarded him with a cool distance. "I take it this wasn't Regina's dress."

"I'm a billionaire, darling, I don't need to have my fiancées share wedding dresses."

"Well, that's good since one leg of mine probably wouldn't fit in a dress that fit Regina."

It sounded suspiciously like jealousy, which was very, very interesting. "You look beautiful, *paidi mou*."

She lifted her chin, fixed her gaze on the officiant. She didn't look at Athan at all. "I'm aware," she muttered, making him smile. "And you should be aware I only agreed to this costume for the pictures you insisted we needed."

"Lucky me," Athan murmured.

He thought she might stab him if she had a pointy implement. But all she had was a bouquet of flowers and a deal to uphold.

Athan nodded at the officiant, a sign for him to begin. And so he did, speaking words of love and fidelity, promises and forever. If it made him a little *itchy*, he supposed it was only because he didn't fully believe in such things.

People were such terribly complicated creatures. Full of malice and spite and hate. Unforgivable mistakes that haunted for a lifetime. And while he'd tried to make his adult life less of all those things rather than more, it didn't mean he expected to be forgiven for what had come before. It didn't mean he trusted anyone to engage in love and fidelity *forever*.

Certainly not the woman saying "I do" who hated him and was only doing this to pay some debts that weren't even really hers to pay.

Who scowled at him, even as he slid a hefty diamond onto her finger.

"You may kiss the bride," the officiant announced happily.

The scowl turned into something a little more like concern. She took a step away from Athan.

"I don't think—"

"Come, *latria mu*. I know how private you are, but we must have a picture of our first married kiss. For the scrapbooks."

If looks could kill, she would have made an excellent hit man. So, before she could mount another argument, he kissed her. Just swooped in, curved his hand around the back of her head and pulled her in.

For the *picture*.

But he was also no fan of denial. He preferred dealing

with a problem head-on. He preferred *action*, and he'd been wanting to know what she tasted like for far too long.

Sweet. Like the sugary confections she was so good at making. As soft in his arms as she looked. A surprising cocoon of warmth, right here as his mouth learned hers.

Because she didn't push him away, didn't even stiffen. He either took her enough by surprise or she understood the importance of the picture to allow him to kiss her.

He wouldn't say she *participated*, exactly. At first. But when his tongue traced the seam of her lips, they parted. When he drew her just that much closer, she went and even *leaned* into him, her hands coming up to his chest.

For a moment he thought she'd push, but she didn't. She just rested them there.

So he went deeper. His fingers threading through her hair, adjusting the angle to really test the contours of her mouth. To glut himself on the confection that she was, here in his arms, kissing him back.

It was a little too potent for public consumption, and he had *just* enough self-preservation instinct to realize that. To carefully pull himself back. To settle himself before he dared look at her.

When he did, she blinked her eyes open. There was a moment of softness there. Her cheeks were pink, nearly red.

Then her expression morphed into *horrified*.

But not unmoved. Her chest rose and fell, and she stared at him in a kind of open-mouthed daze.

"Did you get the photo?" he asked the photographer, not taking his gaze off her. Not dropping his hand from where his fingers were in her hair. His body veritably *buzzed*, every muscle as hard as steel. He might have had a hard time catching his own breath if he didn't have this to focus on.

"Yes, sir."

"Make sure it looks like it's been leaked to the press against our will by midnight."

"Yes, sir."

Some of that *horror* and *not unmoved* started to shift in Lynna's expression to *fury*, so he wisely dropped his hand and turned so they could walk back up to the terrace. He held out an elbow for her to take.

He could all but feel the rage pumping off of her, but she was his wife now. She didn't have to pretend to love him very often, but she was stuck with him anyway.

It was quite the interesting arrangement. After another few moments where she stared at his outstretched elbow, then around the beach, she shook her head and began to walk ahead. She did not take his elbow.

"There's been a delicious dinner prepared," he said, following her in his own leisurely stroll, ignoring the desperate need for *action* raging around inside of him. Though she marched ahead, he kept up easily enough. "The cake, I'm sure, won't stand up to what you would have made, but it will be good all the same."

"I'm not in the least bit hungry," she returned, every word bit off in anger. "I'm going to go to my room." She stepped inside, him behind her. "I'm going to take this ridiculous getup off." She marched over to the stairs. "And I am going to sleep hoping when I wake, the nightmare is over."

He followed her up the stairs, and down the hall. Watching in fascination as she began to rip the little bejeweled hairpins from her hair, releasing curl after curl of hair. A strangely violent movement, followed by a graceful gentle one.

He had a feeling even without anger, this was the heart of her. Strong, careful precision and an effortless elegance she didn't even realize she had, she *was*. He found himself desperate to touch it once more.

She opened the door to her bedroom, but turned to glare at him when he acted as if he might follow.

He held up his hands in mock surrender. "You probably need help getting out of your dress."

"I'd chew out of it with my own teeth before I let you help me." Then she slammed the door in his face.

It didn't bother him. In fact, he found himself smiling. Practically humming on his way down the hall to his bedroom.

He had one year to take down his father.

And one year to seduce his alluring and surprising wife.

Plenty of time for both.

CHAPTER FIVE

Lynna dreamed of that kiss and thus woke in a foul, *foul* mood. She wanted to be furious that he had kissed her without her consent.

But she hadn't pushed him away, and she could have. She hadn't used a strategic knee to make him crumble, and she *could* have. She was well-versed in all the variety of ways to rebuff a man's unwanted advances.

She had let him kiss her because…

Well.

She'd never been kissed. Which she'd never once allowed herself to feel pathetic about. She was introverted, self-assured and had never been able to put up with the foolishness of *boys*, even when life had been easy and happy.

As she'd gotten older, and the world of *men* had offered more possibilities, she'd been too busy. Nose to the grindstone, pulling herself and her family out of grief and financial distress, which left her with absolutely no patience for other people's nonsense.

She had come to the conclusion a few years ago that she would likely always be a virgin, and she'd accepted that. Been happy with it.

"I am still happy with it," she said. Out loud. To assure herself.

So the kiss had…messed up things inside of her. That

was just a physical, physiological reaction. Like yeast in baking. There were reactions that happened in a body just as they did in a bread dough. It was *science*.

She didn't have to want to act on them for the chemical reactions to exist. To find herself surprised and curious *in the moment*.

She most certainly would not let Athan have his mouth anywhere near her ever again. She didn't even understand why he was pretending that he might…see her *that* way.

"Because he's the devil," she told the empty room resolutely, scowling at the crumpled up wedding gown on the floor.

It had made her feel beautiful, and Athan had even said that with a kind of reverence that had made her heart feel… *light* instead of the heavy weight it had been for years.

She hated it.

She pushed out of bed and padded over to her suitcase. She had only brought clothes meant for being a chef. Particularly an event chef. Everything was black, easy to move in and easy to clean.

Drab.

"Well, we have no reason to be anything other than drab, do we?" She pulled out the first pair of top and pants her hands landed on and changed into them. She pulled her piles of hair back into a tight braid.

What she looked like was immaterial. Maybe she was playing the role of wife not chef, but there was nothing in her contract about looking a certain way.

So dressing like the staff felt like rebellion, and that powered her out of her room and downstairs into the kitchen. There were some staff already there, brewing coffee and making noises about breakfast, but she politely and efficiently kicked them all out.

She was going to make breakfast. Part of her was tempted to only make it for herself, let Athan fend for himself, but that was silly if she'd gotten rid of the other kitchen staff.

Besides, if Athan got used to her cooking, he would miss it all the more when they weren't together.

She frowned at herself as she pulled a bowl of eggs from the refrigerator. Not that she wanted him to miss *her*. She just wanted him to be in pain.

She had a *ladenia* in the oven, a fruit salad prepared and was halfway through the cooking the *strapatsatha* when Athan wandered into the kitchen.

Last night he'd worn a tux. He'd looked every inch the wealthy sophisticate he'd been bred to be, and though that wasn't to *her* taste, Lynna did not for the life of her understand his former fiancée's decision to trade in one Akakios for the other.

If you were going to wed the devil, Athan was perhaps the handsomest devil there was. In a tux. In casual clothing. She had once seen him in nothing but his swim trunks and that had *certainly* been an education in the male form.

She did not allow the memory to form in her mind.

"What exactly do you think you're doing?" Athan asked. Not quite with disdain or censure. Somehow he made his tone *curious*, when she knew he was not because it was obvious what she was doing. And he, no doubt, did not want her doing it.

Too bad. "I am going to make the food while I'm here. We had a contract."

"I think the one we signed yesterday overruns the original."

"I *enjoy* cooking, and so I will do it."

"All right. Do I get to make requests?"

"No."

He sighed. "I didn't think so." He watched her as she sliced some bread and put it in the toaster before taking the eggs off the heat.

"Perhaps you can teach me."

"Teach you what?" she asked, paying special attention to how and where she crumbled feta on top of the *strapatsatha*.

"To cook."

"Why?"

"Why not?"

Because I don't want to be anywhere near you. "What possible reason could you have for learning how to cook?"

"So I can make the things I enjoy that you'll refuse to make me simply because I enjoy them."

"Then watch a video."

"Come, Lynna. We needn't be *quite* so antagonistic. We're partners. For the next year."

When he said things like year, and partners, regret seeped into her like poison. Why had she done this to herself? "Partners like our fathers were partners? Should I wear armor to guard myself from the back stab?"

"If you wish."

She *hated* when he didn't get mad in response. Particularly when she was letting her temper get the better of her and she shouldn't.

"Breakfast will be ready in fifteen minutes."

"Excellent." But he didn't leave. He slid onto a stool at the little breakfast counter, got out his phone.

She thought he'd settle into work, and as much as she didn't want him there, that was fine. She was used to all sorts of strange situations while being a hired chef.

But then Athan spoke. "Did you talk to your mother?"

Lynna didn't know that she really wanted to discuss it

with him, but she supposed he had a right to know who knew the truth. "Briefly."

"How did she take the news?"

Lynna tried not to sigh. She actually didn't know. Her mother had neither seemed horrified by the union, nor too happy about it. For both of them, Rhys was the focus. He had been so young when Father had died. Only fourteen. And mother had struggled under the weight of grief those first few years while Lynna had still been away at university and not fully aware of how bad life at home was until that last month.

But they'd both fixed things now, and Mom could hardly argue she'd done the *wrong* thing.

I worry, Lynna. Your father thought he knew what he was doing too and look where that got us.

Father trusted Constantine. I don't trust Athan at all.

But you'll be married to him.

And that had really been it. Her mother had given Lynna a tepid blessing, in between emotional apologies for being such a failure as a parent.

Lynna wanted no one's apologies. Particularly her mother's. Luckily, Rhys was busy at university and Mom would soon enough be distracted by a new home.

"Well enough. She said she'd like to live in Crete, to start."

"I'll have my real estate man compile some potential properties for her to look over."

"Great." And it was, so Lynna ignored the twisting feeling of anxiety in her chest. Mom would get a new house where she wanted to live. Lynna's loan was already paid off, and Rhys's schooling for the year. Good things were in the offing.

She took the bread out of the toaster, and then began to

plate them both a little bit of everything she'd made. When she presented him with a plate and a mug of coffee, he took it all in as if it were some great work of art. Then he grabbed a fork.

"A man could get used to this."

"Feel free."

"Why does that feel like a threat?"

She lifted a shoulder and suppressed a smile. So he could be funny? So what? She had her plate in her hand. She wanted to go eat out on the terrace, but he'd likely follow her. The best bet was her room.

But before she could turn to leave, Athan pulled out the chair next to him.

"Sit. Eat. We should learn how to spend time together without sparring for our upcoming trip to Athens."

"Should we though?"

"Yes, Lynna. We should. There is an entire contingent at AC International that did not like how your father was treated. I can hardly get their support to hire Rhys, to give you all shares, if they think you hate me."

"Maybe they'll oust you and hire me."

Athan sighed and shook his head. "They are afraid of my father. And rightfully so. But everyone knows I'm the only person who could possibly stand up to him. But I need leverage."

"And I'm your leverage."

"You are indeed."

And he was gazing at her like that mattered in some way, like *she* did, when she was only the pawn he was paying dearly for the privilege of having.

Before she could think of what to say, or manage to look away from that dark, dangerous gaze that threatened to poke at her careful, *calm* walls, his phone began to ring.

He glanced at the screen and grinned. "Speak of the devil. Or should I say, devil supreme. Let's have a chat, shall we?" He put the phone between them and answered the call on speaker.

"Hello, Father. To what do I—"

"What the hell do you think you're doing?" a *very* angry voice demanded.

"I'm sorry, sir. I don't follow." Athan feigned a loud yawn. "It's awfully early."

"It's nearly nine," Constantine's voice growled through the speaker. "Whatever do you think you're doing marrying Aled's servant girl of a daughter?"

Athan didn't reply at first, but he looked at her and grinned while taking a bite of *ladenia*. "I didn't realize this was common knowledge just yet," Athan said, after a while. "Just think, if you and Regina had stuck around, we could have had a double wedding."

"If you think doing something so absolutely brainless is going to somehow win you shares and votes, as if anyone in this company thinks of Aled Carew as anything other than a bumbling, *dead* fool, you are even more useless than I gave you credit for."

"Shares? Votes? Father, you wound me. I married for love, of course." This time he winked at Lynna, and she looked away. Down at her plate. To eat. This was the strangest situation she could imagine getting herself into and she didn't know how to deal with it.

Yet. She would figure it out. She always did.

"Love? Did you blind that silly shrew with lies of love?"

Shrew. Well, she was glad Constantine thought so. But silly? No, she couldn't stand that. "I understand why you might see it that way, Constantine," Lynna said, before she thought better of it, before she could rein in her temper or her tongue. "After all, the only person who could possibly love you would have to be blind indeed."

Athan didn't even hear his father's response to that, or maybe the response was simply the click of a phone call ended. But he stared at Lynna in wonder.

He could kiss her. He had never in his entire life seen anyone stand up to his father in such a way. Even her father had treated Constantine as a kind of...untouchable monarch.

He considered following the instinct, considered kissing her here and now as she lowered her head in her hands.

No, not yet. Slow and steady with stubborn Lynna.

"I should not have said that," she muttered.

"Why not?"

"It can hardly be wise to make him so angry."

"It doesn't matter. He'll be as vicious as he can be regardless of how I needle him or don't. A lesson it took me a long time to learn." He went back to the delicious breakfast she'd made him. Yes, he could certainly get used to this.

She turned to look at him with a frown. "Why? You do his bidding. You're his right-hand man."

"I'm his replacement, and he knows it. It was fine enough when I was young and had no ideas of my own, just mimicked his every move, but the minute I balked at that, he turned on me."

"Then how are you still in his company?"

"I'm a savvy man, Lynna. As is my father. He enjoys the little battles we have, always so sure he'll come out on top. Regina is case in point. That's not so satisfying if I'm a beggar on the streets. He wants me close so he can attempt to overpower me, show me up and *win*. And since he often does, I started letting him."

She pulled back, kind of straightened, a look of such genuine affront on her face, he was fascinated by it.

"You *let* him win?"

"Of course. You have to lull an enemy into complacency sometimes." Athan took a sip of coffee. Clearly Lynna did not understand the art of losing a battle or two to win the war.

Unsurprising.

"Regina was supposed to be my first play at rebellion, my first true battle toward a war won. But he figured it out, because of course he did. So, another loss there. But we found a way to attempt a new win, didn't we? This attempt he can't undo, can't manipulate. He knows it, or he wouldn't have called me in a lather. He's usually smarter than that. He's quaking in his boots."

Lynna looked at the phone in clear disbelief. "It didn't sound it."

"Trust me."

"That's one thing I'll never do, Athan." She stabbed a bite of egg with her fork.

It shouldn't bother him. Why should she trust him? And yet he found himself wanting to earn her trust.

Another challenge to meet. Because he *was* worthy, no matter what his father wanted anyone to believe.

She would see. He was certain of it, even if the breakfast seemed to have lost its taste. He was confident because there was nothing else to be.

Athan smiled broadly. "I would wager that the minute we're back in Athens, he'll make an appearance at the house. He'll change his tune a bit. Tell me of all my faults and failings, then offer a handout. Talk loftily about how he'll save me once again."

Lynna frowned at this. "I don't understand."

He studied her. She came from two very honest people. She worked hard—it was obvious in the success of Your Girl Friday. And for the past five years, she had accepted a job from him and pretended she didn't hate him and everything he stood for, while doing meticulous, amazing work.

No, he supposed she'd never understand the games his father played. "Mark my words, Lynna. He isn't done, and because he isn't, this marriage was potentially the smartest thing I've ever done."

"Ironic," she replied. "It might be the stupidest thing I've ever done."

He laughed at that, true enjoyment winding through him. When she let her personality show, there was a glimmer of an interesting woman underneath that hard outer shell.

They ate the rest of their breakfasts in silence. He even let her clean up after everything without complaint. If she felt the need to be chef and cleanup crew, there was really no point to stopping her.

Without a word, she began to walk away from the kitchen.

"Where are you going?"

"To my room," she replied, frowning at him. "I didn't recall you needing to know my every move being part of the deal."

He ignored that. "What about a swim?"

She looked at him with that heavy distrust he was beginning to find frustrating instead of amusing, though he had no right to her trust.

"I didn't bring a suit," she said.

He let his gaze wander. "Intriguing."

Was it terribly masochistic that he enjoyed the cool disdain written all over her face when his gaze returned there?

"There is absolutely no need to pretend as though there is anything remotely…physical about this arrangement."

He let those words settle in the air around them. An interesting point of contention with what he'd said. Not that she didn't *want* him to express physical interest, but that she thought he was *pretending*.

"You don't strike me as a particularly unconfident woman, Lynna, so it's fascinating you wouldn't think there'd be an honest attraction."

"You're a man whore. They tend to like the obvious."

"Funny, I thought being a whore required liking *any and all* kinds."

Her scowl deepened. But she didn't leave the room, and he figured that was sign enough to continue this conversation. He slid out of his stool, casually walked over to where she stood behind the counter.

Her eyes darted to the exit, but she didn't take it. She lifted her chin. And stood her ground when he got close.

Fascinating. Arousing. That her eyes had gotten a little wide, her cheeks a little pink. Her exhale was even a little shaky, and he felt it against his face, leaning this close to her. His whole body throbbed with a complicated want that he refused to think of as a complication.

After all, they were married. Why not enjoy a physical relationship?

He took her hand, the left one where his ostentatious ring sat, he used his thumb to move it back and forth. "Do you need to hear me say it plain?" he asked, his voice low and quiet.

She inhaled sharply, and her words were just as sharp. But her hand was still in his.

"I need nothing from you except holding up your end of the bargain," she said. Clearly, no doubt, but with a hint of a tremor to her voice.

He wanted to press his mouth to the scrambling pulse at

her neck, but instead he held her gaze and spoke quietly but firmly. "The bargain is clear. Contract signed. It is what it is, but you and me are something separate." He lifted her hand to his mouth.

Before he could brush a kiss across her knuckles, she jerked her hand away. "There is no you and me beyond that contract." She pushed at him, and he gave her the space she insisted upon. Let her storm away. Because he could and would take his time.

And she, whether she wanted to admit it or not, was *not* immune to him.

Any more than he was immune to her.

CHAPTER SIX

LYNNA AVOIDED ATHAN for the next two days. It was cowardly, and she *hated* being cowardly, but she hated failing more.

Feeling any fissure of attraction for him, just biological or not, felt like a failure, and she needed to get a handle on it before they headed to Athens.

Today.

She did not think she had any handle on it. Which was lowering, but she convinced herself it was simply like learning a difficult cooking technique. Like making a souffle or macarons. It took time, determination, skill and *practice*.

Avoidance wasn't practice, so she needed to be around him. She would *practice* her indifference all the way to Athens. Because she did not *like* him, no matter how her body betrayed her with its attraction to him.

And maybe he *did* find her attractive, and that all wasn't some trick or ruse. That only meant he had no standards and was likely desperate for anything after agreeing to keep from engaging in any affairs for the duration of their marriage.

Not that him agreeing meant he *would* keep his hands to himself when it came to other women.

Probably especially if you refuse him.

She physically shook her head as if to dislodge that

thought from her brain. It was not her responsibility to…
to…do *that* in order for him to keep his hands to himself.
That was on him and his ridiculous plan.

She'd packed her bag. She'd no doubt need to go shopping once they were in Athens if she was going to be leaving
his house. She didn't mind looking a little blend-into-the-
background and drab if it suited the moment. But she wasn't
going to stand next to him looking like *staff*.

She was his wife.

And no amount of times she reminded herself of that
could make the reality really take root. But she handed her
suitcase off to his assistant when they came to collect them.
She met Athan at the car that would drive them to the airport at the appointed time.

He greeted her charmingly, as if she hadn't been avoiding him for two days, and then chatted inanely about the
weather the whole way to the airport, and then more once
in the air, about what was to come.

"I have arranged a few intimate dinners. Couple to couple, that sort of thing. We won't discuss business. They'll
be friendly outings. I will go into the office this week, normal hours, so you may do whatever you like during the day.
Might I suggest some…shopping."

She scowled at him. Even though she'd been planning on
it, she certainly didn't like to be *told*. "It is hardly my fault
I packed for a *job* and ended up in a *ruse*."

"No, indeed. But you'll need to shop all the same. I'll
have a calendar made up for you, including dress code and
expectations so you can figure out what you need."

She had to bite her tongue to keep from arguing. To argue
with him would be childish. A knee-jerk reaction to being
told what to do.

And Lynna was *never* childish. She was *always* calm

and cool and unbothered by other people's nonsense and attempts to impart their will on her. Whether he wanted to or not, whether he approved or not, she would go shopping when she pleased and for what she pleased.

She assured herself of this over and over again, failing at concentrating on the book she was reading as the flight took them from Mykonos to Athens. They touched down, deplaned, then got in another vehicle.

Lynna had very purposefully avoided Athens for quite some time. Ever since she'd helped Mom clean out their home and put it on the market. When she visited her family, they usually got together near Rhys's school in Thessaloniki or she paid for them to come see her in London when she could manage the expense.

She couldn't help herself from watching the city pass by, feeling nostalgia for a childhood that had been so *simple*. But that nostalgia started becoming dread as they didn't turn into the city center. Instead, they seemed to be driving around and north, very near where she'd grown up. So close that her heart seemed to clutch in her chest.

Would they drive by her childhood home? Where she'd grown up and left at eighteen thinking the world was hers for the taking?

Only to have her stable, loving family's world torn apart.

But the car did not turn down the street that would have led them there. Still, they didn't drive much farther before the car stopped at a gate, and after a few moments, drove through onto a brick drive toward a beautiful white mansion, all classic lines and lots of green surrounding it. So that it felt as secluded as any country estate.

This was not at all what she'd expected. "This is your home?" she asked, suspiciously. "For one single man?"

"I bought it with an eye toward the future. Besides, if I

really need to stay in the city overnight, I simply stay at a hotel. So why not have a comfortable home base?"

An eye toward the future. So he'd bought the house for the beautiful Regina and future children. And still, Lynna didn't think it quite fit. They seemed like such a modern, sophisticated couple and this felt...

Like a home. Like *her* childhood home. And her parents had been Constantine's opposites. Her father used to joke that that was what made them such good business partners. Yin and yang. And she had heard Constantine, on more than one occasion, say he envied the Carew family. For their warmth and their *stability*.

Had it all been a lie? Was *everything* a lie?

"Did you love her?" Lynna heard herself ask before she thought better of it. Before she centered herself in the present instead of the past. Oh, *God*, she should have never vocalized that question. She should have never even *wondered* that question.

But Athan considered this without giving some scathing response or knowing grin. "I liked her well enough. Enjoyed her company. Was looking forward to a life together, getting and building what we had both decided we wanted. But love? I don't think I understand the concept of love."

"What do you mean you don't understand the *concept*?"

"Human beings are selfish and destructive by nature. It's biology. We can decide what we believe is right and wrong, and follow that, but emotions are not...decisions we make. Love is no evolutionary response. So what is it?"

He looked at her expectantly, like she was supposed to know, and know well enough to explain it.

She had no experience with romantic love, of course, but she loved her family dearly. Even when her brother was obnoxious, even when her mother felt more like a burden than an authority figure, even when her father had descended into a bitterness that would take his life.

They were the center of almost everything she did.

And Athan was posing the question as if there was *no* answer, when of course there was. "Love is the things you said. Enjoying someone's company. Wanting to be with them and planning futures together." Lynna thought of her family, her friends. Tried to put all those feelings into words, which was not exactly her strong point. She preferred acts of service to having to *explain* things. But here she was, and she was hardly going to admit to Athan she wasn't sure or didn't know something.

"And it's wanting their happiness as much as if not more than your own. It's caring for them and finding joy in that."

"Interesting," he said. As if it *was*. Which somehow made this whole strange conversation worse. "What about them caring for you?" Athan asked.

It was a strange question to have posed to her. She always took on the role of caretaker, felt she thrived there. The only time she'd really been taken care of outside of childhood was when her friends had rallied around her after her father died, but she'd been so mired in grief she hadn't really, fully recognized what was happening in the moment.

Still, Athan had a point of sorts. For some people. "I… I suppose you'd have to find joy in that too."

"You *suppose*?"

She frowned at him as the car finally came to a stop after circling around a huge fountain. She refused to say anything else on the matter.

"Well, I *suppose* I'll have to take your word for it, expert or not. I certainly haven't seen any evidence that this *love* people are so obsessed with is a reality. Outside of people with nice families, of course."

"My parents loved each other." She said it quietly, and the words felt like they'd escaped against her will. Because she didn't want to be that vulnerable, but it also felt like a strange betrayal not to put that forward.

He had seen her parents. He'd been there when their families had been the best of friends.

She tried to look back on that time from his perspective. His parents had divorced when Lynna had been young and Athan couldn't have been more than a young teen. She remembered him having to spend holidays with his mother, but during the school year he was in his father's custody.

Constantine had never remarried, but there'd been a steady stream of women. Each younger and more glittery than the last—or so Lynna's mother had said once when she didn't think Lynna was listening.

Athan stared at her for the longest time, a faint line between his drawn-together brows. Then the driver opened her door and she pulled her gaze away and allowed the driver to help her out.

Before she could even catch a breath, Athan was at her side. "Welcome home, Mrs. Akakios."

"I am *not* changing my name, even temporarily," she said through gritted teeth, under her breath. Just the thought had her recoiling. Akakios? No. Never.

But Athan only grinned at her. "Let me show you around your new home."

Athan had known his father wouldn't stay away. So, that night in Athens, satisfaction twisted through him as he watched his father's sleek sports car pull up on the security monitor at just a little after ten.

No doubt his father's attempt at a *surprise* visit, but Athan was still dressed for the day. Still debating if he should act *surprised* when Constantine showed up, or if he should play the unbothered protégé.

Ideally, Lynna would be with him. Ideally he could tell her *I told you so*, but she had retired to her room after dinner, despite his attempts to coax her to stay downstairs and enjoy an after-dinner drink.

He'd shown her around the house on their arrival, given her one of the larger rooms in the estate. Then she'd demanded to get a tour of the kitchen. She'd spent over two hours getting acquainted with the layout and where everything was, she'd made a list of cooking and baking items she would need supplied, and she'd studiously ignored him as he'd sat in that very kitchen and, once again, watched her make a meal.

It had been delicious. He had a very good cook for his Athens home, but Lynna had a...special talent. He personally didn't understand how one chef could be better than another when they were all just following recipes, but there was something about the food she made that stuck with him.

Then, despite his best efforts, she had refused to retire to the library with him. Said no to a drink, a swim, a walk around the property. Once she'd cleaned up the kitchen, she'd soared past him and gone upstairs to her room.

Athan was determined to be patient. It was his father's greatest weapon, and Athan needed to use it effectively here. But something about Lynna poked at all the control he'd learned at his father's knee.

But he hadn't gone after her. Hadn't resorted to demands that definitely would not work on someone as hardheaded as his *wife*. He'd spent the last hour awaiting his father's "surprise" arrival, nursing his own after-dinner drink on the sprawling porch that overlooked the sparkling pool. As the sun set, the lights came on inside the water, giving everything an eerie blue glow.

A staff member stepped outside and Athan knew it was *showtime*.

"Mr. Akakios. Your father is here to see you."

"Thank you, Sebastian. Show him to the library. I'll be there in a moment."

He waited five minutes. Finished his drink. His father had spent a lifetime being patient, controlling his anger, hiding his narcissistic impulses. And still, even without any outward reaction, Athan knew how to needle him.

Athan marrying Lynna was something Constantine hadn't seen coming, and he wouldn't be able to let it go until he was certain he had the upper hand in the situation. He'd poke and prod at Athan until he found a weak spot.

But there was no weak spot here. Athan was *determined*.

So, Athan didn't walk back into the house with purposeful strides. He…*meandered*. Half expecting his father to come thundering out of the library demanding to know why the devil he should have to wait.

But when Athan finally reached the library, his father was still in the room. Athan leaned against the doorway, watched as his father looked through drawers. He wondered what dear old Dad thought he might find in a *public* room, in *unlocked* drawers. Did he really underestimate Athan that deeply?

It grated, but it was good, and Athan would use it.

"To what do I owe this late-night visit, Father?"

Constantine straightened, regarded Athan from behind Athan's own desk. He didn't have the decency to look guilty or caught, because the man never thought he was guilty. Anything in service to what he wanted was fair game.

Athan had believed that once himself. And while he had

not murdered Aled Carew, Athan still felt the guilt of his death like a weight around his neck. Because he had used his father's tactics on the man. He had ruthlessly and carefully planned to frame Lynna's father for all his own father's shortcomings.

And still, Constantine had not been *proud*. He'd not reacted positively. He'd only wanted Athan to do more, sink lower.

It had been enough to finally break the spell of Constantine Akakios, and still he likely would have sunk all that lower for Constantine out of sheer habit if it hadn't been for seeing Lynna at the Carew funeral.

"I heard you were back in Athens." Constantine straightened. "Our last conversation was not satisfactory. Since you cannot be trusted to have a calm, direct conversation over the phone, I knew I would need to come see you in person."

It was impressive, really, the blame game his father could play, considering just how calm Athan had been during their last phone conversation.

Unlike Constantine.

But Constantine had a way of speaking, of twisting words, that could have even the strongest man doubt himself.

Athan didn't tonight. "I see," Athan said, though he made sure his expression was one of confusion rather than understanding.

"You have made a grave mistake, son." Constantine shook his head, as if he simply despaired of Athan, when Athan knew what he despaired of was being *surprised*. "I will give you one last opportunity to save us both the hideous embarrassment you're about to cause."

Athan raised an eyebrow. An interesting and impressive

tactic, to use *us* as though they were somehow in this *embarrassment* together.

"And by embarrassment you're referring to…?"

"Your sham of a marriage that was clearly only meant to be a pathetic slap at me."

Pathetic. And yet it had warranted an angry phone call and whatever this was. No, Athan had succeeded quite well.

"Oh, no sham, I assure you." Athan smiled. "We are legally wed and quite happy everything worked out. I suppose the news landed before I wanted it to, but no harm no foul. If you have come to try to pry this wife away from me, I'm afraid that even you will find it impossible. If there is one person I can be assured Lynna will never betray me for, it is you."

Constantine did not bite at that. He kept up the fake tired disappointment. Athan gave him credit, it was an impressive performance, and one he hadn't trotted out in a while. There was a time Athan might have even fallen for the gravely concerned father.

But that time was over.

"I have come to give you one last chance, Athan. One last opportunity to salvage this mess you've made. We will get the marriage annulled, send the Carew girl back where she came from and hammer out a fair deal." Constantine even smiled kindly. "We have been at odds, and I know you are upset about Regina. But this can still be salvaged."

Athan had known marrying Lynna would send his father into a rage, but he hadn't expected it to go *quite* this well. Constantine must be all too aware of how easily members of the board would be swayed to him with a Carew connection.

Constantine sighed deeply. He met Athan's gaze with one of concern. It really was no wonder people fell for his father's act. "I am here to help you, son. If you can be smart enough to take the hand offered, we can fix this gigantic mistake of yours."

Athan didn't laugh, though it was hard to swallow it back at the idea his father would ever *help* him. "I thought you were ousting me?"

"I figured after what happened with Regina, it would be necessary. But the fact you're willing to jump into another doomed marriage proves that I have not hurt anything but your pride. You are still an Akakios, and where I once suspected you'd land on your feet, now I have concerns, son. I want to ensure that you are not left to the wolves."

Son, son, son. Such manipulation. So smooth. So *genuine* seeming. Athan wondered if there was any predator so adept at undermining its prey. For so long, Athan had fallen for it. Twisting himself into whatever knot he could, if only it would make Constantine offer a *good job*, said so damn warmly he'd truly believed he could earn his father's regard.

His father's love.

But it never lasted because whatever task he'd do for his father was never quite enough. And still Constantine kept that carrot of affection right there, within reach, only to slide it through his grasp. Time and time again.

Until Athan had finally grown the hell up. Until he had learned that there was no *relationship* to be had here. They were adversaries. Now and forever.

At best.

"Concerns?" Athan repeated, feigning ignorance.

"The pictures of the wedding hit the papers the night of the wedding because apparently you are not sharp enough to keep these things under wraps."

Athan pretended to consider this. Then he shrugged. "That's one interpretation."

"It is *my* interpretation, and thus *fact*," Constantine said, with a snap to his tone. But he tempered it with a smile. "You're fumbling, son. Let me take care of this for you."

"You know, I was affronted, obviously, at you and Regina plotting against me, when it would have been easier for all involved to just be direct. But Lynna was there, and it reminded me that I do not have to play these…silly parlor games you love so much."

Constantine's gentle expression sharpened. "Parlor games?"

Athan waved a hand. "Stealing fiancées, pitting people against one another, framing others, skimming a little off the top here and there just for the thrill." Athan sighed heavily as if it all exhausted him.

"Are you accusing me of something?" Constantine demanded.

"Of course not," Athan assured him, trying to maintain a wounded expression when what he wanted to do was grin. "I'm simply explaining to you that we're different. You appreciate a puppet on a string, *Father*, and I do not. It's best, surely, if instead of helping me, instead of…how did you put it, not leaving me to the wolves? Let's cut the apron and puppet strings. If I get eaten, so be it."

Constantine's expression was nothing but rage now, but he was breathing carefully. Keeping the explosion inside.

Still, Athan thought he knew how to break his father. And if he could, he had an even larger upper hand.

"Oh, you're worried how this will all reflect upon *you*." Athan shook his head sadly. "And here I thought you were confident enough to stand in your own legacy."

Constantine was across the room in an instant. Violence flashed in his dark eyes, but he did not touch Athan. He clenched his fists at his sides, looked up at his son.

"All these years I've let you fail and fail again. I have saved you from embarrassment. I have been the only thing keeping you from ruin. Now you will fail. Largely. Spectacularly. Publicly. I'm sure the Carew girl will enjoy once again watching her meal ticket crumble into a useless bitter husk."

It was an impressive speech. It was meant to embarrass him, infantilize him, *destroy* any last shred of confidence he might have. And it likely would have worked if Athan hadn't spent his formative years at his father's knee, learning his views on business and dealing with people.

Dad only sought to undercut that which was actually a threat. Which meant Athan's marriage to Lynna had rattled the mighty Constantine Akakios.

Which meant his was a plan that could work. And while he'd already *known* that, it was nice to have his father assure him of this.

"Father, I cannot fathom why you'd be so emotional." Athan went so far as to cluck his tongue. His father's face began to edge toward purple. "Why don't you go on home to my, I mean, *your* fiancée and rest? Please, I give you permission to continue your plans to oust me. And free you of any worry about how I land—on my feet or otherwise."

"People will see through this farce, Athan. I take no joy in ending you, but if it must be done, I will do it. I will ruin you. Once and for all. This is your final chance to be saved."

CHAPTER SEVEN

LYNNA COULDN'T SLEEP. A new place. A new life. So many doubts circling in her head and, worst of all, the low, distracting rumble of Athan's voice playing over and over in her head.

Do you need to hear me say it plain?

She hadn't let him actually say much of anything. But she had spent too much time in the days since imagining what he *might* say plain. What it might feel like to kiss him again. To lose herself in something…

Wrong. Wrong. He is your sworn enemy.

She was just hungry. That's what was causing these ridiculous thoughts. She needed a sweet treat. There had been some options in the kitchen. Maybe she could even put together a sundae. It wouldn't be as good as her usual ones since there were no homemade brownies or chocolate sauce on hand, but it would do in a pinch.

She got out of bed. She didn't *think* she'd see Athan, or anyone else, but she grabbed a robe all the same. It was easier than changing out of the somewhat revealing pajamas. Because all she was going to do was grab a dessert. She'd even bring it back to her room to eat it.

Determined that this would be just the thing to cure her insomnia, Lynna left her room. She found herself…sneaking, essentially. Which was stupid. She lived here too. No matter how little she liked it, she was the owner's wife.

Wife.

If she let that word rattle around in her head, she might start screaming. Maybe run out the front door.

And where would you go? Back to London? Back to all that hard work just to tread water? Just to fail your mother and Rhys?

No. It wasn't an option. She'd made her choice and she had to live with it. For the people she loved most. Lynna had never once accepted failure in herself, and she would not start now.

She crept down the stairs, before she could make her way to the back of the house and the kitchen she heard voices. Low, dark, vicious voices.

Suspicious, she moved toward the sound. Coming from Athan's library he'd showed her upon arrival. It was a lovely room. Not as bright and spacious as his office back in Mykonos, likely to protect the books from too much sunlight. Instead it was made of dark woods and deep colors, but it had been cozy. She'd been able to easily picture herself curled up on one of the oversize chairs reading in front of the fire on a cold night.

In the dim hallway, light from the library poured out. The door was open about halfway, so it was easy to see inside. To see Athan, still dressed as he'd been at dinner, and then Constantine. They spoke to one another in low tones, and Lynna stopped short with the terrible, horrible realization.

They were working together. This was the plan all along. She had been so stupid. So careless. She didn't know what they wanted from her, when they'd already killed her father and won a million times over, but what else could this be?

Her breath sawed in and out, her heart beating loudly in her ears, but then…she remembered what Athan had said before they'd left Mykonos.

He'd been so sure Constantine would arrive the moment they were here.

Her breathing slowed. Was this just some father-son… spat? She calmed enough to actually listen to what they were saying.

"People will see through this farce, Athan. I take no joy in ending you, but if it must be done, I will do it. I will ruin you. Once and for all. This is your final chance to be saved."

Lynna found herself holding her breath, not sure how Athan would react. He seemed determined to overthrow his father, but maybe he would falter? Maybe he would take whatever deal Constantine was offering? Maybe he was all talk and absolutely no wherewithal.

Even as she tried to believe that, she knew in her heart it wasn't true. She could fault Athan for many things, but being weak willed was not one of them.

"You know, it's funny, Lynna called you the devil. And I'm afraid I can no longer do deals with the devil when I have married a saint."

So no, this was not the moment of Athan's inevitable betrayal—one she knew could come at any moment and had to remember that.

She knew he didn't *really* think her a saint, but he wasn't taking whatever his father was offering. And it was clearly making Constantine angry. His voice wasn't slick anymore. It was all venom.

"Do you honestly expect anyone to believe you care for that mousy, pathetic, pudgy *servant* girl? Everyone will know it's a transparent ploy to win over her father's idiotic supporters."

Mousy, pathetic, pudgy servant girl. The absolute gall of that man to narrow her down to his opinion on her looks and her position as a *personal* chef. As if that was all anyone could ever see when they looked at her.

She couldn't hear Athan's response over the roaring in her head. She thought maybe he laughed, but she couldn't be sure.

Because she wasn't about to let that stand. Maybe her marriage to Athan would never be *real*, but now she was bound and determined for Constantine to think it was.

It was rage and pride and a million other things that had her acting. Stupid, mostly, but she did it anyway. She undid the belt on her robe. Her pajamas weren't exactly sexy lace, but the tank top she wore was soft and thin and dipped a little to give a hint of cleavage. She let the robe slide off her shoulders, hook at her elbows.

She pushed the door open farther, trying to make her expression into one of silky promise and intent.

Two pairs of dark eyes turned to her. She feigned shock, rushed to pull her robe together as though she had not expected to find anyone but her husband in his library.

"Oh. Athan. I… I didn't realize you'd been…" she looked from Athan to Constantine, widened her eyes "…distracted."

Athan's mouth curved, dark eyes amused. "Darling, I apologize for not returning immediately. But my father had stopped by to offer his congratulations." He was picking up the thread easily. He held out his arm and she moved across the room to him, let him wrap it around her waist and pull her to his side. She ignored how *warm* it was here, how *hard* he felt against her side.

She had acting to do. So she leaned into Athan, smiled at Constantine, though the smile threatened to curdle at the edges. "It's awfully late for congratulations," she offered, not hiding the censure in her tone.

Constantine's expression was not rage exactly. His color was high, he was breathing a little heavily, but she could *see* the wheels in his head all but turning as he surveyed them.

Then he moved toward them, and Lynna felt a bit like she was being stalked by a lion. It was only Athan's strong arm around her that allowed her to feel…protected. And stopped her from backing away.

Which she was not going to think too deeply about considering she hated both of these men.

Hated.

"Perhaps I have seen the error of my ways," Constantine said, in a low, purring voice when he was close—too close. "You hide your assets, Lynna. Why don't you show them off?" He even reached out, as if he was going to pull the robe off her.

Lynna jerked back in horror and disgust, but then in a blur, Constantine was gone. Well, sort of.

Athan had him pinned up against the wall, his forearm against Constantine's throat.

But Constantine didn't look *scared*, even as Lynna's heart clattered around in her rib cage at the shock of it all. The older man *smiled*.

"Perhaps you should call the police, Ms. Carew," he rasped. "It seems your *husband* has assaulted me."

"If you ever try to touch my wife again, she will be calling the police to report a murder."

"Threats? Athan." Constantine tsked. "This is *shocking*."

Lynna held her breath. For a moment, she was afraid Athan was actually going to commit that murder. It likely wouldn't take him much to crush his father's windpipe right then and there.

But then Athan released him, so abruptly Constantine stumbled a bit before he righted himself. "You'll be hearing from my lawyer," he said to Athan, then strode out of the room.

Athan stood stock-still. He stared at the point on the wall

he'd had his father pinned against. She had never seen him look quite so…dangerous and devastated at the same time.

Lynna also didn't move. She didn't know what to say. It took time for her heart to stop hammering at her, for the fear and thrill of too many things to dissipate.

"I thought I'd find a weak spot," Athan said after what must have been several ticking minutes. He blew out a long, loud breath that left Lynna feeling…

Off-balance. Like she'd stumbled upon a private moment. That Athan might be human instead of the evil demon she wanted him to be.

"Instead, I suppose he found mine," Athan added, somewhat thoughtfully. Perhaps a little too resignedly for her taste.

"A bad temper?" she offered, hoping to get some…response out of him that put them back on their normal footing.

He turned slowly, his gaze met hers, too direct, too potent. "You," he said gravely, that dark voice like an arrow that landed low in her stomach, a pooling, painful heat. "It was never my intention to make you a target."

He said this with a gravity that had too many things inside of her trying to *melt*, but she had to harden herself against him. Maybe he wasn't as bad as Constantine, maybe he'd defended her when she couldn't remember the last time she hadn't had to defend herself, maybe he almost seemed human in this moment, but he was still her enemy.

"You thought I could just be a pawn you got to move how you wanted with no consequences?" she asked, doing her best to sound haughty instead of winded.

He shook his head, suddenly looking exhausted. "Never mind," he said. "I suppose I should call my own lawyer."

"You don't actually think…"

"It's my father's specialty. Poke at someone until they

come undone. Then use their outburst against them either with veiled threats or police action. He will do something, and it will be on my doorstep by morning."

It was awful. Underhanded and awful. So, of course, it suited Constantine to the bone. And no doubt she should leave Athan to deal with it, but...

Well, he had reacted that way in protection of *her*. Now, she wasn't silly enough to believe it was because of some great protective feeling he had toward *her*, or even some inner sense of goodness since he was an Akakios and could have none, but he had done it all the same.

"Come," she said firmly. She walked out of the library, striding for the kitchen. She didn't know if he followed, and she told herself she didn't care. If he came, she would make him a sundae. If he did not, he was on his own for comfort.

She didn't look behind her. She just moved into the kitchen and began to collect everything she'd need.

Once she had everything out, she ventured a look around the room. Athan had seated himself on a stool at the counter and was watching her intently.

"What is this?" he asked, clearly because she'd stopped.

She set the bowls out, took the lid off the ice cream. "It is the makings of a sundae. Subpar, as I do not have the time this late to make the brownies from scratch, or the ingredients to make any kind of sauce, so we will have to do with store-bought."

"You do not churn your own ice cream?" he asked sarcastically.

But she didn't know why that would be sarcastic. She was a chef—and one who enjoyed making desserts as much as she enjoyed concocting savory items. "I do, when I have the time and supplies."

"Of course you do."

She put the sad little store-bought cookies at the bottom of the bowl. The premium ice cream would help elevate them…she hoped. She put a scoop into each bowl.

"Why are you making me comfort food? I'd think you were trying to treat me like a child, but you're making yourself one."

"There is nothing childish about wanting a little sweet comfort after a difficult encounter," Lynna said loftily. "I know I am little more than a pathetic, pudgy servant girl—"

"I know you don't actually believe those things about yourself, Lynna," he said, almost reproachfully.

"No, I don't."

"But let the record show—"

"What record?"

"I happen to think you're beautiful, forceful, and an utterly remarkable chef and businesswoman."

She hated that each compliment landed with *force*, as if she'd spent her entire life waiting for someone to notice what she thought to be true. Which felt far too close to a vulnerability that would leave her doing nothing but repeating her father's mistakes.

She kept her gaze studiously on her creations, no matter how much some strange internal impulse made her want to look up at him.

"You needn't butter me up for me to participate in the war against your father. If I wasn't already enlisted, tonight would have done it."

"I am not *buttering* anything. I am merely stating facts." Athan shrugged, as if it made no difference to him whether she believed that or not. "That was remarkable, though," he finally managed, sounding more like his insouciant self. "Acting as though you were waiting for me to return to bed. An amazing performance. I applaud and thank you."

"I didn't do it for you."

"No, of course not." There was a twisted kind of amusement for the way he said that, but she couldn't quite make sense of it.

She finished off the sundae, slid it across the counter to him. "If he does call the police, and there are questions, *I* am a witness. I will tell them that your father was about to attack me, and you acted in my defense. Perhaps it's an exaggeration, but it isn't much of one."

Athan studied her with steady eyes. When he spoke it was softly, carefully.

"You will make yourself a target, Lynna. My father is a formidable opponent. You were never meant to be anything more than…well, that pawn you mentioned."

"A shame for you then, as I have no plans on being a pawn." She met his gaze with a fierce one. "From here on out, Athan, I am your partner." A partnership with an Akakios was dangerous, but Lynna was no fool. If she was going to be *in* this, it was time to be *in* it.

A willing participant. Aware of the risks. The target she might become. Maybe she'd get burned in the process, but if Rhys had a future, and she could avenge her father in some way, her burns would be worth it.

CHAPTER EIGHT

HIS FATHER'S RETALIATION did not come in the form of police intervention or a lawsuit. Instead, Constantine used
the press.

Athan's assistant was ready the moment he emerged from
his room the next morning, armed with the story.

"So far, no legitimate news source has picked it up, sir, but
the internet is having a field day with a father-son brawl."

"Brawl," Athan said disgustedly. "Don't I wish." It would
have solved nothing, but it would have *felt* spectacular. And
still, it grated, how easily Constantine had played him last
night.

Athan knew he would have reacted in a protective way
to any woman in that situation—and no doubt his father
did as well. *That* had been one of Athan's many failings in
Constantine's eyes.

It was disgusting, and Athan would not stand by while
any woman was demeaned in such a way no matter what
the consequences.

But the tide of fury at his father daring to reach out toward Lynna, the need to immediately stop the look of shock
and disgust on her face at his father's actions, it had all been
so quick—the moment, the white-hot, all-encompassing
fury that had shot through him. He had not thought at all.
He had been too rough, too…reckless.

Now he would pay the price.

"There have been quite a few phone calls and emails asking for you to comment on the story. Ophelia said she will meet you at the office at ten."

"Then let's trust Ophelia to handle it until then," Athan said, referring to his public relations manager, as he walked into the kitchen. "Ignore the calls and emails for the time being. I'm going to eat breakfast then head into the office. We move on, business as usual."

It was surprising him less and less to find Lynna in his kitchen, and it didn't do thinking about the fact he'd now found himself in his own kitchens more over the past few days than possibly his entire life prior.

She never looked up at him. Never greeted him. She always acted as if the food was the only thing that mattered.

"Well, our retaliation has landed," he offered as she studied her pan of eggs. She was twisting around the liquid in an odd little spiral. Everything smelled like heaven.

She lifted her gaze from the pan to him. "I take it you are not to be arrested."

Some of his bad mood lifted at the way she tried to make it sound like she was disappointed, but what he saw on her *face* was relief.

"Not as of yet. Instead, he went with the tabloids." Athan looked down at his phone and read from the article his assistant had sent him. "'An "altercation" at the house of Athan Akakios was reported late last night. Athan Akakios refused to comment—'" He looked up at her. "Not one person reached out to me for a comment before the story was run. How odd." Then he continued to read. "'Constantine Akakios, however, was willing to confirm that he was involved, and that he'd like time and privacy to deal with such an alarming altercation with his own son.'"

Lynna frowned. "But this is a lie," she said with such affront in her voice, he wanted to run a hand over her hair, just to have a sense what naive, innocent outrage might feel like.

"Some will always be willing to lie for the right price. Truths don't matter in the games my father plays. Besides, he was very careful. Much of this isn't a *lie* so much as twisting the story a certain way, with the right words. A Constantine specialty."

"What will we do?"

We. That word had him…off-kilter for a moment. To think of her as a *we.* To be in any kind of *we.* She had said it last night, she planned to be his partner in this, and still he couldn't quite wrap his head around it.

So, he pushed the feelings away and focused on the reality. "I will simply have to weather it. Retaliation won't do. We'll continue our plan as is. That's why he's doing ridiculous things like this. He's terrified my plan will work. So we must remain focused."

The frown didn't leave her face, but she did turn her attention back to her pan. In deft moves, she transferred the food from pan to plate.

"I will go into the office. You will go shopping for our upcoming dinners," he said as she pushed a full plate in front of him. "I normally take my breakfast to go."

"Then go," Lynna replied, preparing her own plate.

But he didn't go. He sat and he ate, and he watched her do the same. The silence was casual, easy. Surprisingly so. He wasn't so naive as to think she'd lost *all* animosity toward him, but he liked to think he sensed a kind of softening.

When he finished his breakfast, he stood. "That was amazing as always." He skirted the counter, and she watched him warily, as he'd hoped.

She held her fork between them as he walked toward her, like she might use it as a weapon.

It made him grin.

He reached out for her arm, gently took it and pulled her to him. "Have a good day, wife," he murmured. "Everyone is supposed to believe us a happy newlywed couple, remember?" he whispered when she resisted. Then pressed a kiss to her hair.

She scowled at him, but she didn't say anything.

"Smile, darling, we're in love."

He got the sense she was about to hurl a fork at him, so he beat a hasty retreat. In a better mood, he rode into the office. He didn't bother to look up any more stories his father might have planted. He focused on looking at the clients currently controlled by people Athan thought would be more sympathetic to the memory of Lynna's father over Constantine's threats. The people who had quietly, carefully and never outright sent little signals over the years that they did not believe Aled had been the one to steal money or make deals with questionable people.

When Athan strode into the office building, there were speculative looks, but no one came out and said anything to him. He met with Ophelia at ten and she outlined a strategy for how to deal with the story. Since most of the dealing with it landed on Ophelia's and her team's shoulders, Athan spent the rest of his day focusing on his *job*. He called clients, read reports, put out small fires here and there.

But when his assistant informed him Ophelia was back later that afternoon, Athan knew not all had gone to plan.

She said nothing as she strode into his office. She placed her phone on his desk, pushed it across to him. He looked at the screen.

Shock Pregnancy Source of Rush Wedding! Beneath the wild headline was a photograph of Lynna. It must have been taken today, as it was in front of a shop in Athens. She was carrying shopping bags and dressed in one of her black ensembles. She hardly looked pregnant, but Athan supposed she didn't have to *look* it. It only needed to seem possible to people.

He looked up at his PR manager, who looked…grim at best.

"She is *not* pregnant," Athan said through gritted teeth.

Ophelia nodded. "Then that rumor will take care of itself in time. I have a meeting with your legal team shortly to go over our best course of action since these headlines are more direct in nature and come from a legitimate news source. But I came by to recommend a few public events with your wife. Along with the altercation story planted by your father, these stories will spread because she's mysterious. So, we must end any mystery. Take her out, show her off and let her story be told."

He wasn't sure how Lynna would feel about that, but he supposed they didn't have much of a choice. "Yes. Consult with Niko about my calendar. The dinners I have set up are nonmovable, but anything else is negotiable if there are events we should be seen at."

Ophelia nodded, collected her phone and turned to leave, but Athan stopped her.

"I want my own story planted. One that questions Constantine's relationship with a woman nearly thirty years his junior, who was my fiancée not that long ago." He knew he was on the right track, and *that* was why he was a target, why Lynna was. But that didn't mean he couldn't make a few targets of his own.

Ophelia shook her head. "Mr. Akakios, if you bring any

attention to your previous fiancée, you will only have people wondering why you rushed to marry Ms. Carew." Ophelia waved her phone back and forth. "That is, if she is not pregnant."

Athan wanted to crush something. Perhaps his father's windpipe. "She is *not*. Find a story then. Something that will have *him* fielding obnoxious phone calls all day. I want it done by tomorrow."

Ophelia looked disapproving, but she gave a nod before leaving. She would do what needed to be done.

And so would Athan.

Lynna found herself humming as she prepared dinner. She loved Athan's kitchen. Whoever had designed it was brilliant. All the items she'd wanted—both in terms of tools and in terms of ingredients—had arrived by the time she'd returned from shopping—where she'd handpicked some of her own supplies as well.

Along with clothes more fitting for dinners with Athan's associates. Many of whom she probably knew, if superficially. Her father had enjoyed bringing people to their home. Mother had enjoyed entertaining. And while her and Rhys had often not been involved in those dinners, they'd often been at the very least introduced, especially as they'd gotten older. Father had wanted them to follow him into AC International.

Lynna had never had any aspirations of business, but Rhys had.

Rhys was the reason for all of this. Because she'd realized that all of Athan's plans would necessitate talking about her father, which she avoided like the plague. For Rhys, she would suffer through it.

Besides, she knew how to reroute a conversation. Mother

liked to reminisce, to get lost in all that *grief.* Lynna preferred to set it aside. To focus on the reality of the situation. So she knew the tricks to turn the conversation to something more…productive, without it *seeming* like she was avoiding the topic of her father.

Father was gone. A tragedy, really, but not one that could be undone. So speaking of the good times, of his warmth and humor before the Akakios family had humiliated and ruined him was…

"Pointless," she told herself fiercely and out loud so her brain got the message.

She began to prepare a salad while her roast cooked, and soon enough she heard footsteps. Her current method of dealing with Athan was to never take her focus away from the food until she knew she was done, until she knew she could handle the…sharp, overwhelming blow that was just…him.

The way he'd grinned at her after kissing her *hair* this morning, all humor and mischief and something that pulled out the strangest sensations in her. Not just…*sexual* feelings, but a matching humor when she wanted to hate him.

She *did* hate him.

But today she was too curious about what might have gone on at his work regarding the tabloid stories to pretend like he wasn't there, or she didn't know if he was or not. So she looked up as he entered.

He wore a crisp suit, though his tie was slightly askew as if he'd loosened it.

She could tell just from the expression on his face that he did not arrive with good news. And something spooled within her chest, an odd kind of…reaction. She could almost picture herself crossing to him and offering him a comforting hug.

Which was the most ridiculous little detour her brain had ever taken. She turned her attention back to the salad. "Have the assault stories spread?"

"Not exactly. It appears my father has chosen to cast a wide net when it comes to stories." He came to stand right next to her, holding out a phone.

With purposeful and careful movements that she considered a pointed retaliation against the things her body *wanted* to do when she felt the *warmth* of him so close, she angled her body away from his even as she took the proffered phone.

There was a picture. A ridiculous headline about their marriage and her pregnancy.

"This is... I was simply shopping." Lynna frowned at the picture of herself. It was not the most flattering angle, but she definitely was *not* pregnant, in any way, shape or form.

But what had Athan said this morning? Truths didn't matter. It was all perception, and she was familiar with the games media played when it came to women's bodies.

"I should have seen this coming," Athan said, sounding apologetic. "An interest in you from the press, spearheaded by my father. His goal is to humiliate, and he is an expert."

Athan seemed genuinely perplexed, which was odd. Why should he concern himself over foolish stories about her?

"Am I meant to be humiliated?" Lynna demanded, eyebrows raised. "Perhaps if it were true, but it is not."

He stared at her for a full beat. Blinked.

She was *almost* amused that he did not have a quick, smooth rejoinder. *Almost.* "A woman's body will always be picked apart, Athan. Perhaps I am not used to it being *my* body splashed across tabloids with lies told about *me*, but this is hardly new. Even if your father spearheaded it, this is the kind of thing women in the public eye deal with."

"I don't like it."

She laughed, though with a touch of bitterness. "Oh, well if *you* don't like it, something must be done."

"My PR team is on it. They suggested going to a few events of our own accord so you don't seem mysterious enough for people to want to make stories up about you."

"What kind of events?"

"Balls, charity dinners, anything that will have you dressed up and on my arm and lots of pictures available for anyone who wants them. The more it seems I'm hiding you, the more Constantine will have ease in poking at you."

She hated the idea. Small private dinners with her father's old coworkers was one thing. She felt like she excelled in small group situations. But *balls*? Pictures? She much preferred her place in the kitchen.

And she was hoping to avoid pictorial evidence that this year she'd signed herself up for had ever occurred.

Her phone trilled and she saw that the work wives were calling. It gave her the perfect out to leave this conversation and have a few moments to decide how *she* wanted to proceed.

"I have to take this. When the timer goes off, pull the pans out of the oven."

He frowned at her. "I hardly think—"

But she didn't listen to his protests. She strode out of the kitchen and answered the four-way video call.

Her friends faces all appeared, and she could immediately tell they all looked concerned.

"Hello. Is everything all right?"

"We've all seen the stories. The picture of you shopping," Irinka said. "We want to know if everything is all right with *you*?" She said this almost at the same time Maude offered—

"You're not actually…"

"Good God. *No.*" Lynna looked over her shoulder as she hurried up the stairs. Athan hadn't followed her, thank goodness. "I haven't slept with him," she whispered fiercely.

"No one could blame you," Irinka offered.

Lynna made it to her bedroom door and hurried inside, closing the door behind her so no one would overhear this ridiculous conversation. "*I* would blame me. For the rest of my life."

"You did marry him," Maude pointed out, *oh so helpfully.*

"Not to have sex with him. To clear my father's name. To give Rhys a future."

Her friends were all silent at that.

"We're all very sorry you've made your way into the tabloids and have to deal with this gross body shaming stuff," Auggie said kindly. "What can we do?"

"Nothing. It's…nothing. Weird, but it hardly matters what some strange websites post about me. Apparently I have to go to some glittering events now, let my picture be taken, take away the *mystery.*"

"That's very smart," Auggie said.

Lynna wrinkled her nose. Maybe it was, but she wasn't used to getting dressed up and having her picture taken. She wasn't used to being a *story.* Maybe it'd be one thing if she was actually in love with Athan, married to him for all the right reasons.

But she wasn't.

"Once you know what events you'll have to attend, send me the details and I'll send you some outfit ideas," Irinka offered. "Though I'm sure Athan has a stylist on hand."

"I trust you over anyone Athan employs."

All her friends were silent for a few minutes. And even

though they were all currently in different places, she could almost *feel* them giving each other looks.

"Are you sure you want to go through with this, Lynna? Because we can come rescue you anytime. You don't have to fight this battle on your own."

She thought of Constantine smiling while Athan had him pinned against that wall. She wasn't *alone*, per se, even if she didn't trust Athan fully. "No, I'm good."

She wanted to have a hand in making Constantine pay.

So she'd have one, even if it meant balls and pictures and stories. She'd do whatever it took to give Rhys a future.

And ruin Constantine's.

CHAPTER NINE

MORE STORIES CAME out day after day. And each one enraged Athan a little more. Especially since they'd started to focus on Lynna. Not just the pregnancy rumors, but a gross exaggeration of the loan Athan had paid off for her and what that transaction might *mean* about their relationship.

Yes, Constantine had found his Achilles' heel, because Athan did not feel quite so calculated and careful when the stories made Lynna out to look bad.

He'd phoned Ophelia so many times she'd stopped answering his calls. She'd managed to plant a few stories in the press about Constantine, but none had taken off with the fervor that stories about Lynna did.

Their first public outing would be this weekend, but they had to make it through tonight's private dinner first.

Henry and Bethan Davies were their guests. They were the first dinner he'd scheduled because they were the easiest targets. Henry had been Aled's childhood friend who Aled had brought into the fold of AC International before Athan had been born.

Henry's loyalty would lie with Lynna over Constantine, Athan was certain. Even with Constantine's threats and Athan as a go-between.

Lynna had suggested that instead of going out, Athan host the Davies in his home and allow her to make the meal.

He'd had reservations about it looking like his wife was *staff*, but in the end, she'd won him over. It would feel like family. Like a home-cooked meal. Appealing to the sentimental, which was the whole point of marrying Aled Carew's daughter.

Still, he was having a hard time shaking his foul mood when he returned home. Until he hunted Lynna down. She was in the dining room. Everything was set up for a fine dinner, and she was clearly going over the entire tablescape to make sure it was perfect.

She wore black slacks that somehow appeared both elegant and comfortable. She wore a short-sleeved sweater the color of eggplant. Her hair was swept up in a more elaborate twist than he was used to seeing from her. A delicate gold chain hung around her neck, and little diamonds winked at her ears.

He did not know how she could make him feel like he'd been electrocuted in an outfit so simple, so casual. But he wanted to trace the line of that necklace, feel the soft warmth of her skin, more than he wanted to deal with Henry Davies.

"The hors d'oeuvres are ready and set out," she said, as if ticking points off on some internal list of hers. "Petros will serve the rest of the meal. I added some Welsh touches to the menu. It will offer an easy way to segue into talking about my father that doesn't feel calculated."

He thought of what she'd said about being his *partner*. He knew she wanted revenge against his father, but he hadn't expected...*this*. Her actually working *with* him. Because all of this was...

"You are brilliant."

She stopped a little short, straightened her shoulders. "Of course I am."

She had an unshakable confidence. He'd seen that in her,

year in and year out. The way she took his jobs, the way she acted unaffected—for the most part—by who and what he was every time he brought her into his home to *be* his staff.

But there was something about the way she reacted when he complimented her that hinted at some tiny…vulnerability, and it made him even more furious that his father had turned her into his preferred tabloid target.

But he had to set aside all those frustrations and put on a smile when the Davieses were announced. He had to play the role of gracious host. It was a role he'd always been good at, but Lynna added a special touch. Where he would have been tempted to play on the memory of her father, she always drew the conversation back away from Aled. So that even the most cynical person could not have accused them of a mercenary dinner in an effort to gain support.

But there was enough of Aled's ghost haunting the dinner that Henry no doubt felt it. With the right moves, Henry would associate Athan with Aled instead of Constantine, and once he promised to bring Rhys Carew on?

Athan was certain he would have a steady ally in Henry Davies.

When they said their goodbyes, Henry took Lynna's hand in both of his. He squeezed. "It was so good to see you doing so well, Lynna." His smile wavered, emotion in his eyes. "I miss your father very much, but you brought a piece of him back to me tonight."

Lynna blinked, a bit like she'd been struck. Then she managed a smile, but it was not warm.

"It was good to see you, Henry," she said, not engaging in the topic of her father at all. She pulled her hand from Henry quickly. "If you'll excuse me."

Then she strode away quickly. To smooth over her abrupt exit, Athan walked Henry and his wife to their car, speaking effusively of Lynna's culinary talents and inviting them to come back another time.

But he was a bit confused by Lynna's odd exit, so he went to find her once the Davieses were seen off.

When Athan returned to the dining room, she was collecting dishes. Clearing the table. Which they had an entire staff ready and waiting to do. She must have stopped them.

"Well, I think that was a success," she said brightly. *Overly* brightly. Too brisk with it too. She was moving in quick, efficient movements, but there was something underneath it. A shake. That *vulnerability* she always seemed so desperate to hide.

"Your father was a good man who made an impression on many people."

She stopped what she was doing. Her eyes were hot as she pinned him with a glare. "I see no point in discussing that with *you*."

"Or with Henry, apparently."

"We could sit here and tell old stories, reminisce about how wonderful he was," Lynna said. Her words were clipped, her movements back to efficient but a little jerky as she pulled a stack of plates high. "But the truth and reality is he's dead. Grief is a wasted emotion."

He was shocked to hear her say so, if only because it reminded him a bit of his father. Who had never had any patience for *feelings*. Things must be done regardless of them, or so he'd always intoned at Athan.

Usually when they had to deal with the topic of Athan's mother. Athan's feelings about her. Elena's feelings about the custody agreement.

And Athan to this day felt regret for the way he'd dealt with his mother before he'd realized his father was the enemy. He'd tried to rectify the relationship with his mother, but it remained tenuous at best.

Hardly the topic at hand.

"Lynna." He crossed the room. He had never once been gentle with his mother, and he'd regretted it these past few years of trying to rebuild himself into a decent enough man. So he tried to be gentle now, with Lynna. "There is nothing…wasted about feeling grief for your father."

He stopped her movements by softly putting a hand at her elbow. There wasn't so much as even a tremor in her voice or her arm as she pulled away from him and met his gaze with those blue eyes.

She kept everything so…locked away. Carefully hidden behind that cool distance she employed so well. He had believed this was a sign of strength, of confidence, but now… he wondered.

Because he had seen her at the funeral. Devastated. Undone. She *had* feelings.

Grief is a wasted emotion.

Did she think *all* emotions were? Except maybe hate.

"There is no one in here to pretend for," she told him, as if him offering comfort had to do with pretend.

"I was not *pretending.* I was offering comfort, as you seem upset."

"I'm not upset. I'm fine. Or I would be if you'd leave me alone and let me clean up."

He *almost* believed her. She had a talent for taking all the emotion out of her voice. For seeming so perfectly fine you never worried about her.

Which was probably the point. It was no hidden mystery that *she* was the thing that had kept her family together. *She'd* taken out the loan to pay for her brother's education. *She'd* dealt with everything.

He found he liked knowing he'd released her of some of those burdens. He'd gotten what he wanted out of it—her married to him, so he knew he shouldn't feel like he'd done something *for* her. It had been for him.

Because he wasn't selfless.

Case in point, he found himself thinking about the moment he *had* gotten underneath all those walls she held up against him. A moment she'd *surrendered*.

When he'd kissed her on their wedding day. Wedding. Because she was his wife. And maybe she hated him, but that didn't mean she didn't *want* him.

All these years, he'd only seen the cool, calm outside. But he'd never seen that flicker of emotion underneath.

But it had been there. This whole time. Which meant her grief was there, just as her anger and frustration were.

As her desire might be.

He moved closer to her, lured by the idea. Desire. That kiss on their wedding night. What might lurk underneath her carefully curated surface?

"Did I mention that you look beautiful tonight? Ethereal." And she did. He'd found himself losing the thread of conversation more than once when he'd caught sight of her smiling at Henry or taking a delicate bite of the food she'd made herself. The sound of her gentle laugh had knocked into him like a blow on more than one occasion.

It all suited their purposes. Made him look in love with her. Which was all that mattered. At least, when they were around people connected with AC.

Now they were alone. And nothing mattered except what he wanted to matter.

He moved closer still. "I could hardly focus on the task at hand."

"Stop that," she snapped.

"What?"

"We are husband and wife in name only. It's fine enough to pretend for an audience, but I don't want to hear… I don't need your compliments, Athan."

He liked the way she said his name all clipped, reproachful. "Need? Of course not. But you don't want to hear that I think you're beautiful? That I spent just as much time considering the angles of how to win Henry over to our side as I did the precise spot on your neck I'd like to put my mouth."

Her eyes widened for a moment—and perhaps it was arrogance, but he liked to think it was a moment of anticipation—before her eyes narrowed.

"I am *not* going to be your plaything."

"Oh, it isn't *play*, *omorfiá mou*, I assure you."

She shook her head, made a fed-up kind of noise, then hefted a stack of dishes and tried to sail past him. But he knew her well enough or was getting there. He knew just what to say to stop her in her tracks.

"Why are you running, Lynna?"

She didn't take another step. She stopped abruptly, shoulders straightening. "I am not running. I have dishes to do."

"Lynna. Come now. Surely you can come up with a better excuse than that."

She whirled to face him, temper flaring, the stack of plates wobbling dangerously in her arms. "I have held up my end of the bargain this evening. I did an impeccable job."

"You did."

"So. There is no need, there is no…place for this…whatever game you're trying to play."

"It couldn't be as simple as finding you attractive, being married to you, and wanting to taste you again. It has to be a game?"

The plates clattered, but she firmed her grip. "I don't

know what would ever give you the impression that I'd want you to touch me—"

"Perhaps our wedding when you kissed me back." He smiled at her. "You liked it when I kissed you."

Temper was heightening her color. Maybe he would have liked to find a different emotion to coax out of her, but at least anger was *something*. She didn't cut that one off abruptly, and he wanted more.

Because he wasn't a selfless man, and in this moment, he didn't even want to be.

"We all have temporary bouts of insanity now and then," she said acidly.

But it did nothing to dim his smile. Her barbs were always so well-placed, so *funny*, even if she wasn't trying to be. "Insanity or no, that is not saying you didn't like it."

"Perhaps I'd like kissing a frog," she returned archly.

It made him want to laugh. It made him want to put his mouth on her. To undo the twist of her hair. To see what she was hiding under all those layers.

"Well, as long as you'd enjoy it. You know, you don't have to like a person to have sex with them. Good sex, at that."

She lifted her chin and immediately shot back. "I'd hardly share my body for the first time with someone I hate." Then something in her expression shuttered.

She hadn't meant to let that slip.

First time.

She whirled away from him, marched from the dining room to the kitchen, the plates rattling against each other as she moved.

Maybe he should have let that be that, but… She was so self-possessed. So beautiful. He couldn't fathom that she would… Why wouldn't she have *shared her body* before?

He followed her into the kitchen. "Why have you been hiding?"

"Hiding?" She made a scoffing sound as she set the stack of dishes into the sink. "I have no interest in putting up with a man simply because he might, and I feel *might* is the operative word here, offer a bit of physical pleasure. I have had much more important things on my plate. Sex is for people with lots of time and freedom from consequences."

It was meant to be a dig at him, but it didn't bother him that she might consider him part of that. "Indeed, indeed. But see, you have already decided to put up with me for other reasons, so why not get pleasure out of the deal?"

She opened her mouth, but no sharp rejoinder came out of it. He watched as she scrambled for one.

And came up empty.

The want was like a drug now. A potent, yearning, tangling thing deep inside. All the more irresistible because he saw *something* in her reaction.

Oh, he was under no illusions she would ever *like* him, but that didn't mean the elemental chemistry that sparked between them couldn't be explored. And he was becoming more and more convinced *she* wanted to explore it, if she could ever get past her own stubborn nature.

"You know, Lynna," he said, moving slowly closer. Watching as her breathing got more shallow, but she did not retreat. She did not hold him off. She watched him with an expression full of curiosity warring with a wariness. "I could make you feel things you've never imagined."

She made another scoffing sound, but she did not rebut the statement. Didn't push him away.

"With a touch, a taste. You have no idea what I could show you. You only have to say the word."

She let out a shaky breath, but her gaze was steady on his when she responded. "Don't hold your breath."

He smiled at her. Stayed in this space just a whisper away from her while seconds ticked on. While he watched the effect of his proximity wash over her. While he felt his own body tighten, yearn.

It was a dance. Or maybe *fencing match* was more appropriate. Lunge, parry, retreat. Build up to the final moment of surrender.

She *would* surrender.

"Enjoy washing dishes, *omorfiá mou*," he offered on a sultry murmur. Then turned and walked away. More than pleased at the little outraged sound she made at his retreat.

She washed the dishes. Cleaned the kitchen and dining room from top to bottom even though the staff tried to help, but she shooed them away. She worked herself into a state of exhaustion, or tried.

But even after she'd showered and crawled into bed, late into the night, she could not stop thinking about those words.

You know, you don't have to like a person to have sex with them. Good sex, at that.

It was terrible, though better than thinking about the sharp lance of pain she'd felt at Henry bringing up her father. The man he'd been. *Before.*

She didn't want to think about *before* Constantine had betrayed her father any more than she wanted to hear Athan's words echoing in her mind, feeling like a caress against her skin.

In her *mind*, she knew she had no desire to encounter *any* of what Athan described. Not with *him*. The confections she made for herself were all the physical pleasure *she* needed. Always had been, always would be.

Her body seemed to be on a different planet of under-standing. One that kept reminding her she didn't have to *like* him to have sex with him. He *was* her husband. And what was this if not the opportunity she told herself she'd never have?

A period of time where her responsibilities were mini-mal. A sexual encounter with him required no emotional investment. No potential for conflict or complication, be-cause they didn't like each other and they would divorce after they took AC back. After Rhys was instated.

An opportunity.

She shook her head, there against her pillow. That line of thinking was absolute insanity. A sexual encounter with the devil? That would leave marks. Scars. He'd be the first man she was with *forever.*

I bet he's really good at it.

She rolled onto her stomach and groaned into her pillow. Where did thoughts like that come from? She didn't want to think that way. But just like her body reacting to him—his presence, his words, his gaze, *him*—her brain seemed to have a will of its own.

Lying here, *feeling* her own body, was a recipe for disas-ter. And the only way she knew how to fix it was to feed it.

It was how she'd dealt with her grief, her anxiety, her stress—a bunch of pointless emotions that accomplished nothing. Feed the feeling, and it went away. The perfect solution.

Maybe she'd ended up in the kitchen every single night of being here, making herself a sweet treat and pretending it was a decadence and not a distraction. Maybe there was no pretending tonight, but if she lay in this bed, she might be tempted to take care of the desperate ache inside of her herself.

Which would be fine, if it wouldn't be *him* she pictured or imagined while she did it. And if she allowed herself that, how would she ever face him again?

How was she going to weather this feeling, this *yearning* she didn't want to have but was there all the same for a full *year*?

No. Food was the answer. Pretty much always.

She got out of bed and wrapped the robe around herself. Pretending it was the chill and not the buzzing layer of lust making her skin prickle.

She crept her way downstairs in the dark like she'd done more often than she should. She could move around the kitchen without turning any lights on—the outdoor lights of the patio enough to illuminate her way.

She moved into the pantry. She didn't need ice cream or the whole rigmarole of a sundae. This wasn't that dire. She was *fine*. She'd just grab a cookie or two—she'd made her own now, so they weren't pathetic store-bought ones. She just needed some sugar to cap off the night, and then she could and would go to sleep—no thoughts of Athan anywhere to be found.

Never mind that she'd had a very large slice of apple cake with dinner. That didn't count.

Once she was in the pantry, she pulled her phone from her robe pocket and turned on the flashlight. She quickly located the cookies she'd made yesterday and packed away in a jar. She procured two—only two—then replaced the jar's lid and turned off her flashlight.

She would go back upstairs, crawl into bed, eat her cookies, and then she would be able to settle and—

The room flooded with light. She jumped at the surprise, made a little screeching noise, then squinted against the brightness.

It didn't take a psychic to know who would be behind her when she turned. She closed her eyes for one second. *You are not giving in to whatever this is, Lynna. Not now. Not ever.* She would be strong. She could be strong.

Then she turned.

He'd changed his clothes. Was this what he wore to bed? A soft T-shirt that outlined the impressive muscles of his body, and sweats that rode low on his hips. His feet were bare. His hair was even a little mussed, as if someone had been running their fingers through it.

She tightened her grip on her cookies and her phone and tried to ignore the errant thought that she'd like to do just that.

"What are you doing in here? It is the middle of the night," she hissed at him. Even though it was his house, and his right.

"I know what goes on in my house, Lynna darling," he returned, all but lounging there against the pantry door-frame. "And every time you struggle to sleep, here you are." He smiled, the smile of a devil—handsome and *tempting*.

And she knew better than to succumb to temptation.

Except...

She still hadn't come up with any good reasons to resist the temptation. Except the whole "hating him for ruining her father's life" thing. It was easy when Constantine was the topic of conversation to focus on the fact Constantine had been the mastermind of all that, but she needed to remember Athan was no innocent party.

No matter how handsome he looked.

"Did you come looking for dessert, *omorfiá mou*?" he asked, like a sultry promise.

He had to stop calling her that. He had to stop speaking Greek in that low, delicious rasp of a voice. He had to stop *this*.

Because if he didn't, she might be forced to reckon with the fact that part of her had…hoped for this when she'd come downstairs.

Part of her had wanted exactly this. Fantasized *this*.

Him finding her. Pursuing her. Not letting her refusals stand. Because she couldn't allow herself to give in, but if he…

He moved toward her and she was…trapped, essentially. In the pantry. Any retreat would require pushing past him.

"I find sleep difficult when I have…other things on my mind as well," he said, too close now. So she could feel the heat radiating off of him. So they were *both* in this pantry room. "What were you thinking about, Lynna?"

He reached out, touched a strand of her hair, then tucked it behind her ear, tracing the shell of it. A shudder of feeling went through her. How could that be such a jolt, such a pleasure? It was simple. Her *ear*?

And what if he touched you other places?

She tried to shake her head, but it wouldn't move. She was transfixed. By the shadows on his face in this dim room. By the sound of his breathing—not quite controlled. By the way his scent—something piney and luxurious—seemed to overtake any food smells in here.

She had *not* come down here hoping for this. She had come here for…

His hand cupped her jaw. His body was against hers now.

She could push him away, for a second she wondered if that's what he was waiting for, in this moment where he simply stood there and held her face. Then his head bowed.

"Let me taste you," he whispered, his breath dancing across her mouth.

She shouldn't let this happen. She certainly shouldn't lean *toward* him like she was eager and willing and—

And then his mouth touched hers. How easy it was to forget one's entire moral compass when lips like his were involved. Sure and in control, as though she didn't have to worry about anything except melting into him.

When she always had to worry about *something*.

But her mind simply…emptied. The heat of it all was incomprehensible. How she could be at the center of such a range of things and still be whole? Herself?

She wasn't cognizant of dropping the cookies or her phone, didn't even mourn the loss. Her fingers were too busy finding purchase in the soft cotton of his shirt as his tongue swept into her mouth.

It was wild and maybe desperate. A lack of control from both of them. Like the wedding, but more. Because this had been building. He'd made it build over the past week and she'd tried to put it off, but all she'd done was give more kindling to the fire, so it erupted bigger and hotter and more devastating. A wildfire burning through her.

Dimly, she was aware he unknotted the tie in her robe, that it was tugged off her arms. That losing her grip on his shirt meant she needed a grip on *something*, and maybe that should be his face. The rough prickle of a day's growth under her palms. A sensory overload, here in his *pantry*.

His mouth slid down her neck. His hands were huge and gripped her waist. His mouth a sensual assault against the sensitive crook of her neck. She was shivering, panting, desperate for something she knew she should not want. Not with him. Never with him.

Then she felt the warmth of his hands *under* the soft, thin material of her pajama shirt. His fingers splayed wide, he slid those large palms up her sides, eliciting sparks and an unfurling of need so potent she didn't know how anyone survived this.

His fingers stopped just under her breasts. Her skin tingled everywhere, and she didn't know how to move, how to get him to touch her. Everywhere. Anywhere. More.

Except, she should push him away. Stop this madness. His mouth was on her shoulder, and she could almost...*almost* think.

"Is this what you want, Lynna?"

She did and she didn't. It was too much and not enough. How would she live with herself if she went through with this?

How would she live if he did not push her across this delicate edge? His thumbs brushed against the underside of her breasts and she did not recognize the sound that escaped her, so close to surrender and freedom—two things she could not allow herself.

Ever.

"If it's not, tell me to stop, Lynna," he said, a low, luring rumble against her skin. But then he pulled away, looked her right in the eye. His mouth was amused, arrogant.

She wanted to punch him.

Kiss him. Forever.

"If you don't want it, simply say the word. *Stop.*"

It felt like a dare. It felt like a lifeline. *Stop* felt like the only choice between this or an oblivion that would take her over, take her under. When she had to be strong and herself.

Who would she be if she lost control? If she let someone else handle everything there was to handle? What tragedies would befall her this time?

"S-s-stop," she managed.

And he did. Immediately. He pulled his hands back and held them up like surrender. He took a step away from her, and then another. His gaze never left hers, and there was nothing but a grim kind of amusement in his expression.

"You know where to find me when you change your mind, *omorfiá mou.*"

Some strange part of her wanted to stop him. As he turned and moved out of the pantry. Demand he stay and finish this.

But he walked away. Like it was easy. Like nothing was rioting around in his body like it was in hers.

She had *felt* his erection against her body. Maybe she wasn't well-versed in the male body, but she knew enough to know that.

Why would he just...walk away?

Because you told him to.

So it was wrong she felt disappointed. It was *ridiculous* she felt disappointed. But that was what settled inside of her. Frustrated, thwarted desire. Huge, yawning disappointment.

And the bastard probably knew it.

CHAPTER TEN

A FULL THREE days later, and Athan still had not quite recovered. For the most part, Lynna had avoided him, which was satisfying. She only bent her pride like that when something *had* affected her, so there was that.

But he could not seem to rid himself of the echoes of that kiss. It kept ringing in him like a bell. And he could not recall a time, even if he went back to his reckless, hormonal teenage days, when one woman had ever affected him on such a level.

It felt like a bad omen of too many losses to come, and yet he could not change course now. She was his wife. And maybe he realized, even if she ended up meaning too much, it would only be his due to lose her, really. Maybe this was all just a grand sacrifice toward allowing her to hurt him the way he'd once hurt her family.

Or he was losing his mind.

Either way, there was no way to go but forward. They were going to a charity ball tonight. To be seen and photographed together. To introduce Lynna to anyone and everyone. To end any questions that Constantine's tabloid parade had stirred up.

When Athan strode down the stairs, she was already standing by the door waiting for him. He would have glanced at his watch to see what time it was, but he could not take his eyes off her.

She was perhaps the most beautiful woman he'd ever seen. She tried to hide it, keep so many things understated in her usual day to day, but in the ball gown, there was no hiding how striking she was.

It was a dazzling sparkle in bronze. It nipped in at the waist, hugged her hips. Her arms were bare, pale and mouth-watering. There was a smattering of freckles on both shoulders, and he nearly missed a step at how badly he itched to taste each one.

He had teased himself with a taste, the most basic feel of her the other night, and it was eating him from the inside out.

Was he even breathing? He felt as if every atom of his being had been frozen into place.

But he forced himself to look away, at the stairs. At his watch, then back at her. And then when he'd gotten himself under control, he smiled at her.

She was scowling at him. "I was told to be ready at seven. It is ten past," she said, sounding like a scolding schoolteacher.

"It is not my experience a woman is ready to go on time."

"Then your experience is lacking. I am *always* on time."

"Yes, I suppose you would be." He offered his arm.

She eyed it as though it were some kind of trap. Her scowl never changed, especially when she hooked her arm with his and let him lead her outside to the car waiting for them.

The driver held the door open for them and Athan helped her in before skirting the car and getting in on the other side. She was rearranging her skirts, studiously *not* looking at him. He supposed she had no reason to, but it was interesting to watch her now as they drove, when she had nothing to do.

She was not so good at pretending he wasn't there when she couldn't distract herself with cooking.

"The dress is beautiful."

Her chin came up a fraction. "Thank you," she said.

Her hair was pinned up in strands, much like it had been on their wedding day. Colorful jewels winked at her ears. She kept her profile to him, elegant neck, lofty expression. Regal, all in all.

"You must have to work very hard to make yourself look so drab on your jobs."

Slowly, she turned to look at him, affront in every inch of her expression.

Maybe he'd done it on purpose. Maybe he couldn't quite help himself. Some sort of deep-seated need to get her to look at him, react to him. Childish, no doubt.

But she *was* looking at him now.

"Drab," she repeated, as if she didn't quite understand the word when applied to her.

He wanted to laugh. There was something so...*something* about her. The way she said things, the way she held herself. Her sharp, dismissive reactions to him. The vulnerable way she accepted a compliment. He wanted to puzzle through it all.

He decided it all suited their purposes. His near obsession with her. This want. Everyone would see it and assume it love. People loved that little fantasy, almost as much as if not *as* much as they loved a salacious tale.

Every picture would reflect a man besotted, and if he was, he supposed no matter how strange and out of character it was, it was not like he believed in some end goal of happy-ever-after. He could try to be a better man, but being a *good* one forgiven for all his past transgressions was impossible. So…

"All that frumpy black."

"I am *staff* when you see me. It is my job to blend in."

"And now you are my wife." He liked to say it. Out loud. Watch the way she tried to hide her reaction to the word. Sometimes a wince, sometimes a scowl. Would she spend a year scowling over it, or could he potentially get her to enjoy some piece of it?

When they beat Constantine, maybe. When he talked her into bed, definitely.

Because he would and they would enjoy their time—or at least, he would endeavor to. Then they would part. Both having gotten what they wanted, more or less.

He did not know why the thought left him feeling *restless*. Moody. But it wasn't the thought. It was just this aching, persistent *want* he'd brought upon himself for being fool enough to touch her.

"Ophelia has the biography ready to go. Once the pictures begin to circulate, she'll make sure it's distributed."

Lynna's response was muted. She'd approved the biography and knew the reasons behind why so many people were interested in her—thanks to Constantine's stories. But he knew she wasn't fully *comfortable* with the speculation about her as a person.

Still, she was going through with this. Still, they were *partners* in this. It was a new experience Athan had not expected to enjoy so much.

When the car arrived at their destination, Athan got out of the car and went to her side to help her out himself. He opened the door, held his hand out. She hesitated, and he knew it was because any physical touch reminded her of that moment in the pantry.

She had wanted him every bit as much as he'd wanted her. He should not have taunted her into telling him to stop, but he wanted no confusion.

If she wanted him, she would have to make that choice herself. Not leave it up to him. Not give herself an *out* when it came to the responsibility of her own choice.

"Smile for the cameras, *omorfiá mou*. We have a crowd to dazzle."

Lynna had tried to prepare herself for people wanting to take her picture. For a charity ball, for a reminder of the glittery life her parents had once led and she'd had a few glimpses of before her father had lost everything.

It was a lot, and yet none of it was more than trying to deal with her reaction to Athan, and his obnoxious determination or need or *whatever* to not ignore the little spark of chemistry that seemed to exist between them.

When he could, and should, just as she was trying to do.

She kept telling herself to prepare for her body's reaction to him. She kept assuring herself time would allow her the ability to brace herself, to ice it and him out.

But no amount of *bracing* changed the reaction inside of her. He'd walked down his elaborate stairs in his simple if elegant and well-appointed tux, and she'd struggled to breathe normally ever since.

Sharing the back seat of the car with him. Having him help her out of the car, his hand on her back as he'd guided her into the crowded room of sparkling people. It felt as though someone had shaken up an entire carbonated beverage in her chest, and she was nothing but an explosion of bubbles.

And lower, a deep, throbbing *pang*.

And maybe all of these things could have been weathered, but people were watching her every move. Her picture was being taken at every angle. She had *known* this was the purpose of tonight—for people to see and take pictures of her with Athan. So people stopped creating some mystery behind who she was.

But no amount of knowing prepared her for the discomfort that itched over her skin. It wasn't about confidence. She knew she looked good—Irinka had helped her from afar, and she had hired her *own* stylist to help prepare for the evening. But that didn't mean she was simply comfortable with being...looked at? Perceived? Whispered about, quite assuredly.

It was discomfiting, but worse was when it wasn't discomfiting at all. When Athan kept his hand on the small of her back. When he introduced her to people, procured her a drink, never allowed anyone to separate them for even a moment.

And all those concerns about the wider world around them seemed to melt away.

He was like a mountain, looming there. He was beautiful and made her breathless and there was something *immovable* about this *knot* that sat in her stomach, tying tighter and tighter until every faint touch from Athan had her reliving that pantry kiss and *yearning* for all that more he'd promised in words, and she'd stopped.

When Athan led her out to the dance floor, she didn't even notice the flashbulbs. His hand engulfed hers, he drew her close, and it felt as if they were the only two people in the room.

In the world.

You hate him. You hate him. You hate him. Why was that so hard to remember with his hand at the small of her back, with the easy way he swayed her to the music?

"We have danced together once before," he said, his voice low and rumbling next to her ear. He *had* to feel the tremor go through her. "Do you remember?"

She had purposefully not allowed herself to remember. It had been before she'd left for university. Before he'd betrayed her father. That hazy time of *before* when she had been happy and carefree enough to believe the world was hers for the taking.

Even when the dashing Athan Akakios had stepped in to offer a dance at the party her father had thrown for her eighteenth birthday. He had smiled at her crookedly, and teenage fascination had fluttered there in that moment.

He was older, too handsome to be fair, and she had known his offer to dance was something her mother had finagled, not something of Athan's choosing. But he had been kind about it.

Even in that moment of thinking he was dashing and fun, she hadn't had any real dreams of a romance between her and Athan *specifically*. But she hated here and now remembering that too much had started in the moment. The belief that it would be silly to waste her time on the foolish boys at school when there were *men* out there who knew how to handle themselves. Athan was five years older. He'd no doubt still seen her as a child, but he'd given her a glimpse into what adulthood looked like. How a *man* behaved himself.

She'd told herself then and there she would wait for the right man, never waste her time with *less*.

And at university, in the *before* of it all, she'd held everyone up to the standard Athan had set that night. Charming and polished and gentlemanly…with just the *hint* of something like mischief and danger dancing behind all those polite manners.

Not for her. She knew it hadn't been for her, but she'd dreamed of a time when it might be.

"Your dress was navy blue," he offered when she said nothing to his original question.

She looked up at him in surprise. Why would *he* remember that?

His mouth was curved, his eyes self-deprecating. "Trust that I did not *wish* to remember that detail at the time, as you were so young, but it was the first time I had to accept you were no longer…a childhood *buddy*."

She could only stare at him, as the music drifted around them and Athan moved her through the song. His body in perfect accordance with hers.

He had *seen* her in that moment, when she'd been quite certain she'd only been a duty to get through. In the here and now, it left her…rocked, when it shouldn't. It didn't matter. After all, look what he'd done after all that?

"Perhaps you should have continued to consider me a *buddy* and concerned yourself with not betraying my father," she said quietly. Now wasn't the time to have a discussion or argument about her father, about Athan's betrayal, but she needed to put that wall back between them. Somehow it had gotten unsteady, and she needed it strong and sturdy.

"You know, we have not actually ever discussed that."

Something that felt far too close to fear seized her, but she knew what to do with fear. Stamp it out. "Nor will we."

He looked down at her, a strange, considering expression on his face. "Why not?"

She could not meet his dark gaze, and the faint look of something that *appeared* like concern, but couldn't be. Athan Akakios had no *concerns* for her. "It's over and done. There is nothing to discuss."

"Ah. Best to box it up, set it away, push it down?"

"Yes." She didn't care if it was considered emotionally healthy or not. It had gotten her here, and maybe this exact here was a borderline disaster, but it was a moment in time. Her life was on the right track. A good track. She was setting Rhys up for every success, and once she got out of this, she would go back to the work she loved.

Then he said the next words, low and in her ear. "It is still there, Lynna."

An unbidden lump began to form in her throat. Tears wanted to spring to her eyes, but she swayed to the music and fought off the wave of emotion. Maybe all her feelings were there, but what did it matter if she never thought about them? If she never took them out and poked at them?

It did not matter. She would never let it.

And she did not cry. Even when Athan pulled her slightly closer, like he was offering some kind of comfort she didn't want and wouldn't take. Not back at his house when faced with the topic of her father's old friends missing him. Not now, simply because he'd reminded her of a time before… and wanted to speak of what happened.

What *happened* was Athan and his father had ruined her family's lives. Intended consequences or not, they had done that. Whether the feelings about that were *still there* or not didn't matter.

She got to choose how she dealt with them. Which was not at all. You could only control yourself, so she would.

And when he led her off the dance floor, in the direction of the exit, she was determined, *so determined*, to not let all these emotions get the best of her. Because chemistry, desire, lust—they were just emotions, right? Or science at the very least. Things that could be controlled with the right parameters put in place.

Outside the air felt cool. She could almost breathe again. She could set all that happened inside away.

Best to box it up, set it away, push it down?

Yes. Forever. That was how she'd survived the past five years, and how she'd survive the rest. *Always.*

Athan helped her into the car when it came around, and she made to settle herself with as much distance as possible from him, there in the back seat.

She *knew* he noticed, but he said nothing and made no attempt to scoot closer. Honestly, it was somehow worse when he seemed able to control himself…because then it felt like she should be better at this. Less…teetering on the brink of a terrible decision.

"Now that the pictures have been taken and will start to circulate, the biography Ophelia drew up that you approved should begin to appear in the media tomorrow," Athan said, as if he had not mentioned her eighteenth birthday or her father or feelings at all back inside. "There might be some who are still interested in digging deeper into you, but the basic facts will help dispel some of the rumors my father has planted. And we can add more to the story as needed, but the pictures tonight will go a long way to take away the mystery, to undercut his leverage."

Lynna hated this part of it, but she hated more that Constantine should get to call all the shots and morph how the public interested in Athan Akakios might view her. It wasn't that she felt in any way shape or form protective of Athan's reputation—because obviously he deserved whatever he got. And she wasn't all that concerned with hers—couldn't be, when she'd watched how easily someone else could ruin a reputation. A name. A family.

She had not allowed herself to really nurse that anger—it was unproductive, and she'd had to be productive. She'd had to pick up her family or else they would have sunk. But now, it was tempting.

Surely anger would keep herself from giving in to this… *thing* burning between her and Athan that he seemed so bound and determined to stir up.

"We will need to continue to make public appearances over the next few weeks. No doubt Constantine will have a rejoinder, and we must be ready to deal with it," Athan continued as they drove.

"And you would know all the devious and underhanded ways to do that," she said archly.

She could *feel* his gaze on her, but she didn't dare look at him, even in the dark of the back seat of the car. She kept her gaze resolutely on the glittering Athens passing by outside her window.

"I would," he said evenly, and it was completely and utterly unfair that he could make her feel small when he'd always been in the wrong and she never had, at least when it came to him.

She refused to say anything else the whole drive home. No, not *home*. *His* house. One she wouldn't even have to live in for the entire year. Once they had won enough AC International people over, she would go somewhere else. Anywhere else. Back to London or maybe to his Norwegian home in the fjords—far, far away from *him*.

When the car slowed to a stop, Athan got out of the car and before she could manage to scramble out herself, he was there. He helped her out of the car again, and he didn't immediately let her go. He led her to the front door, her hand in his. His grip was firm, but she could have pulled her hand away with a decent yank.

That hardly screamed *happily married* couple though,

and it would allow him to see too many emotions, when she hoped he saw her as an emotionless robot.

Oh, how she wished she could be one.

Once inside, she did pull her hand out of his grasp. She offered no good-night, no words of anything. She simply marched for the stairs. She wouldn't run. She *wouldn't*.

But part of her thought maybe she should.

He wasn't following her though. Still, when he spoke, his words were loud and clear, even though she had the impression he was still standing by the door while she was hurrying up the stairs.

"I want you, Lynna."

It was stark. Plain. Said in his dark, low voice it was like the most intimate touch. She had to squeeze the banister just to steady herself, had to stop so she wouldn't trip.

If words can have this kind of effect, what could he *have?* It was one of those errant, terrible thoughts she couldn't allow herself to give in to, but their frequency and potency just seemed to grow. Day by day. Second by second.

She could hear him take the steps behind her, but it was the fact she could *feel* him, some force he exuded. Closer and closer, until she knew without even looking that he was right behind her.

"Do you believe that?" he asked, his voice a low rumble far too close to her ear.

The strong thing to do would be to turn and face him. To tell him that his feelings were immaterial, and he could not keep pressing this point. This…*whatever* between them. The not strong but maybe smart thing would be to run. All the way up the stairs, into her room, and lock the door.

On herself.

Instead, she answered the question she shouldn't, eyes closed, voice little more than a whisper. "Yes." She wished she didn't believe it. Wished she could believe he was a user manipulating her.

But she had seen the way he watched her. She had *felt* him kiss and touch her. She wouldn't put it past him to use it against her, but that didn't mean he didn't want her at all.

"And you want me," he said, his finger grazing the line of her neck. It sent a wash of sparks through her. A shudder she couldn't suppress. "Whether you like it or not."

He was not asking her a question. It was a clear statement, and still he said nothing else, touched her nowhere else, like he was waiting for an answer to a question he hadn't asked.

She could lie to him. It would be so easy. Meet his gaze. Say *no* and walk away. She had the strength, somewhere deep down, she knew she had the strength.

But the other night had showed her that he was hardly going to act on that desire if she said she didn't want him to. Which meant, to find some *release* from all of this, she was going to have to admit to him, out loud, that she wanted it.

And, by God, she wanted it. When was the last time she'd gotten what she wanted? When was the last time she'd had the opportunity to think of nothing but her own wants, needs, desires without repercussions?

Because what could be the repercussion here? He rejected her at some point in the future—when she didn't want him to *accept* her, so that hardly mattered? Nothing could take away one night. She could have this one night and know…

"Yes," she whispered in spite of herself.

But he did not touch her again. Did not turn her to face him. Did not do any of the things she hoped he might so it could feel like he'd…lured her into this, tricked her.

"Then why hold back?"

She finally steeled herself to turn to face him. Tipped her

head back to meet his gaze. "I hear tell devils are charming enough, but then you eat the apple and all hell breaks loose."

His mouth curved, all dark, dangerous intent. Thrilling and perfect. "Hell is not always so bad."

It was unfair. Resisting him was too hard, and hadn't she had enough hard? Wasn't life hard enough without fighting so damn much? Marrying him had been an easier way out than scraping by…why not take this easier out as well?

His gaze moved over her face, like he was drinking her in, and it was a heady thing, to see his desire stamped all over *his* face. To know he wanted her, surely as much as she wanted him if he was doing this, pushing this.

But he still didn't touch her. "You will have to admit to me that this is what you want. You will have to say it, show it. So that when tomorrow comes, even if you still lie to yourself, you will not be able to lie to me."

"What does it matter?" she asked, a little desperately. Because it shouldn't, if this was nothing.

But his eyes were a blaze. A sun to get lost in and blinded by. "It matters."

CHAPTER ELEVEN

HER EYES WERE the sea, a tantalizing blue that would drown a man who wasn't careful.

Athan wanted to drown. He wanted to glut himself in her, and only this line he'd drawn in the sand helped him hold on to his tenuous grasp of control. His body ached for it, throbbed with built-up desire. He could hear his own heart in his ears, beating wildly, even as he kept himself still and in control on the outside.

She might want him, this, but the woman had ironclad control. He would not be at all shocked to watch her walk away. Or to be forced to walk away himself.

Again.

Painful, impossible, and yet he kept putting himself in that same position. Like he wanted to punish himself, over and over again. "You must be sure."

"I'm not sure of anything," she said, and he thought perhaps it was the most truthful she'd ever been with him, which somehow felt like a gift. One to be careful with.

"But I am tired of fighting for everything," she continued, and her hand lifted, rested on his chest. She stared at it there for a moment, before lifting her gaze to his. "I am tired of scraping by. I am *tired*. And for once, I deserve a reward, no matter how much I might come to regret it."

She moved closer, tilted her head back. He read determination in her expression. Maybe some wariness, but not confusion, not conflict.

"Ah, *omorfiá mou*, you will regret nothing," he said, wrapping his arm around her waist, pulling her close so he could feel the contours of her soft body against his. "Pleasure given and taken requires no regrets." Then he claimed her mouth for his own. Only his.

She tasted of a sweetness he could not identify, so unique it was to her. Haunting, obsessive. Three times now, he had earned a taste of her and there was no end to the ways it wound through him like a drug.

It would not end with a taste here. Not tonight. He broke the kiss, but only long enough to lead her up the stairs, quickly. To his room. It was dim inside and that wouldn't do. He released her hand and moved to turn on the lights in the room.

There was a flicker of uncertainty in her then, but he returned to her, nudged the straps off her dress, then reached around her to push down the zipper. He took his time, enjoying the feel of warm, soft skin against his hands. Though his blood pounded in his ears, in his sex, he would not hurry this.

She was a delicacy, and he had no idea how often he'd be able to enjoy it, so he would take his time. He would savor every moment, every inch.

Every soft sigh, every huffed out breath, every sharp inhale. As he slowly peeled the dress away from her. She held his gaze the entire time, all uncertainty gone. A fire in her eyes, but complete stillness in her body. It did something to him he did not fully recognize. Unleashed a kind of desperation he'd never felt.

He felt like a gladiator in the ring, ready to take on anything. If death were an end, it would be worth the journey getting there.

And still he took his time, baring her to him. Pale and soft. Sweet and sharp, wrapped up with all that *control*. She was impossibly strong, forged in too much adversity. Too much taking care of others.

Tonight, he would take care of her. This pale goddess in front of him. He reached out to trace the strap of her bra, a confection of lace and frills that surprised him considering her no-nonsense demeanor.

Before he could do any more than that, she reached out, pushed the suit jacket off his shoulders. He shrugged it off, watching in fascination as the only sign of any sort of nerves or heightened feeling was there in her eyes. Not in her steady hands, her serene expression. Just in the stormy blue.

Once his jacket was gone, she stepped ever so slightly closer and reached for his collar. For just the quickest moment, her fingers trembled, but she stilled herself. She undid the first button, her concentration on her fingers as she moved down the column of buttons.

Her shoulders were back, all determination to see it through. And since she was, he let her push the shirt off his shoulders. He simply watched as she decided what she wanted.

Her fingers trailed down his chest, his abdomen, taking their time. Torturing him, and she knew it too if the little curve of her mouth was anything to go by. She undid the belt with deft fingers, though she took her time.

When her eyes lifted to his, it was a lightning strike through his body. A rumbling thunderclap that threatened to change the very landscape around them.

And still they only stood, eyeing each other, stillness on the outside, storms internally.

"Are you going to make me do all the work?" she asked, her voice thready.

"That depends," Athan returned, watching the beautiful pink of heat and desire chase across her skin. "Do you want to do all the work?"

She didn't reply right away, as if taking it into consideration and weighing the pros and cons. "No, I don't." Always so careful. Always so measured.

He wanted to rip that all away from her—the weights and responsibility that had built that inside her. He wanted to tear it to pieces, give her nothing but wild abandonment and not a second thought.

"Then allow me," he said, or maybe growled, and he let it go. That tenuous grasp on control, everything that held him back. Because she had unleashed this.

Everything imploded then. He grabbed her, kissed her, devoured her without worrying about anything but how much more he wanted. With more speed than agility, he rid her of the rest of her garments, walking her back toward the bed.

He began to pull the pins from her hair, let them drop. He didn't watch the bouncing curls as he had that first night after the wedding. He cared not how elegant her hair might be tonight. He only wanted his hands in it.

Soft and silky and smelling of some kind of spring fruit. New and faint but intoxicating all the same. He buried his nose there, his hands tangled, his body its own torture chamber of restrained need, throbbing desire.

He needed her underneath him. He needed his mouth on her. He *needed*. He lifted her onto the mattress so that he could see her, sprawled out naked in his bed.

His bed.

He had dared not imagine *this*. Her spread out on his bed, as if marking it as hers. A concerning revelation that he might never be able to forget her there, naked and fascinating. So strong and yet she wanted him. *Him*.

He could have stood here forever, simply drinking her in, but he was afraid it was altering something inside of him. He needed to touch, to taste, to make her his.

Because there was only her as he moved over her, and everything he finally wanted to experience with her. The way her skin felt under his hands, the way her sigh sounded and felt against his ear. The taste of her, deep and potent and true.

He splayed his fingers wide, moved his hands over her abdomen, her thighs, encouraging them apart.

His name on her lips, not with disdain or that infuriating cool detachment. Hoarse and desperate and wanting. Wanting *him*.

He followed the path of his hands, tracing open-mouthed kisses down her body, while she moved, urging him on. Her breath in staccato gusts. Her movements wild and desperate.

For him. For this. For them.

He moved her legs wider, settled between them for a taste. But when she stilled, so did he.

"You only have to tell me to stop, Lynna." He waited, bracing himself for the inevitable guillotine. It was too much, too fast. He should have—

"No, don't stop," she said. Maybe her voice was breathless, but the words were clear. An order.

One of the few he would gladly obey.

Lynna felt like a top, spinning out of control. And Athan and this weren't at all like she'd expected. She'd known there would be pleasure, the sparkling fireworks of their kisses, his touch, his voice had showed her that in a million ways— it was why she was even *here*.

LORRAINE HALL 125

But it was different naked. Brighter and hotter and more all-encompassing than even those kisses that had given her some reprieve from all her thoughts, anxieties and heavy responsibilities.

This was like…she wasn't even herself. She was just skin and nerve endings. Need and desire in a throbbing, desperate storm.

It didn't matter that she'd never done this, that Athan was touching the most intimate parts of her, that she could feel him hot and hard against her own skin. It only mattered that she find the peak of everything her body was building to.

His whiskers were a scrape on the inside of her thigh. His hands on her hips a firebrand as he moved her just how he wanted. And then his mouth, his tongue, *inside* her, lighting fires she'd never dreamed possible.

Until it all tightened into one spot that exploded, shuddering through her like an earthquake. Like *finally*. Echoing, echoing, turning her body lax, languid, sated.

What had she been doing with her life? Why had she thought sex could be a waste of time when even just this in this moment was all-encompassing and everything?

Nothing else mattered. Nothing else rated. Just this pleasure, this heat, just *him*. His mouth, his hands, his body now ranging over hers.

The dark, dangerous intent in her eyes, so potent, so desperately *just* out of reach, she felt no nerves, no concerns. There was nothing inside of her but anticipation as he rolled the condom on himself.

And when he was on top of her once more, nudging inside of her, impossibly large, she could only look at his face. A face she'd known for so long. A face she'd once had vague girlish fantasies about, a face she'd once hated, but it had always been too handsome. Too *him*.

He whispered something to her in Greek, something she probably could have parsed if her brain was functioning beyond the moment. But he was filling her, and it was too much and not enough all at once, but there was a freedom in that. In the *everything* of it all.

His hand clamped at her waist, the impossibly hard length of him deep inside her body. It was too much intimacy and not enough. The way each movement reverberated through her like a drum. And it built, higher and higher, a soaring, joyous climb to new heights.

With his voice in her ear, his body on hers, a perfect symphony of utter freedom and joy. Until it all crashed, a throbbing, potent delight.

He pushed against her, hard and firm, staying there on a guttural, conquering sound as the ebbs and flows of her own release stretched out, settled in. Winded and relaxed, she trailed her hand down the hard plane of his back.

She had never once believed a person was anything more than exaggerating stories of sex that made it seem other-worldly and worth sacrificing or risking for.

Now she knew different.

Athan's warmth slid off of her. In the dim light of the room, she watched as he removed himself to an en suite bathroom.

She felt…sleepy. With absolutely no desire to rush into thinking or action. She just wanted to lie here and absorb every last pulse of pleasure until there was nothing left.

But when he returned, still beautifully naked and too handsome to be fair to anyone, the tiniest inkling that she needed to *act* began to stir.

But before she could, he returned to the bed, tucked her into his body, the blanket tight around them, his arms tight around her. And it was…nice. This quiet moment, after all the storms had receded. Calm and nice and for a few fleeting seconds, the responsibilities that lay heavy on her shoulders were still gone.

But she began to be aware of them again. "I should go back to my room," she said, though she didn't move. Because *shoulds* had always governed her, but it didn't mean she *wanted*.

"Why?" he demanded, his face buried in her hair like he could simply inhale her whole.

She had a million reasons, but she could really only seem to verbalize one with him so close, with the bed so warm and comfortable around her, weakening her resolve. "It seems reckless."

His gaze moved over her face, as if taking in every last centimeter. Then his mouth quirked in that lazy way of his, a contrast to the seriousness in his eyes. "Then be a little reckless, Lynna."

CHAPTER TWELVE

WHEN HE AWOKE the next morning, a slow blinking intro-
duction to day, it was with Lynna still in his bed. Her dark
hair sprawled out against his pillow, his shoulder. Her eyes
were closed, so her long dark eyelashes created a little fan
against her cheek. Her skin pale and pink against the soft
fabric of his sheets and the air around him smelled faintly
of strawberries.

Of her.

And it created an odd weight in his chest—not unpleasant, but strange and perhaps a little disconcerting for its
weight. For the fissure of uncertainty it sent through him,
but when twined with the deep-seated satisfaction, there
was nothing really to be done about it. It was simply something to endure.

Her eyes began to blink open. Blue threaded with silver,
carefully awakening and shaking away the last tendrils of
sleep. When her eyes focused in on him watching her, he
noted the wariness that lingered in the edges of her expression, but her pretty mouth curved ever so slightly. So he
pressed his mouth to the corner of that smile, and felt that
smidge of wariness melt away.

Heat curled inside of him lazily. Instead of that potent
slap of lust like last night, this was gradual. A gentle ocean
wave that would eventually swell and overtake them both.

But for now, he rode the gentle. The slow. The natural, swelling stirring. Her soft sighs, the beautiful blooming give of her mouth, her body, as without anything spoken, they came together. In slow moves and quiet gasps and pleasured sighs.

He talked her into the shower, into pleasuring her there, drunk on the feel of her, the sounds she made, everything that made up Lynna. His wife. *His* and only his.

When she finally left his room, insisting she needed her own things and to make breakfast, Athan hummed to himself as he prepared for the day. Perhaps he would be a little late to the office, but he would not miss any meetings if he took his time with breakfast.

Less than thirty minutes later, he was dressed and on his way to the kitchen certain his good mood could not be dimmed. All his goals would be realized in short order, and then he could spend the next year enjoying his beautiful wife.

Perhaps it felt like too short a time, but no doubt by the end he would be ready to move on. Everything would be settled then. Everything would be right.

He would make certain of it.

She was already in the kitchen, cracking eggs into a bowl. She was not dressed in black, though she was dressed casually. Soft pants the color of summer green and a loose sweatshirt to match. Her hair was pulled back into a ponytail that bounced as she moved.

When he paused in the opening of the kitchen to watch her, sure she would continue with her preparations as she had every other day leading up to this one, she didn't. She stopped what she was doing and looked over her shoulder at him.

She was more potent and addicting than any substance could be. Because it rearranged something inside of him, this change. This *admission* on her part, no matter how small, that something had changed.

And he wanted to make that permanent, in ways he failed to understand. The need to do something that held her here, right where he wanted her, was too big a need, a desperation to set aside.

She must have read the intent in his gaze because when he approached, she held him off with a hand to his chest, studying him with those blue-gray eyes that spoke of a million questions and uncertainties and suspicions. It made him want to take away every last one. To give her every answer and assurance she needed.

"Do you think this is wise?" Before he could answer that, she shook her head, presumably at herself. "Let me rephrase. I know being *wise* is not your concern, even if it is mine, I only mean, should this really be...a recurring thing? Is that best?"

Best. "Who knows what's best?"

She clearly did not like this answer, because she frowned, and didn't drop the hand that held him off. "I do. I *always* do."

She sounded certain, but it sounded like someone trying to convince themselves more than any certainty.

"Lynna." He tried to imbue his tone with a gentleness, which was rusty, or perhaps new and never truly used before. "We are to be married for a year. I see no reason not to enjoy what there is to enjoy for that time, then go on our way at the end."

"What if we should tire of it before then?"

He laughed in spite of himself. Tire of it? He grinned at her. "If you think you could tire of it, I will have to prove you wrong. Over and over again."

He watched her try to fight a smile, and it thrilled him

that it was a fight. That she didn't quite succeed in hiding her amusement. And since she didn't, he pressed his luck. Lowered his mouth to hers, but stopped a whisper away, listening for that little sound of sharp intake so heady and uniquely her.

That *pause* where she decided to move forward or not. Where want fought with reason and safety and whatever else Lynna Carew concerned herself with.

"We should start right now," he murmured, his lips so close to hers she no doubt felt the movement on her mouth. And then he kissed her, gentle, slow...perhaps even sweet, though the notion was as foreign to him as this wholesale obsession that only seemed to grow, no matter how many tastes he got of her.

Whatever she had been doing was forgotten because she held on to him. Melted into *him*. And nothing existed except this kiss and the sweet, perfect response inside of her.

Until someone behind him cleared their throat. Twice.

Athan managed to drag his mouth from hers, looked over his shoulder at his assistant and scowled. "Perhaps now is not the time, Niko."

"Perhaps," Niko agreed, but he didn't leave and that was the first indication that something was wrong. Moreso when he continued to speak. "However, I think you'll want to see this, Mr. Akakios. Immediately."

Athan wanted nothing to disturb this moment. He wanted nothing of the outside world right now, period. "If my father has stirred up another false story..."

Niko shook his head. "Not your father, sir."

Dread arrowed dead center, drowning out all those good feelings he thought invincible. If it wasn't his father...

Niko moved forward, tablet outstretched. Athan took the object from him and read the screen.

A Mother's Regret. Why Elena Akakios fears her son's temper and what his sudden marriage means.

Athan did not read the rest. He wasn't certain his eyes worked anymore. He felt perhaps as if he'd been flipped upside down, like someone was hanging him out to dry by his ankles.

His *mother.*

He felt a hand on his back. Gentle pressure. "Athan." Lynna's voice. "What is it?"

Athan had to clear his throat, and it irritated him that he did. "Apparently my mother has decided to weigh in." Athan tilted the screen so Lynna could read.

Her hand didn't move from that spot on his back, like she was holding him up, offering him comfort. And so he held himself very still, until the thought of her breaking the contact sounded worse than him deciding when and how to lose that warmth.

He stepped away from Lynna, handed the tablet back to Niko.

"But…why?" Lynna asked, soft and confused, and he was no doubt fooling himself to think she might actually be concerned. Because sure he had talked her into his bed, but based on chemistry and lust.

Not *feeling.*

Which seemed good in the moment because there were too many feelings rioting around inside of him, none of them finding center or purchase. All out of his control.

But why?

Athan did not have answers for that. Why indeed. Because while he knew his relationship with his mother was… complicated, he would have thought her hatred of Constantine would have trumped their…issues.

Instead, she had come out against him—no doubt at Constantine's behest. Perhaps there was more to the story. Manipulation, coercion. Constantine had many tactics up his sleeve.

Athan had just lost the plot. He'd been distracted by Lynna, when he should have been focused on all the ways Constantine could try and destroy him.

Or perhaps your mother should have warned you.

He set that aside. He had not warned his mother any of the times he'd betrayed her. He had certainly not warned Aled Carew before he'd upended Lynna's father's life. In reality, this was all no doubt his just desserts.

Because the human condition was betrayal and hurt. In between whatever glimpses of goodness and pleasure a person could find, there was only *this*.

But that didn't mean he wouldn't fight them or fight for himself. Even if he had to clear his throat again. "I assume Ophelia knows?" he asked Niko.

"Yes, sir. She's doing damage control. She'll meet you here once she has more to go on."

"No. Not here. At the office. I must go into the office. I have meetings this afternoon."

"Ophelia did not think that best. Her instructions were to stay put."

"Well, *I* think it is best. I will not let this affect my work. That's what he wants." But it wasn't his father. It was his mother. "You needn't break the news to her. I will handle it."

Niko hesitated, but only for a moment. After a sharp look from Athan, he turned and left the kitchen.

"Athan, perhaps you should stay here," Lynna said. "Listen to Ophelia. She is your public relations manager for a reason."

He looked at Lynna then. Really looked at her. She had something like *concern* in her expression, in the way she had her hands clasped together. And for a strange blinding second, he wanted to listen to her. He wanted to believe she was concerned, that she did care.

That someone could.

But he knew better, and so did Lynna.

Which left something sharp and painful lodging in his chest. So perhaps his words were more curt than they needed to be, but they needed to be said either way.

"You needn't pretend you suddenly care simply because we slept together, Lynna."

Lynna felt the words like a slap. She should not have been surprised that he might lash out, but she found herself taken aback anyway. Perhaps not so much at the words as her reaction to them.

Not anger, but something that felt far too close to hurt.

Luckily the idea that her ever traitorous heart might be so completely worthless as to feel *hurt* because Athan Akakios might be a little harsh infuriated her.

"And you needn't pretend we are any less partners against your father simply because we did. This is about AC International. This is about Rhys. It is about clearing my father's name."

He held her gaze, and perhaps if it simply stayed cool or blank or angry, she might have softened, but the fact she was stupid enough to think she saw *hurt* there had her sticking to her guns.

"Of course it is," he returned. Coolly.

And that would not offend her, because there were no secrets here. No feelings. A night together in bed didn't change what they were to each other. That was all physical—and the physical needed to be put away to deal with this.

For the people who meant most to her in the world. So

what did it matter if he was *cool*? If he lashed out? She was a problem solver, and she would solve this problem if he would not.

"It seems an epically bad idea to ignore the instructions of your PR expert in the midst of a PR crisis."

"I will not *cower*," he all but growled.

"No, but you will need to make the right choices. And to do so, we need to understand where this came from."

Athan turned away from her then. His back was stiff, his shoulders tense, and she had the oddest impulse to move forward and smooth her hands over all those contracted muscles. Like when she'd reached out and touched him when Niko had dropped the news.

But that had been too close to crossing lines, confusing motives. Perhaps the pleasures of last night…and this morning…did not have to *end*, but only if they could keep those lines clear. Only if it did not get…confusing. For either of them.

So, they had to focus on the task and moment at hand. They had to solve the problem.

"Why did he go to your mother?" she asked him. "Why did she turn on you?" Maybe if they understood that, Ophelia could somehow undo this.

"I grew up at my father's knee, Lynna. That meant a hefty disdain and mistreatment of my own mother. She has every reason to turn on me."

There was clearly more to that story, and she opened her mouth to demand it. Then she stopped herself. This was partly her fight, but not totally. And Athan had a whole team of people to deal with this. He didn't need her.

And, maybe, there was some *small* part of herself worried that if she heard the story she'd have empathy for Athan because, while she had issues with her own mother, they all stemmed from dealing with tragedy. Her mother had never once turned her back on her children, and it felt so wrong to think any would.

She went back to making breakfast. It was something she could do, and he would need to eat. And then she didn't have to think about a boy whose parents did not love him. Who had presumably used him as a tool, and still did.

But that only made her think about the truth of the matter. Athan's parents had not been married for some time, which meant whatever Athan thought he did to his mother at his father's knee was nothing *recent*. "You were just a boy when your parents divorced."

"I was thirteen," he said starkly, as if that refuted what she said, when of course it did not.

"That is a boy. Rhys is nineteen, and I hardly consider him more than a boy, no matter how brilliant he is and how well he'll do once he graduates into the real world. Thirteen is a *boy*." She didn't know why she felt so adamant about that when she could not doubt that he'd done terrible things to his own mother.

It was the Akakios way.

"Well, this *boy* followed his father's example. I was cruel and manipulative with my mother. Just as I was well into my twenties, I followed his orders, danced to his puppet strings, and thought we were both right and clever and *good*, while she was wrong and someone to be pitied at best."

He did not look at her as he said any of this. He was staring out the window, something bleak and sad on his handsome face. Enough sadness to make sympathy twist deep inside of her where it didn't belong.

Then he whirled on her, suddenly and with a snapping anger.

"Would you like to know when that changed for me?" he

demanded, eyes blazing. There was something about that question that felt like a threat.

So she shook her head. "No."

"I did not think so." He gave a bitter laugh that made her feel uneasy. With herself. With her understanding of everything—most especially him. But then he sighed. "I suppose since I'm staying put, I shall go for a swim. Please send someone to fetch me should Ophelia arrive." Then he strode out of the room.

Lynna let out a slow breath of relief, mostly. Because he was staying. Just as she'd wanted him to. As his PR manager had *wanted* him to. The smart thing—it really had nothing to do with her.

Yet she couldn't help but think she had solved that problem for him. If she hadn't been here, he would have gone into the office. Which was no doubt what Constantine wanted—another confrontation.

But Lynna had convinced him to stay.

And that meant far more than she could let it.

CHAPTER THIRTEEN

WHEN OPHELIA ARRIVED, Athan had already swum until his muscles screamed. He could barely lift himself out of the pool. Then he sat there, dripping water while she told him every last piece of information from the article.

Against his wishes.

It was truths mixed with lies, and all of it continued to be a tarnish on his reputation. All of it made it harder for anyone who might have a soft spot for the Carews to follow him—not just because they might believe the stories that he was violent and betrayal personified, but because they also might be concerned that Constantine's retaliation to any defection would be stories about each of them.

No doubt Constantine knew all their secrets.

"I cannot avoid my work, my office simply because of this," Athan told Ophelia, gesturing at the tablet she read from.

"No. But when you do go into the office, it must be with calm. With a plan. All of these stories, Constantine's little wars against you, they are meant to get under your skin. And then, once he has, prove every single one of them a fact."

Athan was well aware. That night in his library had been an obvious indication of that, and yet… He was struggling to find that clear, determined detachment.

His mother had essentially called him a monster in the

press, and maybe he was. No, there was no maybe. He *had* been. He had tried to make amends these past few years, but he supposed this was evidence that it did not matter.

What was done was done. There was no fixing all the lives he'd hurt. And that overwhelming realization that there was nothing to be done about it, that these years of trying to *fix* it were pointless and worthless made it feel impossible to act, to move.

"Mr. Akakios?" He could hear the slight concern in Ophelia's tone, and he almost laughed. That his dogged PR manager would suddenly have concern for him must have meant he was truly in bad shape.

He inhaled deeply, let it out slowly, trying to hold on to a course of action. He needed to get into work, nothing changed that, but…

He heard a door slide open and glanced over, sure it would be another staff member to deliver some new blow. But it was Lynna.

She had changed into dark slacks, a button-up shirt the color of sunshine. Her hair was pulled back into a simple twist, and she looked…office ready.

"I am going to go into the office with you." She looked him up and down. "I suppose you'll want to be clothed first, though."

"Why would you go with me?" he asked, truly confused.

"The point of this entire endeavor is to win over anyone who might still be loyal to my father over Constantine. They have seen me at dinners, at the ball, but they have not seen me in the same place my father once worked. They should, and what better time than now? To prove I don't believe these stories."

He turned to look at her, all prim and determined. Strength personified, but… "Do you not believe them?"

Something flitted in and out of her expression too quickly to analyze. "You are capable of many terrible things, Athan," she said firmly, "but I take exception to your parents, who are clearly not above reproach, trying to tear you down like this. It is wrong, so we'll do what we can do to right it. I'll come with you, make the rounds for a little bit. Then, tonight, we'll have dinner with the Aritis as planned. Does this suit, Ophelia?"

"It does indeed, Mrs. Akakios."

She stiffened at that, but she didn't correct Ophelia at the *Mrs. Akakios*. "Then I suggest you go get ready, Athan." She glanced at her watch. "Quickly." She strode inside without anything else.

Athan didn't move at first. Too many confusing, whirling feelings were battering around inside of him. But Ophelia studied him with her sharp, assessing gaze.

"You might want to keep her around." Then she too left.

Athan knew he needed to move. To go get ready for the day. To put on that suit of armor that would allow him to walk down the halls his father had built and stolen, Lynna on his arm, and not *react*.

But it felt as though yesterday he had known exactly who he was and exactly what he was doing, and now…after last night, after this morning, he didn't have a clue. Too much like that night after Aled Carew's funeral, when he realized what a lie his father had sold him.

Except now it felt less like lies exposed, and more like truths…just out of reach. Ophelia's words, echoing in his head like a curse.

Keep her around.

Lynna didn't care for the way she was feeling, which was why she'd set it aside. Locked it down. There was a problem to be solved and she intended to solve it.

If it helped Athan, it was only in the service of *not* help-ing Constantine. If she helped Athan, it was only holding up her end of this bargain to get what she wanted. Rhys settled for life and her father's name cleared.

Perhaps he did deserve whatever befell him, but she couldn't help but think it rather awful that Athan's parents had *both* turned against him. Obviously, Constantine had no ground to stand on, but Lynna had watched Athan in the aftermath of both his parents' bombshells.

Constantine stealing away his fiancée had made him angry, but it hadn't *hurt* him. His mother's words in that article had drained all the color from his face. Lynna had been actually concerned about him in that moment.

Before she reminded herself he deserved everything he got, and that her only focus was Rhys's future and clearing her father's name.

But that meant aligning herself with Athan. So when he came down the stairs, dressed crisply for a day at the office, she followed him outside to his car. When he climbed into the driver's side, she got into the passenger's.

They said nothing. Athan drove adeptly into the hustle of Athens proper, and to AC International.

A building she hadn't been in for almost a decade. Anxi-ety began to build inside of her, no matter how she tried to set it aside with everything else. She did not wish to be as-saulted by memories of her father.

People would no doubt want to talk about him with her. Why had she thought this was a good idea?

Rhys. Think of Rhys's future. She could do that, and it wouldn't be so difficult to maneuver every conversation into one about the future rather than the past. She would never understand why so many people wanted to live in the past, the loss, the *pain*.

Marching on was only ever the answer. Athan pulled his car to a stop in his parking space, but before he turned off the ignition he looked over at her, something thoughtful and strange in his expression.

"I am struggling to understand why you are doing this for me."

She pretended to look through her purse. "I'm not. I'm doing it for Rhys and my father's name." But she felt his gaze on her, like he was studying every inch of her face for some inkling that there was more to it.

There wasn't. There couldn't be.

He got out of the car, and so she did too before he could get around to her side and help her out. But she could hardly avoid touching him completely if the point was to look like she supported him.

So she let him put a hand on her back, gently guide her to the elevator. She tried not to think of that hand, of *anything* from last night. Or this morning. She focused on her goal. On divorcing herself from any emotion battering her, because this wasn't about *feelings*.

It was about fixing a problem. Halfway up, the elevator stopped and let in an older man who looked vaguely familiar, though Lynna couldn't place him right away.

"Athan," the man greeted. He looked at Lynna briefly, but didn't greet her.

Usually Lynna didn't mind being ignored, even when it was meant to be a slight, but the pompousness of greeting only one of them really struck her the wrong way today.

"Mr. Giordano," Athan said in return. "You remember Lynna Carew, I'm sure, as you worked closely with her father. Lynna, this is Regina's father."

Once again, the man looked at her, then said nothing.

The *gall*.

"Well, I take it you've seen the news," Mr. Giordano said pleasantly enough, his gaze on the elevator doors instead of either of them.

"If you're referring to my mother's appearance in the tabloid scheme against me, yes I have indeed," Athan replied, and he sounded quite carefree about it, which gave Lynna hope that he had recovered from this morning's...blow.

"And it doesn't concern you?" Mr. Giordano asked, looking back at Athan with something like overly acted skepticism in his tone. "Perhaps it should, young man."

"You know what would concern *me*?" Lynna offered, managing to sound pleasant despite how much she wanted to wring the man's neck. "Why someone seems so bound and determined to attempt to make my husband out to look like a problem, when there is not a shred of evidence that he has actually done anything wrong."

When Mr. Giordano's cool dark gaze turned to her, she smiled blandly at him. "But I suppose we all have different concerns, of course," she added pleasantly enough.

"I suppose it makes sense you'd think so." He looked back at the elevator door. "If I recall, your father was a bit of a criminal as well."

"I wonder what determines if someone is a criminal," Lynna mused, or pretended to anyway. "Because I think there's something a little criminal about supporting your daughter marrying a man thirty years her senior just so you can feel more important in your job."

The elevator door opened, but Mr. Giordano did not get out. He turned to stare at Lynna. And Lynna knew she shouldn't have said it. She knew she should not enjoy the surprise, the horror, the slowly dawning fury on this man's expression.

But she would not listen to anyone criticize her father.

"Lynna, darling, perhaps this is not the time," Athan murmured in her ear, but he sounded amused more than censoring. "If you'll excuse us," he said, maneuvering himself between Mr. Giordano and Lynna and ushering her out of the elevator space.

Giordano said nothing, and Athan held her tightly by the elbow and walked her down the hall. He made a motion to a trim man behind a desk, then opened a door and guided her inside, closing the door behind them.

"I thought you had come here to help, not start fights."

"No one will call my father a criminal to my face."

"And here I thought you had supernatural control. Why, you have pretended not to hate me for so long, I almost believed you actually indifferent."

Lynna did not want to engage with that topic. She tossed her purse on the luxurious leather couch and stalked over to the huge window that looked out over Athens. She crossed her arms over her chest and tried to breathe.

She usually *did* have better control. She should have kept her mouth shut. *This* wasn't her fight. "It isn't as though Giordano is going to vote with you anyway."

"No, I don't suppose he will, but I don't need to stir up my enemies when my father is stirred up enough. And my mother, apparently."

Lynna closed her eyes, breathed in and then out. It wasn't like her to lose her temper so easily. Athan was right, she'd spent five years pretending she was mostly indifferent to him when he was her second sworn enemy.

And now you've slept with him. Perhaps a lack of control in all things is your punishment.

She wanted to laugh at herself. The thoughts were dramatic and that wasn't her. Time to screw her head on straight. She took a few more breaths then turned to face Athan.

"All right. No more fights. Moving forward, I am as detached and bland and pleasant as they come." She even offered him one of her patented bland, polite smiles.

But it faltered when he stepped close. When he reached out, fitted his large palm against her cheek. Making her entire internal wiring go haywire.

"I don't mind watching you fight, Lynna," he said, his voice low and gravelly, somehow it always felt like friction against her skin, and now that she had let herself intimately know what all that friction could *do*, it heated her bloodstream even more.

She wanted to pull away. To center herself. She was letting too much get to her. Giordano. Athan. All of this corporate nonsense. When her only goal was her family. Her only focus *them*.

But she was Athan's wife here. They wanted people to believe it was true. They needed her father's supporters to believe it was true. So she had to endure the touch.

Endure. If only she could convince herself it was a hardship.

A knock sounded at the door. "Come in," Athan said, though he did not look away from her or even drop his hand.

The man from the desk, probably another assistant, entered. If he thought anything of Athan standing so close or his hand on Lynna's cheek, he didn't show it.

"Your meeting is here, Mr. Akakios. I have put him in the meeting room."

Athan nodded, and finally dropped his hand. But he didn't look at his assistant or anywhere away from Lynna.

She should look away, get a handle on her heart scrabbling about in her chest like what had happened last night changed anything between them, when it absolutely did not.

But she held his gaze anyway.

"My wife would like to see some of her father's old friends," Athan said. "Make sure to help her find anything she needs."

"Of course, sir."

"I'll be back in an hour or so, and then we can go to lunch. Perhaps with Henry. We'll see who's available." He leaned in, brushed a very chaste kiss across her cheek. "Behave, Mrs. Akakios," he murmured in her ear, before turning and walking away. Out of the office.

While she stood, off-kilter and…too many things to name. She hadn't even given him a dirty look for calling her Akakios.

"Mrs. Akakios?" the assistant said, and she realized he must have said something she hadn't heard before that.

"I should be able to find my away around," she offered, sounding breathless even to herself. "If I have any troubles, I'll let you know."

The assistant nodded and left and Lynna closed her eyes, took a deep inhale. This was a problem of her own making, and she solved everyone's problems. Including her own.

So she straightened her shoulders and set out to charm her father's old associates.

CHAPTER FOURTEEN

ATHAN WENT INTO his meeting somehow feeling…lighter. He knew Lynna had not been spiteful toward Mr. Giordano *for* him. It had been for her father. And really, it hadn't been wise.

Still, the way she had defended her father had loosened some of the knots tying him tight. The fact she was here and on his side. He could almost believe she didn't hate him anymore.

But letting himself believe that was a recipe for disaster. For having the rug pulled out from him again. He needed to hold on to the simple fact that what she had done, what she would do, had absolutely nothing to do with *him*.

Because even if it did, he would only betray her.

He went through his meeting feeling oddly detached from everything, but it had gone well in spite of himself. If his clients knew of the article from his mother, they had not mentioned it or acted as though it affected their trust in him.

Athan wondered how long he could make that last.

When he returned to his office, it smelled faintly of strawberries, but Lynna was not in it.

Which was good as he had phone calls to make before they went to lunch. He sat down at his desk, looked at his phone and the people he needed to call.

He did not call any of them. He should, because this was

not the time or place for a personal call, especially since
Ophelia had warned him against trying to smooth this over
before they understood what Constantine had offered his
mother to get her to turn on him.

But he called his mother anyway.

He didn't expect her to answer. Elena was very good at
avoidance when she wanted to be. The last summer he'd had
to spend with her before he'd been a legal adult who did not
have to follow his parents' custody agreement anymore, she
had jetted off to an entirely different country and left him
alone in her home in Patras for the summer.

Yes, she knew how to avoid him when she wanted to. He
could hardly blame her. Whether she'd been there or not,
he'd always used his father's words against her. That she
was weak, at fault for anything that went wrong, a *mistake*.

So desperate to earn his father's love, he'd decided to
thwart his mother's.

So he was more than a little surprised when she answered,
sounding tired and vaguely offended. "Athan, hello."

Athan didn't bother with a greeting. He simply didn't
have it in him. "What did he offer you?"

His mother was silent on the other line. "You have caused
me much harm over the years, you know," his mother said.

"Yes," he agreed. Because he could not deny it. He had
been thirteen, tasked to choose between his parents. They
had always made it sound like they'd given him a gift by
having him choose.

It had never felt like one.

But he *had* made the difficult decision, and he had done it
as his father wanted. How could he be an Akakios at AC International if Father was not in charge of his schooling? How
could he expect to inherit a company if he spent his days
being spoiled rotten by his indulgent and indifferent mother?

And so, he had chosen Constantine. And so, every summer spent with his mother had felt like torture. He had been cruel to her. In his teenage years, he had avoided her, ignored her, lashed out at her. In his early twenties, he had done his father's bidding to do what he could to make sure she got as little money out of Constantine as possible.

He had not treated her well. He had failed her. But…

"Did I really cause you more harm than Constantine? That you would choose his side over mine?"

"If there are sides, you chose yours, Athan. Your father is a terrible man, but you're on the same side. So… Does it matter whose side I get paid by? I'll happily say something nasty about your father in the press for the right price. But don't forget, Athan, *you* chose him."

So did you. But he supposed that wasn't fair, though he couldn't quite articulate why. He only knew…he had made mistakes here. And he thought he had made some steps to rectify them, but apparently not.

"I am sorry, Mother. I have tried to make amends. I don't understand why…" Athan didn't have the words. He should have planned this out. He shouldn't have called. "I do not need to pay you for any stories. That isn't why I called."

There was another moment of silence. Terse. Had she really expected a payday from both of them?

Probably.

"Then why did you call?"

To understand what I can do to make this right. To save myself from all my mistakes. To find redemption somewhere, maybe. "I suppose I simply needed to know," he said to his mother.

She made a pained sound. "Why do you both torture me like this? Why am I always caught in some Akakios war? I only want to be left alone."

And yet she'd taken Constantine's money. Gone to the press. That was hardly being left alone, but who was he to judge?

"Very well, Mother. Goodbye." He hung up. Then laughed at himself as he scrubbed his hands over his face. What a pointless endeavor. When would he ever learn?

He pushed away from his desk. He would find Lynna. They would have their public lunch, smiling and acting as though nothing mattered. He would ignore this story and it would go away. It didn't matter. All that mattered was winning enough shares to kick Constantine out. To fix AC.

You couldn't count on people, but you could depend on a business you controlled.

He stepped out of his office, and immediately saw Lynna a few meters down the hallway. She was standing with Henry Davies, they were smiling as they chatted. She seemed to glow like the sun.

He stopped for a moment, struck by…her. The sight of her, the *feeling* that worked its way through him every time he saw her. More potent, more impossible to ignore by the day.

He did not believe in love. But he remembered how quietly and earnestly she'd told him her parents had loved each other back on their first drive to his home in Athens.

So maybe it was love, here inside of him, but what could he do with it? She hated him. She was here for Rhys, for her father's name, and he… He knew what he was. No matter how he tried to make himself into a good man, his past mistakes would always be there. Would always define him.

There was no forgiveness in this world, that he knew. His mother had proven it to him.

Lynna lifted her head, and her smile did not dim. She waved him over. An invitation into the sunshine that seemed to surround her. The *strength* she exuded.

It could never be his, he knew. His failures would always be there in the way. Even if she set them aside for this short marriage, it would not be forever. There would be no miracle of forgiveness because miracles did not exist.

So he did not have *hope*, but what he did have was time. A little time to pretend that he could be forgiven, that he could be a good man. So, much like he'd said to Lynna last night, why not enjoy while it was here in front of him?

It would all end soon enough, regardless.

He moved down the hall, fixing a bright smile on his face. "Are you up for lunch, Henry?" He slid his arm around Lynna's waist easily enough, and she didn't even stiffen. It felt natural, and right.

"I'm afraid I can't today. You two should go enjoy yourselves. You hardly took a honeymoon. Enjoy the time you have before you start a family." The man winked, then walked away.

Lynna had stiffened at the word *family*, and he felt a little stiff himself. Though he'd never considered such a thing, just the word seemed to conjure images of blue eyes in small dark-haired children.

Horrifying.

He *wanted* it to be horrifying.

"We should go," Lynna said. Was it just him that she sounded a little robotic?

But he could hardly worry about that, as he had to yet again clear his throat to speak. "Yes. We should."

Family.

That word echoed through her, in Henry's Welsh accent that reminded her of her father, maybe *felt* like her father's word now, rattling around inside her head.

There'd been a time *family* had been in her future plans.

Find a good husband—a kind, good, affable man like her father. Have a few children.

Then… She didn't want to think of *then*. The disillusionment of who her father had become, tangled indelibly with his untimely death. Then there had been no point to her plans. The only thing with any meaning was to take care of Mother and Rhys. That had been enough.

It *was* enough. Because this fake marriage she'd engaged in was a sham, not some chance at a family. She didn't care for Athan, and that would be the only real way to start a *family*.

So why that little moment in time seemed to nestle into her brain, she did not understand. Did not want to. It had to be boxed away with all the rest.

Once the year was up, all these things she didn't want to deal with wouldn't matter anymore, and she'd never have to handle them. They were irrelevant blips in time, best disregarded.

She had a subdued lunch with Athan. They barely spoke. They didn't really need to. The entire purpose of her being with him today was simply optics. That whatever stories might abound—online, in print, in whispers—she was by his side.

And anyone who had once supported her father could be by his side as well. It was a symbol, and it did not require more than just being here. She told herself this was fine, because of course it was, and there was no reason to feel any concern or worry over the fact he barely spoke.

No innuendo. No sly jokes. No smiles meant to make the heat creep into her cheeks. He ate as though the weight of the world rested on his shoulders, and she could not stop thinking about the word *family*, and the way his parents had failed him.

She didn't absolve him—he had made mistakes as an adult, and even if they came from some trauma as a child, that didn't mean he hadn't done harm. That didn't mean there was forgiveness to be had.

"Would you like to return to the office, or home?" he asked her when they were walking out of the restaurant.

"I think I should return home to prepare for tonight's dinner," she said, feeling formal and stiff.

He nodded, and so they got in the car and he began to drive.

Home. *His* home. Not hers. Ms. *Carew* not Mrs. Akakios, even if she'd now allowed too many people to call her the latter today.

The car ride was silent. She supposed he must be in his own mental world of wheeling and dealing and coming up on top when it came to his father's horrible schemes. Just as she was in her own mental world of…confusion and frustration and *nothing* she liked.

So she would go back to the Akakios home, and calm and silence her thoughts with the restorative act of cooking a meal.

Not long before he would turn into his own drive, he spoke. With no preamble, he simply offered: "I called my mother earlier."

She didn't immediately respond to this. She turned to study his profile. He had a vague frown on his face, and she wasn't altogether certain that he'd really planned to tell her that.

But it stirred something inside of her. A frustration. An anger. Even when she told herself he deserved anything he got, the idea his mother could be the person doing it just made her angry. No matter how she tried to stop or push away that anger.

"And what was her excuse for this attack?" Lynna asked, frustrated with her own bitterness. She slumped back in her seat and told herself to stop *feeling* so damn much.

He sighed. "Constantine paid her to."

Lynna shook her head. She should have known, and still it stoked her anger only higher. "But…surely she has no loyalty to Constantine. Her loyalty should be to her son."

"I chose Constantine over her. Why shouldn't she do the same?"

The words didn't make sense, no matter how she turned them over, and his vague frown but otherwise blank expression did nothing to help clarify it to her. "What do you mean?"

"When they divorced. I was given the choice who I wanted to spend the majority of the year with. I chose him, not her."

The shock of it wound through her like a blow—though she didn't, *couldn't* care. Except… "You were a boy." And she remembered him as the boy he'd been when his parents had divorced. He hadn't yet hit his growth spurt, and yet because he was older than her, she'd seen him as a kind of…giant. If not in stature, in who he was.

"Does it matter what age?" Athan asked, sounding tired.

"It should. They never should have put that decision on you." And they should not be having this conversation. She was developing too much empathy for him. Allowing herself to be too…taken in.

Wasn't that what Constantine had done to her own father? Softened him, manipulated him, made him believe they were friends. The *best* of friends. Brothers, almost.

"I don't see why my age should matter. I was old enough to understand and they gave me a say."

A thirteen-year-old. Old enough to understand the complexity of an adult marriage? She didn't want to absolve Athan, and she would never absolve the adult version of him, but she could hardly stand the injustice of putting that decision on a *child*. "They gave themselves an out. For any responsibility. And as far as I can tell, they have continued that. Putting all responsibility on you and none on themselves." She made a scoffing noise, couldn't help it. "They're both despicable."

"I would assume you of all people would think I deserved it."

He did. He *did*, no matter how much some strange part of her wanted to balk at the idea. "You deserve much, Athan, but what you might have done as a boy isn't part of that. A parents' role is to protect their children, and your parents failed you. This is a rare case where you are not to blame."

"Is that why you do not ever wish to speak of your father? You were disappointed in him since he stopped protecting you?"

Everything inside of her went cold. It wasn't true, of course it wasn't true, so the fact the words felt like a blow was little more than…than…than… "My father was exemplary in all ways," she said stiffly.

"What happened was not his fault, I suppose, though I did not personally stop his heart from beating," Athan continued, as if this was a conversation they were going to have. "But in dying, he did not protect you. And it doesn't seem your mother did much protecting in the time since either. Quite the opposite. You have handled everything for your family since your father died."

She could hardly breathe through…anger. It had to be anger twisting her lungs and causing a terrible pain in her chest. Her parents weren't like Athan's. And her position wasn't like Athan's. Because she hadn't been a child, no one had stopped protecting her, and she had behaved correctly. Always. "*I* was an adult when all of this happened. I have made my choices, and I stand by them. You—"

"You were at university," Athan interrupted.

"Yes. I was an adult, living on my own while I saw to my studies. My mother lost the man she loved, everything she'd counted on, and she had Rhys to raise. All I did was help financially. This was not some…some…lack of protection."

"You felt the need to solve the financial constraints of your family as a university student. On the heels of losing your father, whom you loved."

Her throat was closing up, and she refused to let that happen. "It isn't the same. My father's financial situation he left us with was not his fault. My mother did not…put any responsibility on me. And neither my mother nor brother have ever turned to me for money, so, it is wrong to compare them."

He sighed. "So, I am correct." He gave her a wry kind of look that wasn't like himself at all. Too…sad, almost. Which was hardly fair. "It is my own fault that my mother has turned on me."

Why she felt the struggling need to defend him was beyond her, but she bit her tongue and said nothing. She would not… If he wanted to think his boyhood self was to blame for his current problems, well, that was his problem. She would not defend him.

He did not deserve defending. Not after comparing her parents to his. When she had never had any doubt her parents loved her. When she had stepped up because she *could*, not because she was forced to. When her father…

She did not want to think of her father.

They arrived back at *his* home and she got out of the car. He did not. He was going to drive back into the office for a few hours, as he should. Hopefully Ophelia would have a new plan of action for his PR, but it didn't matter if she did or not.

Lynna would focus on her end of the bargain. Pretending to be his wife to get the amount of shares needed to rid AC International of Constantine. Making it a place for Rhys, because he wouldn't be so high-and-mighty about calling himself an adult and telling her to butt out if she got him this.

She would be back to focusing on the important things.

With some space from him. Space. Necessary, important space. To settle all this that was unsettled inside of her. Because none of this was productive. None of it solved a problem.

It is my own fault that my mother has turned on me.

How dare he say that, sounding as though his heart had been ripped out. How dare he think that when he was an arrogant, self-absorbed reprobate who did *not* sit there blaming himself for his parents' terribleness.

She whirled back to face the car. He rolled down his window and she stomped toward it, angry at herself but unable to stop.

"You were a boy. Your parents are wrong. You have done wrong things as an adult, and these things I will never absolve you from, but that doesn't make your parents right. You should know that. Believe that."

They stared at each other, for too many beats. Her heart was battering about in her chest. What was he doing to her? It wasn't supposed to be like this. It wasn't supposed to *feel* like this. All her control was slipping and she couldn't let that happen.

She would turn into her father if she did. Letting her life fall apart over pointless, useless emotions. She wouldn't. She couldn't.

She whirled away again. Back toward the front door. She needed to find some safety to put all this swirling emotion *away*. She heard the car door slam and knew he was coming after her and still she did not stop.

She would not deal with him. Not until she was in control. Not until…

His arm curled around her elbow and he turned her to face him. Her on the top step, looking almost even with him at the middle step.

He said nothing. She said nothing. She struggled to breathe and blinked at the incomprehensible tears in her eyes. She refused to name the pained, hurting thing she saw in his gaze.

It had nothing to do with her.

Nothing.

"Athan… Don't…" And she didn't know exactly what she was telling him not to do, because all he was doing was standing there. His arm on her elbow.

She didn't know what she wanted to avoid, only that there was this…fear inside of her. Like something too big, too hard was right here in front of her. If she stopped it, everything could go on as it was.

If she didn't stop it…

Whatever horrible consequence that would befall her was lost as he lowered his mouth to hers. Slow and careful, the press of his lips gentle. Soft. A lull, a carefulness that twisted inside of her, loosening knots, poking through holes in a foundation she'd been desperately shoring up for five years.

All at the mercy of *him*. This. This…thing that happened when he touched her. She wanted it to be physical. Devoid of any and all emotion, but there was something about him. Something she wanted to curl herself around and protect, soothe, help.

And that was easy enough to pretend away when it was passion, when it was a buildup over weeks of want she had pushed down and ignored and denied.

It was something else entirely right now. When his hands were gentle, his kisses soft. As though this thing that sparked to life between them was breakable, and he did not want it to break.

She needed to break it. Smash it to bits—with refusal, with harsh words, with *anything* that would stop her heart from feeling this swollen and vulnerable and not her own. She needed to break this hold he had on her. Now. *Now.*

She couldn't.

It felt too special, too vital. Like a gift, like care. Like everything she'd run away from for so long and yet…some small kernel of the girl she'd once been still yearned for this.

Someone who wanted something more from her than all the acts of service that kept things running smoothly.

She knew what she needed to do, she understood her responsibility—stop this, whatever it was—and for the first time in her life, she could not do her duty.

She succumbed to him, to her heart instead. She kissed him back, wrapped her arms around him and held on for dear life as birds trilled around them on a pretty summer afternoon.

CHAPTER FIFTEEN

ATHAN WAS COMPLETELY UNDONE. For days, he had been certain that this *thing* with Lynna was lust and lust alone. Something to burn out eventually. Oh, he enjoyed her. Respected her. Always had. But he had known she did not feel the same, and so he had known this—she—was a fleeting moment.

But that little speech at the car, the fervor in which she absolved a small piece of him. No, not the things he'd done to her family, but all those twisted childhood mistakes…

No one in his entire life had ever… Too much was expected of him. To be his father's son. To be an Akakios. Savvy and smart, charming and powerful. There had been no room for mistakes, only punishments.

Only the driving fear he would never be good enough.

And perhaps he was following old patterns, kissing this woman he could never be good enough for. He had harmed her in ways she had said herself she could never forgive.

And still he kissed her, not in desperation, not in a fervor of lust, but in some small, gentle world where even if he *knew* better, he *felt* good enough. For a moment in time, he felt like hers.

If she could kiss him back, hold on to him, allow him to sweep her up into his arms, maybe there was still hope somewhere that she could be his. And that that would be all they needed.

He carried her inside and up the stairs like she was precious because she was. Strength and fragility were not opposites, not in Lynna. Both were her, a complicated twist. And he wanted to bask in her strength, protect those fragile pockets inside of her.

He wanted, he wanted, he wanted, and she didn't. Not the depth and breadth of this emotion that seemed to swell inside of him.

But she at least wanted this.

So he would deliver. He would enjoy. She would not forgive him for what he'd done in the past, but she would allow him this. And he *was* an Akakios, so he would take it.

He spread her out on his bed, the golden light of a summer afternoon washing over her. And he worshipped the goddess she was, the revelation she was. With his mouth, with his body. While she sighed into him, met every knot of pleasure with her own unspooling response.

And still, they did not rush. It was as if there was no outside world, only them, only coming together. Only sighs and sweet words and the way she came apart for him, over and over again.

Until he followed her into bliss, until there was nothing left to give one another, because they had given it all. *All.*

And he wanted that all. Forever. This should be enough. How could a man such as him ask for more?

But he supposed, that was the answer. To end this horrible hope, this *chance*, he had to ask for more.

So she would tell him no.

Lynna thought faintly of the dinner she needed to make. She really did not have time to doze here in the warm afternoon sun. And no doubt Athan needed to return to the office and see to his business.

But they both lay sprawled out on the bed as their breathing steadied.

She did not think about the gentleness, the emotional feelings that had swamped her. She was too good at boxing those up and shoving those away and focusing on whatever else.

In this case, she could enjoy the physical echoes of pleasure in her body and not wonder why they had seemed so important and life altering in the moment.

Emotions would never change her life. She'd made a promise to herself.

So it was absolutely incomprehensible when Athan rolled her over to face him, looking grim and haunted and said, "I think we need to discuss your father."

It was like being slapped across the face, and she didn't for even a minute understand why he would say such a thing. Why he would... No. *No.*

She tried to edge off the bed, but he held her firm. So she gathered up all the ice and disdain she could muster—naked and still beautifully sated. "I believe I've made it clear that is not on the table."

"It is on *my* table."

She kept his gaze and did not let herself think of the emotional toll of the words as she delivered them. "I don't recall ever acting as though *your* table mattered to me."

There was a silence, heavy and awful, because she felt *guilty* for saying something that was only the truth. That was only necessary. But she hated that it might land and hurt all the same.

He released her and she scurried off the bed. She needed

to dress. To go handle her duties. To get away from all *this*. What had she been thinking?

"Do you know when I realized my father was the devil and I did not want to follow in his footsteps to hell?" he asked softly.

He did not give her time to say *no* or put her clothes on and flee. He just kept speaking as she scrambled about searching for clothes.

"It wasn't when I hurt my mother by choosing Constantine, by being cruel to her."

She found her shirt and nearly wept with relief, but he kept right on going.

"It wasn't when I betrayed your father. It wasn't even when I began to suspect that no amount of turning myself inside out to please Constantine would earn his approval or love in the immediate aftermath."

"I refuse to listen to this." She considered putting her hands over her ears, but even she could not lower herself to such a childish gesture. She pulled her shirt on with jerky movements, one of the sleeves was too twisted to allow her arm to get through and she did not know where her underwear was, so she simply put on her pants without them. She stalked away, half-dressed, in a panic she did not understand.

But he followed her out of his room, into the hall. Of course he followed, because he did not listen. He did not respect her lines drawn in the sand. He was an Akakios and did as he pleased. *Always*.

"It was when I saw you after your father's funeral."

She froze, unable to walk another step. She looked down, half suspecting an actual blade to be stabbed through her chest so visceral was the pain.

She never thought about that day. Not ever.

"Hiding. Crying. *Sobbing*," Athan continued. Saying all the things she'd promised herself in that moment she would never allow again.

Because she'd had her family to consider, to protect, to *save*. There was no time for tears. But in that one small moment, when she thought herself alone, she'd given in to the wave of grief that had taken her out at the knees.

It was the lowest point of her entire life. Not because of the funeral, or not only because. But because she had felt so alone and afraid and overwhelmed. Because she had known from that moment out, everything was up to her. For Mom. For Rhys, whether he appreciated it these days or not.

All because of the man she'd idolized. He had been a good father. He *had* been. Mostly. Until... Until.

It had been impossible not to blame his death on the way he'd stopped taking care of himself, so obsessed with revenge. To blame it on the way he'd leaned into alcohol. The nights she'd had to handle things because he was either passed out or crying. It was the Akakioses' fault he'd become that, she had no doubts.

But her father had disappointed her wholly in his reaction to their betrayal. He'd stopped caring about anything that wasn't revenge.

A revenge he hadn't gotten. A revenge she'd somehow taken the mantle of now, without fully realizing it.

But she was not like her father. Not anymore. She wouldn't get revenge with obsession, or emotion. She would find it with her own wits. Her own choices. She would give that to the family her father had left behind.

But now Athan demanded to throw emotion into it? No. No.

She turned to face him, half-dressed in his hallway. He

wasn't in much better shape. Pants unbuttoned, no shirt, feet bare.

What *was* this? Some alternate reality where she did not have control? Where she did not make the right choices? She hated it. Worse, when he continued to speak, so stern, so determined, so *vulnerable*.

"I realized, in those six months before Aled's death, that nothing I did would please my father, but I still thought I would live that way. That I was supposed to live that way. And then I saw you crying, and the consequences of what my father and I had done. Real consequences, untenable, unfair consequences. Not just against a stranger, but against someone who had been a *friend*."

Tears—those tears she had controlled so long now—were threatening and she hated him in this moment more than she ever had for bringing her to this point. "Do you think I should forgive you then?"

"No, *latria mu*, I know you will not."

"Then what is this? Why are you doing this?" And she didn't sound strong like she wanted to. She sounded like a small child, begging.

"I don't know," he said gravely. "I only know that… I cannot pretend this has not gone farther than we planned. I cannot pretend that you do not mean something to me, Lynna. I cannot pretend that this thing I did not believe in, this thing I did not think existed, would take a hold in me."

He should have just shot her. At least then this would be over.

But it was clear now, he would not end this. So she had to. So she turned and ran.

But his words followed her down the hall. "I love you, Lynna."

She practically dove into her room, shaking as she desperately tried to turn the lock. He would not and could not follow her, with these…words. With this bizarre game he was playing.

She leaned against the door, breathing hard, looking around her pretty room and how happy it looked in the afternoon light.

She would not stay in this place. She would not *do* this. She would find some other way to end Constantine.

And she would never, ever see Athan again.

She rushed forward for her suitcase and haphazardly began to throw things into it. Anything she'd need to travel back to London.

All the while she ignored the tears streaming down her cheeks and pretended she was fine.

Fine.

CHAPTER SIXTEEN

ATHAN KNEW SHE would leave. He could have stopped her. He considered it. But in the end, he thought maybe he should just give up. What had fighting gotten him?

All that fire, all that determination, and it didn't seem to matter anymore. Let his father be a criminal. Let Constantine kick him out of AC.

Maybe all this time, deep down, he had known. AC didn't matter as much as he wanted it to. It was Lynna he'd wanted to make things up to.

And he'd finally pushed her and himself to the point where they both had to accept that was impossible. The mistakes he'd made—from childhood on—defined him. Were unforgivable. And he realized fully in this moment, knowing she was gone, that he'd still held out a small kernel of hope that there was forgiveness, absolution to be found.

More fool him.

Eventually he got himself together enough to return to his room, get dressed appropriately, and then texted his assistant to meet him in his library.

There were things that needed to be done, and as much as he might have been happy to let it all go, let it all explode in his face, he would rather go handle his business than sit in his room feeling sorry for himself.

Plenty of time for that later. With a bottle of Scotch to drown it all out.

He went into his library, found himself inexplicably caught in the memory of the way Lynna had swept in their first night here while he'd faced off with Constantine and been…perfect.

Beautiful and savvy, and even though he'd made the mistake of physically lashing out at his father, she had only taken it in stride.

The way she took so much. Too much, likely. Piled on her own shoulders, and he knew better than to want to take the weight off her shoulders. It was there because she wanted it to be.

But he liked to think, sometimes, he'd distracted her from it. Relieved her of it for a time.

What a fictional world you've created for yourself, he thought sourly, skirting his desk and sitting down behind it. He'd left most of his belongings at the office, and that was where he should be now, but how could he face it?

When Niko entered, Athan leaped into orders immediately. The sooner he tied up any loose ends, the sooner he could go drink himself into oblivion.

"I will need you to cancel tonight's dinner. Also, set up a meeting with Ophelia here when she has a moment. Lastly—"

Christos appeared in the doorway. Instead of the normal blank expression, he appeared harried. "Mr. Akakios—"

But a blustering young man pushed past the butler, marching right toward Athan, blue eyes flashing. His security would have intervened, but there was something about the man that had Athan standing as he waved off anyone on his staff who was poised to act on his behalf.

Even as the man—boy?—reared back and punched Athan square in the jaw. "Where is she?" he demanded.

It took a few moments to fully recognize his assailant, to put him in the context of everything that was happening.

"Rhys." Athan rubbed his jaw. It had been a solid blow. He'd likely had some boxing practice.

Lynna's brother. All grown-up—or close to it. Nineteen and rangy, angry and determined.

But that did not explain his sudden appearance. "Well, this is quite the unannounced visit."

"Where is she?" Rhys demanded again, his fists still clenched like he might punch again. "Get my sister in here immediately."

"She's gone." Athan touched his finger to his lip. It came back with a smudge of blood. Fascinating.

"What the hell does that mean?"

Athan studied the youth, trying to make sense of what was happening. Then he decided *sense* didn't matter. Why not just lead with the truth.

He was done playing all these foolish Akakios games. He just wanted some…reality.

"Well, she'd had enough of me, and she left. I assume back to London, though it's possible she went to see your mother. She was upset."

"Then she would not have gone to Mother," Rhys muttered. He paced the entry, a whirlwind of energy and emotion.

"While I'll admit most blows are only my due, to what do I owe the pleasure of this one?"

Rhys whirled on him. "How could you marry her? How could you involve her in any more Akakios bullshit? I don't know what she was thinking."

Athan could not quite follow. "That was weeks ago."

"Yes, and apparently my mother and Lynna did every-thing they could to hide it from me. I've been busy with exams, but once I heard... What was she thinking?"

He clearly asked this of the ether, not Athan himself. It surprised Athan though. Lynna had been adamant about telling the people she loved the truth about their marriage. But she'd kept it *altogether* from Rhys?

"What the hell do you think you're doing?" Rhys de-manded, of him this time.

Athan couldn't say he cared for a teenager *demanding* things of him. "A great many things, Rhys. None of them any of your business."

"Lynna is *my* business, and what she does in her incessant need to make things right for me are my business. What did you promise her? How did you manipulate her? Why can't you leave my family alone?"

Valid questions, all. And an interesting way of phrasing. *Incessant need to make things right.* Yes, that was Lynna to a T. Even when she didn't want to, she seemed unable to let a wrong thing stand.

But the bigger question was why couldn't Athan leave the Carews alone. And now he knew why, and it had every-thing to do with Lynna. And very little to do with the *boy* currently accusing him.

"Sit. Have a drink."

Rhys eyed the chair, then Athan. There was a clear in-ternal war.

"We will discuss all your questions," Athan said, mov-ing around his desk and toward the decanter and glasses housed on the counter.

On a huffed-out exhale, Rhys slumped in the chair, suddenly looking much more his age. A little petulant, a lot confused, but plenty of anger and determination still snapping in his blue eyes.

Athan did not think the truth of the matter would stop that anger any, but maybe just like earlier today with Lynna, he wanted to see how far he could push things. Prove that this really was all a mess he could not clean up. So he wouldn't be so damn determine to try.

He poured them both a drink, handed one of the glasses to Rhys. He took it, seemingly more out of rote manners than any want as he did not take a sip.

Athan did. To fortify himself. To get a head start.

"Your sister agreed to marry me in order to attempt to wrestle control of AC International away from my father. This included a loan payoff for her, a position for you at AC once your studies are complete and a public apology to your father, clearing his name."

Rhys gaped at him, reminding Athan a bit of a fish.

"Loan. What loan?" the boy finally managed to demand.

Athan considered telling him, but then figured this was a step beyond his place. Though if he stepped out of his place, would Lynna return to yell at him?

That was too tempting, a desperate urge to have her back, and he could not give in to it. Perhaps he was beyond help and forgiveness, but he would not be *pathetic*.

"Maybe it is your sister you should be asking."

"Of course it is! But she keeps all of this from me. Treats me like I'm still a baby. She needs to take care of everything herself. And I have tried to tell her, now that I'm older, I don't need it. But she doesn't listen."

Athan heard what he didn't think even Rhys realized he was doing. Confiding in Athan—though he be the enemy—

unloading his burdens and frustrations. Not smart, really, but Athan appreciated it all the same as Rhys continued.

"*I* am the man of the house, and she treats me like a… like a fragile pet. So much so that she married *you*." Disgust dripped from his enunciation. "Her sworn enemy. All to…take care of everything when she didn't need to. Why does she do it?"

Rhys was older than the last time Athan had seen him, and he was definitely capable of taking care of some things, but still too young and immature in some ways to carry the whole weight of it.

And so, he was laying it at Athan's feet, and for a moment Athan felt bowled over that anyone should come to him whether they meant to or not.

"Because she loves you, Rhys."

Rhys's gaze was sharp then. Some of that childish bluster tucked away as he straightened in the chair, looked right at Athan. "If she'd talked to me, she would have found that I have no desire to work for the company that killed my father."

As barbs went, it landed no doubt as the boy had intended. "Companies can't kill people, Rhys. Only people can. My father and I took care of that."

Rhys scowled at him, but with a surprising eye roll. "I don't blame you. Or *only* you. I don't even blame your bastard of a father or only him either. My father's death was caused by an ego failure of every man involved, and *I* will not repeat history."

Athan found himself…oddly moved by that. It wasn't *forgiveness*, but a dismissal of blame. A *failure*, yes, but not a murder.

"So I want nothing to do with…" Rhys waved a dismissive hand up and down Athan "…whatever this was. You'll release her."

Athan wasn't *keeping* her, but he supposed he didn't need to make that distinction to Rhys just now. "And what of your father's name?"

"I don't care about my father's name. I don't care about your money or influence. I will build my own, on no one else's sacrifice."

Rhys did not say this with bitterness, but because Aled Carew's name meant so much to Lynna, it was a shock, and a painful one, to hear Rhys dismiss their father's legacy so simply.

"Your father was a good man. A good father."

"I know. Lynna has made certain I know. But he was not a good father to her in his final days. Or the good husband he'd been to my mother. They think I was too young to understand, and maybe in some ways I was, but I have seen it clearly since. Lynna idolized him. And even in his final mistakes, he was not a bad man. But he had failed her. At, I think, the worst time."

Athan could not help but think how adamant she'd been today. That he'd been a boy. That his parents had failed him. He knew she had not wanted to absolve him of anything ever, but her sense of fairness had not allowed for anything else.

Maybe she had balked at the comparison of his parents to hers, and maybe it hadn't been fully fair, but it was not… *unfair*. It was not *wrong*. Lynna *had* been failed.

If her brother would say it, how could he think differently?

"When my father died," Rhys continued, "I was too young. To understand, to feel betrayed. Mother and Lynna had to deal with the reality of not just losing someone they loved but losing their image of him. I only lost a father. They lost…a world."

It was very thoughtful and insightful for a nineteen-year-old. "Lynna mentioned you were brilliant."

His grin was a flash, quick and handsome. No doubt on the cusp of devastating once he grew into his shoulders, his face. "I cannot disagree." Then the smile died and he sighed. "I care nothing for the past you're all embroiled in. So I came here to tell Lynna that. To stop this ridiculousness and divorce you immediately. Since she isn't here, I'll tell you. It ends. Now."

Athan felt an odd twin surge of emotion—on opposite ends of a spectrum. On the one hand, no one ordered him around. Rhys did not get to swoop in and end things—regardless of whether Lynna and he had done that already.

But there was a little swell of something like pride or relief, that Lynna *did* have someone in her corner willing to fight for her. Even if it was a bit too late for all this bluster.

"I am afraid that what Lynna decides to do is up to her. But if it comforts you any, she has left despite the fact that I find myself desperately in love with her. And as she will never forgive me, or even have a discussion about the emotion, I will likely spend the rest of my days a failed lovesick moron."

Rhys straightened a little, studied Athan as if he wasn't sure whether to believe him or not. "That all sounds a bit dramatic."

"It feels it."

Rhys studied him with narrowed eyes, but some consideration in his expression. "What would an Akakios know of love?"

"Nothing, I assure you. I'm as surprised as anyone. Well,

except perhaps your sister. She didn't take such confessions well."

Rhys snorted. "She wouldn't. Nor would she appreciate dramatics."

"No, indeed."

But Rhys did not stand to leave. He did not say good riddance. He sat in the chair and studied Athan with surprisingly empathetic eyes.

"She gets her way because she stonewalls every other way out. She controls things because she's had to, and now she's afraid to let go."

Afraid. Athan blinked at that word. Lynna did not appear to be afraid of anything. Ever. She had always stood her ground. Maybe she pushed certain things away, but…

No, not just pushed. She had *run away* from him. Not because he'd done anything terrible. But because she hadn't wanted to hear his words. She hadn't wanted to have a rather simple conversation, all in all, because it involved feelings. Complicated ones. Grief—that *pointless* emotion as she'd once called it.

She'd always held her own in a fight. Snapped back with barbs equal to the task. But when it came to the soft, she fled. Time and time again.

This was a revelation, but it did not change the bottom line. Athan looked at his desk, unable to meet Rhys's blue gaze any longer. "She will never forgive me," he muttered.

"Maybe. Does that change how you feel though?"

"Not me, no," Athan agreed. "But one doesn't simply… bully their way into a relationship, Rhys. I hope that is something someone has taught you along the way."

Again, the boy rolled his eyes. "Of course, but you're missing the point. One of Lynna's very adamant lessons is that we must do the thing regardless of how we feel. I happen to think she's taken it to extremes, but I give her lee-way as she's taken so much on her shoulders. You, on the other hand, have no leeway. So, you must do what needs doing regardless."

"And what needs doing, pray tell?"

Rhys shrugged. "*That* is up to you."

Athan had spent every moment since he had witnessed Lynna crying at a funeral making decisions that were up to him and only him. Every plan, every retaliation against his father, every *step* had been his.

Was he really so ineffectual as to give it all up simply because he'd realized *why*, and his why of loving her didn't matter because she didn't love him back?

But she had come to his bed. She had let him touch her with all that soft vulnerability she was so afraid of. Maybe there was no forgiveness, but maybe there was love. Maybe there was something.

Maybe…

Athan studied Rhys. Up to him? Maybe it was time to make some changes. "Perhaps it will be up to us."

"Us?"

The idea began to form, like all the best ones did. Quick and on the fly, with nothing but obstacles in the way. "I'd like you to come with me."

Rhys frowned suspiciously. "Where?"

"London."

"Why?"

"I think I have a plan for you, Rhys Carew. Are you man enough to find out if you're up for it?"

Lynna had arrived at her flat in London in a cold, dark drizzle. Fitting. Everything felt cold and dark and a little too oppressive, but she'd been exhausted enough to fall into her bed and go to sleep.

Not for long. She awoke when it was still dark, far too early in the morning, and couldn't go back to sleep.

Athan's words haunted her. It was like he was here, whispering the same thing to her over and over again.

I love you, Lynna.

Why would he say such a thing? Why would he *think* such a thing? She wanted to believe it another manipulation. A betrayal. She would be falling for the same tricks her father had fallen for if she believed him.

But…

Athan was not Constantine. He never had been.

"It doesn't matter," Lynna told herself, out loud, so she'd be more inclined to take it on board.

She tried to distract herself by making an elaborate breakfast, and it worked for a time. Until she got to plating, and realized she'd been thinking of a breakfast for two.

She ate two bites, then threw the rest away. A waste, she knew, but she couldn't talk herself out of it. She'd never be able to eat it without *feeling* now.

She needed work. Real work. She'd go into the office, get some accounting done and try to set up her next destination job. Somewhere far away. Maybe she could go to Los Angeles. Tokyo. Somewhere, anywhere outside of Europe.

It was still early when she headed into the office. Even if one of her friends came in today, it wouldn't be so early. As they so often worked remote, the office was just a home base of sorts. It wasn't rare that they were all there together, but it was getting to be more so with Auggie and Maude involved in whole other lives besides just their work now.

So she was more than a little shocked to walk into the offices, *very* early, and find all three of her friends there.

Sitting in the cozy little main room, almost as if they were waiting for her.

She closed the door behind her, studied them. "What are you all doing here?"

"When you texted you were coming back to London yesterday, we knew something was wrong," Auggie said. "So, we figured you'd be in early."

"Nothing is wrong."

"You look terrible."

Lynna didn't bother to make a face at Irinka. "Are you guys hungry? I could whip us up some breakfast."

It wasn't likely there was much in their kitchenette, but she'd find a way, she decided. She strode into the room, all of her friends trailing after her even though there wasn't really the space in the kitchenette for the four of them.

"What's going on, Lynna?"

"In what regard?"

"In the regard that you married Athan Akakios. There were *pregnancy* rumors about you in the *press*. We barely heard from you for weeks. And now, with very little warning, you're back, sans your husband."

"It's very simple. The arrangement no longer suited, so I came home." She opened the little pantry. There was some pancake mix, but unless someone had stocked the fridge in her absence, no milk or eggs to go with it. Could she manage from scratch?

"It doesn't seem all that simple."

She moved to the refrigerator. "Why not? I'm back at work." No milk. What were her other options?

"Well, you have a tendency to panic cook for a crowd when something is wrong," Auggie said.

"In other words, you like shoving food in people's faces so they can't talk to you," Irinka added.

Lynna looked at none of them. "I'll run to the store. Pick up some things." But when she turned to the exit, all three of her friends were standing next to each other, blocking the doorway. She managed to keep her expression bland. "What are you wanting from me, ladies?"

"The truth," Auggie said earnestly.

"The truth is as I said. Athan could not uphold the terms of our deal. He wanted…" Lynna hated that she faltered. "It was too complicated. He was…confusing things."

"What things?"

"All the things!" Lynna almost shouted, but she held herself back at the last minute. She straightened, focused. "It was ridiculous. I don't know what game he was playing. I don't know what I was thinking letting him touch me, but it's over now."

"So you *did* sleep with him," Maude said, as if that had been a very involved discussion somewhere along the line.

She wasn't going to think about it. "It doesn't matter."

"I mean, historically picky Lynna takes a lover kind of *does* matter," Irinka pointed out.

"I assure you, it does not," she said, adopting her haughtiest and most *don't touch this subject with a ten-foot pole* tone. "He was complicating things. I did not want to. So I left."

There was a beat of silence, but still her friends did not move.

"Did you fall in love with him, Lynna?" Auggie asked gently.

Love? Why was everyone so suddenly concerned with *love*? She scoffed. "How could I love him? He betrayed my family. He all but killed my father. Purposefully destroyed his legacy. How can you even ask me that?"

"That didn't answer my question. Do you *love* him?"

Lynna shook her head. Her throat was almost too tight to speak, but she had to. "I don't want to."

"Still not an actual answer," Maude said, but not without a gentleness to her tone.

A gentleness Lynna wanted nothing to do with. "What the hell do you want me to say?"

"The truth," the three of them said in unison.

"He ruined my father's life. On purpose." She remembered him as he was. So cocky and arrogant. So like his father. But there had always been a warmth in Athan. A kindness Constantine did not have. Even her father had seen that, though he'd never counted it as a mark against Constantine. Only a positive for Athan.

Because he'd seen them both as two separate people, instead of one Akakios conglomeration. Before.

Before.

"Lynna. Buck up, now," Maude said brusquely. "It isn't like you to ignore the truth of a matter."

But emotions weren't truths. They were weapons. They upended everything. She couldn't stand the thought of being upended again.

But aren't you anyway?

No. Because she had her work and her family. And maybe everything about Athan made her feel turned inside out, but she wasn't *upended*. She was a little frazzled, but not...

The doorbell to the office rang out loud in the silence.

"I'll get it." Irinka disappeared and Lynna tried to get her wits about her. She wasn't going to think about love. She wasn't going to be *interrogated* by her friends.

She knew what she'd promised herself, what needed to be done, and none of it could be derailed by something as stupid and pointless and *painful* as love.

Particularly loving an imperfect man.

When Irinka returned, she was not alone. But Lynna could only stare at the man next to her. How much older he somehow looked than the last time she'd seen him—only a few months ago. These teenage years seemed to go by in blinks while her brother turned into a man with every one.

There was always a pang of pain and pride at that, how quick the time stamped itself across her little brother. Who was no longer little and far too close to adulthood for her liking.

But not yet.

"Rhys. What are you doing here?" A horrible thought gripped her. "Is everything all right? Mother—"

"Mother is fine. Athan brought me."

"Athan…" And then there he was. Standing behind Rhys. This man who'd upended her life. Upended her *soul*. With her brother. But… "What's happened to you?" she demanded of Athan, noting the faint smudge of a bruise on his jaw.

"A gift from your brother," he offered.

Too many things jangled inside of her. She wanted to scold Rhys. Touch Athan's bruise. Run far, far away. Again.

"Don't worry," Rhys said. "We made amends on the flight over."

Amends. *Amends.* What the hell was Rhys thinking? What did Athan think he was doing? "You shouldn't be here," she said firmly to Athan. "I told you—"

"And I told you I love you. Which I have come to determine trumps everything you told me, since none of it was true."

"Maybe we should go," Auggie whispered, but Athan must have heard because his gaze flicked to her for only a second.

"No need. I do not mind an audience," Athan said, all arrogance and certainty that had Lynna…off-kilter. Panicked.

When she never panicked. She was in charge. *She* decided.

But Athan kept talking. "In fact, I think with someone as stubborn as Lynna, I should need it. So when she inevitably changes her mind—"

"I am not *stubborn*. No more so than—"

"—she will have people to remind her what happened here."

"Nothing is happening here," she snapped, panic and something she didn't want to analyze having a battle in her chest. "My brother has taken a leave of his senses, and we shall put them to rights. Athan, you may go. Rhys—"

"May I?" he returned silkily.

She ignored him and focused on Rhys. Who should be *at school in Greece*. "I don't know what you're thinking making some kind of pact with the devil—"

"*You* married him, Lynna," Rhys said with a shrug that was too much like Athan. "What does that say about your decision-making?"

She whirled on Athan, feeling more and more like she was losing a grip on something. Something she needed. "You have gone and turned my brother against me as if that will somehow get you whatever it is you want? It won't."

"Actually, I came to him."

She looked from Athan to Rhys, tried to find some solid ground. "What?"

"Granted, I came to him to find *you*, and tell you what a mistake you were making dealing with an Akakios, and how I don't need you sacrificing yourself for me. But since he was there, I told him the same."

"We came up with an alternate plan," Athan offered.

"One that serves all of us. Or could, if you weren't so stubborn."

She was both incandescent with rage, and something else. Something far more terrifying. A twisting, growing thing deep inside of her that she could not get a handle on. Could not set aside.

She wanted to throw her arms around him and hold on for dear life. She wanted alternative plans and going back to Greece and all the things it was not smart to have.

She had to be smart. Everything was up to her. She gathered herself as best she could and looked at her friends. "I want you all to leave." She looked at Rhys too. "I need to speak with Athan alone."

There was a lot of silent exchanging of glances, but in the end Auggie managed to corral everyone out of the kitchenette so it was only Lynna and Athan.

Lynna made sure there was as much space between them in the small space as possible. "What is this?"

"It is me fighting for you, Lynna. I know that's hard for you, but I think it might be necessary."

"No one needs to fight for me."

"Not your friends? Not your brother?"

She was silent. She knew they *would*, but that didn't mean she wanted it.

"We all love you."

"Stop saying that!" she shouted. And it was a shout, and the tears were threatening. It had been so long since she'd cried before last night, and ever since making her deal with Athan everything had been so tenuous. Too tenuous.

She turned away from him. She'd rather die than have him see her cry.

"Why should I stop saying it?" Athan asked gently. And

she felt him come up behind her. She could have moved. She could have stopped him.

But she let him put his arm around her, pull her against him. If she leaned… Wouldn't everything fall apart? And still, she couldn't seem to stop herself. He rested his chin on her head and she felt like she could breathe for the first time in too long.

"I have made mistakes," Athan said quietly. "I will always regret them, but I have also learned from them. I have changed who I am. If I could go back and change what I've done, I would. But since I cannot, I must make the best of what's left."

"There's nothing left," she whispered.

"You. You are the best of everything. And you are here, as am I."

A tear slipped over, and she held herself very still. Maybe he wouldn't see. Maybe he wouldn't notice.

"Perhaps I have nothing to offer you—"

She whirled to face him then. How could this arrogant man so consistently undermine himself? "You are clever and funny and kind, in spite of yourself. And—"

His grin spread. "And you are too quick to defend me in spite of yourself, *latria mu*. I do not know that I deserve it, but I want it."

"Athan."

He reached out, brushed the tear off her cheek. "And I think, once you get passed your fear, you will find you want it to."

"I am not afraid. I am *exhausted*. I am tired of fighting so hard."

"Then stop. You do not need to fight. I will fight for you. Alongside you."

She wanted to believe him. The yearning for that release was so sharp in her chest, she could scarcely breathe around it. But… But… How did she believe in this? How did she let these feelings win when she knew how dangerous they could be?

"My father loved you, you and your father."

Athan nodded, and she could see the hurt in his gaze, hated that she put it there.

"And we betrayed him. I cannot argue with you. Perhaps you can never forgive me for my role in that. I would hate this, but I could understand, I could accept. If you told me you do not, could not love me, I will accept it. This has always been your choice."

She wanted to. Wanted to find the words. She didn't want to determine if they were true. She didn't want to understand her feelings.

But he said one last thing, one last thing that upended everything that she'd so desperately been holding on to.

"Choose me, Lynna. I cannot change what I have done, I cannot fix the past, but I can build us a future. All of us. You and me, your family. I promise, I would do everything in my power to make it right."

Six years ago, she had stood in front of her father and begged him to stop. Begged him to choose his family instead of his revenge. The people who loved him, instead of the people who didn't.

Choose us.

He had refused.

He had died.

If she lied, if she turned away from Athan, would it eat her whole? Would she be making her father's mistakes? Would she become him? Would she be ruining a future all because of their past?

The answer was simple. She could keep running from it,

but that wouldn't take it away. As Athan had once told her, no matter how she boxed it up, it was still there.

So maybe the lesson was to deal with it. To take it out and *feel* it. *Choose* the people who loved her—perfectly or not.

"I will still work," she rasped out.

He was so still. So careful, and he studied her with that gaze that reminded her too much of yesterday, when it had seemed as if his mother's betrayal had made him fragile.

He wasn't. He was here. But still, she couldn't stand to be the thing that made him careful. Not anymore. "And I think we should live in Athens," she continued. "If I am to choose you, if we are to stay married, that is the house to do it in."

"Are we to stay married, *omorfiá mou*?"

"Naturally," she returned, meeting his gaze and studying his beautiful face. It seemed surreal to end up here, but here she was, and wasn't she an expert at making the best of her situation?

Maybe she was afraid, but she had been afraid for so many years now. She had survived. Helped build a business. Kept her family afloat. And now here was someone who wanted to add to that, support that, be her partner in that.

It would be stupid to ignore that because she was *afraid* of everything she felt, everything she'd been through.

"I love you, Athan."

He enveloped her in a hug, hard and with a relief she felt wash over her too. All that tension, all that *fight*, for what? When this was what was waiting for her?

It wouldn't be easy or simple, but it would be right. It would be…a partnership. Where they each carried some of the weight, instead of her insisting it only be on her shoulders.

"Come home with me, Lynna," he murmured into her

ear. "We'll stop fighting the past. We will build a future. Forget AC International. Forget Constantine. It will be us."

Lynna let out a long, steadying breath. *Us. Future.* Yes, that was exactly what she wanted. It was exactly what they'd have.

EPILOGUE

ATHAN AKAKIOS HAD not always been a man of his word, but he built himself into one. With his wife by his side, it seemed a foregone conclusion even when things were tough.

After Rhys's graduation, he partnered with Athan in his new business venture. Instead of trying to hurt Constantine, they focused on building themselves. Lynna continued to work for Your Girl Friday, taking the jobs that suited and refusing the jobs that didn't.

There was not a moment of regret that he had married her, regardless of the circumstances in which their marriage had started.

When she was pregnant with their first child, her mother came to live with them, and Rhys often did as well on breaks from university. With the Carew family under their roof, Athan felt he finally had a real family. One built on forgiveness. Joy. Even in the face of loss and pain.

Lynna gave him a son first, named Aled, after a good man who had made mistakes and left them all too soon, but had loved them all the same. Three years later a daughter with Lynna's sky blue eyes joined their family.

Lynna mothered with love and joy and grace. She cried with and for their children. She fought with and for him. That strength of hers never once faltered, but as time passed, as they grew—individually and together—she learned to lean, to ask, to express.

And he learned to be the kind of man his father had not been. He learned to be a man he could be proud of. And while he'd always regret his mistakes, he had learned to accept that mistakes were part of it.

So he forgave. He asked forgiveness. And most of all, he loved. Surrounded by a family made up not just of Carews, but of Lynna's friends and husbands, all of whom acted as aunts and uncles to their children, and offered cousins in return.

When Dikaios Global, the partnership between him and Rhys, began to really compete with AC International, Constantine once again tried to ruin the Carews and his own son.

He failed.

"I'm proud of you," Lynna had told him one night, tangled up together long after they'd put the children to sleep. "Not because you finally took Constantine down, but because it doesn't matter that you did. You and Rhys built something for you, for us."

Athan pressed a kiss to her head. "It is satisfying, I can't lie, but I also realized long ago that no matter what happens in business, Constantine's life is much sadder than mine could ever be. I have love and family. He has nothing but his own poison."

Lynna squeezed him tight. "Speaking of your family, I've been thinking." She smiled up at him. "Perhaps we should consider expanding that family once again."

He grinned down at her. "Wife, you have the best ideas." He kissed his beloved wife deeply and set about to do just that.

* * * * *

MILLS & BOON®

Coming next month

ROYAL BRIDE DEMAND
LaQuette

'Reigna.' He called her name with quiet strength that let her know he was in control of this conversation. 'I am Jasiri Issa Nguvu of the royal house of Adébísí, son of King Omari Jasiri Sahel of the royal house of Adébísí, crown prince and heir apparent to the throne of Nyeusi.'

Her jaw dropped as her eyes searched for any hint that he was joking. Unfortunately, the straight set of his jaw and his level gaze didn't say, 'Girl, you know I'm just playing with you.' Nope, that was a 'No lies detected' face staring back at her.

'You're…you're a…prince?'

'Not a prince, *the* prince. As the heir to the throne, I stand above all other princes in the royal line.'

She peeled her hand away from the armrest and pointed to herself. 'And that makes me…?'

He continued smoothly as if they were having a normal everyday conversation and not one that was literally life-changing. 'As my wife, you are now Princess Reigna of the royal house of Adébísí, consort to the heir and future queen of Nyeusi.'

Continue reading

ROYAL BRIDE DEMAND
LaQuette

Available next month
millsandboon.co.uk

COMING SOON!

We really hope you enjoyed reading this book.
If you're looking for more romance
be sure to head to the shops when
new books are available on

Thursday 24th
April

MILLS & BOON

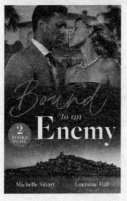
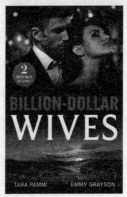

afterglow BOOKS

Afterglow Books is a trend-led, trope-filled list of books with diverse, authentic and relatable characters, a wide array of voices and representations, plus real world trials and tribulations. Featuring all the tropes you could possibly want (think small-town settings, fake relationships, grumpy vs sunshine, enemies to lovers) and all with a generous dose of spice in every story.

♪ @millsandboonuk
◎ @millsandboonuk
afterglowbooks.co.uk

#AfterglowBooks

For all the latest book news, exclusive content and giveaways scan the QR code below to sign up to the Afterglow newsletter:

SCAN ME

afterglow BOOKS

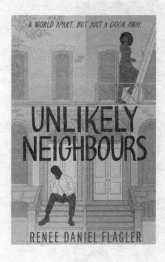

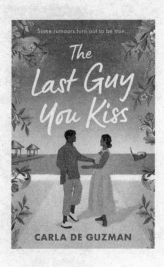

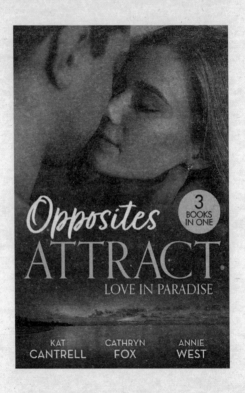

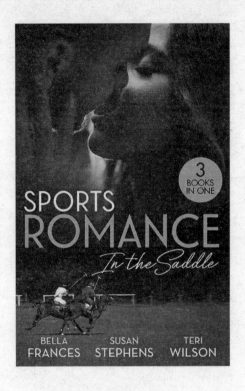

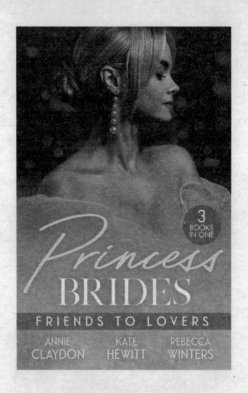